The Savannah Betrayals

Will Ottinger

Pocol Press
Clifton, VA

POCOL PRESS
Published in the United States of America
by Pocol Press
6023 Pocol Drive
Clifton, VA 20124
www.pocolpress.com

© 2018 by Will Ottinger

Publisher's Cataloguing-in-Publication
Names: Ottinger, Will, author.
Title: The Savannah betrayals / Will Ottinger.
Description: Clifton, VA: Pocol Press, 2018.
Identifiers: ISBN 978-1-929763-80-1 | LCCN 2018939062
Subjects: LCSH Dueling--Fiction. | Savannah (Ga.)--History--19th
century--Fiction. | Historical fiction. | Mystery fiction. | BISAC
FICTION / Historical / General | FICTION / Southern
Classification: LCC PS3615.T92 S28 2018 | DDC 813.6--dc23

Library of Congress Control Number: 2018939062

COVER PAGE: *The Code Of Honor—A Duel In The Bois De Boulogne,
Near Paris*
Wood engraving by Godefroy Durand, *Harper's Weekly* (January 1875).

ACKNOWLEDGEMENTS

My sincerest thanks to Roger Paulding and the writers' group at Scribbler's Ink in Houston. Their critiques were always on target. My editor, Dr. Roger Leslie, deserves credit for sharp eyes, as does my friend and reader, Jon Harbuck, for his review of legal matters in the book.

In Savannah, Preston Russell, my long-time friend and accomplished artist, provided guidance, courtesy of his non-fiction books and many articles on the city's history. In addition, special thanks are due Ms. Ellen Byck, lifelong Savannah resident, for her generosity and guided tour of the Old Jewish Colonial Cemetery, a rare and very special treat for outsiders. The fine old work, *Savannah Duels and Duellists 1773-1877* by Thomas Gamble, was a tremendous resource in understanding matters of honor and anger that prompted so many residents to tempt fate.

Finally, special loving tribute to my wife, Sandra Cobble Ottinger, my sounding board and long-suffering supporter for her encouragement and proofreading. And last but not least, to Gus, our red male tabby for his keyboard 'assistance' and unfailing company. Any and all other errors and oversights are solely my own.

DEDICATION

As always, for Sandra and my children. And for the timeless beauty of Savannah and the Low Country.

"Savannah spurned all suitors..."

John Berendt
Midnight in the Garden of Good and Evil

*"It was no time for those of sluggish temperament,
for the pacifist, for those who shrank from violence
and bloodshed."*

Thomas Gamble
Savannah Duels and Duellists 1733-1877

Chapter One

March 3, 1836
Charlton Street
Savannah

Wavering yellow candlelight transformed the dining room into a bleak confessional. Jesse Caine looked across the table at his father and dreaded the next minute. The rotund cook warily scurried past him, her footsteps the only sound other than the subdued rattle of silverware. Aware of the tension in the room, she eyed the two men and retreated to the kitchen.

Earlier in the day Jesse had passed the city's mayor on the street who glanced oddly at him without speaking, looking back over his shoulder as though Jesse carried plague. He'd put the slight down to civic preoccupation, but the scene replayed now as though offering a warning for what he was about to say. The memory delayed the collision with his father a moment longer and he raised the wine glass to his lips, then abruptly set it down, the claret's pleasure stolen by deceit. Later, the confrontation seemed almost insignificant given the whirlwind that followed, but within that moment, Jesse's entire world revolved around the words he was about to utter. Once spoken, he'd shatter a trust. What would he then become? No matter. Tell him and be done with it.

"There's something I must tell you."

Ambrose Caine, taken aback by his son's abrupt tone, looked up. A small man, his drawn features confirmed that time and sickness had conspired to pilfer his spare body, the physical dissolution abetted by a wife who no longer existed. Now a patchwork man, his shoulders were bent by sorrow, hands spotted and heavily veined, hair grayed in less than two years. On his worst days he presented the sad image of a street indigent seeking a quiet place to die.

"Charlie Ruston's consented to a duel," Jesse said. "I've agreed to act as a second."

His father lowered his fork with a slight tremor. He started to speak, but Jesse plunged ahead. "Randall Tyree's challenged him. An argument concerning a young woman."

Ambrose slowly shook his head. "Randall and his father are educated men, and Randall can be a charming dinner companion, but he's lethal, Jesse. Charlie should never have trifled with him."

"I know what he represents."

"And you agreed to take part?"

"I won't lie to you."

"I wish you had," his father sighed.

1

Ambrose Caine loved his son with an unbending Calvinist discipline meant to mold him into a good man. Overcome with disappointment at the double admission, he looked away.

Jesse folded his forearms on the linen tablecloth. "Tyree insulted the girl." He heard his argument's weakness but pressed ahead. "Charlie felt her reputation was at stake."

Ambrose looked up, his eyes troubled. "And this girl is important to Charlie?"

It was a fair question. "She's an acquaintance."

Ambrose shook his head again. "One of Charlie's many acquaintances, I assume." He sighed, the silence lengthening until he met Jesse's eyes. "So you broke your word to me over this travesty?"

"You put me on a leash." Jesse immediately regretted the words but could think of no other defense. "I can't allow him to face Tyree alone."

Laying the napkin aside his father sat back. Creases appeared around his eyes like dry stream beds and he massaged his temples as though the pressure might drive out his son's declaration. The cook appeared from the kitchen, but he waved her away.

"You're swimming in dangerous water," he said. "Georgia fools and the hotheads in South Carolina lead this nation in duels. This city..." He paused. "It's sealed-off gardens and rigid conventions tempt the worst in too many men." He choked off a cough, took a careful sip of water, and softened his tone. "I may sound like a hidebound old man, but I tried to teach you that principles and integrity provide order. Without them, emotions rule our lives."

Both of Ambrose's brothers had been killed in duels on the same day, and their presence now sat as ghosts at the despondent figure's shoulder. Ambrose tried to gather his words. Lips drawn tight as wire, he stared at the ceiling as though salvation was etched into the plaster.

Jesse recognized the posture. The old man was tough; he'd survived desertion and he'd survive a well-meaning mistake by his son. His father covered his mouth and erupted in another coughing spasm. Helpless, Jesse waited until he wiped his lips.

"He's my friend." Jesse could offer no other defense; he'd failed in two attempts to stop the madness. Trapped, he faced a Gordian Knot of impossibilities with no escape.

Go with Charlie or accede to the wishes of the disappointed figure across from him.

Bound by his mother's abandonment, Jesse's devotion to his father had grown stronger, but his friend required an equal measure of loyalty, the connection forged by years of shared pain and trust. The ordeal would provide an hour's diversion for Randall Tyree, but Charlie

2

faced a sterner test. He might suffer a minor wound, a painful mark of courage—or he might never walk away.

Twenty-nine years old, Jesse preserved his Shawnee mother's sharply-defined features. Lanky and angular in frame, his dark gray eyes reflected like chipped flint in the room's candlelight, sleek black hair and raised cheekbones revealing half his heritage. The city forgot its well-defined manners and whispered delicious innuendos about his appearance. Uncertain where he belonged, he grew up reserved and reticent in mixed company.

Ambrose Caine hacked into the napkin again, embarrassed by blood-stained teeth. Pink fluid rattled in his lungs, the organs losing the war within his waning body.

"Understand why I have to be there," Jesse pleaded.

"No, I cannot understand!" The words exploded in a rare outburst of anger. "Both my brothers died in senseless arguments," Ambrose rasped. "They were good men, but their judgment failed them and they died at the hands of scoundrels dressed as gentlemen." The tired eyes searched the ceiling again. "Our family's had more than enough scandal for two lifetimes."

"You must admit there are insults a court of law can't redress," Jesse insisted. "That a true gentleman must answer for his behavior."

"I admit to no such thing. This 'death before dishonor' nonsense is..." Ambrose's breath left him in a rush of defeat. "Justice is not to be administered on some desolate piece of ground." He placed both palms flat on the table, his voice hard. "When's this travesty to occur?"

"Day after tomorrow. At the old Oyster Point Plantation."

"Fitting. And you'll be there?"

"I have no choice."

"You once promised me..." Ambrose began, but coughing halted his protest. He swiped his mouth and concealed the bloody napkin in his lap. "A senseless waste if Charlie throws away his life on this." His eyes fell again. "I've seen waste. Your mother..."

The words opened old wounds as though the mention of her broke an unspoken covenant. They lapsed into silence among the simple but elegant furnishings. Only a few of her belongings remained, mournful remnants of betrayal. The house had been converted into masculine browns, solid grays, and off-whites, refurbished to alter her imprint. For Jesse only a blurred aquarelle of her remained. He remembered the late afternoon when he returned home to find his father hunched in the shadows of the front porch, hands clasped together as his dreams withered like month-old fruit.

Ambrose Caine had unwittingly unearthed the dead past. His drawn face studied the tablecloth as though it offered a map out of his rekindled sorrow. Jesse recalled her final days in the new house, the silence punctuated by single word responses, his father casting distressed glances at her as though she'd become a guest. Jesse never discussed their altered relationship with his father, imagining she pined for a lost heritage. But Jesse was wrong; her longings proved much closer to home, and she ran away a speculator with visions of finding their fortunes in Florida.

"When I came home and found the front door open, I knew the unthinkable had happened." Ambrose closed his eyes but the memory sharpened. "I never told you that I found her gold chain and crucifix hanging from the doorknob to our bedroom. A totem, I suppose, to ward off evil spirits that might follow her." He lifted his eyes, softened by memories Jesse could only guess. "You never needed to know such things."

The scandal quickly become public knowledge, grist for people who reveled in others' misfortune, festering until she died of yellow fever a year later. The humiliation bound him closer to his father, but the treachery lingered, setting him apart more than ever, a half-breed whose Indian blood demonstrated he could never be fully trusted. Except for Charlie, friendships were tossed aside like chipped bowls. He shoved aside his dinner plate and started to reply when a fist pounded the front door.

The cook bustled past them and quickly returned from the foyer, hands knotted inside her apron. She looked first at Jesse as though begging for assistance before she turned to the elder Caine.

"Mr. Caine, Sherriff Dew's asking for you," she stammered. Her eyes flicked to Jesse. "His deputy's with him and he's carrying manacles, sir."

John Dew, a heavy-shouldered bear of a man, brought the ripe smells of his jail into the narrow hall, a polished nickel badge gleaming under the foyer's crystal chandelier. An underfed deputy fidgeted beside him and displayed a smaller badge. A set of heavy manacles in one hand, the deputy ogled the carpeted staircase and parlor's fine furnishings. Neither man removed his hat.

"Mr. Caine," Dew grunted. "Jesse."

His father offered his hand, but Dew ignored the gesture.

"Is there a problem, John?" the elder Caine asked.

"I've a warrant for your arrest."

Ambrose gave a tired smile. "Is this a hoax by my friends?"

"No, sir, it is not."

"Arrest for what?" Jesse demanded.

"Fraud. A great deal of money is missing."

Stunned, Ambrose managed a single word.

4

"Ridiculous."

Jesse confronted Dew. "Who brought these charges?"

Dew drew back and removed a folded paper from his coat pocket. "Judge Fraley reviewed the complaints, and had me swear out a warrant. The matter concerns the canal project. A number of citizens were cheated, including the mayor."

Jesse reached for the warrant. "I don't believe a word on that paper."

Dew stepped back and slipped the writ into his pocket.

"We've evidence you sold fraudulent investments," he said to Ambrose. "Your partner Colonel Tyree confirmed your handwriting. Word is both the Colonel and his son lost a large sum." He squinted at the well-appointed parlor with a hint of avarice. "More money than I've seen in my lifetime."

"I sold investments to no one," Ambrose said.

Behind them, the cook burst into tears. The deputy gawked at the sobbing woman and shifted his weight, the rusty manacles out of place against the richly-patterned paisley rug.

"That's not for me to determine, Mr. Caine." Dew shot Jesse a warning look. "Bring his horse around front."

"Give me a minute to get properly dressed," Ambrose said.

"Just get your coat. Jesse can bring other clothes later." The deputy stepped forward with the chains and Jesse pointed at them.

"There's no need for those," he said.

"I have orders." Dew reached past him and lifted the bottom of his father's waistcoat in a perfunctory check for weapons. The deputy stepped forward with the manacles and Jesse snatched them away.

"Damn your orders."

He and the deputy wrestled for the chains until his father and Dew separated them. The cook wailed and Ambrose turned to her with a raised hand.

"Be still." Then to Jesse: "Saddle Mercury and bring him around." Jesse hesitated until his father gently shoved toward the rear of the house. "Go on. This can be quickly sorted out."

Jesse glared at Dew. "I'll ride with him. Unless you wish to chain me as well." He stalked out the back door and saddled his father's favorite horse, then his own. He led both to the street where the three men stood waiting. Encumbered by the chains his father mounted the mottled gray with a small groan. Dew and the deputy fell in behind them.

Only the hum of night insects disturbed the deserted street. Jesse ignored shafts of lamplight from windows that cast striped patterns across their path as he struggled to comprehend what had just occurred.

To his shame, he remembered Dew's assertion of proof and found doubt scraping the edges of his mind. Unbidden, the word *disloyal* crept into his thoughts. Uncertain if the label applied to him or his father, he buttoned his collar and tried to ignore of the jangle of chains beside him. Was his father merely bewildered, or ashamed he'd exchanged his dinner for manacles? The coming day might well witness a pointless death, abetted by disaster if his father's life dissolved into ruin.

The jail's unadorned outline loomed ahead, and phantoms from Jesse's past gathered in the shadows around the procession. For the first time since returning to an empty house a year earlier, he found himself alone again.

Chapter Two

Early Next Morning
The Caine House

Jesse stood before the full-length mirror and adjusted his black cravat. He brushed his most expensive coat and held it toward the light. The assembly of human vultures waited for him, but whatever the day brought, he would maintain appearances for his father's sake. They'd searched the confused figure at the jail the previous night and led him away to a subterranean cell. Unnerved by the medieval conditions, Jesse had gripped the iron bars until his hands ached.

More than respectability, the coming day required human sustenance, a light and healing balm to point his way out of hell.

He fed Aristotle and led the horse from the carriage house, caressing the soft black muzzle. Jesse waited as the animal displayed its displeasure at being saddled again. With a final pawing of the leafy ground, the animal acquiesced to whispered assurances and Jesse mounted.

The morning chill mated with wind and layers of high Sirius clouds, the weather defining the regions pernicious weather, the sea and inland rivers conspiring to hold spring in check. Wind bullied trees' skeletal limbs newly tipped with green buds, dried leaves scattering in the cobbled alley like frightened mice. Jesse touched Aristotle's flanks with his heels and emerged onto Abercorn Street. The horse picked its way over wheel ruts crested with dried mud as Jesse rode past workmen bent at their labor in city squares. Originally intended to drill militia, the palm-filled blocks of open space provided pastoral relief from encircling homes, schools, and businesses. Fronting the squares, squads of slaves dotted the stone steps and porticos of columned houses, while others stood on ladders and cleaned spotless windows. He appreciated Oglethorpe's meticulous plan, but the city had turned its back on him, diminishing its meticulous and symmetrical beauty. The cold wind flayed the hem of his thin coat as though determined to match his mood as he neared the jail. Ahead, two stylishly-dressed men appeared on the sidewalk.

Ellis Wilford and Nathanial Moore turned at the sound of hoof beats and stopped. Friends and occasional hunting companions, Jesse reined beside them.

"Ellis. Nathan."

The two glanced at one another as though waiting for the other to speak. The shorter cleared his throat and breached the prickly silence.

"I assume you're on your way to see your father," Wilford said.

News of the arrest had spread rapidly. "It's a misunderstanding, nothing more," Jesse said.

Slender and professorial in manner, Wilford adjusted rimless glasses and spoke as though addressing a stranger. "My uncle lost his life's savings. He's collapsed. His doctors say he may not survive the shock."

Jesse removed his hat and rested his forearms on the pommel. "I'm truly sorry, Ellis."

Nathanial Moore, a taller pugnacious man, stepped closer. "Ellis won't call your father a crook, but I will. What's happened is a damned outrage. He stole from people who trusted him."

Jesse bristled. "My father's done nothing wrong."

"A judge and jury will see it differently," Moore snapped.

Jesse recalled Dew's assertion of written proof. "I'd appreciate your forbearance."

Moore shoved his smaller companion aside and leaned closer until his shoulder touched Jesse's boot. "Your father proved himself unworthy. He robbed us, he and his Indian whore—"

Jesse jerked his boot from the stirrup and kicked Moore in the chest. Moore lost his balance, stumbled backward, and sat down heavily. Jesse jumped from Aristotle and shoved Wilford aside. Jesse ignored his cries he loomed over the fallen figure, seeing only a helpless enemy at his feet, resisting the impulse to kick Moore until the world redressed its wrongs. He caught his breath and looked sharply at Wilford who stepped back, palms raised toward Jesse. The day had just begun and everything he valued was slipping away.

Moore struggled erect, fear trumping his anger. Jesse climbed on Aristotle and spurred away without looking back, a pinwheel of raw emotion tearing at him. The horse sensed his apprehension and skittered to one side as a gust of wind struck its flanks. Mouth dry, Jesse tightened his grip on the reins, fully comprehending blind rage for the first time, and how easily he could tip into the abyss. He'd long known rage formed a part of him but kept in check. But things had changed. Less than a day after Dew's appearance, the city was closing its doors to him, seeing a gangrenous intruder in its midst. Highwaymen who robbed them. Bonds of friendship had slipped their traces in a matter of hours. If God had a master plan in designing Savannah's flaws, He'd never let Jesse in on the joke. He recalled Moore prostrated at his feet, face contorted in fear.

I could easily have killed him.

An incoming squall climbed the city bluff and swept up the Savannah River from the sea. The broad expanse of lazy water defined the city's northern boundary, and the drizzle glossed Savannah's few paved streets. Jesse bent his head as an insistent flurry tapped against his hat. Ahead, hulking stone monstrosity appeared through the rain.

Erected sixty years earlier by Tories to imprison the city's patriots, two stories of unalterable ugliness marked the squat structure. The ominous pile of granite slabs resembled a derelict mausoleum, its ugly bulk blighting nearby homes in its shadow. Inside, the first floor was a monochrome wasteland of stark wooden chairs and scarred desks, the tableau infected with despair, the stagnant air leaving a stale gray taste in Jesse's mouth.

Dew's emaciated deputy recognized him and reluctantly got to his feet. Wary after their confrontation, he led the way down stone steps to the lower level without speaking. The stairwell smelled of lye, the stones underfoot spongy. Jammed into cast iron sconces, sputtering candles and sweating walls lost their war against the encroaching mildew and residue of boiled cabbage, the miasma overlaid with the stench of caged men. The odors grew stronger as they descended into the lower depths. His reluctant guide opened an iron-strapped metal door on a small landing, leading them deeper into Stygian depths. At the bottom of the evil-smelling stairwell, a drowsing sentry, shotgun across his lap, guarded the third landing. The man scowled at the deputy for interrupting his nap and unlocked the door without opening it.

Jesse found himself inside a murky passageway. Cells lined both sides of the passage, and he resisted the urge to clasp a handkerchief over his nose and mouth. A few cells emitted the watery glow of candles that backlit faces pressed against rusty bars. The reek of unwashed bodies and night soil grew stronger, and he fixed his eyes on the far end of the passageway, ignoring pleas and angry epitaphs, aware a more dire confrontation waited for him.

The deputy unlocked the last barred door on the right and assumed his station a dozen steps from his father's cell. Ambrose rose and managed a tentative smile. His breath plumed, vapor thick with cold and damp. The frail figure appeared a disheveled beggar, his frame shrunken overnight as though sucked dry, crepe paper skin brittle in the smoky candlelight. A translucent blue vein pulsed in his neck. Jesse chided himself for looking away; hours seemed to have mutated into years, the feeble figure mirroring dejection—or guilt. Hunched on the edge of the bunk Ambrose Caine looked up from the forbidding walls.

"Did you bring the Defoe?" he asked. "I sent a boy with a note."

Jesse reached inside his coat and handed him the small leather-bound volume.

Ambrose placed the book on the soiled mattress. "Given my circumstances, *Robinson Crusoe* seemed an appropriate companion. If I'm here awhile, you'll have to serve as my man Friday."

Seated on a three-legged wooden stool Jesse tried to ignore the cries and wails from the other cells, waiting for his brain to assemble questions and healing words.

"Dew was kind enough to relate the charges against me," Ambrose said. "'Fraud and felony theft. Taking funds under larcenous pretenses,' he termed it." He placed a hand on his son's knee, his reedy voice desperate.

"I never solicited money from anyone. According to Dew two men swindled investors using my written authority for the past week. You know I was in Milledgeville acquiring property rights for the canal, but Dew claims my trip was a ruse."

For a moment his eyes turned bright with an engineer's zeal. With the Colonel's backing, they'd planned a canal to pierce the heart of Georgia. Colonel Fletcher Tyree. Scion of business in the city, an oracle of acumen and advice. Their dream began with statewide fanfare and high hopes. Excited at the engineering challenges and potential profits from barge revenue, Ambrose Caine threw himself into the project. He and the Colonel rapidly completed several miles of open canals leading from Savannah into the state's interior, envisioning an efficient transportation system. The Chatham Canal System would cut deep into the state, reducing the cost of transporting cotton to the port city.

Ambrose's right hand listlessly indicated the surrounding walls. "My role in the project concerned only the construction challenges. I surveyed the proposed route. I designed canal locks and ensured stronger embankments, leaving all financial matters to the Colonel."

Jesse subdued his flicker of misgivings, silently cursing his seeds of skepticism.

His father shook his head "It's unbelievable. I don't deny signing off on financial estimates," he declared, "but why shouldn't I? As a partner I spent my own money for the initial surveys. We hadn't reached the stage that required additional funding." He looked away wistfully, momentarily back at his drawing board. "So many technical problems to resolve."

A coughing spasm rattled his chest, Exhausted, he wiped his mouth and balled up the handkerchief to conceal flecks of blood. Jesse handed him a fresh handkerchief.

Whatever the truth, this hole will conspire to kill him, he thought.

"I never solicited a dollar," his father said. "You must believe that."

It wasn't fair, Jesse thought. *Fair*. The word was an imposter. The world had robbed his father of a wife, leaving a ruined husband and motherless son in its wake. Now, 'fair' raised its Janus face again, catastrophe arriving at his front door again with a warrant in hand.

Jesse pulled the stool closer. "We were invited to the Westbury's home tonight." The invitation seemed a mundane matter, but he needed to present a semblance of normality for his father's sake.

Ambrose nodded. "Go. You need to be there, if nothing else to show you've done nothing wrong."

"It's happened too fast."

The older man gripped his knee with surprising force. "Remember that you'll be seen in a different light now. If you must attend Charlie tomorrow, don't say or do anything rash. There are people who will seek revenge."

Jesse stared at the grimy floor. Had his father demanded perfection of him while concealing his true self? He hated the thought, but if he'd cheated those closest to him, both their lives were a lie. He had to see the evidence for himself.

His father lowered his voice. "I know it was hard on you when your mother left. I drifted for days with only the canal to keep me sane."

Jesse could not lift his eyes from the floor, a rush of anger directed against the bent figure. The rock of his life, a gentle man of principle, tottered on the edge of a ragged mattress, assaulted by inmates' curses and screams beyond the bars. Had his father hidden a different face all these years? Jesse searched for answers among the dirty stone slabs under his feet. After his wife disappeared, it was possible his father decided to find another life, a better one. He was a trained engineer, after all, and his grown son could take care of himself, so why not start over somewhere else. It was a jarring scenario but plausible, and if his father had joined the ageless procession of men tempted by easy money, the rumpled figure would most likely say anything to evade the consequences, ruining both their lives in the process.

He stood and signaled to the jailer, a hand on the bony shoulder. After promising to return the next morning, he trudged up the dim stairs behind the deputy, anxious to feel sunlight on his face.

Melissa and Howard Westbury were lifelong friends. Having delayed his departure as long as possible, Jesse dressed in formal attire and rode slowly to their home. He dismounted in front of the columned house where a liveried slave took Aristotle's reins.

The well-proportioned three-story house dominated the north side of Telfair Square, one of the city's largest dwellings. The front door stood open to the night air, the interior ablaze with candlelight as voices rose from the interior. The skies threatened rain and he removed his cape as a slave carefully folded it and disappeared inside. If he'd timed it right, he was the last to arrive.

An elderly black butler waited in the hallway, a tray of champagne balanced in one hand. Jesse took a stemmed glass and wondered if Randall Tyree was included on the guest list. He gathered his courage and started down the entrance hall. Melissa Westbury spotted him and turned back to two couples without acknowledging him.

Jesse drained his glass. A long evening, he thought.

Howard Westbury appeared from the study, a compact man in his fifties who wore rimless spectacles and spoke with a clipped measured cadence, his position solidified by the enormity of sheer wealth that cowed more prominent families. One of the South's most prosperous marine supply merchants, he gave Jesse a tight smile of welcome.

"Jesse. Glad you could join us."

Jesse took the offered hand with relief. "I hope so."

"I give no credence to the charges," Westbury said, aware several heads turned in their direction. "I know your father. He's incapable of such a thing."

Grateful for an ally, Jesse said, "I only hope your guests feel the same."

"No doubt they do," Westbury said with as much zeal as he could muster.

A dinner bell chimed and Jesse followed him across buffed hardwood floors to the dining room where an elaborately set table waited for twenty guests. At the far end a brick fireplace large enough to hide several small children, boasted waist-high brass andirons, twin French doors flanking the elaborate mantel. The table's expanse of white linen displayed meticulous settings of silver and crystal that glowed softly beneath regiments of slender candles. For no discernible reason the somber setting reminded Jesse of a fashionable wake. Standing around the room, women competed for attention in the latest fashion trends, subtly admiring or disdaining one another's choices. The men, somberly dressed, seated them at assigned place settings and Westbury positioned Jesse several chairs to the right of his own. Most of the guests seemed intent on imagining Jesse had become invisible.

Seated across from him, Randall Tyree met his eyes with a sardonic smile.

"I'll give you credit, showing your face tonight," he said.

Jesse formed a reply, but thought better of it. Thirty-five years old, Tyree had inherited his family's lineage of delicate features. Flaxen-haired and delicately handsome to the point of frustrating a portrait painter's nuances, a single white scar marred his right cheek. Bead-black eyes concealed whatever color remained, a nocturnal presence buried in their depths. Had Greek sculptors carved his image, they would have passed over his deeds and produced only a cold marble image with patrician features to recommend him. Famous along the entire southeastern coast, his notoriety spread throughout entire United States, rooted in a dozen duels that killed six men, wearing his reputation without regret or apology. The next day's duel was the talk of the town, and either Melissa Westbury had a misplaced sense of humor, Jesse thought, or she desired assurance of a lively evening. Tyree began a conversation with an attractive woman on his left, ignoring Jesse as a server filled his glass. Jesse scanned the length of the table. He recognized most of the men, but Fletcher Tyree, the city's *eminence grise,* was absent from the evening's festivities.

Hemmed between an elderly dowager smelling of face powder, and a taciturn young woman who studiously inspected her plate when he tried to engage her, Jesse sought an escape. Neither woman acknowledged his presence or attempts at conversation, and he resigned himself to a long evening, his foreboding confirmed.

Midway through the first course, a man to his left, knife and fork in hand, leaned past the old woman and found his eyes. "I take it you're here to defend your father?" he asked in a presumptive voice. The room quieted with abrupt suddenness as though St. Elmo's fire ran along the length of the table.

"I've no need to defend an innocent man," Jesse said. He sensed the futility of his reply as faces around the sumptuous table remained uniformly blank.

A woman at the far end buried her face in her napkin, her voice quaking. "We lost half our savings, plus the money my husband borrowed."

A second woman beside her bowed her head without looking at Jesse. "We've lost everything as well. Everything."

Tyree held up a hand. "Ladies, perhaps my father and I can offer assistance," he said, glancing at Jesse.

"But you and your father also lost a great deal, did you not?" the woman asked.

"It's the least we can do."

Melissa Westbury stood and went to the crying woman, patting her shoulders as she smiled compassionately at Tyree. "You're most kind. We all know you and Colonel Tyree lost a great deal of money as well."

Tyree inclined his head. "We do what's expected of good citizens."

"An educated man such as yourself is aware of the needs of others," Melissa said.

Tyree raised his glass. "The university taught more than the classics, Melissa. Ambrose Caine robbed innocent people."

"He's robbed no one," Jesse shot back.

"Ah, the cry of the bereaved son," Randall retorted dryly.

Jesse looked along the length of the table, the high-ceiling room pierced by silence. His father could not have done such a thing, he reasoned, not to these friends and neighbors. But friendships became brittle when investors blindly rushed toward the promised land, then protested their avarice when the windfall failed to materialize. If the written evidence proved valid, why would his father remain in the city with stolen money? Why not vanish and enjoy the rewards?

"The sheriff and Judge Fraley say the evidence marks him as our thief," Randall said.

"Nothing's been proven," Jesse replied. "Your education was lacking if you condemn a man before his day in court."

"An education you obviously lack," Randall said.

"Dueling seems to have been your chosen subject."

Randall nodded agreeably and addressed the assembly of guests. "Most of you are aware our country's history is replete with duelists. Hamilton. Burr. Even our own Button Gwinnett after putting his name to the Declaration of Independence. He applied the code when it served to redress personal insults. Other founders knew certain offenses could only be satisfied on the field of honor." He looked pointedly at Jesse.

"And it cost him his life," Jesse replied, "though he chose pistols to resolve his differences. You and your friends prefer the use of swords. That gives you the advantage over the untrained."

"Then it serves to ensure good manners. The blade's a more elegant choice for gentlemen. If you're intent on defending Charles Rushton here tonight, understand that he appreciates the sword's finer points." He inclined his head with a half-smile. "If the ladies will forgive the pun." The smile disappeared when he looked back at Jesse. "Would you prefer we throw rocks at one another, or possibly you'd prefer the bow and arrow."

"Charles Rushton's no duelist," Jesse said.

"Then he requires a lesson in manners."

Howard Westbury held up his hand. "Gentlemen, this is not the time or place."

"I quite agree," Randall said. "I only bring to Mr. Caine's attention that his friend committed a grievous error of judgment."

"Only in your narrow world."

Tyree smiled at Jesse. "Does this mean we're no longer friends?"

"Enough," Westbury demanded.

Melissa Westbury rose and stood behind her husband's chair. "You were not invited here to pick a quarrel with Mr. Tyree. In fact, you were invited over my objections."

"Melissa!" her husband scolded.

Jesse laid his napkin beside his plate and stood. "Then I apologize for my presence. Enjoy your evening."

He bowed and walked to the front door, boot heels loud on the waxed floor. A slave followed him outside and draped his cape over his shoulders. He swung into the saddle and spurred Aristotle away from the brightly lit windows until he reached the darkened house on Charlton Street.

Chapter Three

First Daylight
The Caine House

Jesse hated the early morning. The world lingered in gloom, walls and window suspended in melancholy. Closing his eyes he sank back onto his pillow. The gauzy rags of sleep slowly dissipated as he recalled the previous evening's debacle and dejected figure in the cell. He listened in vain for sounds of movement within the house, any indication the memories were a dream. Unable to accept what had occurred only hours earlier, he closed his eyes and crept into the imaginary cave he'd dug as a boy.

He'd created his lonely sanctuary as a boy, a solitary church with no walls where he could retreat when his skin marked him an outsider. As he grew his circle of friends had grown smaller, and affronts became common. He tried to follow his father's dictates to remain above smaller men, admonishments to judge others by merits, not failings. Perfection in friends represented an impossible human condition, he told Jesse. Without evidence of intent to do harm, he bore the mantle of a renegade in an imperfect society.

Despite the warnings, fist fights and retaliation marked the passing of his boyhood, a quiet rage passed down through his mother's blood. Had she infected him with a contagion scorning forgiveness, requiring none herself, transferring a code from mist-shrouded mountains? In the aftermath of her disappearance, he'd damned his heritage, refusing to look at his reflection when he passed mirrors. To his father's dismay his singular image increased the bitterness. Unable to shed his half-breed legacy like snake's skin, he faced down stares, using his fists when pushed beyond his limits.

He shaved in cold water and selected a white shirt and narrow black trousers, wondering what constituted acceptable dress for a duel. Sitting on the side of the bed with a flush of shame, Jesse shoved away his reluctance to make good his promise. Charlie had always stood by him when other schoolboys hurled 'half-breed' and 'squaw boy' at him. He'd fought by Jesse's side, insults and jeers carrying a heavy price for the tormentors. Ambrose Caine frowned at the cuts and bruises he brought home. 'You're no different from them', he repeatedly reminded him. 'Know you're their equal and walk away.'

His friend bore no burdens of birth, but managed to snap the slender filament between honor and common sense. Any rational reason for the affair with Tyree was trivial at best, and Jesse hoped the ride to the plantation would come to nothing. Blades might never be lifted. An apology. A handshake. Peace. But Jesse knew his friend too well. It wouldn't happen that way.

He donned a black swallowtail morning coat and looked around the room a final time without lighting a lamp. "Damn it, Charlie," he murmured to the darkness, "it's too early for this nonsense," knowing the last word was poorly chosen for what the morning demanded of him.

Carrying his boots in one hand he closed the bedroom door and made his way downstairs in his stocking feet to the darkened kitchen. He pulled on high-top boots, pausing again to listen to silent rooms once abandoned by his mother—and now his father.

A scrim of boot-top fog hugged the ground, the humid air smelling of wet bricks and decaying leaves. Half-hidden in the mist, houses emerged like familiar phantoms. Jesse looked at the unlit windows where innocents slept, blissfully unaware of the travesty where he was expected at first light.

Inside the carriage house he saddled the gelded stallion and led it into the deserted alley, winter adamant in its refusal to relinquish its fading grip on the coastal lowlands. The bay tossed its head, skittish at abandoning its warm stall. Jesse stroked the heavily muscled neck and the horse quieted, moist black nostrils emitting small clouds of cold brittle air, buckles and harness jingling. Jesse pulled the head down and blew his warm breath into one ear to calm the animal.

"I don't want to be out here either," he whispered to the stallion.

Swinging into the saddle Jesse buttoned his coat collar for the hour's ride to the plantation. Jarred by the hard canter, he shivered and cursed himself for not wearing a heavier coat. The bay's stiff-legged trot seemed calculated to annoy him, but he preferred the spirited animal to his father's docile gray, taking perverse satisfaction in controlling the willful beast. He halted at Chatham Crossroads, the two country lanes bordering a stubble field and ditch filled with frosted brambles. Rail fences lined the road like dashes on an empty page. A lone squirrel sat atop a fencepost, a furry decoration that fluffed its tail and returned Jesse's inspection. Hands jammed beneath his armpits, Jesse shivered and looked down the road.

He and Charles Rushton had grown up side by side, their parents' houses cheek to jowl. They'd shared their first taste of whiskey, and traded heady stories of unraveling, untying, and unbuttoning the mysteries of young women, inseparable co-conspirators. When a fire killed Charlie's parents, the two became brothers without the bonds of blood. Now Charlie faced the consequences of defending a young woman's reputation, a girl he barely knew. The strict code duello offered a tempting potion to salve injured pride, a remedy Jesse doubted would lose its luster in the light of day.

A bulky figure appeared from the fog atop a black mare of good blood. Charles Rushton's tailored coat showed white ruffles at the cuffs and an upturned collar, his riding boots polished from toe to looped pull as though attending a cotillion, a leather scabbard secured across his saddle pommel. Heavy-set and half-again Jesse's weight, he touched the brim of his top hat with a sardonic smile and ignored Jesse's discomfort. He leaned across and shook Jesse's hand with an embellished shiver.

"A chilly morning, Mister Jesse Caine." Rushton briskly rubbed his broad hands together with exaggerated discomfort. Despite the chill, perspiration dampened his forehead. He peered down the empty road and frowned before he gave Jesse a concerned look.

"I heard a far-flung rumor this morning. My neighbor says your father's accused of theft."

"Not so far-fetched. John Dew arrested him two nights ago."

Rushton reared back in the saddle. "That's absurd."

"Nevertheless, he's sits in the city jail."

Rushton backhanded the air with a dismissive gesture. "Damned fools, whoever they are. When I complete this morning's business, we'll find who's responsible for this claptrap."

His loyalty unfailing, Charlie would side with his father no matter the circumstances.

"I'd endure it more readily if we returned home," Jesse said. "It's too damned cold for this nonsense."

Rushton laughed. "You heathen savages are supposed to be warriors of the woods, inured to the elements."

"Go to the devil."

The generous smile flared, then faded, replaced by a look of resignation. "In any event, it can't be undone. I respect your feelings about these affairs, but I must follow my own."

Jesse withheld a dismissive sound. Two decades of disagreements had only bound them closer. Meeting with Randall Tyree's seconds, he'd twice attempted reconciliation without success, and Jesse now sensed a subdued melancholy beneath the glib manner. Shivering with cold and buried inside his coat, his anger spilled over at the prospect of what awaited them.

"This concerns a shop girl whose name you've likely forgotten."

Charlie blinked and searched his memory. "Her name was Barbara, and Tyree left me no choice."

"Dammit, Charlie, you selected a formidable opponent to test your notions of chivalry," he snapped. "Ignoring Tyree was the wiser choice. You know the bar at the City Hotel breeds these incidents like rabbits."

Rushton lifted his reins. "No reason to be so glum. I can take care of myself far better than you imagine."

"Being a pig-headed bastard was never your most endearing trait," Jesse said.

Rushton laughed and spurred the saddle mare, flinging bits of dirt and shell. The squirrel skittered back on the post and watched the riders until the road was deserted again.

Oyster Point Plantation provided a lesson in failure. The long-dead owners had come and gone with the tides, leaving few footprints. Scattered tabby remnants sat beneath gloomy oaks, thick branches bent low as though weary of watching over the ruins for the past century. An untended graveyard of forgotten names bespoke of monuments to a squandered fortune. Acres of marshland and brooding trees guarded the remains, and even in the morning darkness, an aesthetic eye could see where the manor house once occupied a slight rise of ground; trees festooned with pointed beards of gray Spanish moss completed the ominous setting. Only yards away Hope River, a misnamed ribbon of sluggish tidewater, snaked its way through acres of Spartina marsh grass. Scarcely navigable at low tide, the rivulet meandered past the grounds, the stench of wet pluff mud spoiling the bucolic setting. Rot had claimed the dock, leaving nothing to reveal the owners had once breached the expanse of reeds. Hordes of tiny fiddler crabs scuttled across the glistening shoreline, the birthplace of ocean life fermenting beneath mats of tide-flattened reeds. Across the prairie of reeds the emerging sun silhouetted the tree line with the illusion of salvation.

Jesse and Charlie reined beneath the nearest copse of oaks. Windom Salter, Rushton's other second, watched them dismount. Jesse nodded at Salter whose closely trimmed black beard glinted with frost. Beyond him, a narrow swath of ground cut through a lane of decomposing leaves, a man-made scar on the landscape. Carefully prepared along a north-south axis, the path sat at right angles to the rays of the rising sun.

Salter refused to meet Jesse's eyes. Jesse handed his reins to a slave as Rushton removed his hat. Sitting on the damp ground, he pulled off his boots, and slipped on low-cut shoes. The morning sun lit the glade, bathing the ground in pale pink, and everything suddenly seemed a terrible mistake. Charlie stood and Jesse gripped his forearm.

"This is foolhardy. The girl means nothing to you. No one will think you a coward if this stops here."

Salter joined them. "He's right, Charles. Listen to him."

"It's gone too far." Rushton forced a rueful grin. "Besides, I never liked the arrogant bastard."

Randall Tyree stood a few yards away, his back to them. Charlie's careless words had presented an opportunity, and Tyree reveled in role of the injured party. Friends surrounded him and cast glances at his opponent, searching for signs of fear or remorse. Bundled in black overcoats, they reminded Jesse of impatient crows, a well-dressed audience drawn by primal curiosity. The glade's tranquility remained undisturbed except for the murmur of voices and horses tended by slaves on the nearby road. Jesse searched the crowd for allies but saw only thinly disguised masks of excitement and the prospect someone might die. Looking more closely he more saw each face imbued with relief they were excluded from the morning's proceedings.

Charlie slid the epée from its scabbard, staring down at it. He held up the flawless length of tempered steel and a hint of anguish touched his eyes. Walking away from Jesse and Salter, he slashed at the carpet of dried leaves, rethinking his impulse of chivalry.

Fear clotted Jesse's throat and he turned to Salter. "I should never have consented to this."

The bearded cotton broker crossed himself. "Too late now. This thing will play out as God decides."

Tyree's seconds motioned them forward and Jesse walked into the clearing on numb legs. An older individual, shirtsleeves rolled to his forearms, joined them, a small black leather satchel in one hand. Harris Moorehead was a doctor, his presence a familiar specter, his attendance required by the rules. Tyree glanced at him and assumed an attitude of boredom as though he was about to engage in a foot race where he might suffer nothing more than a twisted ankle.

Harper Jerrard, the morning's master of ceremonies and Tyree's closest friend, motioned Charlie forward. Dressed in a formal knee-length frock coat and silken gaiters, his center-parted black hair and elongated features reminded Jesse of a disreputable undertaker who buried his clients stark naked. Jerrard laid out the affair's rules in dry tones, restraining a smile each time he glanced at Tyree.

Rushton and Tyree removed their coats to reveal loose shirts as he spoke. Like actors taking center stage, the white garments glowed in contrast to the desolate setting. Jerrard completed the instructions, and Jesse walked quickly to Charlie.

"Charlie—"

Rushton ignored him and strode away, sword clutched in his sweaty fist, knuckles white. Without looking back, he twisted his shoulders inside the unfamiliar shirt, his back damp despite of the morning chill. Unruly brown hair fell into his eyes and he pushed the locks aside, avoiding his opponent's amused scrutiny.

Founder and president of the city's Foil and Blade League, Tyree feigned a yawn and glanced around the plantation, a study in boredom as though irritated to interrupt his morning. Jerrard whispered in his ear and Tyree laughed, the sound intrusive beneath the cathedral of century-old oaks.

Jerrard motioned the two men and seconds forward again.

"Gentlemen, your weapons."

Jesse and the other three seconds measured the length of both epées against one another, inspecting bowl-shaped hand guards. The tips, meticulously sharpened and designed to penetrate rather than slash flesh apart, were not touched.

I need to stop this, Jesse thought. He'd harbored an ill-formed notion he might avert the fiasco before it started. He looked at the road where his horse waited, and wondered if his unexpected departure might provide additional time for reconciliation. The expectant assembly of onlookers grew quiet, the clearing's tranquility disturbed only by plaintive cries of marsh birds that pleaded for dawn to appear. Winged coveys gyred in agitated circles above clusters of eager men.

Too late, Jesse thought, his heart falling. *Too late*.

Rays of sunlight brushed the tips of marsh grass, and his heart sank as Rushton and Tyree faced one another, swords at their sides. Jesse joined Salter a few yards away, and stood at right angles to Charlie and Tyree; the other seconds faced them, creating a human crucifix.

Tyree stepped away and held up his hand. He bowed to the crowd and turned back to Rushton.

"I condescended to meet you, though you and your associates merely play the roles of gentlemen." Tyree delivered the slight as though reciting the day's price of cotton. "You need only to admit to my superior powers of observation about your tart. Then you and your friends can return to your breakfast of greasy pork and day-old biscuits."

Color rose in Rushton's cheeks. "You may cordially go to hell."

Tyree shrugged and rolled his shoulders." Then your breakfast will turn to dust waiting for you."

Jerrard stepped between them, eyes alight. He spread his arms in an obscene benediction and slowly raised his hands together until they were a foot apart. Rushton and Tyree lightly laid their sword tips against his outstretched palms. He looked at both men.

"Ready. Begin!"

Jerrard quickly stepped away and Rushton lunged. Randall Tyree parried the thrust and stepped to his right. He flicked his blade against the other epée, the ring of steel obscene in the quiet glade. He parried Charlie's next two thrusts and lowered his blade as he circled him, left hand on his hip as though encouraging another attack. He stopped and suddenly lunged. His blade slipped past Rushton's guard but stopped short of its target.

Charlie stumbled away and blinked sweat from his eyes. Tyree brushed aside a series of tentative thrusts and circled again, measuring, prolonging. He turned his back and swiped his blade at the earth as if its presence offended him.

Shirt soaked and cold against his back, Charlie struggled for air, his breath visible.

Tyree turned and lowered his blade, inviting another attack. When it came, he easily swept it away, stepping aside and directed his blade at the ground again. Catlike, he executed two flawless thrusts. Charlie, chest heaving, parried both at the last second. He seemed on the verge of speaking when Tyree lunged again and drove six inches of steel into his throat. Eyes wide, Charlie uttered a childlike sound as a finger-thick stream of blood erupted from his neck. He blinked once and stumbled forward. His knees gave way and he collapsed, almost falling against his killer. Tyree stepped back and allowed him to fall face down.

Jesse and Salter rushed forward. Moorehead swore and shoved them aside, holding a cloth against the wound. Several men turned the limp body over. Confused, his eyes blinked once, then closed in resigned acceptance. Jesse touched a bloodied sleeve. He rose, the body at his feet empty waste as his father had predicted.

A matter of a few hours had swept away his world. He wiped his slippery fingers on his trousers and stared down at the body. Too numbed to hear Salter's condolences, he brushed clinging damp leaves from his knees and watched four men carry the lifeless body to a waiting wagon.

A sharp crunch caught Jesse's ear, and he turned to see Tyree jam his epée into the spongy earth, cleansing the blade. He swabbed the steel with a handful of damp leaves and caught Jesse's eye.

"A dreary way to begin one's day," he said with a dry smile.

Salter touched his arm but Jesse shook it off. He pointed to the blood-stained earth.

Tyree shrugged. "You know how the game's played."

"Killing is not a game for your amusement."

Randall gestured at the group behind him. "It's what they expect."

"I don't consider dueling a spectator sport."

Tyree shrugged again and feigned contrition. "You saw I was open to a retraction, but he chose otherwise." When Jesse only stared at him, he said, "I told you last night, poor decisions bring consequences as your father discovered." He smiled. "But you have my sympathies. His arrest must have come as a shock on top of your mother's infidelity." He glanced toward the wagon. "You'd best attend your father now. He has more need of you than a dead friend with a careless mouth."

Salter was saying something but Jesse did not hear him. In his dreams Jesse often saw a painted figure beside a pyramidal fire, beckoning him forward to join a blood ritual. The image lingered but he forced it away. An angry or careless word would leave his father defenseless.

Tyree turned and rejoined his circle of admirers; others lingered in small clusters, talking in hushed tones as if reviewing the merits of the city's latest play. A slave led Aristotle to the edge of the clearing, and Jesse heaved himself into the saddle, the reins slack in his numbed fingers, waiting until his vision cleared. It would be a simple matter to confront Tyree and repeat Charlie's mistake. But his father's life outweighed revenge. If he failed to save him, the days ahead promised an end to life as he knew it.

Thoughts tumbling over one another, Jesse slumped in the saddle, steeling himself for what awaited him. Sunlight pierced the trees, burnishing the plantation's remains with false hope. Avoiding the stained leaves, he turned the horse's head toward a city that would awaken to find Charles Rushton dead and his father a common criminal. Spurring Aristotle into a gallop, he put the killing ground behind him without looking back.

Chapter Four

Jesse never recalled the ride from the plantation, one life tragically ended and another in ruins in the space of a day.

He unsaddled the horse and led it into the stall. Inside the house, the empty rooms ticked and groaned as they collected the morning's feeble heat. He tossed the blood-stained shirt in the rubbish bin and selected fresh clothes. Dressing, he recalled Randall Tyree's certainty about his father's guilt. Worse than a callous judgment, what if he was right. Was there more to the wreckage of two lives? Was his own guilt entangled with a dead mother who'd created a half-breed, then left him to deal with the consequences? Had there been disagreement and arguments with his father he'd never witnessed? How did anyone accept parents had feet of clay, their lives filled with mistakes and failings?

Standing motionless by the window for a full minute, he allowed the black water swamp of anger to surge through him. His father sat in jail, and Charlie and his mother were dead. The temptation to avenge his friend returned, an act others would view as a friend's right of retribution. His revenge would be noble, even virtuous. He basked in the fantasy until he realized it could only end in his death, leaving his father at the city's mercy. Whatever happened, he would try to maintain appearances for his father's sake. He brushed his best coat and held it up to the light. More than redemption and respectability, he required a healing balm to point his way out of hell.

He led Aristotle from the carriage house again, caressing the soft wet muzzle. Unsettled at being saddled for a second time, the agitated horse nickered and tossed its head as Jesse whispered assurances. He mounted and rode toward the river.

Samuel Cohen's law practice occupied the drab structure on a wide boulevard aptly named Liberty Street. The three-story building narrowly escaped the definition of disreputable. Its clapboard exterior thirsting for paint, peeling boards revealing the first signs of dry rot. A refuge for guilty and innocent alike, the office offered a haven open to rich and poor in the city's center. Possessed of a piercing legal mind, Cohen traced his lineage back to Portuguese Jews who helped settle the city. The displaced arrivals had quickly assimilated into the colony six months after Oglethorpe climbed the river bluff to claim his New World charter. He needed every colonist he could scrape together, and welcomed the small colony of Jews to the New World despite the

Trustee's specific instructions to exclude Hebrews. For his part, Cohen broached no peers in the city or state. His worship at the temple meant little to unfortunates who crossed his threshold; those inconvenienced or interned by the law remained blind to race. Vindication, if it existed, dwelt in Samuel Cohen's legal skills.

Jesse walked past an unhinged shutter and pushed open the front door. A brass bell jangled in a cold anteroom. Two young law clerks shivered at simple desks jammed against the far wall. A table overflowed with writs, petitions, while a backlog of legal pleadings and maneuvers smothered the floorboards beside elevated stools. Absorbed in life and death and property issues, the young men hovered beneath lamps and tried to ignore Jesse, aware in all likelihood more work had just walked through the door. One of the clerks, a blanket draped over his shoulders, reluctantly looked up, asked Jesse's name, and slipped from his stool. Possessor of thin gloves and a woolen hat, he escorted him to a varnished door. The sallow clerk knocked and Jesse found himself in an overheated office with the feeling he was expected.

Warmed to discomfort by a roaring fireplace, the office presented a distant universe from the other side of his door. A large Queen Anne table served as Cohen's work space, cherry surface waxed to a soft sheen. A framed Revolutionary War flag hung above the mantel, a gilt-framed map of Boston behind the cluttered table. Two rocking chairs flanked a comfortably upholstered wingchair, the furniture assembled on a splendid Kerman rug, the room a clear dividing line between the aspiring and the successful.

Samuel Cohen worked in shirtsleeves, bent over an ornate table, quill in hand, face concealed behind a tower of books. Fifty-two years old, his body radiated restrained energy bound within a thick-set torso. He stood and smiled at the city's newest pariah. He moved on his toes with a dancer's grace, the ease of confident movement well-known in courtrooms across the state. Dark curly hair showed no gray, his closely shaven cheeks blued with the day's beard. Six inches shorter than Jesse, his ears were oddly stunted and his square hands terminated in blunt fingers and distorted knuckles. A ridge of scar tissue divided his left eyebrow into two equal halves, and he occasionally squeezed the dark eye closed as though it served no purpose. He gripped Jesse's hand with surprising force and indicated an oversized wingchair.

"I know about your father," he said, settling behind the table. "Bad news travels of its own accord." He frowned. "I wish you were here under more favorable circumstances."

"You're his best hope to put this behind him."

Cohen rose and tossed a superfluous log into the flames; embers popped and boiled up the chimney and a burst of heat assailed Jesse.

Cohen showed no discomfort and thumped Jesse's arm as he resumed his chair.

"This is a lovely city in the summer, but colder than a marble tomb in winter," he said. He regarded the fire with satisfaction, oblivious to perspiration on Jesse's forehead.

"I was born here, you know," he continued. "My family moved to Boston when I was a child. I hated the abominable winters and returned to Savannah, expecting year-round tropics after listening to my father's unending complaints of the heat." He smiled and laced his fingers over his waistcoat. Accustomed to years scrutinizing and assessing the desperate and despairing who crossed his doorsill, he laid one hand atop a law book and waited for Jesse to plead his case.

"I wish to retain you to defend my father," Jesse began.

Cohen held up the hand. "I expected as much, but I cannot."

"If it's money, I'll place our home as collateral against your fee."

"It's not money. A friend allowed me to see the proof assembled against your father. To say the least, it's formidable."

At a loss to refute him, Jesse said, "I've not seen the evidence."

Cohen sat back. Known for his unorthodox legal tactics, he enjoyed an occasional gamble around the edges of the law, especially in capital cases where the stakes were high. Favors were owed him in certain quarters and it seemed only fair a son should see what his father faced—and his refusal to represent him.

"Did you ride?" he asked.

When Jesse nodded and Cohen collected his coat, the lawyer said, "There's a way for you to understand what you face. If you'll remain quiet. Bring your horse around back."

The two men rode from the office building without speaking. Near the river Jesse followed Cohen down a side street to the city courthouse. They secured the horses in an alley behind the building and Cohen tapped lightly at the rear door. A small balding man opened it, his countenance falling when he saw the attorney. The pinched bespectacled face peered past Cohen at Jesse who saw a high-ceilinged room jammed with filing cabinets.

"Brewster, I need favor returned," Cohen said without preamble. "Your sister's husband has overcome his addiction, I hope? No further arrests?"

Eyes closed, the clerk nodded, resigned to a life shared with an unrewarding in-law. The little man ushered them into his world of wooden filing cabinets and overflowing wire baskets. He quickly shut the door and locked it. The air smelled of old paper, a sterile desert of plat books and bound documents. Cohen turned to him.

"Now if you'll be so kind as to find work in the front office, I'd appreciate you making certain we're not disturbed," he said. "I only want a quick look at some old documents, and we'll be gone. Come back in five minutes."

Brewster disappeared and Cohen locked the connecting door behind him. He strode to a cabinet. Fingering rows of files, he withdrew a four-inch folder. He untied the restraining cord and placed the pile of paper on a table, saddened by the shock on Jesse's face.

"I'm told there are more," he said.

Stunned by the size of the stack, Jesse picked up the top document.

Cohen leaned against the door. "You only have a few minutes."

Short of breath Jesse flipped through the stack of promissory notes, confidential agreements, and revenue forecasts. He understood little of the canal's construction details but quickly recognized the file represented a mountain of evidence, all in his father's familiar handwriting. The telltale odor of cloves wafted from every page. He skimmed each page, peering closely at the writing and distinctive signature, all set down in his father's personal scarlet ink. The sterile room fed on the spice until the odor sickened him. A harmless conceit, the spiced ink was a blend of ground soot and cloves combined with an unknown coloring agent. A closely-guarded concoction, nothing more than a small vanity, it now pressed a jury's dagger against his father's throat.

Jesse picked up a magnifying glass from the table and examined a promissory note, the careful script all too familiar. He ran his fingers over the words as though touch might erase a calamity of his father's own making. A drop of perspiration fell onto the final page. Angry and bewildered, Jesse crumpled the document and flung it across the room. He stared at the miniature scaffold of evidence. The signature and handwriting were unmistakable.

What salvation existed in the obvious?

He glanced at Cohen who read the day's newspaper, his eyes averted. Impulsively, Jesse stuffed a half dozen pages inside his shirt. He'd seen no inventory and needed time to clear his mind. The pilfering betrayed Cohen's trust, but he needed to confront his father. He quickly restored the stack.

Cohen retrieved the crumpled document from the corner and smoothed the paper. He rebound the file and replaced it in the cabinet just as Brewster slipped into the room. Cohen nodded his thanks as he and Jesse walked out without another word.

In the alley, Jesse allowed the attorney to walk ahead of him. He hastily arranged his coat over the documents and they rode away.

Back in his office, Cohen placed his forearms on the desk and chewed a corner of his mouth. The papers stuck to Jesse's bare skin and he looked away.

"Letting you examine evidence would not please my silk stocking colleagues," Cohen said, "but you needed to see what your father faces. And I'll confess another secret since we've ignored legal boundaries. Knowing your father's reputation as I do, forgery came to mind when I first saw the documents. I'm not an expert, so I allowed two colleagues to inspect the signatures. I won't reveal their names, but they know your father quite well." He shifted uneasily in his chair. "Both agreed there was no doubt about the signatures. The notes and signatures are in his hand."

Jesse did not move, fearing a rustle of paper.

"Representing your father would be a misuse of my time and your money," Cohen said. "I do not waste my clients' money nor my time in hopeless causes. My current case load is overflowing and I won't deceive you. What you saw is a veritable ocean of credible evidence." He sat back. "I'm sorry, but I cannot devote sufficient time to build a credible defense."

The documents stuck to Jesse's chest, the faint aroma of cloves wafting upwards beneath his shirt. He slowly stood, hating that he'd deceived Cohen, but what was the damage if he now refused to help his father?

"Then I'll find someone with sufficient confidence to defend him." He slammed the front door shut and left the office without offering his hand.

Jesse squinted at the half-full bottle of whiskey that whispered answers. The golden liquid glowed in the kitchen's single lamp, and he accepted the fact he was drunk. The window presented a grim black rectangle, morning an eternity away. He picked up the unlabeled bottle, curious what he'd consumed for the past hour. He'd found the pedestrian bottle in the back of the liquor cupboard behind the finer whiskies. After several confused moments, he recalled its provenance: His father acquired Monongahela whiskey for his foremen and rougher elements among the engineering profession. What the whiskey lacked in refinement, it made up for in potency, and Jesse required its respite. He'd inspected the stolen documents again, then jammed them into a desk drawer, distraught at the sight of his father's handwriting. He needed a friend more than ever, but Charlie was dead.

I'll never hear his counsel or laughter again, not in this life.

The lamp shown wavering images on the kitchen walls and covered him in shadow. He embraced the gloom. He downed his drink and filled the glass again. The whiskey promised an understanding even though his brain duly informed him that he'd passed his normal limit. He ignored the warning and wondered if the liquor's rapid entry into his brain had anything to do with being a half-breed. He'd always experienced a sense of profound loneliness when he drank, and he wondered if alcohol increased his feelings of isolation. They claimed whiskey made Indians crazy, but did the weakness apply to half-Indians? He grinned, picked up the bottle, and considered the possibility. Was he half again as drunk as a white man might find himself under the circumstances? Did his blood breed a weakness that bore watching? Too disorientated to work out the reasoning, he thumped the bottle on the table and frowned at it.

God grant me mercy if I can't find solace in a bottle.

But the bottle's relief provided only a maudlin haze that bordered on black humor.

"Solace be damned," he informed the walls. "My father sits in jail and Charlie's dead."

Vaguely amused that he'd stated the obvious to an uncaring room, he splashed more whiskey in the glass and considered his father's plight. Nothing to be done tonight short of a jail break, he reasoned. And no remedy for Charlie inside his coffin. He drained the glass. No justice for a friend or his father. No justice for a sick old man.

Unless Randall Tyree ceased to exist.

Jesse rose unsteadily to his feet. He allowed the room to stabilize and pushed away from the table. In the hall, he clutched the newel post and conceded that tradesmen's rough whiskey indeed had its advantages. He placed his foot on the first step and waited until the stairwell stopped spinning, pleased with his caution. At the top of the stairs, he steadied himself with one hand along the wall and opened the door to his father's bedroom. He weaved to the bed and sat down heavily. He resisted the temptation to fall back and let the night pass, and instead found matches on the bedside table and lit the lamp.

He removed a stubby percussion pistol from the drawer, his father's sole protection against intruders. Behind the weapon, he found a small powder flask and box of percussion caps. Squinting down the muzzle, he poured powder into the barrel and spilled black grains onto the bed quilt. He brushed them onto the floor and gingerly thumbed the percussion cap into place. Pleased with his dexterity, he eased the hammer to half-cock and slipped the pistol in his pocket, its weight comforting.

At the kitchen table he poured a final drink. Reeling, he saddled Aristotle with muttered reassurances, the horse skittish as if sensing its owner's uncertainty. Jesse pulled himself into the saddle and spurred toward the river. Patches of moonlight lit the street, a flickering kaleidoscope of light and dark blurring his vision. Along Bay Street, brighter pools of lamplight bathed the sidewalk in an amber blush. Midway along the street the City Hotel windows glowed in the darkness. Two immense brass lanterns guarded the entrance.

He tied Aristotle to a hitching post and touched the pistol in his coat pocket, his eyes blurring as he stepped into a wall of light. To his left, the expansive mahogany bar beckoned. He turned his back to the noisy room and called to the bartender. Down the bar, Samuel Cohen was engaged in conversation with two men, one finger vigorously tapping the bar's wood surface. Beyond him at the far end, surrounded by friends, Randall Tyree stared at Jesse.

Jesse met his gaze, the whiskey reasserting itself, the pistol insistent against his hip. Rage spilled over the edge and he saw Moore again, helpless at his feet. Voices around him faded into a cloud of sound. The flocked walls and tobacco smoke slanted, revolving under three enormous chandeliers. Somewhere in the smoke a piano struggled to be heard above the din.

Tyree turned back to his friends and Jesse's fingers closed around the checkered grip. If I kill the bastard, he reasoned, at least sit in jail alongside my father, waiting to be hanged for an act long overdue. Pleased by the clarity of his reasoning, he downed his drink, unable to banish the memory of Charlie Rushton's ruined throat.

Do this scornful city a favor and join Charlie at the same time.

He looked back down the bar at Tyree who met his unfocused gaze. Several associates looked past his shoulder at Jesse and laughed. Cohen turned in the same instant and saw Jesse. The tavern blurred, the floor tilting. Jesse ignored Cohen and fixed on Tyree. He slipped his hand into his coat pocket.

Cohen appeared beside him and glanced down the bar at Tyree. He leaned forward to block Jesse's view and slid two silver coins across the mahogany.

"Allow me to make amends for this morning," he said, pressing against Jesse's arm. "My manner must have seemed abrupt in light of your situation. I can only assure you my decision doesn't reflect on your father's guilt or innocence."

The barman placed two drinks in front of them. Jesse downed his in a single gulp and aware he slurred his response. "My father needs your help."

"I wish I could provide it."

"Then do it!" Jesse exclaimed. The mirror behind the bar shimmered under the lights as heads turned toward them.

Cohen lowered his voice and spoke slowly. "Your father faces a calamity of monstrous proportions."

Jesse belched and grunted. "Your somewhat elevated reputation indicates otherwise."

"I'm no match for such evidence."

"Then I can only surmise your reputation is constructed of fragile material."

Randall Tyree and Harper Jerrard started toward them, and Jesse's hand slipped into his pocket, tightening his grip on the pistol. Cohen moved closer and clamped his hand over Jesse's wrist.

Tyree stopped beside Jesse, leaned on the bar, and lifted his glass toward Cohen. "I hope we're not interrupting legal matters, counselor. Every sinking ship requires a lifeboat, does it not?"

Cohen tightened his grip and Jesse flinched in his iron-like grasp. "Jesse, it's time we left."

"No, no." Tyree grinned. "Stay. We'll share a drink and discuss the whereabouts of the two ghosts employed by his father."

"You bastard." Jesse tried to pull away from Cohen who bumped against him without loosening his grip. Jesse winced as powerful fingers dug into his wrist bones.

Tyree bowed to him. "I'm at your convenience." He raised his voice for the crowd's benefit. "A half-breed and Savannah's most esteemed shyster. A fitting combination." Nervous laughter spread along the bar.

"I do not discuss my clients in a public house," Cohen replied.

Tyree gave an exaggerated bow to more laughter. "Then you're a match made in heaven."

Cohen propelled Jesse from the tavern, and he stumbled as the whiskey caught up to him. Laughter followed them. Outside, Cohen tugged the pistol from Jesse's pocket. Braced by the night air, Jesse mumbled a protest as Cohen steered him toward Aristotle. Mounted, Jesse swayed in the saddle and stared through the tavern's lighted window.

"You came close to getting yourself killed in there," Cohen said.

Jesse swayed in the saddle and squinted at the blur of the lighted doorway.

Damn Cohen's logic. I'll go back and... What? Murder Randall Tyree? Or be killed by him?

Cohen held the horse's reins. Laughter erupted again from inside, and he followed Jesse's glassy stare.

"I have your pistol," he said. "In any event, you're too drunk to hit the floor."

Jesse looked down at him, the fog clearing. "What you said in there about being a client. Have you changed your mind?"

"Come to the office at nine tomorrow morning."

Chapter Five

March 8
Morning
Samuel Cohen's Office

The fireplace blazed in its full glory.

Cohen, dressed in a plain morning coat with a snug high collar, savored the heat and rethought his decision. Jesse Caine sat across from him, his hopeful face glazed with alcoholic sweat. Cohen's inspection of the evidence left few avenues of defense. He'd represented many men who'd stepped beyond the law's boundaries, and evidence indicated Jesse's father had succumbed to the lure of easy money.

"I only just learned of Charles Rushton's death yesterday," Cohen began, grimacing as he rearranged a few papers. "Too much time spent behind these closed doors shields me from what happens beyond them."

"It was a murder," Jesse declared. Head precariously balanced atop his neck, he feared sudden movements would be his undoing, resisting the temptation to move his chair away from the hearth. "Legal under the law, but outright murder in my estimation."

Cohen's expression softened. "I agree, but nothing justifies your impulse last night." He opened a drawer and placed the small pistol on the table. "Killing Tyree in a barroom brawl would have seen you hanged, nothing more."

Jesse sheepishly pocketed the small weapon.

"Your drunken interpretation of justice last night did nothing to return Charles Rushton to life or assist your father," Cohen warned. "If I agree to his defense, you must swear not to get yourself arrested. I don't have time to defend two Caines."

Jesse gingerly nodded, edging from the fireplace.

Cohen smiled at his discomfort. "Have you recovered?"

"Almost."

"Work many times interferes with important matters," Cohen said. "Such as finding a reason to put Randall Tyree behind bars. He's a dangerous man, and poor fortune seems intent on stalking your family. Stay away from him."

Jesse started to protest, but Cohen cut him short.

"Here's my first piece of legal advice: You should not have involved yourself in the duel, or shown yourself at the City Hotel."

"Charlie Rushton was my friend."

"You were drunk last night," Cohen said. "It did not help your father's cause."

Jesse ran a hand over his sweaty face. Chagrined by the truth, he'd added drunkenness to his dubious lineage, coming close to murdering a man.

"It won't happen again."

"And Rushton's duel," Cohen insisted. "What possessed you to attend after your father's arrest?"

"Tyree forced Charlie to call him out." Jesse repeated the argument he'd given his father. "He had no choice."

Cohen sighed and folded his large hands atop the desk, inspecting them. "Barbaric. The State's prohibition against dueling is toothless, and our city's Anti-Dueling Association provides amusement for those sanctioning the practice. Both attempts to outlaw the custom died like newborn gulls in a hurricane." Color rose in Cohen's face. "You're aware these same people employ the Sheftall cemetery as a dueling ground? Old Mordecai Sheftall must be spinning in his grave." He shook his head. "If my race took offense at every slur, Mickve Israel temple would be a dry goods store."

Jesse smiled weakly and shifted his chair. Less than five minutes in the heat-baked office, and his coat clung to his back.

"Your father. He's well?" Cohen asked.

"Conditions in the jail are killing him." Jesse wiped perspiration from his upper lip. "Can you arrange bail?"

Cohen shook his head. "I can try, but emotions are running too high. A great deal of money's missing, and the victims fear your father might flee the city. In this instance, the desire for punishment overrides compassion. Many who might have interceded are counted among the list of victims. They feel no obligation, and I must admit with some justification, given the evidence."

"Friendship," Jesse mumbled.

"Friendship has little to do with it," Cohen said. "You saw the evidence. Combined with the embezzled money, your father should expect no consideration unless he's proven innocent." He shook his head. "It's the largest hoax since the Yazoo Land Fraud twenty years ago, so I won't mislead you. Worse, there's little in the way of a customary defense open to us."

Jesse stared into the fireplace, unable to argue. "I recognized the handwriting," he said softly. "Nothing remains but to find the two men."

Cohen gazed out the window, wishing he could convert cold sunlight into reassurance.

"I know my father's innocent," Jesse said despite the signature and distinctive ink. "I'll stand by him, no matter the evidence."

"A successful defense requires more than a son's faith."

"So what do we do?"

"What you propose. Find the two men."

"Common sense says they fled the city long ago," Jesse offered.

"In all likelihood."

Jesse looked up helplessly at the black tinned ceiling. "And the documents?"

"A friend assures me more are being collected. I fear you saw only a trickle of the documents to come." Cohen turned his chair sideways, lost in thought before he turned back.

"The written evidence appears unassailable, at least to the naked eye," he said.

Jesse nodded at the obvious as doubt crept from its lair. Cohen only described what he'd seen with his own eyes, and it was obvious the seasoned attorney harbored few illusions.

Cohen chewed his lower lip and weighed his next words carefully.

"There may be a chance to refute what you saw," he said. "A slim possibility."

"You doubted what you saw?"

"Think about it a moment." Cohen tapped his fist on the desktop. "Our sight often deceives us. We watch magicians pull rabbits from hats. Playing cards vanish under our nose. Seeing such wonders, of course, does not mean they're factual."

"We'll require magic to make the documents disappear."

"Or another kind of magician," Cohen replied. "Since the documents aren't going away, our best hope is to cast doubt on them." He shoved aside a law volume as if its presence offended him, but kept his hand atop the cover. Picking up a writing quill with his other hand, he tapped his teeth with the tip, choosing his words with reluctance. "We must shatter a jury's certainty about their authenticity. Give them pause."

"How?"

Cohen twirled the feathered pen. His brow knitted in indecision, he considered what he was about to suggest. It meant plowing new legal ground and possibly risking his reputation, but he saw no alternative and he'd never backed away from a challenge.

"We need to prove the eye can be led astray," he said. "There's someone in Boston. A person skilled in uncovering forgeries. An expert in falsified documents. It's a reach, but more than we have at the moment. She —"

"A woman?"

Cohen jammed the quill into a crystal inkwell and assembled a confident face. "A skilled professional. The fact she's female is irrelevant. I talked with a colleague during my last trip to the city. He speaks highly of her. She's made a life study of comparative handwriting, as she terms it, and she figured prominently in a recent Boston case."

The possibility offered the first thread of hope since viewing the evidence. If his father created the documents, nothing could save him. The answer lay in uncovering a clever forger if one existed. But who? A faceless back-office clerk with champagne tastes? A traitorous business associate? Professional criminals who disappeared forever? Had someone seen an opportunity and performed a sleight of hand that now threatened his father's life?

"A forger? For so many documents?"

"We're not concerned with quantity. With the amount of money that's involved, the thieves would go to any lengths."

"Will a Georgia court accept her testimony?"

Cohen opened the fat black and brown volume and turned to a bookmark he'd placed earlier. "I've researched the matter. Comparative analysis is new legal ground, but several cases involving falsified handwriting were successfully heard by high courts in Massachusetts and Connecticut." He donned a small pair of metal-rimmed spectacles and ran his finger along a paragraph: *Valid consideration of fraud based on handwriting comparisons are deemed admissible. Such evidence may be allowed if contentions of fraud are grounded by court-verified comparison.*

Cohen closed the book. "Both decisions were ground-breaking precedents. More importantly, they allowed comparisons to exemplars, the defendant's actual handwriting, that existed *outside* of the evidence."

"But will a Georgia court allow such a precedent?" Jesse persisted.

"A fair question, but we're left few choices unless the men who sold the notes are arrested and exonerate your father. I'll move for a preliminary hearing and make the argument pre-trial. In any event, I don't believe there's any possibility of having the charges withdrawn. But I'll warn you: Precedents or not, defenses claiming forgery have always been controversial." He considered how best to impress upon Jesse that the new science represented more than a legal sleight of hand. It represented a breakthrough for defense counsels although in its fledgling state, accepted after centuries of study and technical treatises.

"Handwriting analysis bears the stigma of being new," Cohen explained. "Many people claim the ability to discern an individual's personality through the study of their handwriting." He gave a half-smile. "According to my Boston colleague, Miss Pendleton dismisses such claims as fraudulent. She focuses her opinions on scientific comparisons of true and forged documents." He studied the dwindling flames as if considering more wood.

"Others believe in something called phrenology," he continued, "The theory purports that criminals can be identified by bumps on their head," he said with an amused smile. "So we indeed face the possibility the court may dismiss the comparative rulings as legal aberrations. New spheres of law frighten timid judges who don't like seeing their decisions overturned."

"Will this woman come to Savannah?"

Cohen removed the glasses and rubbed his eyes. "She might. But I must warn you. She has a sharp mind, but I'm also told she's not one of your delicate Southern belles."

Jesse waved his hand. "If she represents a glimmer of hope, I'll gladly accept her lack of social amenities."

Cohen frowned. "Even if we're successful in proving forgery, discredited documents alone may not be sufficient to produce an innocent verdict. Emotions are too high. We need the two agents who sold the notes to create the certainty of reasonable doubt. Also, there's the problem of not having documents to convince the woman," he said. "My friend allowed us to inspect them, but they're otherwise under lock and key until the trial. If someone discovers I showed them to you, I'll find myself practicing in another state."

Jesse suppressed the guilt of his larceny. "A trip to Boston will take several weeks. What if the trial occurs before I return?"

An enigmatic smile. "I plan to call in other markers to ensure the trial doesn't appear on the docket for awhile. I can make a strong case for the time needed to prepare a thorough defense."

Jesse marveled again at Cohen's reach and influence in the city. At the same time he wondered if Cohen grasped at straws, dangling the woman to sustain Jesse's hopes, or did he intend to use the strategy to test the innovative legal concept. None of his conjectures mattered. A sea voyage with stolen documents paled in comparison to the consequences for his father.

"I'll book passage," Jesse said.

"Just so you realize it's a gamble, not a guarantee."

Jesse's doubts about guilt or innocence resurfaced, but he needed the truth. "Someone placed my father's head in a noose," he said. "I need to know what happened, no matter the consequences."

Chapter Six

Same Day
The Danford House

The sky draped itself in funeral gray, sanctioning the disaster that singled out his father out for retribution. The city's best legal mind had yet to offer a viable defense, any chance of acquittal vanishing like a tiny shell beneath the waves. Even Cohen's agreement to represent his father formed only a spider's thread of hope. Making off with a few documents had been an impulsive act, but Jesse needed to verify the evidence to his satisfaction. The wind freshened and flattened the horse's ears, and he buttoned his coat.

God knows how a few sheets of paper can reverse what's happened, he thought.

The wind persisted and Jesse held his top hat in place. Aristotle settled into an easy canter for a change and allowed him the anticipation of seeing Victoria Danford. His desire for the city's premier actress had remained undiminished from the first night he'd seen her on stage. Idolized by the city, she'd overwhelmed his senses in an offering of *Othello* where she'd burned brightly as the tragic Desdemona. She formed the apex of unfulfilled longing. Enduring his longing for her, she cost him sleepless nights as he resisted easier offerings along the waterfront.

The wind quickened. Trash danced and swirled through the streets as the first raindrops struck palm fronds that quivered from the gentle blows. Aristotle skittered sideways until Jesse calmed him with a tight rein. The Danford home required only a short walk from his home, but arriving at her front door soaked and windblown like a wet mongrel was not the image he desired, especially in light of his father's imprisonment.

Larger drops popped against his hat as the small frame house appeared. Sheltered against his body he removed the documents and slipped them into his saddlebag. He jogged to the porch, his eagerness increasing as he slapped raindrops from his coat. A yank on the bell pull. The door immediately opened as if Victoria Danford had watched his approach.

Pale blond hair carefully pinned above flawless skin, she looked quizzically at him as though she found a stranger on her porch. Taken aback, Jesse could only stare at her. Dressed in a bottle-green taffeta dress, a frilled linen handkerchief peeked from her left cuff. Like all beautiful women, she fully appreciated her effect on men and framed a smile as Jesse swept off his hat. Quickly recovering, she beamed at him and kissed him lightly on the lips.

"Jesse, come in before the rain finds you."

He draped his hat and coat on the wooden hall tree. She took his hand and turned back to him. "You appear well, given your calamity."

"It's because I made time to see you." Rumor and gossip traveled quickly.

The parlor, enclosed by heavy brocade draperies, sheltered the room against the unseasonable chill. Ornate lamps dispelled little of the gloom, but the room smelled of lavender, milled soap, and the warm scent of fresh starch. A framed array of Victoria's small watercolors dotted the walls, her talent displayed to visitors. Small but carefully decorated, the space appeared as pristine as an Easter setting without the lilies. Her mother's footsteps echoed from the kitchen, Franklin Danford dead the past two years.

Jesse sat next to Victoria on the buttoned velvet couch with engraved rosewood armrests, a new addition since his last visit. He placed his wet hat on the floor. Unable to take his eyes from her, he understood again why she captivated the city.

"A dreadful day," she said, touching her hair. "The news about poor Charles Rushton, now this awful story about your father." She took his hand. "Is he well?"

"Given the jail's conditions, I only hope for the best."

Victoria's family had always ignored his stigma. Unable to take his eyes from her, her concern shone like an oasis in the sands. Anxious to somehow explain the events, he squeezed her hand.

"Samuel Cohen's agreed to represent my father, and I've an appointment with the mayor tomorrow."

Rain slapped against the window and a slip of wind forced its way past the thick draperies. Victoria interlocked her fingers with his, her fingertips cold. She briefly squeezed is hand and released it, plucking the handkerchief from her sleeve.

"There's talk of you being implicated as well," she said, kneading the lavender-scented handkerchief.

Implicated.

It struck Jesse that everything had been meticulously arranged to point directly at them. If his father had indeed succumbed to temptation, had he worked alone or employed accomplices? Did he harbor flaws Jesse had never imagined? But why incriminate his only son, and why remain in the city with the money in hand? Nothing made sense, but doubt crept from its cave again. Studying Victoria's lovely face, he wondered if she'd reshaped her feelings for him in the space of a single morning.

"This will all be quickly resolved," he said, at loss to say more.

Martha Danford bustled into the room. Arms outstretched, Victoria's mother's voluminous skirt rustled across the carpet. Jesse rose and she crushed him against her ample starched bosom with a flurry of sniffles. The fair-complexioned woman resembled her daughter but carried the accumulated weight of her years. She held him tightly and patted his back until she leaned away and composed herself. She grasped his hands in hers.

"Your poor father. We only heard this morning," she said. She sat across from him and two orange tabbies quickly commandeered her abundant lap. "It has to be an awful misunderstanding. I've known him for twenty years. He'd never do such a horrible thing." She smoothed her skirt and smiled at Victoria.

"Have you asked Jesse to stay for lunch?"

Victoria balled the lace handkerchief in her fist with a small frown. "Jesse has much to do," she said. "We mustn't detain him."

She stared at her mother and an abyss yawned beneath Jesse's feet. The familiar surroundings shifted, suddenly alien. Had Victoria assembled a performance, a role in a sympathy play constructed for his benefit? He got to his feet.

"Another time," he said, managing a smile.

Martha Danford brushed away the two cats and stood with a glance at her daughter. "We'll keep the invitation open. We're here for you, you know that."

Are you really? Jesse wondered. He searched their faces and realized how desperately he would need them in the coming days.

Victoria reassembled her smile and offered her hand. He kissed it, and her mother bid him goodbye, leaving them alone. Jesse pulled Victoria to him, and she returned his kiss, her lips moist as though contradicting her abruptness. Confused, he pulled back and silence overtook them.

"This can't come between us," he said.

She kissed him again and he picked up his hat and let himself out. The door clicked shut and he stood on the veranda, glad to see the sun divide the clouds. Her kiss lingered, but new misgivings stole the pleasure. Despite their assurances, he feared mother and daughter found themselves caught up in the riptide of opinion.

Coat collar turned up, he pulled himself into the saddle, grateful the rain had stopped. The parlor drapes stirred and for a moment he imagined a pale face behind the panes. Crediting the image to his imagination, he turned the horse's head toward home.

Chapter Seven

March 5
9:00 AM
City Exchange Building

The ostentatious stairwell spiraled upward toward the third-floor landing, the City Exchange interior smelling of new-sawn wood and damp mortar. A morning thunderstorm rolled toward the bluff where the new building stood, and beyond the tall mullioned windows the river added touches of briny water and river waste. At the top floor, Jesse stopped at a window to check his appearance in the glass, frowning at the image. An Indian, he thought, his father an accused thief and his mother an adulterer. He hastily chastised himself, but he'd seen the pile of evidence, and if the failing man walked out of jail a free man, Jesse had to prove the charges represented an unbelievable mistake. He continued to stare at the pane of glass with a dispirited smile.

Nothing to it, he thought. Just disavow the eight-inch stack of documents in his father's handwriting.

Above his head a ladder ascended up the wall to a ceiling trapdoor, leading in turn to a cupola atop of the building. The steeple edifice was home to an immense brass bell recently purchased from Amsterdam to alert Savannah's citizens of disasters and momentous news. Rain lashed the window and he wondered if the city fathers planned to ring it when he stepped into the mayor's office.

A single door stood open at the far end of the hall. Tobacco smoke partially obscured the spacious room's interior. Through the haze Jesse made out Mayor John Sanderson behind his expansive desk at the far end. Conversations halted and heads swung toward Jesse as he entered. He recognized a state senator, the city treasurer, two ship owners, and a red-faced bank president. Wreathed in tobacco smoke, the assembled consortium of power and money fell silent.

Sanderson looked up and waved him forward. He heaved his bulk from a high-backed chair without offering his hand. "Jesse, we're glad you've come," he boomed.

Taken aback by the sea of apprehensive faces, Jesse said, "I didn't know you were in a meeting. I'll come back."

"No, no, join us." Sanderson's smile tightened with anxiety as he leaned over the desk. Endowed with weighty jowls and sausage-thick fingers, his voice was surprisingly high-pitched for a man of such generous proportions. As though commanding a podium to coerce voters, he fixed a practiced smile on Jesse.

"Close the door behind you, son."

Tobacco smoke ruled the air, ranks of familiar faces funereal as sets of eyes fixed him without a nod of recognition. Dark suits encircled him like shark fins. Men that Jesse had known his entire life looked at him as though he'd been reborn a Chinaman overnight, an assembly of barbered and well-dressed Huns measuring an enemy. He walked past rows of glass-front bookcases and sensed he'd entered an unexplored sea, one that maps labeled *Here Be Dragons*.

Aides scuttled about the room and placed standing ashtrays and gleaming spittoons next to its inhabitants. A boy placed a chair in front of Sanderson's desk, and the mayor brusquely motioned the aides outside. He waited until Jesse was seated and cleared his throat.

"Jesse, we want to..."

A rotund man seated beside Sanderson sprang to his feet. "We want our damned money back, that's what we want!"

Turnip-shaped, the man's face contorted with anger. President of Savannah's largest bank Jacob Belden leaned past Sanderson and speared Jesse with barely concealed malice.

"Your kind won't elude us, you can be sure of that."

"*My* kind?" Jesse resisted the impulse to leap across the desk.

Sanderson caught the banker's sleeve. "Sit down, Jacob. That's why we called him here."

"My father's done nothing wrong," Jesse managed.

A lanky man with a heavily-lined face crossed his legs with a satisfied air and pointed his cigar at Jesse. "Ambrose Caine marked us for fools. We'd expect you to defend him, but we didn't come here to have shit shoveled at us. The sheriff's provided the assistance we require for now."

Heads nodded, faces marked with panic born of desperate men. Once counted as friends, the well-dressed posse assumed the roles of embarrassed victims, pity and tolerance banned from the room. The rain outside fell harder, attacking the windows, and sultry heat thickened in the airless office. An aide cracked a window as the storm swept over the building and the room grew darker, a spray of rain gusting over the sill.

At a loss Jesse looked at Sanderson. "I'm here to help resolve this."

"We can ask no more," Sanderson replied in a practiced campaign tone. He picked up a sheet of paper and exhaled loudly. "Jesse, we have a calamity on our hands." He found his magisterial voice and raised it for the sake of constituents in the room.

"This entire deception was perpetrated in less than a week." He paused for effect. "Close to a million dollars has been stolen from these good men."

The room spun. A million dollars? Impossible. He never imagined that much cash existed within the city, but deception and secrecy abounded. He looked at the anxious faces and ran the sums in his head. Fifty thousand dollars per man, less for some and more for others without counting those who wrung their hands at home. Sanderson must be mistaken.

"Impossible," Jesse muttered aloud.

Belden leapt to his feet again, "Impossible? I'll show you receipts for my money. Then, your claim of impossibility can go to hell!"

Sanderson dragged the banker back into his chair as Jesse rose to face him. "Jesse, I'm sure you see our position. The losses will ruin many of us. Tell us what you know, and we'll do our best for your father if the money can be recovered."

They're not interested in the truth, Jesse thought. He scanned the faces of those seated closest to him and smelled a silent rage. Helplessness settled on him like a coffin lid as he realized the assembled mob possessed little concern with due process. Panic had trumped presumption of innocence; the de facto jury wanted its money back, and rendered a guilty verdict before his arrival.

"You've all have known Ambrose Caine for years," he said. "He's no thief."

A moon-faced ship owner stood, hands trembling with anger. He raised his voice and overrode the outbursts. "Two men contacted each of us individually," he shouted. "Armed with authority to do business in your father's name. Showed us detailed plans and the agreements signed by other investors, even the company's revenue estimates. They warned we'd forfeit our return if we discussed details with anyone outside the list."

Incredulous, Jesse said, "You never confirmed any of this with my father?"

"Your father supposedly left town on business," the man said, "but I recognized his signature. The condition of secrecy was explicit."

Jesse marveled at their greed. "Colonel Tyree will refute all this."

"The Colonel and his son lost over $100,000," Sanderson interjected. "I myself lost almost $25,000." He grimaced and wiped his face, a tremor descending his substantial girth. Disasters of this magnitude invariably clung to administrations, creating sad processions of forgotten politicians and nameless has-beens. Sanderson did not intend to join their ranks.

"A clever scheme, Jesse," he said, "aided by your father's standing in the city." He looked around the room at abashed faces. "To our eternal sorrow, we abided by the agreement's terms until it was too late."

Delayed facing the truth in hope of enlarging your bank accounts, Jesse thought. He studied the patterned carpet as a fresh wave of anger erupted. Sanderson held up his hands for quiet and picked up two documents.

"This morning, your bank informed me $10,000 was deposited in your father's account several days ago," he said. "Another $5,000 in your name. Both slips were signed by your father."

Jesse opened his mouth to reply when Belden bounded from his chair a third time. Clenched fists supporting his considerable weight he leaned over Sanderson's desk. "Couldn't wait, eh, Caine? Well, you won't spend a damned penny when you're sitting in jail beside your thieving father."

"I know nothing about deposits," Jesse shot back.

"And swine fly too!"

"Sit *down*, Jacob!" Sanderson yelled. His face oiled with perspiration, he stood and removed his coat. Flinging off the garment, he pointed a finger at Jesse, his electoral performance ended.

"This isn't a social gathering, Jesse. We're here to get our money back."

Outcries erupted again and Jesse scanned the room a final time. The mob sought his father's scalp, and he had no answers and nothing to gain from threats. He started for door amid shouts of protests, compassion and reasoning destroyed by embarrassment and financial ruin. Sanderson and Belden joined in the chorus and bellowed for him to sit down. Jesse paused at the door. The only person to stop the nightmare was locked in the lower depths of a cell only blocks away.

"Gentlemen," Jesse said, "I assure you my father took no part in this."

He closed the door on the shouts, praying the promise was true.

Chapter Eight

March 6
City Colonial Cemetery

Mourners stood around the grave in small clusters, shivering. Thick with promised spring rain the gray sky abetted the funeral service; colorless clouds hoarded the cold and refused the benediction of sunlight for Charles Rushton's last moments above ground.

Spread over several city blocks, a spiked steel fence surrounded the Colonial cemetery. Drifts of withered wind-blown leaves piled against arched burial vaults. A pantheon of Revolutionary War heroes and forgotten names populated tree-shaded plots as encroaching tree roots sought the interred, heedless of former glory or forgotten honors. Smothered by encroaching gray lichen, nature worked to slowly reclaim stone and human remains with equal disdain.

In a back corner near the sidewalk, a mound of black soil exuded decay from newly-turned earth. Around the grave, mourners pressed closer against one another, seeking warmth. Their eyes avoided the pit, unwilling to contemplate the inevitable reality of their future. Several blankets of flowers covered the mound, petals quivering in the wind, murdered by the cold. The largest spray leaned against the foot of the grave encircled by a black ribbon with silver-embossed words: 'An ending too soon'. The attached card was signed by Randall Tyree. Jesse ripped away the silken sash, drawing intakes of breath from onlookers.

With no relatives or social acclaim, Charlie's final farewell ended quietly. A white-collared minister mumbled a short prayer and waved a last benediction. Anxious to retreat from the cold, the crowd quickly dispersed. A few bundled souls filed past until Jesse stood alone above the grave. Only the cook and housekeeper approached him, round pink faces reddened by tears and the cold.

"We come to pay our respects, Mr. Caine," the cook said, her cheeks damp and wind burned. Her companion nodded and sniffled, chewing her lip." We knew you both since you was nothing but tykes." Heavyset with oval faces they were many times mistaken for sisters. The teary spokeswoman edged closer to her companion and cleared her throat.

"We hates to leave you at a time like this," she mewled, "but you can understand our position."

"You'll find work. List me as a reference." He gave a wry grin at their obvious embarrassment. "Or maybe not, given the circumstances."

"Oh, Mr. Caine, we don't believes the talk about your father."

Jesse raised his hands in understanding.

"It's just that we're both maiden ladies."

He handed each an envelope. "There's enough to tide you over until you find work." The gesture produced more tears. The women thanked him and clutched the envelopes. Wiping their faces with a shared handkerchief they left him alone by the grave, pausing only once to look back at the lone figure.

After a few minutes, Jesse bid his friend farewell and walked from the graveyard, avoiding families who wandered the drab grounds, pausing with curiosity to read inscriptions on weathered tombstones and roofed sepulchers. Unable to lift his eyes from the chipped sidewalk, he passed beneath the wrought-iron archway. The biting wind, indifferent to his grief, pursued him as his day suddenly accelerated downhill.

A fashionably-dressed man and gangly woman hurried toward him. The taller woman clutched a pink and white parasol, her husband assuming the role of a minor appendage. The Middletons were acquaintances of his father, city fixtures well aware of their fortunate heritage. Trailed by a male slave, the pair slowed and inclined their heads toward one another, arranging their faces as though digesting an unpleasant breakfast. Jesse forced a smile and doffed his hat when they blocked his path. The wife drew her husband closer as though seeking protection, the slave peering past them at Jesse.

"Virginia. Paul."

The wife pulled a cashmere muffler closer around her neck as an additional defense. "I imagine you attended the funeral," she said

"We chose not to attend," Paul Middleton said as though they decided to decline an unfashionable dinner invitation. He aimed his walking cane at Jesse's chest. "We don't believe in these sordid affairs of honor. To depart this earth in such fashion is little more than premeditated suicide, a sin against the scriptures." He briskly lowered the cane. "Frankly, we're appalled by your involvement."

Virginia Middleton lifted her sharply angled chin. "I would think you'd distance yourself, given your father's disgrace."

Jesse stared blankly at them and cursed himself for not crossing the street at first sight of the couple. Earth had covered his friend only minutes earlier, while his father coughed away diseased lungs in a dank cell, buried without the benefit of a coffin. Jesse searched his memory and tried to recall if Paul Middleton had occupied a chair in the mayor's office. He could not suppress a sense of guilty pleasure, wondering if they were among the victims. A special breed of social lemmings, their kind rushed after the tide of opinion, seeking comfort in conformity and condemnation. Like mindless fiddler crabs that ruled the marsh's mud flats, they scuttled for their holes when confronted by their own folly.

"Charles Rushton was my closest friend," Jesse said evenly. "He lived a good life, even in his foolish moments. If he was with us today, he'd defer his opinions until my father had a fair hearing, a basic courtesy ignored by many of his friends."

Middleton raised his cane again, but Jesse swatted it aside. Startled, he stepped back. Aghast, Virginia Middleton edged behind him. After a second both recovered their composure and brushed past Jesse who knew their backs were not the last he'd see.

Jesse crossed the street, heading toward the river. His temper calming he strode past the Independent Presbyterian Church. Its three steeples, stacked atop each other, reminded him of an ambitiously decorated wedding cake. Despairing of human foibles and the failure of religion to change man's worst tendencies, Jesse marveled at nature's resilience. All around him flowers and shrubs blossomed into life, spiting the weather, wind rattling palm fronds like ancient parchment.

Wood smoke thickened the morning air. Regal homes, new and old heirs to the original squares, rose two and three-stories in Federal and Regency styles. Attached walls concealed private gardens and lined the sidewalks like fort ramparts, walling out interlopers and curious eyes. Sunlight anointed the houses in muted sepia tones, adding a measure of artistic splendor, as though their owners warranted more than the mundane facade of bricks and mortar. Like all who enjoyed an abundance of money the lavish interiors reflected expensive conformity, displaying a rigidly required orthodoxy to match their neighbors' tastes.

A hundred years earlier, financially distressed British debtors, Irish convicts, and persecuted Jews fleshed out Oglethorpe's adventure, conquering personal misfortune and converting themselves into New World gentry, in the end delivering revenge on the English courts. Nature's accents and the city's designed beauty seemed only fitting for families close by the Savannah River, a mythical boundary between the fortunate and the toilers.

In spite of its in-bred faults, Jesse loved the seductive and reclusive city. Compelled by its significance, the inner city shunned Jesse's affection. The best families politely discouraged him from courting their daughters, the taint of forest blood unsuitable for descendants of those cast out by the courts. As he grew older, Jesse came to understand his anger wasn't fueled by envy or jealousy, but rather a yearning to share in Savannah's fraternity of beauty and opportunity. The city's unspoken strictures gnawed at him in a manner he never fully understood. Now he faced reprisals and vindictive retaliation.

He lengthened his stride, the river's pungency finding him before the bluff came into view. He ignored the few heads that turned his way, anxious to find a flagon of rum and his friend's sympathetic ear.

He passed a white-painted wooden building crowding the sidewalk. Single-storied with shuttered windows, a polished brass plaque announced the forbidding structure as 'The Foil and Blade League - Members Only.'

To the uninformed, the building housed a traditional French *salle*, a school that taught the finer points of fencing for a fee. Cards, drink, and wagers occupied its members when not dancing to the tune of the fencing instructor. The 18th century exercises seemed a harmless diversion, time and fashion having bypassed fencing as a means to settle disagreements. The art had given way to gunpowder, but League members ignored the new egalitarian era. Sons of the city's best families created new rules for gentlemen. Any commoner might shoot a gentleman in matters of honor, they argued, so League members passed a decree, deeming the blade the only acceptable weapon to settle disagreements, a gentleman's weapon, they claimed, designed for more refined sensibilities. Percussion firearms might represent modern thinking, but placing one's life in the hands of frightened rabble holding a pistol: unthinkable. No dignity existed where any dirt farmer could remedy an insult by hurling an ounce of lead. Others might abide the democratic concept of cap-and-ball, but League members were permitted to rebuff challenges that required crude weapons with no disgrace attached to the refusal.

Jesse harbored no such fine distinctions. Dead meant dead, the ultimate end game. To his mind everyone fit into the same size hole, and the dead never came back to boast or complain how they died. The intricacies of response and counter-response were meaningless; the formal choice of weapons formed no part of his world.

His thirst more insistent, he crossed Bay Street. Dodging puddles and wheel ruts filled with horse droppings he passed rows of brick and wooden buildings that dominated the river bluff, their backs to the river that flowed five stories below. The structures lodged cotton brokerage firms, lynchpin of Savannah's wealth. Tasked with negotiating the sale and shipment of the white blossom, burlap-bound bales were shipped to Europe and northern states in the holds of sailing ships where distant mills and factories spun the prickly boll into gold.

A curved set of twenty stone steps led down to the wharves. Deserted on Sunday morning, the cobblestone street below echoed Jesse's footsteps as he descended. At the bottom the worn black and brown stones, ballast dumped from arriving ship holds, sloped toward River Street.

Shrill *screees!* pierced the morning calm as gray and white gulls wheeled overhead. Funneling beneath the wharves, the river reflected flinty sunlight, its surface caramel in the hard sunlight. A procession of sailing ships crowded bow-to-stern, towering over a flotilla of smaller boats at anchor in the river. Tethered to cleats and enormous steel bollards ships gently swayed in the languid current. Brine-coated tar and rotting barnacles dominated the air. Topped by furled sails, rows of planked hulls rode high with the tide, gunwales pressed like a procession of wooden forts against the pier. Several hundred yards across the river, pyramidal steel buoys marked the channel that flowed past the desolate expanse of Hutchinson Island, the last sliver of Georgia before South Carolina's border.

Negotiating over cobblestones slick as waxed eggs, Jesse crossed River Street and stepped onto the pier. Hawsers of thick rope lay coiled like drowsing snakes, undisturbed by sailors and longshoremen who languished in sporadic sunlight on their day off. Three rats skirted a bare-chested sailor sprawled in an alcohol-induced coma. The greasy trio sniffed a bare foot before Jesse's arrival chased them beneath a warped plank.

Bars and taverns lined the riverfront, ragged sisters of the stately cotton exchange buildings built atop them, a separate city of patched walls pocked with shuttered windows. An array of whorehouses masqueraded as boarding houses and beckoned to the sad and uncaring, offering a variety of sin beyond dim doorways. The river's stench grew stronger as Jesse walked the waterfront, and a prostitute, breasts precariously restrained by a thin dress, yelled at Jesse from an open window. A gaggle of seamen passed a bottle and encouraged her sales pitch, jeering at Jesse who ignored her bored promises of bodily delights. Other sailors leaned against ship rails, spectators to the morning's diversion.

Jesse made for a hanging sign adorned with a busty wooden mermaid entwined around a ship's anchor. The Mermaid's Promise embodied what passed for waterfront refinement. Low ceilings. A shoebox fireplace. A dirty basement beneath its floorboards housed a circular pit where rich men carried brought trained terriers to wager on the number of rats killed in an evening's sport.

Jesse ducked inside the low doorway and ancient sawdust crunched underfoot, the shavings harboring unnamed filth. A single lantern lit the interior, and a plank bar fronted a mirror silvered with the years. An obese woman leaned on the rough board, tinted red hair cascading over fleshy arms. Her plump fingers lingered near a length of lead pipe, sleepy eyes expertly calculating the resale value of Jesse's clothes.

"Jesse!"

A silhouette raised a hand from a rear table as Patrick Kerrigan got to his feet. Irish as a potato, Kerrigan had done work for his father. Unlike many peers, Jesse harbored no ill feelings toward Hibernian immigrants. Transformed into laborers and soldiers and criminals, the Irish imported toughness and blunt humor, accompanied by a keen longing for what was denied them in the British Isles.

Kerrigan's disreputable broad-brimmed hat rested on the table in front of him, a floppy felt affair with an improbable yellow band. The easily-recognized hat served as a garish badge of authority, proclaiming him lord and master among longshoremen. Fools ended up in the river and back-talk earned broken bones. Ten years past Jesse's age, he easily sustained his 250 pounds, his scarred hands capable of mayhem. An inquisitive face displayed more cunning than intelligence, his features a slab of Irish beefsteak reddened by sun and wind. Curly black hair with unruly muttonchops completed the aura of someone not to be taken lightly. The easy smile quickly disappeared, and despite his well-earned reputation as a brawler, he'd worked for Ambrose Caine, providing a pool of laborers for the canal's construction.

The tavern was empty except for Kerrigan and the heap of feminine flesh defending the plank bar. Jesse dodged worn and splintered tables and dropped into a chair. He grasped Kerrigan's calloused hand, glad to have something solid beneath him.

Kerrigan squinted at him. "Damn, man, you look like a corpse's ugly brother. How much sleep have you managed?"

"Enough."

"I mightn't known you on the street, but then you don't often visit us common folk and Geechees along the river."

Jesse raised two fingers at the barkeep. "A good thing," he said. "Few down here know who I am."

Kerrigan grunted. "Your troubles matter little to most in my domain. There's a small passel of them what knows about your father's troubles, but you ain't viewed as part of it. Not yet, anyways. They only see another toff come down here to find a whore, or make money off their strong backs."

"You mean none of them were cheated by someone named Caine. Otherwise, you'd pull me from the river with a knife between my ribs."

Kerrigan flashed a humorless smile. "Aye, unless I was one of them what was robbed. Then, the blade would be mine, and I'd let the crabs have their way with your lordship's ass."

The red-haired bartender plopped down two tankards and flashed Jesse a gap-toothed smile, assessing the resale value of his soft boots. Kerrigan waved her away and waited until she waddled behind the bar.

50

"How's your father?"

Jesse wagged his head. "Sicker than he lets on. No one in his condition can survive that pit for long. Unless I get him out, he'll die in there."

"What news of the two who peddled the rubbish?"

"Nothing. No trace of them."

The barkeep wiped the table behind them, bringing a wave of body odor that rivaled the hardiest stevedore. Jesse buried his nose in the flagon and took a swallow of less than Barbados's best. The woman sidled closer until Kerrigan shot her a look and she returned to the bar. He lowered his voice and uttered the only apology Jesse might ever hear from him.

"I'd most likely kill the man who cast doubts at my old Da, God protect his soul, but could your father be involved in this thing? I hear things down here, so I'll ask you. There's them claims he's a clever crook, though I ain't one of 'em."

Jesse took a scalding swallow of warm rum and said nothing about the documents he'd inspected. "He's not capable of cheating anyone," he said, as much to convince himself as Kerrigan. The certainty died in his mouth and he shrugged to hide his doubts.

"I've employed Samuel Cohen to represent him."

"Pah!" Kerrigan banged down his tankard with a thump. "Most likely he'll do little to help your father. Too little profit in it. This city tolerates Jews, but I don't trust none of 'em. Never have. And they don't like us bogtrotters neither."

"He's no equal in the city, Pat, and I need him. If you find yourself in trouble, he's definitely the man you'll need."

Kerrigan grunted. "I couldn't afford the likes of him."

He jammed a finger in his ear and scratched. He pulled the finger away, inspected it, and lowered his voice again with a wolfish grin. "Then again, maybe he'll find a clever way to save your father, even if your father turned highwayman. People change, and your father may be one of 'em. Money's a strong master, the finest temptation under heaven for those in high and low places, so I'll ask again. Do you believe he's telling all? That he took no part in this thing?"

Too exhausted to consider the insult, Jesse peered into his tankard. His father faced the loss of all he owned and what remained of his life. With more than a million dollars missing, maybe the money *had* appeared an acceptable risk to ease his final years. Kerrigan only asked the same question Jesse had asked himself. But the situation seemed oddly skewed, missing an array of pieces Jesse couldn't connect. A man as smart as Ambrose Caine didn't leave such an obvious trail of evidence and remain in the city. Why not take the money and run? And why involve his only son? The handwriting, however, trumped all reasoning, clear and unmistakable although his father claimed he'd been out of town when the bonds were peddled. Without substantial proof to the contrary, Jesse's world was fast dissolving like salt in water.

"He's my father," he whispered hoarsely. "We're both lost if I don't believe him."

"I hear something else in your voice."

The lumbering bartender returned with a grimy rag to wipe the table beside them, inclining her bird's nest of red hair toward them. Kerrigan rose halfway from his chair.

"Ruby, if you don't keep your lard ass behind the bar, I'll forget what a darlin' you are."

She scurried away and Kerrigan leaned closer. "All kinds of sons of bitches down here," he muttered. "Can't trust them or their like." Jesse raised two fingers toward the woman, then let his hand fall to the greasy tabletop. Awash in cheap rum, his words slowed.

"Whatever you hear is my fault," he declared. "I see flaws, even in my father." Disheartened by the admission he raised one shoulder, remembering the cluttered office in the courthouse that housed the evidence. "Maybe he saw an opportunity and took it. Like you said, money overwhelms even good men."

The bar maid waddled to Jesse's side with two tankards and cocked her chin at Kerrigan, ignoring his stony glare as she flounced away with the empties.

Kerrigan took a drink. "I may sound like a defrocked village priest, but who isn't ruined in some way? Only blithering fools deny that."

Jesse drank deeply, the coarse rum smoother now. Part of him wanted to refute Kerrigan. Instead, he drained the tankard and motioned to the woman. Kerrigan pushed down his arm and shook his head at her.

"You'll find no answer in there."

"Then where? I'm down here because I've lost most of my friends."

"Don't be a fool. You only rent friends, you don't own them. Most of 'em bolt at the first sign of trouble, when they've no further need of you."

Kerrigan glanced at the obese woman and lowered his voice. "I once found a bit of trouble and your father lent me money. Probably saved my life." He leaned sideways and spat into the sawdust. "Charity it was, but I couldn't afford to turn it away." He looked out the empty doorway. "Even if he's guilty, thieves have a kind gesture or two in them."

"What can I do?"

"Find the two bastards who sold the horseshit."

Jesse closed his eyes, resigned to a fruitless search. The two strangers had vanished as though they'd never crossed the city limits, phantoms who might not exist.

"Most likely professional thieves," Kerrigan offered, "gutter trash who're long gone. But be careful whatever you do. Randall Tyree killed your friend for nothing more than his pleasure. Wealthy men lost money, so they'll say good riddance if someone skewers you."

"I'm no duelist."

"Then buy a pistol," the Irishman said sharply.

Jesse shook his head, but the snare waited, the pit always a few steps ahead of him.

"Then you're doubly a fool," Kerrigan said. "There's them what'll take your life in payment for what they lost." Kerrigan brushed his mouth with the back of his hand. "You once told me you gave your word to your father. Pardon me for sayin' so, but it was a promise made to a cuckolded husband grieving for his two dead brothers. Best you rethink the words if you're called out."

"I made him a promise, Pat."

"It might just get yourself killed if you bury your head in the sand, boy. Is that what you want?" He leaned across the table. "We're ruled by change, every mother's son of us. Promises won't mean much when you're branded a thief and a coward. What happens when some fool posts you in the City Market?" Kerrigan looked at the door. "You know this city. Them in their big houses and fancy fencing club don't care about the likes of you and me. They're always in the right, and the rest of us can cordially go to hell." He leaned back, his brogue stronger. "Sooner or later, you'll be fightin' if you want to show your face in this city." He pressed harder. "And what about your lady friend, the lovely actress? Do you think she'll have any feelings for you if you're branded a coward? I'll keep my ears open along the river, but one day you'll need more than a Hebrew lawyer and a river rat like me."

Jesse ran his finger around the mug's rim and recalled his encounter with Nathanial Moore. "I almost killed a man two days ago."

Kerrigan laughed and fell back in his chair, slamming his palm on the tabletop. "Well, that's a start. If things gets worse, come to me. Maybe there's a way to repay your father's charity. I have a friend, an expert with the blade. An odd one, he is, but knows what he's about."

Jesse shook his head and the rum slowed his words. "I'm not crazy enough to pick up a sword." He waved his hand at the bartender.

Kerrigan placed a scarred palm over Jesse's mug and shook off the woman. "Believe me, you'll fight when the time comes."

"Won't save my father," Jesse slurred.

"You'll fight," Kerrigan insisted. "You've an Irish temper, even if your granddad was a coal-grimed Welshman and your mother a heathen Indian, pardon my saying so." Kerrigan leaned closer still. "You'll have to fight. Too many dandified jackasses lost money."

Jesse's head swam. "I didn't steal it."

Kerrigan grasped his sleeve. "Listen to me. If you're challenged, I can help. Will you remember that?"

Jesse nodded and the floor tilted beneath his chair, the rum burning his throat. He scattered coins on the table and struggled to his feet, clutching the back of the chair.

Kerrigan watched him weave through the doorway and stared after him. He leaned back and counted the money with a grin before shoving half in his pocket.

"Ruby darlin', bring me a full bottle."

Chapter Nine

Same Day
Afternoon
The Fletcher Tyree House

Seven blocks from the Mermaid's Promise, Colonel Fletcher Tyree closed the twin doors to his study. Motionless for a full minute, he assessed the trappings of naked wealth. Twisting the gold signet ring around his index finger as he surveyed the opulent room, satisfaction close to complete. Decorated in a style he preferred to call 'masculine elegance'—much to his deceased wife's chagrin—it served as a refuge from her prying eyes and uneducated curiosity of associates who understood little of what they saw without his enlightenment.

The house was approached by a patterned brick walkway through a scrolled wrought iron gate. He bristled each time he walked out the gate to be confronted by the Owens House on the opposite side of the square. William Jay of Bath may have designed the charming house, he thought, but his own was its equal, if not its clear superior.

Inside its walls he'd designed a compact museum, a rummage of fine art and artifacts unrivaled in the city. He crossed the room to his 16th century burled walnut desk, his hand lightly trailing across the fronds of two live palms in elaborate Chinese urns, as though nature provided the means to cleanse the air of his acquisitiveness. In front of the desk, he turned and admired his favorite pieces, each arranged to be enjoyed from his leather chair, two tall windows illuminating two painted Chinese screens. Next to them a collection of lacquer boxes, scrolled with ivory designs and gold inlays. A life-size 13th century Italian bronze of Hercules presided over an English gaming table said to have belonged to Beau Brummell.

Well-proportioned for his sixty-eight years, Fletcher Tyree settled into his chair. He carried himself with as much aplomb as age allowed, a worn railroad spike of a man, solid but showing signs of rust. His undiminished mane of white hair easily marked him on the street, and he bore a remarkable resemblance to his grandfather, a captain in Oglethorpe's personal guard, a detail he pointed out to visitors who ogled the oil portrait above the Italian marble mantle. Running his hand over a crystal globe atop a fluted gold base on his desk, he gazed out the louvered window behind his desk. Six male slaves, identically clad in gray broadcloth, kneeled in the garden below, the lush plot concealed from the world's curious eyes by surrounding walls. He watched until satisfied the slaves understood his instructions about the boxwoods, then surveyed the courtyard's design of baroque fountains and classical statuary.

A single arrow justified all this, he thought, his status and possessions paid for by a chip of sharpened Cherokee flint. Forty years earlier he'd crawled a mile back to camp to warn his militia company of a pending Indian attack. The act proclaimed him a hero and elevated his status another notch. Abetted by a sharp eye for business, both above board and borderline legal, his fortune had grown steadily. The bit of edged stone remained in his thigh, occasionally jerking him awake at night, but confirming his right to enjoy whatever he desired. This house, this room. Even the blackamoors in the garden. He possessed more than any man needed, but brushed away the irrelevant notion of need. He'd long ago discarded justification where necessity ended and possession became entitlement.

Now the pinnacle of his collection beckoned, delivery promised within the month. He harbored regrets about what had been required to acquire the painting, but guilt stopped short of recrimination. The need to possess overrode what principles remained in his life. The passing of years and life's travails earned whatever pleased him.

Satisfied with the oft-practiced justification, he leaned heavily against the window frame and fixed his eyes on a small vine sheltered along the windowsill. The delicate green tentacles tenaciously gripped the glass pane, a basic tenant of survival. The climbing plant thrived, far removed from the week's events, and for the briefest instant, he envied its simple needs for nothing more than water and sunlight.

He selected a cigar from an inlaid teak humidor. Lighting the blunt cheroot, he savored the tobacco's bite. The most current addition to his collection sat in the center of the desk: an ivory Geisha, a delicate umbrella held above her cocked head. Light from the window glinted off his heavy ring as he reverently turned the statuette over and noted the Japanese artist's markings. The signature, well-known to collectors who could afford his work, added to his pleasure.

He moved the statuette to one side and clicked open a gold pocket watch. His son was late. Again. He snapped the engraved cover shut and inspected his hands, frowning at the mottled flesh as he waited for his only son's appearance.

Sixty-eight years old, he thought, Unbelievable.

He acknowledged an uneasy armistice with the stranger's face each morning as he shaved, time now measured in lost friends falling like withered leaves around him. The passing years had done their work, bringing him closer to death than the womb. Waiting for the inevitable had become a daily game, but he'd conquered the terror of dying. At peace with the thought he marveled at his acceptance, curious only of the time and manner in which he'd die. Life was now defined by objects that pleased him, arousing a yearning to acquire more, amazed at the creations of those endowed with gifts he could only imagine. Thankful for their talent and the time remaining to admire his newest addition, he decided to make the Geisha a permanent addition to his desk.

The study doors opened and Randall Tyree crossed the room without acknowledging his father. He beamed at his father and tossed a black cane on the nearest chair, slinging his topcoat over it. Fletcher frowned as his son leaned over and removed a cheroot from the humidor. He lit it and tossed the match into a potted palm

"You're late," he said. "It would be an extraordinary event if just once you abided by my wishes."

Randall flopped into a Bergére chair and squinted as the cheroot's smoke burned his eyes. "I lunched with my very good friend, *Monsieur* Charbonneau, a rapacious creature." He waved at the biting smoke. "He experienced a vexing trip from New Orleans after ignoring my advice to enjoy a more leisurely journey. The little French prick worried I wouldn't pay my debts." Randall gave a short laugh. "Imagine that he thought I might cheat him, as though a Tyree were capable of such a thing."

Fletcher rose and went to the window. Two slaves paused in their labors below to dip water from a wooden bucket. They saw him at the window and returned to their labor.

"He insisted I pay my debts immediately," Randall continued, "and was surprised when I paid him in cash." He inclined his head at his father who continued to observe the slaves. "You were most kind to advance the funds, dear father. It appears I'm once again welcome in his elaborate establishment on the Gulf."

Fletcher regained his chair. A look of disgust replaced his annoyance with the slaves' efforts. "Your associate's a grasping creature. New Orleans is fit only for whores and thieves," he said. "A kingdom of bordellos, pretenders preening about in silks as if they're polite society. No place for a gentleman."

Randall studied the cheroot's glowing top. "Ah! And we're far superior to such lowly beings, are we not, dear father. Besides, I have little choice but to visit the city you detest. There's not a decent gambling house or indecent whorehouse within a hundred miles of Savannah that caters to my tastes."

The elder Tyree stubbed out his half-smoked cheroot. "I detest being responsible for your debts to this Charbonneau person. I hope you've learned you don't possess sufficient skills for expensive games of chance." He studied the familiar figure as though a stranger sat before him. "I withdrew a hundred thousand dollars from the bank to complete your scheme, money we supposedly invested with Caine. It was a simple enough to convince people we'd also been duped by my partner. All their money's lying fallow in my safe like so many cabbage leaves, not earning a damned cent."

"*Our* scheme as you term it." Randall fingered the scar on his cheek. "And I suppose your desires did not enter into the plan?" He gestured at the reserved space on the wall behind his father. "The little Van Dyke portrait you lust after, the fat Dutch burgher. Has it suddenly released its hold on you?" When his father glanced away Randall aimed the cheroot at the wall. "Or do you plan to fill the space with a dreary little oil of sheep in some squalid English meadow?"

Fletcher blanched, but pleasure keened in his chest when he thought of laying hands on the Van Dyke. He'd possess the painting to the exclusion of all others. The thought caused him to become slightly lightheaded. He'd risked everything to own it, a haunting likeness of an anonymous Dutchman, the canvas suffused with enticing yellows, reds, and royal blues. The image beckoned to the viewer, the Old Master's brushstrokes applied like finely creamed butter, the rich tones practically edible. His *needed* to possess the small masterpiece, no matter the cost. He'd completed negotiations a week earlier. The New York dealer's demands amounted to legal extortion, but a final payment guaranteed his ownership, preventing other collectors from possessing what he rightfully coveted. Still, given his long relationship with Ambrose Caine, the act represented the highest price but he's had no choice. If only I'd not wasted my reserves on the acreage near the river, he thought.

"There should have been another way," he muttered. "Ambrose Caine was a friend."

Was it too late to turn back, he wondered? The money was locked away except for payment to their accomplices. No one had any clue of their involvement. What if all the funds mysteriously appeared at several banks with anonymous instructions to return the money to their rightful owners? He'd many times skated along thin edges of business ventures, but this was different. He and Randall became common thieves in the end, clever ones, but the conspiracy pursued him like a ravenous beast. He looked dolefully at his son and kept his voice level.

"I should never have let you talk me into this madness."

"But you're not grieving over your decision," Randall said. "My presence at the Westbury home last night confirmed we're seen only as victims. I even assumed the role of a benevolent benefactor to those in need." He laughed. "We can afford compassion."

When his father made no reply, he took pleasure in knowing he'd cut close to the bone, that regret assumed a distant position in his father's hierarchy . "We took advantage of a moment, nothing more,"

Randall said. "It's more money than either of us could have earned in two lifetimes. Acquaintances at the jail tell me your concerns about Caine will be short-lived. The old man's sick. When he dies, the door closes forever on the matter. It'll all fade away when no other culprits are found. We'll then simply join the ranks of poor souls who invested unwisely."

"And Caine's son?"

Randall shrugged. "He's engaged Samuel Cohen but neither have an inkling what happened. They'll nose around, but when Caine sees the evidence, his ardor will dim. Even if his father escapes indictment, Savannah will force both from the city. We'll never hear of him or Cohen again."

"Cohen." Fletcher frowned. "He's clever and tenacious."

"When he learns of the deposits in their accounts, his ardor will dim."

"The deposits in their accounts had merit," his father admitted, "but it's money gone forever."

Randall Tyree inclined his head. Despite his father's complaints, the deposits drove the spike of suspicion deeper, a small price to pay to guarantee the Caines' ruin.

"This forger of yours," Fletcher Tyree persisted. "Can he be trusted to remain loyal?"

Randall gave an enigmatic smile. "We're not in the loyalty business." The smile broadened. "Marvelous talent, really" he mused. "No one disputes the documents' authenticity. A jury will not deny what it can see and touch."

"And these two brothers you hired?" his father demanded. "We paid them well enough, but who's to say they can be trusted? You admitted the one has a loose tongue."

Randall regarded him closely, surprised how much the man had aged in the past month. He removed the cheroot from his mouth and frowned at the stubby tube of rough tobacco; his father's taste in cigars approached the abominable.

"I'm afraid he's met with an accident," he said, enjoying the other's look of dismay. "Neighbors discovered his body last week near his Asheboro home. His head had been caved in. North Carolina authorities concluded he fell astray of an unruly horse. But there's no need to be concerned, dear father. His brother's more reliable and may yet prove useful to us. But if he proves greedy or talkative, there are other horses that can't be controlled."

Fletcher paced the window as though it offered refuge, his voice barely audible. "We've descended to the level of common criminals."

"We'll *rise* to whatever's required to keep us safe," Randall asserted.

"And if something happens you haven't foreseen? If young Caine gets too close to the truth, then what? I've lived long enough to know how capricious plans can be."

"My God, you are the consummate worrier," Randall exclaimed. "Whatever happens, I can deal with anyone who becomes too curious. No one will plague us, I assure you."

Fletcher Tyree regained his chair. He drew the fragile statuette closer and submerged his alarm in its graceful lines. "I'm well aware of my weaknesses, but I can't understand what drove you to attempt this." He looked up at his son, his disappointment evident. "I haven't entertained the vaguest clue about you since you were a boy. Your mother gave up all hope, but I believed in your future. We had more than enough money to live our lives as gentlemen."

"Gentlemen." Randall gave a slight smile. "I assume we retain the designation euphemistically."

Fletcher looked aggrieved. "It's a matter of station and how one carries himself." He looked around the luxuriously appointed room and calculated the combined value of what he saw. "One day you'll inherit this. What do you want other than your toys and swords?"

Randall's smile vanished. He closed his eyes and visualized the tall containers of marbles. Agates of red and blue and green. Yellow cat eyes. Orbs filled with rainbows from almost every country in the world. He possessed a universe of small glass planets that filled his house alongside battalions of toy soldiers, confidants since boyhood. The miniature soldiers never struck him, or demeaned his dreams and pleasures, requiring nothing except his admiration and the warmth of his hands when he held them. At the lowest points of his boyhood he'd sat motionless for hours and watched sunlight illuminate the lifeless battalions he commanded.

"What do I want?" Randall pretended to mull the question, then spread his arms wide, pleased the answer would infuriate his father.

Life!" he exclaimed. "One without the dreary encumbrances of labor and uncertainty. Without toil and worry about the next dollar's appearance. I desire nothing but the day itself."

He indicated the lavish surroundings. "I was ten years old when I decided not to become you," he said. "That I'd *pursue* life and not try to possess it. Privilege has its obvious advantages, but can you remember what life was once like, when you anticipated more than a wooden crate delivered to your door? I don't want Old Masters, dear father. I want to face a man across a space of two yards, risk everything on my skills. I desire women and the delight of removing each layer of their clothing, and I want the pleasure of the best gaming tables. "

"You can have all that, if that's what you wish. In a few years, you'll inherit all this."

"Years? I care for nothing beyond next week. There's no guarantee of the canal's success." Randall smashed the cheroot in an ashtray. "It began with flag waving and parades and speeches by you and your friends, but we might never see a penny from it. You know your history. Even successful men fail and vanish. Only a few end up in dusty books no one reads."

Fletcher massaged his eyes with the heels of his hands. He should never have listened to his son. Clever as he was, blunders happened with even the best of plans, ghosts who crept up beside you and suddenly woke you in the dark of night.

"Your mother warned me," he said. "She asked me not to send you away to college. She feared the experience might ruin you, and she was right. You squandered what was offered and never saw fit to graduate."

"Classes were an unending bore, but I excelled at fencing. And the northern belles were charmed by my *uncultured* accent, so not everything was counted as a loss." For a moment he considered titillating his father with more intimate memories.

"And there were the delights of The Rake's Club," he mused, "a marvelous New York institution that carried on the traditions of England's Hellfire Club. An enlightened fraternity of the most delicious debauchery. What better education could you and mother have purchased for me?"

Fletcher Tyree sprang forward and swept the ivory carving to the floor in a rage. The Geisha crashed to the floor, its head and umbrella snapping off. Aghast, he stared at the disaster of his own making.

"God damn it!" he blurted. He knelt and collected the pieces with trembling fingers. Disgusted and dismayed, he tossed the shattered remains on the desk. "We sent you away to be educated, not indulge your base desires."

"Fencing permits me to defend our good name, dear father." Randall had never spoken to his father of the delights of dueling, and he knew of no way to convince his father of the blade's purity. "There's something else." he said. "A rare tonic when one walks into the arena to risk all in a single instant. Afterwards, every moment's sweeter if you survive the encounter. No painting or cold marble likeness can approach the sensation."

"Your talent and observations are most impressive."

Did his father understand nothing? Randall rubbed his unlined forehead with his fingertips, tired of the sparring. "My skill works to our advantage. People will hesitate before accusing us of complicity in the matter."

"And if one day you find your talents unequal to an opponent?"

"Then I will be duly surprised," Randall replied lightly. "But there's no one in the city I fear."

Fletcher pushed at the figurine's severed head with his thumb. "In which case, I suggest you avoid strangers. All adversaries are not created equal."

"A sensible observation, but my instructors taught me well."

When his father fell silent, Randall adopted a more conciliatory tone. "But I left New York's delights and returned to you, did I not? I didn't belong there, and Savannah would never accept my classmates. This wonderfully accommodating city is doubly suited for my talents."

Randall gathered his coat and cane. As a boy, he'd spent hours among the room's treasures, cowed by their importance to his father. "You taught me to love all this, but not one of them ever loved me in return," he said. "I wanted your admiration, but you held me up to your friends as though I was simply another acquisition to marvel at."

He paused at the door before a glass cabinet. He opened it and removed a delicate porcelain figure depicting a ballerina gracefully poised on one toe. He held the translucent shape to the window's light, the piece weightless between his long fingers.

"I imagine you lose sleep plotting your next acquisition," he said, turning the figurine as if it danced in his hand, "dreaming what you'll possess next." He admired the play of light on the figure's glazed surfaces. "As you observed moments ago, life is indeed fickle and worrisome, particularly when you concern yourself with threats to your comfortable world."

Randall released the figurine and it shattered on the parquet floor. He nudged the bits and pieces with the tip of his cane and mimicked a sigh of regret.

"I'm your assurance such things never happen," he said.

Chapter Ten

March 7
Morning
Savannah City Jail

Jesse followed he deputy down the dismal stone steps, its collection of fetid odors familiar now. The jailer's key rasped in the cell lock, and he forced a smile as the stooped figure painfully rose from the soiled cot.

Jesse gripped the frail hand, the flesh feverish despite the chill seeping from stones slick with condensation. Half-hidden beneath the tangled thin blanket, a crumpled handkerchief showed red at its edges. Eyes ringed purple from a sleepless night, Ambrose Caine searched his son's face for new hope. He shoved away the handkerchief and faced Jesse who sat on the cell's only stool.

"Is there anything I can get you?"

His father smiled wearily. "Out."

"Samuel Cohen's agreed to represent you." Jesse avoided his review of the evidence.

"Good, good." His father hacked into the handkerchief and Jesse winced at the rattle of wet phlegm. "He's the most competent lawyer in the city."

"I asked Patrick Kerrigan to keep his ears open on the docks. He knows the rougher trade."

Ambrose Caine regained his breath with a half-smile. "Interesting allies, Cohen and Kerrigan. Kerrigan helped me find surveying crews, but he's a little too rough and too Irish for our genteel friends. He is more clever than he appears, and he's constantly on the lookout for money." The half-smile faded. "Better to have him with you than against you."

Jesse remembered their conversation in the tavern. Even if Kerrigan managed to locate the two swindlers, there was no certainty they'd absolve the dejected figure, possibly claiming they were pawns, that his father masterminded the scheme. Jesse resisted the temptation to press for the truth. He did not want to hear the words if they destroyed two lives.

He's my father, for God's sake! he thought. *No matter what I saw at the courthouse, I can't believe he'd deceive me and so many friends.*

They fell silent and Jesse examined the cell's damp walls as though they might blurt the truth. The exhausted face across from him dulled his heart but failed to allay his lingering fears. Unable to tamp down suspicion, he allowed the silence to lengthen. The deputy shifted his weight outside, the jangle of heavy steel keys breaking the stillness.

"Sanderson made it clear he'll offer no help, nor will others in positions to assist us. Most were victims as well."

"I suppose Sanderson claims he lost money."

Jesse saw no point in recounting the irate assembly or his encounter with Belden. "Sanderson saw the evidence. All the documents bear your signature."

"Impossible," his father murmured.

"Several claimed they recognized your signature. Notes in your handwriting offered rates far above market." Jesse recalled the familiar ink and signature, but he shook his head. "What I don't understand is why they handed over money without your personal assurance."

Ambrose fixed him with a sad smile. "Greed," he said. "And the illusion of preferential treatment. Easy money loosens the tightest pockets. As for the offerings being in my handwriting, I have no answer."

Jesse looked away. "Cohen claims there's overwhelming evidence."

"Whatever occurred was carefully executed," his father said, rubbing the back of his neck. "No suspicion was aroused, mine least of all."

He appeared at a loss, but Jesse wondered if Ambrose Caine was an ordinary man after all. Had the lure of easy wealth blinded him? Had a more base man concealed himself all these years, hidden inside the most important person in Jesse's life?

"There's more," Jesse said. "Sanderson claims a large deposit appeared in your bank account. More was deposited in my bank. Fifteen thousand dollars total."

His father blinked and could only shake his head.

"Give me something, anything, to refute these charges," Jesse pleaded, the memory of hostility and acrimony in Sanderson's office still fresh. "With your arrest, no one's searching for the culprits. I could be arrested as an accomplice with no one left to defend either of us."

"What of your prospects with the Caldwell firm in the face of all this?"

Jesse waved aside his father's concern about his job. A partner of Caldwell and Associates had appeared at his front door at first light, bringing welcome news of paid leave until the courts absolved his father. If the case went to trial, Jesse's feared the reprieve would quickly evaporate.

"Locating those responsible is all that matters now. If we find them, we'll soon have the truth. I haven't talked with the Colonel, but he'll help any way he can."

His father suppressed a cough and wiped his eyes. "Maybe, but whatever evidence they've compiled isn't going away. If you don't find the men, I'll be at the mercy of judge and jury."

"I'll find a way," Jesse said without the slightest indication how that might occur.

His father rested a hand on his son's knee. "I know you'll do everything."

Unable to fashion a reply, Jesse looked away and called for the deputy.

Chapter Eleven

Same Day
Mid-Afternoon
Downtown Savannah

Jesse rode from the law office to the jail. The deputy led him underground and he faced the broken figure again, unable to reconcile his father in the desolate surroundings.

They talked for an hour, and Jesse booked passage to Boston thirty minutes after leaving the cell. He left the ticket office, guiding Aristotle past rainwater ponds along Bay Street, breeding grounds for belligerent mosquitoes that welcomed the late arrival of spring. The prospects of a sea voyage lifted his spirits for a few seconds.

Ahead, a sleek black lacquered carriage rolled to a stop in front of a millinery shop, gold trim contrasting with the muddy street. An elderly negro man in faded blue livery jumped from the driver's seat and folded down the carriage's metal step. Victoria, her mother, and a young female companion emerged, chattering as they alighted from the imposing vehicle. All three carried umbrellas and held their skirts high above the dirt-caked sidewalk. The driver reclaimed his lofty perch and tugged at his starched collar.

The shop's front window advertised the latest Paris fashions and displayed bonneted mannequins as proof. Jesse dismounted and entered with the usual male trepidation of trespassing on forbidden territory. Several shoppers turned as he closed the door. Heads close together, they peered at him with wide eyes over busy fans.

Victoria talked with a shop girl at the rear, shaking her head. The clerk lifted a pink satin turban from Victoria's golden curls and replaced it with a velvet green contrivance, a long yellow feather curled to one side. Adjusting the frilly concoction, Victoria raised her chin and examined her reflection. She saw Jesse's reflection in the full-length mirror and quickly removed the hat.

"Jesse," she said in a hushed tone, aware others watched them. "Whatever are you doing here?"

He removed his hat and bowed. "I thought I might offer my expert opinions about women's hats." She seemed the only female worthy of the expensive creations.

Martha Danford latched onto his arm. "Your father's situation and condition have improved, I hope."

Jesse started to reply, but Victoria steered him away from her mother. She pointed at a tall stack of hat boxes. "I'm here to pick up my new hats. What are you doing here?"

"I just came from Samuel Cohen's office and saw you enter."

Victoria gestured out the window. "Mother and I acquired a new carriage. We became tired of being hauled like freight in filthy rented coaches."

"Did you also hire the livered driver to convey you?" Jesse teased.

More shoppers entered and joined the circle of whisperers that stared unabashedly at them until Jesse swept off his hat and bowed to them with an extravagant gesture. Embarrassed, the faces swiveled away.

Martha Danford ignored the gawkers and joined her daughter. "We purchased Aaron from a family whose fortunes fell in disrepair. Victoria negotiated a most reasonable price for Aaron and the carriage." She smiled, seemingly content to have joined the ranks of slaveholders.

"I never concerned myself with money," she sighed. "Franklin managed all our financial matters. Thankfully, Victoria inherited his skills."

"Workmen converted the tool shed in back," Victoria added. "Aaron seems quite content there."

"I'll hear next that you've moved into a manse on Oglethorpe Square," Jesse teased, "conducting weekend soirees for the city's better families."

Victoria frowned. "Is that such a bad thing?"

"Nothing was further from my mind. If it pleases you, it pleases me."

"Victoria has such a wealth of understanding about money," Martha Danford interjected. "Since Franklin's death, she's become my rock in financial matters. I left the matter of the estate's assets to her, and I'm amazed how well we manage under her guiding hand. Do you know she acquired a new pianoforte manufactured by John Broadwood of London?"

"Mother," Victoria retorted sharply, "Jesse has no interest in such things."

Jesse changed the subject. "Samuel Cohen is devising a defense."

Victoria seemed taken aback but locked her arm with his, her peevish demeanor altered in an instant. "What wonderful news. What clever maneuver has he planned to blind a jury?"

Jesse started to tell her about Elizabeth Pendleton but realized how ludicrous it might seem. An unknown woman in Boston without credentials. Little choice remained but to travel on blind faith and Cohen's assessment. The documents appeared in his father's hand, but Cohen might have a point; eyes were many times fooled. The question remained if the expert would make the arduous journey to Savannah, and even then, could she successfully refute documents?

"I prefer not to raise hopes too early. I'm sailing to Boston in hope of providing a new witness."

Victoria bit her lip. "How long will you be gone?"

"I've booked passage on the *Abraham Reed*. Given fair seas, I should return within three weeks."

Victoria's expression remained questioning. "I know you're trying to help, but how can you leave him just now? Shouldn't you remain to bolster his spirits?"

"The trial will be delayed until my return."

"When do you leave?" Martha Danford asked.

"In two days."

She patted his arm. "You must do what you deem best. It's in God's hands."

Jesse remembered Salter's similar prediction before Charlie Rushton's death. He'd long ago decided a distant pantheon of deities allowed men their carefully laid plans, only to scatter them to the winds as their private joke.

Their covert inspection of Jesse satisfied, shoppers left the store. Victoria beckoned to her friend, and Jesse helped the three women into their coats. Martha Danford called to the driver who secured the hat boxes in the covered boot. He pulled down the entry step and assisted the women into the carriage. With a pulse of excitement he took Victoria's gloved hand and helped her inside.

She looked down at him from the coach window, her hand remained atop his. "Why not change your plans. Come see our new production instead. We'll make an evening of it."

"This is something I must do. I'll return as quickly as I can."

Victoria gave him a listless smile and removed her hand. She tapped the carriage roof with her umbrella handle and Aaron flicked his whip as the carriage splashed away.

Chapter Twelve

March 9
Noon
The Fletcher Tyree House

Bored, Randall Tyree sat across from his father. Warm leather and horse sweat wafted from his dusty clothes and he arched his back to reach the thigh of a life-size marble statue behind his chair, blank eyes looking down at him. A small stone gargoyle attached to the wall behind his father's desk glared malevolently at his fondling. As a boy, Randall hated the grotesque decoration, fearing his father might order the creature to descend on him if he disobeyed.

"You smell like horse," Fletcher said to him.

"A ride with a lady friend to Isle of Hope. I assure you *she* did not smell like a horse." He grinned and waited. "Surely you didn't summon me to discuss my bathing habits."

"No."

When his son seemed more interested in stroking the sculpture than responding, Fletcher picked up a sterling letter opener and tapped it against the desk pad. The temptation of returning the money had diminished, but his guilt remained each time he heard Ambrose Caine's name or met a friend who invested money. The drumming grew louder, a test of wills. In all his years of business dealings, his son always held odd sway over him in matters of opportunity. The silent standoff ended when Fletcher tossed the opener onto the desk.

"Tell me again why Caine's traveling to Boston."

"Jesse Caine will go to any length to protect his father," Randall said, "even employing a charlatan who claims she can distinguish variations in handwriting." He patted the statue's calf and looked up at the empty eyes. Crossing his legs he continued as though explaining the obvious to a child.

"He's wasting his time. Our forger is exceptional. Gifted, in fact."

"And our other two associates?"

Randall brushed a coating of dust from a boot toe with a handkerchief. "One brother met the unfortunate accident in North Carolina. He wasn't long mourned by his sibling who is back in the city. He'll ensure our good fortune continues without interruption."

"I don't like employing such rabble."

"You don't have to *like* it. He's paid for and will do what I tell him."

"You're certain young Caine's leaving the city?"

Tyree stuffed the handkerchief into his pocket. "His passage is confirmed. The *Abraham Reed* sails tomorrow."

"Why is he leaving now? His father's trial could be scheduled any day."

Randall's patience neared an end. "The woman in Boston, remember? She's part of Cohen's defense."

Fletcher twisted in his chair. "I don't like it."

Randall struggled to keep his voice under control. "If you don't have the stomach for this—" He heard two maids in the outer room and lowered his voice. "You've never cared for my opinions on anything other than business matters, but you're in my world now which tolerates fewer strictures," He gestured around the sumptuous room. "Sit here among your baubles and let me decide the best course."

His father swiveled his chair and looked at the empty space on the wall behind him, exciting a spark of excitement. Earlier that morning, the Philadelphia dealer occupied the chair where his son sat. Arrival of the Van Dyke was expected within the month, the transaction completed except for the final payment. With the funds concealed in his safe, more treasures were within his reach: A sumptuous Rubens he'd long coveted, plus several Da Vinci sketches the dealer dangled in front of him. Anticipating the additions, he quieted his apprehensions.

"I rely on your judgment."

"Your confidence's well placed, dear father."

The gargoyle leered down over Fletcher's shoulder. "Madness," he muttered, not knowing if he referred to himself or his son.

Kerrigan spotted the feathery wisp of smoke behind a wall of crates. He stepped away from Jesse and yelled at the stevedore. The man hurriedly knocked the pipe against his boot heel and jammed the meerschaum in his jacket pocket. Avoiding Kerrigan's baleful glare, he trotted toward a gang of workmen manhandling a cargo of lumber into a ship's open hole. Kerrigan scanned the docks for more malingerers before he turned back to Jesse.

"Can't trust none of 'em 'less they feel your eyes on their backs. Now tell me again why in hell you're sailing off to Boston."

Jesse propped his back against a ragged cube of baled cotton, a single valise and thin leather folio at his feet. Gangs of workers ambled past them toward a row of ships docked along the quay. The *Abraham Reed*, moored a few yards away, sat ready to sail within the hour. On deck a blue-uniformed mate yelled instructions to stevedores who manhandled luggage and the last of the cargo aboard as Kerrigan watched the loading.

"Cohen's arranged a meeting with a woman in Boston," Jesse said. "A handwriting expert specializing in uncovering forgeries. She'll inspect the evidence against my father if I'm able to convince her to return to Savannah with me."

Two longshoremen rolled a squeaking cart up to them. Jesse moved away from the burlap-wrapped bale and they manhandled it onto the trolley, avoiding Kerrigan's surveillance as they rolled the handcart toward a ship. The bale tottered and they grabbed at it, swearing loudly. Workmen scoffed at their efforts until Kerrigan scattered them with a torrent of curses. He turned back to Jesse and shook his head.

"Jesus, Joseph, and Mary. A woman, is it now. You're depending on this witch's magic to save your father."

"Unless you find the two men."

"Waste of time." Kerrigan crossed his hairy arms. "Rumor says there's a barge full of evidence against your father. Ain't no jury goin' to believe but what they see."

"The woman's all I have, Pat. I've run out of options."

"Them two crooks. There's your answer. Find 'em, and I'll make 'em sing."

"And if you never find them?"

Kerrigan shrugged. "Just watch yourself up there. Boston's a lovely lady with a club under her fancy skirts."

"I'll back within three weeks if the weather holds. I'm told the *Abraham Reed's* a fast ship."

Kerrigan admired the clipper's sleek hull with a practiced eye. "That she is. Two hundred feet of good American timber with a proven crew. She'll take good care of you."

The wind picked up, and Jesse turned to inspect the sky above the riverfront buildings at his back. The temperature suddenly dropped, and he hunched inside the Benjamin coat as seagulls scattered to seek calmer perches. He looked again at the ship's graceful hull and his spirits lifted. A possible solution waited a thousand miles away for his arrival, and the voyage offered escape from two scandals and a dead friend, a temporary refuge if only for a few days. Straw and wisps of cotton swirled around the two men's legs, the quickening wind hurling bits of debris into the river. Banks of easterly clouds blotted the horizon, and a fresh gust rippled the water, rattling ships' halyards in the rising wind.

Kerrigan jammed his hands in his trouser pockets and beamed at Jesse. "These spring howlers will likely fill her sails more than a land crab like you will enjoy." His mouth twisted into a grin, a face seamen reserved for land-bound innocents. "With a following wind, you'll most likely feed your dinner to the fishes, but you'll likely make Boston Harbor in four days."

Jesse looked at the ship as its hull against the dock. Four days and nights at sea seemed suddenly less appealing, never having spent more than a few hours on open water. Whatever his hesitations, he'd seek out a strange woman who might prove a savior or waste of his time.

Jesse picked up his luggage. "Keep your ears open while I'm gone. Go to Cohen if you hear anything. We've no guarantee this woman will consent to help my father."

"Don't put your faith in charlatans," Kerrigan warned, "especially the female variety."

"I'll take help where I find it, Pat."

"You believe Cohen?"

Jesse nodded and Kerrigan extended his callused hand. "Law and order it is then."

They shook hands just as massive drops of rain splattered the planked dock as though trying to destroy the wood.

Chapter Thirteen

The gale thundered across the Atlantic and crashed into the *Abraham Reed* the day after the clipper slipped anchor. Slanting rain and demented wind lashed the ship and shoreline as though both were age-old enemies warranting punishment. The storm worsened through the night, starless skies assuming the role of a disinterested witness, shrouds of black clouds content to benignly observe the clipper's battle against the sea.

Below decks, wind probed between caulked bulkheads into Jesse's tiny cabin, intent on destroying the vessel and all on board. The prow cleaved two-story rollers of black-green water and burrowed its sleek snout into towering waves. Listing at a frantic angle, the ship's builders pitted the vessel's strength against an enraged ocean. Floods and waterfalls of seawater crashed over the decks above him as he clung to the edge of his bunk and waited for relief or death. Jesse rolled from side to side in his bunk, fighting off bouts of nausea and banishing any thought of food. The cabin bulkheads bore down on him, a soaked wooden cage lit by a solitary brave candle. The walls danced before his sleepless eyes, offering no escape until the storm relented and they sighted Boston—or the ship broke apart.

An immense wave crashed broadside into the hull, and the ship keeled over at an alarming angle before righting itself for the thousandth time. The collision tossed Jesse against the bulkhead like an apple in a pail. Inches from his face, rivulets of seawater streamed down the planked bulkheads, the cabin a prison of snaking waterfalls. He turned over and watched the oilskin pouch swing wildly from the bulkhead hook, thankful he'd double-wrapped the documents and packed them in the sealskin bag. He gritted his teeth and averted his eyes from the pendulum as bile rose to his throat.

He groaned and recalled Kerrigan's crooked smile. Damn him. The Irishman had known what the sky promised as they talked on the dock that morning. 'Watch the horizon, and you'll be fine,' he'd said, but going on deck risked a midnight swim.

The fatty aroma of fried pork from the galley seeped under his door. Jesse tried to vanquish the existence of food, but the greasy odor clotted the cabin. He held a sodden pillow over his face, congratulating himself on his stamina. Unable to keep food down, he'd foregone all meals since the previous morning. His stomach knotted, and he dry-heaved into the pillow; his curses aimed at the sea. Damn all hell, he'd been born a landlubber, not a sailor.

If they find me dead of starvation, at least I won't be discovered in a pool of vomit.

The clipper shuddered like a wet dog, then snapped upright before it inevitably rolled in the opposite direction. Wind shrieked through the ship's bowels, and Jesse focused his thoughts on Boston. The woman might or might not decide to help him, but good intentions meant nothing if the sea battered the ship into splinters.

Unable to face another minute trapped inside the pitching cubicle, Jesse swung his legs over the side of his bunk. Bracing himself, he pulled on his jacket and the flat leather cap he'd bought for the voyage. Weak and dizzy, he staggered out of the cabin, a sober drunk on watery legs.

The passenger salon ran the length of the passenger interior, both walls flanked by doors to identical cabins. The deserted narrow passageway offered little escape. Lighted by four lanterns the deck tilted crazily. Faint cries and moans rose behind the doors, and Jesse gagged at the stench of vomit and overflowing chamber pots. He groped past two long dining tables and heavy wooden benches, all knocked askew like toys in an angry child's nursery. Clutching an overhead beam, he lurched toward the ladder at the far end of the heaving passage. He clambered up and for an instant imagined he heard the soft click of a door behind him.

Jesse heaved open the hatch. A blast of icy wind almost drove him half-way down the ladder. Seawater poured through the opening. He stumbled up the rough steps, fighting for balance. When the deck righted itself, he grabbed the deckhouse railing beside the door and pulled himself outside, slamming the hatch shut behind him.

The black world around him tilted and pitched, an asylum of wind and rain, yards of sailcloth tested to bursting in the crosstrees above his head. Jesse peered along the slanted deck, amazed at the storm's malevolence, the sea an enraged wilderness that cared nothing for trespassers. Wind ripped off his hat and hurled it into the darkness. Ahead, the bow disappeared in impossibly angled rain, the sky onyx-black. Nailed in place, he clutched the rail with both hands as the ship's prow cut through the monstrous sea, cleaving off the tops of white-capped swells. Seawater lashed and drenched him. Lightning threw ghostly white shadows on the deck, the wind's fury louder than the accompanying thunder. Astonished by nature's fury, he clung to the rail, trying to recall what had possessed him to leave the safety of his cabin.

He ducked his head and swiped water from his face. The sea around the *Abraham Reed* created a universe of deep swells and ragged whitecaps, the wave tops blown into frothy white spray. Mesmerized by the violence, Jesse tightened his grip on the rail and shuffled toward the bow. The sails swelled and snapped, joining the rigging in a mournful chorus, the topsails invisible in the night sky. Jesse dragged himself forward with both hands, spitting rain and seawater as he hugged the deckhouse wall. Secured by block and tackle contrivances, lines quivered and shrieked like penitent sinners, the enraged waves indifferent to his survival.

He squinted aft, but the stern and helmsman were invisible, the blackness complete. He reached the corner of the deckhouse where the handrail ended. Only a void of blackness remained in the direction of the bow. No way to go forward.

Wiping his eyes, he ducked his head against the wind and retraced his steps. Lightening cracked along the horizon and the image of the frail figure in the cell returned.

My father deserves the best defense I can muster. I'll do whatever—

The blow glanced off his skull.

Stunned, he fell to his knees and glimpsed a bearded face, a club raised to strike again. Dazed and ears ringing, he lunged forward and crashed into his assailant. Both men fell heavily to the deck and skidded across the rain-slick planks, crashing into the ship's unyielding railing, the last barrier above the sea.

Pinned beneath the heavier man, Jesse grabbed the club with both hands. The man hit him with a fist, and Jesse's head bounced off the deck. His vision watery, he lost his grip on the lead club. The man's arm lifted again just as the bow collided with a wall of water. The impact lifted both men off the deck and threw them back down. The club rolled out of sight.

Rough hands lifted Jesse to his feet and jammed him against the railing. Bristly whiskers scratched the side of Jesse's face. The feral eye glowed brightly as his attacker's grip tightened. The ship keeled onto its side, and Jesse glanced over his shoulder at waves a few feet away.

"Over you go," a harsh voice grated.

Jesse's feet dangled in mid-air, his body arched over the railing.

No!

He drove an elbow into the man's throat. The calloused hands lost their grip and his attacker slammed against the railing. The figure lunged for a rope, missed, and tumbled over the side. Jesse caught his jacket in one hand, grabbing the rigging in his other fist.

The dark form dangled above the hungry waves, mouth agape, the single eye pleading. He yelled something, but wind snatched away the panicky words.

Jesse tightened his grip, struggling to keep his grip on the dead weight. Palm burning, his hand slipped down the sodden rope. Legs braced against the rail, the dead weight threatened to pull him into the sea's embrace alongside the one-eyed man—unless he released the jacket.

He stared down at the terrified face and screamed against the weight. His hand lost its grip just as muscular arms suddenly encircled his waist.

A wiry elf of a seaman bundled in a dirty mackinaw held him fast, both his feet braced against the railing. Grunting, he reached past Jesse with one arm for the man's jacket. The wet lapel ripped away and the attacker plummeted into the sea with a terrified cry, the sound stolen by the wind.

Jesse's savior waited until the ship righted itself, then shoved him toward the deckhouse railing. Holding his arm tightly, the seaman pushed him toward the salon, both clutching the railing. He forced open the hatch, and they clamored down the steps, sealing out the storm. Drenched and shaking, water poured from his clothes. Jesse indicated his cabin, and the man followed him inside.

"I seen it, sir, seen it all," the seaman gasped, eyes wide as Jesse collapsed onto his bunk. Water ran from his rescuer's weathers and pooled around seaman's boots. "You tried to save that poor fellow, but it weren't no use. Too much weight for the two of us. If I hadn't come along on my watch, you'd have gone overboard with him."

His hand afire, Jesse cradled his arm, shivering. The left side of his face swelled, the skin tight and burning, and his breath came in irregular gasps. He looked up at the little man who likewise trembled from the cold.

"Thank you," Jesse croaked. "You saved my life."

His breathing slowed and the sailor gaped at him, neither knowing what to say. The man's slicker glistened in the candlelight as he pushed back the hood. A pinched weather-beaten face stared at Jesse.

"Lucky for you I was just startin' my last watch. What was you two doing up there?"

"I was sick," Jesse lied. "We both needed air."

"If you don't mind me saying so, sir, the deck weren't no place to be gettin' fresh air."

Jesse nodded and stripped off his sodden coat. Whoever had tried to kill him came close to his completing task if the little man hadn't appeared.

"You all right, sir? I need to tell the captain straight away," the seaman said. "No way I could save your friend, not in this storm. Good as dead the moment he went over the side."

The sailor touched his hood and left. Jesse stripped off the rest of his clothes and draped them over the single chair. His hands stopped shaking but the pain reminded him how close he'd come to swapping fates with his attacker.

My god. Someone tried to kill me.

The sailor believed he'd witnessed a rescue attempt. Jesse hoped their combined stories would prevent an inquiry, that the vessel's master accepted his version of events. An official inquiry might entail days or weeks of delay in an unfamiliar city, while his father edged closer to trial.

But who was the man who tried to kill him? Who wanted him dead? The killer had followed him aboard, obviously intending to murder him. Jesse sat heavily on his bunk, his head 'reluctantly clearing as the ship rolled without letup, his survival still in doubt if there was more than one killer. No matter the outcome, all doubts about his father's innocence had vanished, erased by the single eye peering down at him as he struggled against the railing. If he'd ended up in the sea, someone remained very rich, and his father died alone.

Jesse gingerly opened and closed his fist, the palm raw and burning, a painful reminder how close he'd come to death.

We'll reach Boston tomorrow, and if someone wants me dead, they'll try again.

Whoever they were, they made a mistake leaving him alive.

Every item in the cabin dripped or sagged with water, but the walls and deck no longer pitched, the storm dissipated during the night. A collection of pointed hammers pounded the inside of Jesse's skull. He touched the painful lump at his hairline and winced as he sat up. One hand braced against the bulkhead he peered into the tiny mirror above the fold-down desk. The left side of his face glowed deep red, the eye partially blackened.

He lifted the pouch from the bulkhead and removed the black waterproof case. The documents were dry and untouched. He reread Cohen's letters to the Boston attorney and Elizabeth Pendleton, recalling his wry warnings that Jesse would find both "different", a knock on the louvered cabin door interrupting his thoughts.

He replaced the documents and opened the door to find the diminutive sailor with his woolen watch cap in one hand. The captain was asking for them, the man said, as though they'd received a summons from God, a near truth in the seaman's universe. Jesse donned his coat and assured his savior he'd explain his rescue to the ship's captain. He followed the worried man on deck, amazed at the benign sea around them, so different from the previous night's raging beast.

The interview lasted only ten minutes. Jesse corroborated the tale of events as the little seaman had interpreted them. The captain, more than willing to accept their stories, listened indulgently, satisfied the ship's owners would suffer no liability from the incident. He praised the seaman's courage, wished Jesse a pleasant stay in Boston, and ended the meeting. Outside, Jesse gave the little man fifty dollars, far more than he could spare, but less than the value of his life.

Shaking the sailor's hand, Jesse made his way forward to the bow. Wind-bloated sails bulged above his head, the wind barely harrowing the sea's surface, waves no higher than spring plowing furrows. Free of angry whitecaps, the water slid docilely alongside the hull as the temperate wind propelled the *Abraham Reed* northward, satiated by the sacrifice of a man who deserved to die.

Jesse leaned against the rail and looked aft where the ship's wake covered his assailant's grave. The captain said his name was Mincey, but it meant nothing to Jesse. The breeze soothed his battered face, a healing companion as he turned and peered over the bowsprit at the northern horizon that might hold answers to the unfathomable. Cohen believed the woman had powers to refute the obvious, but Jesse's doubts about her *bono fides* remained in limbo. If she agreed to help, he and Cohen placed a life in her hands. But first, he had to convince her to return with him to Savannah.

He closed his eyes and gripped the railing until his skinned hand throbbed. Accepting the pain as penance for his earlier doubts, he silently asked his father's forgiveness. In the terrifying moments suspended above the sea, his suspicions had washed away with his attacker. Someone had hired the one-eyed man to feed him to the sea, assuring an innocent man died in jail. His guilt pulled at him until he buried it forever and forced away the last residue of shame.

Vertical silhouettes appeared from the sea as Boston's towers and church steeples emerged against the cloudless sky. The profiles sharpened his anticipation and Jesse returned to his cabin.

Chapter Fourteen

March 16
Boston
Same Morning

Jesse gingerly grasped the gangplank rope and stepped onto Lewis Wharf, his raw hand throbbing. A frigid gust of northeastern wind defied the calendar's proclamation of spring, the air a colder cousin to Savannah's timid chill. Patches of snow persisted in the dock's shadows, tops crusted with dirty ice. The cold wind-swept harbor housed a metropolis of ships, a forest of masts and furled sails riding at tide as though fashioning a nautical city that obscured the ocean beyond, vessels nestled against multiple docks that stretched seaward like blunt fingers.

Jesse hefted his satchel in his uninjured hand, the portfolio beneath one arm. He shook off the cabin's cramped confines and paused at the bottom of the gangplank. He rolled his shoulders in relief and surveyed the expanse of neatly stacked cargo, spaces between the crates forming narrow paths for stevedores and arriving passengers. The week's haul of cod and every variety of ocean rot brought Savannah's wharves to mind. Despite the similarities, he found it difficult to accept the two cities shared the same ocean. Boston appeared to be Savannah times ten.

Three grey and white gulls perched atop pilings and measured him as a potential meal. Jesse wound through the canyons of cargo, sidestepping bustling sailors, beggars, and well-dressed Bostonians as he made his way from the waterfront. He sensed the ship's motion with every step and glanced behind him every few yards, recalling the single malevolent eye glaring down at him as he dangled above the sea. Sweating despite the chill he slipped into the first alley and searched for a second assailant, though god knows how he was supposed to recognize an assassin amongst the crowds. His back pressed against the wall, he scanned the flurry of bodies that ignored him. He endured the alley's stench and slowed his breathing, but only a few people glanced at the figure lurking in the alley. The rustle and clatter of the overflowing city assaulted his ears with the rumble of carriage wheels, and hard-edged voices. After a full minute he stepped from the lane, glanced in both directions, and hailed the first Hackney carriage he saw, instructing the driver to take him to Fresh Pond Hotel in Cambridge, lodging recommended by Cohen.

The carriage maneuvered past hurrying pedestrians and wheeled conveyances of every description; wagons and carts cluttered every intersection, sidewalks jammed with hordes of city dwellers. His bruised face cooled by the stream of air, he sat back on the unpadded seat and marveled at the city. Gas streetlights, Boston's latest marvel of technology, lined the sidewalks, the stately procession of ornamental lampposts announcing progress. Boston could only be described as a city bent on claiming its place in the world, while Savannah huddled beneath her insular cloak.

The carriage skirted Faneuil Market, then clattered past City Hall's peaked spire. Endless warrens of alleys and narrow streets paraded past the open window until Jesse lost all sense of direction, adrift in a strange city. He thought of the bearded man hired to kill him, unable to prevent the image of black waves as powerful hands lifted him from the storm-ravaged deck. He twice leaned out the window to check behind the carriage until the coach bustled over the new West Boston Bridge that spanned the glassy Charles River.

On the other side of the river, Cambridge assumed the face of Boston's small sister. Modest shops and houses lined dirt and cobbled streets. The carriage halted before an imposing three-story wooden building, and Jesse paid the driver. In his second-floor room he bathed and changed from shipboard clothes into a more presentable appearance, frowning at his bruised face in the dresser mirror. Downstairs, Jesse showed the desk clerk the woman's address. Elizabeth Pendleton lived a short walk away.

The white saltbox cottage faced a cobbled street, fronted by an undersized porch. Sheltered by a slanted overhang, two pots of withered flowers guarded the front door. Jesse knocked. Footsteps sounded on bare floors and a spare young man cracked open the front door. His shoulder jammed against it, the face, appeared haggard and cadaverous, younger than Jesse. His clothes bore deep wrinkles and stains as if he'd not removed them since the previous night. He inspected Jesse's blotched face and glanced at the folio in his hand.

"No drummers," he said, starting to close the door.

Jesse caught the edge. "I'm here to see Miss Pendleton." He pushed Cohen's letter through the strained opening. "I have a letter of introduction from my attorney in Savannah."

His shoulder wedged against the door, the slim guardian sighed, his unshaven face impatient. He opened the letter, read it, and inspected Jesse again. He reread the missive and reluctantly stepped aside as Jesse entered. Letter in hand, he slouched down a narrow hall without looking back. Jesse followed his surly guide who ushered him to a warren of paper and lamps. The sparse furnishings reminded Jesse of Cohen's anteroom where the two clerks labored. Paper of all variety littered the bare floor, and more documents sat in stacks against the walls. The sweet aroma of sugary tobacco pervaded the cluttered room, and a single vacant chair beckoned to unlikely guests.

Seated behind a chest-high desk Elizabeth Pendleton reigned over the paper universe. Flanked by two oversized oil-burning sconces, lamplight fell on black hair that cascaded past her narrow shoulders. The dark river of glazed silk fell forward over her face and obscured her features. Unaware of the two men's entry she held a thin cigarillo between two fingers, studying a document through a large magnifying glass. A diaphanous cloud of pale blue smoke floated above her head. Notwithstanding the obvious affection for tobacco, she appeared regal on her elevated perch, a timeless archetype of her gender. Poised above the paper she did not look up until the unkempt young man spoke.

"Lizzie, this man has a letter from a Georgia lawyer, a Mister Cohen," Elias Pendleton said.

The woman straightened and inspected Jesse, her irritation evident at being interrupted. Jolted by Caribbean blue eyes, Jesse appraised her with equal scrutiny, surprised by her grace and beauty as she slid from the high stool. She crossed to the fire and tossed the cigarillo into the flames without acknowledging him. He detected an obvious limp despite her attempt to mask the flaw. When Jesse stared a second too long, she met his inquisitive stare with weary boldness.

"Yes, I have an impaired leg," she said with a glare. Seated again, she made no attempt to hide her disdain at his disheveled appearance. "A very obvious *flaw* on my part."

Her brother handed her the letter. The lamps cast flickering highlights over her hair as she read Cohen's introduction. Jesse failed in his attempt not to stare at her. The sweet pall of burned tobacco scented the air, the unexpected aroma enhancing her exotic appearance. Her skin bore a similarity to his own with the hint of a foreign inheritance. The olive hue ran well past the sun's tan, a field of smooth flesh. She wore oriental pantaloons of dark blue satin over a loose white chemise. Flaunting current fashion, she wore her long hair loose. So black it shown like deep indigo it obscured her face as she studied the letter. The image of a Gypsy floated unbidden in Jesse's mind, and had she flaunted a single gold earring, he'd have accepted it as a truth. She exuded something indefinable, exceedingly feminine, a woman men turned to look at, then turned back and stared again.

The tobacco's sugary presence persisted in the small room. She looked up and in spite of her brusque manner and unconventional appearance, she captivated him, her eyes shining with the unapologetic fervor of a zealot. Shifting the clear blue eyes from his face, she glanced at Cohen's letter again. She skimmed the words and caught him staring when she looked up with obvious distaste. She handed him the letter and shook her head.

"I'm not interested."

Jesse's heart fell. "Miss Pendleton, Samuel Cohen is acquainted with your efforts through an associate in Boston." He heard the urgency of his plea. "He regards your work as sound. He recommended I seek your help."

She leaned on the slanted desktop and glanced at her brother with a knowing smile. "And *why* are you in need my services, Mr.—Caine, is it? Are you another of those desperate men looking to save himself or a family member who's broken the law?"

"My father's innocent, Miss Pendleton. The evidence against him is comprised of documents purported to be in his handwriting, but I've no means of proving them false."

"Of course," she sighed wearily as though the words produced an unpleasant odor. "Fabricated evidence. My brother Elias and I are sought out by many who clutch documents of all varieties. They have no avenues left other than the distant hope of proving them a forgery."

Her brother gave an abrupt laugh, the disclaimer obviously an opening gambit with many who sought her help. Jesse's confusion showed, abetted by the fact that the folio he held contained stolen documents, that an entire city believed his father guilty. She pointedly ignored his discomfort and fixed him with a smile void of humor.

"The guilty clutch at a cripple like me, sir. Damaged as I may be, I represent their last hope."

"I traveled from Savannah because Samuel Cohen thinks highly of your work," Jesse said. "He and the Boston attorney mentioned in his letter hold you in high regard. My father *is* falsely accused, and Cohen believes you to be our only hope."

She rose from the desk and limped to a low table. She removed a cigarillo from a blue porcelain jar. Her brother bent to the fireplace and lifted a sliver of burning kindling. She cupped his hand and drew deeply at the miniature cigar, brushing fine strands from her forehead. She caught Jesse staring at the cigarillo.

"I'm not an addictive," she said." Three a day, not one more." She cocked her head and eyed the bruises on his face to change the subject.

"It appears someone disagreed with your father's innocence."

Her brother laughed again. Increasingly irritated by their manner, Jesse said, "A stranger tried to kill me during my passage here."

Elizabeth studied him a long moment and shrugged. "I suppose you brought samples of the evidence." She curled a corner of her mouth upward and glanced at her brother. "They all arrive clutching paper," she said to him.

Jesse held his temper. "May I sit?" he asked. She indicated the sole chair. He opened the folio and removed two sheaves of paper. He handed her the first stack. "People claim this is my father's hand." Then the second stack. "And this is verified correspondence from his office." He indicated the first group. "I'm told the prosecution has ten times this amount."

"And the authorities *allowed* you to remove these papers?" she asked.

"Not exactly." Admitting to larceny did nothing to strengthen his plea. "I was told you'd want to inspect the evidence."

"So you've broke the law and desire me as an accomplice in your theft of court property."

"I did it to help my father."

Staring at his damaged face, she hesitated before placing both stacks on her desk. She removed a document from each pile and leaned close to study them side by side. The scent of cloves filled the room. She wrinkled her nose and passed the magnifying glass over the papers, looking from one page to the other.

She sat back. "Examining documents entails a great deal of work, and your actions and appearance do not inspire confidence." She returned the documents to him. "My services involve a trip to Georgia, and I don't hold with states abiding slavery. I do not work for those owning other human beings." She reached to a table behind her and thrust a broadsheet at Jesse, a new fervor in her voice.

"We've begun the crusade in Boston."

Emblazoned as the *Liberator*, the foolscap shouted anti-slavery sentiments from every column. Jesse's face warmed as he read virulent anti-Southern proclamations. Slavery long ago proved abhorrent to him, but he did not view the institution as inherently ingrained in all Southerners. Justification of the practice was morally bankrupt, an opinion shared by his father, their position marking them as enemies among Savannah's wealthy slaveholders.

"I appreciate your opposition, Miss Pendleton," he said, "and I reject the institution. Neither my father nor I own slaves." He returned the broadsheet to her. "Without meaning to appear argumentative, you're undoubtedly aware the slave trade began here in Massachusetts, not in the Southern colonies."

Elizabeth Pendleton flushed. "Be that as it may, Mr. Caine, I have many other obligations." She swept her hand at envelopes and documents scattered around the desk. "I'll look at what you've brought. Come back tomorrow."

Disappointed, Jesse picked up his carrying case. She drew daintily on the slender cigar and resumed her perch behind the desk. The interview at an end, Elias ushered him out the front door without a word where Jesse found himself once again in the company of dead flowers on the porch.

Jesse re-crossed the Charles River next morning into Boston. His coat wrapped tightly about him, he gazed at the city as the coach rattled over the new bridge. The city reawakened his fascination, but the disappointing meeting with Elizabeth Pendleton dimmed his ardor for the wonders surrounding him. Unless the bizarre woman used her alleged powers to refute the documents, he had no idea where to turn next. His helplessness burgeoned as the carriage wound through streets crowded with early risers of all dress and shapes, none of whom cared a whit about his father or the missing million dollars a thousand miles away.

The carriage stopped before a newly constructed brick and terracotta building on State Street. Its imposing elegance shamed its neighbors, rising above the sidewalk like a temple. A polished plate to the right of brass-adorned double doors announced the law offices of Harpe, Golden, and Rothstein. Jesse paid the driver and got out. He looked up at the structure: Five stories of scrubbed red brick, decorated with elaborately carved masonry and rows of gleaming windows, the facade designed to create awe for its august occupants. He smiled and compared the brick palace to Cohen's uninspired quarters. Somewhat surprised when the doors admitted him, he stepped into a foyer of marbled stone.

The waiting room overflowed with defendants and plaintiffs, faces angry, expectant, or frightened. With all the chairs occupied, people leaned against the walls in earnest conversation, their lives, futures, or fortunes in the balance. Jesse crossed the crowded room and handed Cohen's letter to a male secretary who barely glanced at it. Dressed in somber black. Jesse assumed the harried attendant guarded the unmarked door behind him.

The sentry scanned the letter a second time and brusquely told him to wait. He disappeared through the door and left Jesse standing awkwardly beside the desk with no place to sit. Counting over fifty people in the room, he was startled when the secretary reappeared with an apologetic smile, ushering Jesse through the massive door and gently closing it behind him.

Thaddeus Harpe's office smelled of many things but largely new and very old money. It also reeked of tobacco, old books, and worn leather, the mixture absorbed and embedded in patterned carpets heaped atop one another to banish the audacity of footsteps. Brown and black law books lined floor-to-ceiling bookcases, and a desk large enough to serve family dinner dominated a pair of casement windows overlooking the street. Stained glass enlivened the upper panes, admitting a rainbow of light in sharp contrast to the austere office. On the desk sat an array of brass and glass inkwells, and ornate three pipe stands. Six decorative tobacco jars completed the clutter that almost obscured the squat balding figure.

Harpe cleared his throat and appraised Jesse with periwinkle blue eyes. Jesse guessed him to be in his late sixties. The man quickly came round the desk and enthusiastically pumped Jesse's hand, a toothy smile lighting his scrubbed cherub face.

"Mr. Caine, Mr. Caine. Do have a seat."

Jesse sat in an oversized leather chair capable of seating two lumberjacks. Harpe resumed his chair and brushed aside a pile of depositions. He held up Cohen's letter with a toothy grin.

"How *is* Sammy?" he asked.

It took a moment for Jesse to realize that Harpe referred to Samuel Cohen, Jesse never having heard anyone refer to the feared attorney as Sammy. Still grinning, Harpe selected a long-stemmed pipe and dipped it into one of the jars, packing the bowl with a thumbnail as he examined his visitor. He lit the carved bowl with a long match, smoke billowing above his head. His expression narrowed, an uncompromising slyness behind the jovial exterior as he waited for Jesse to speak.

"He sends his regards," Jesse managed.

Harpe nodded with a burst of renewed enthusiasm, "Good. Good. We miss him in Boston. Never understood why he opened his practice in the South. No offense, Mr. Caine, no offense, I assure you." He drew deeply on the pipe and aimed the stem at Jesse.

"Did he tell you his sordid background? No? A boxer, a bare-knuckled fighter, and damn fine city champion. Sammy Cohen." Harpe's tone turned wistful and Jesse recalled the broken knuckles and severed eyebrow, fist-hammered clues he'd overlooked.

"Won my share backing him, yes, I did," Harpe exclaimed. "Disappointed when he was accepted into law school. Amused as well, I can tell you," he chattered, "but proved his worth in a courtroom as well as the ring, he did." He wagged his head with a look of disappointment. "Nay, never picked another winner after he pursued the gentler occupation. Never again. Lost my share of wagers since then, indeed I have."

He sucked contentedly at the pipe, looking as though gambling losses were pleasures rather than financial inconveniences. A look of nostalgia crossed his face, and he rested his round head against the chair, content for the moment in his memories. Colored rays from the stained glass adorned his glossy dome as he refocused on Jesse.

"So what brings you to Boston, Mr. Caine?" He inspected Jesse's face. "You're not by chance a boxer, are you?"

Jesse waved his hand. "A slight altercation, nothing more." He saw no profit in relating the attack aboard ship "As his letter states, Samuel Cohen represents my father in a case of fraud," he began. "He recommended Elizabeth Pendleton as someone who might prove the evidence against him was falsified. He said you had experience with Miss Pendleton, and that I should seek your opinion."

Harpe laughed and settled his chin on his chest. "She's a strange one, I grant you, but the woman knows what she's about. Proved an employee robbed my client blind in his own office. Remarkable woman in many ways. Remarkable, I say again."

"I found her disconcerting."

The lawyer chuckled, enjoying Jesse's look of consternation. "So you've met her," he said. "Her value's surely not found in her social manner." He leaned over the desk and took aim with the pipe again. "But she's clever by half again, sir. She speaks with a new certainty. If you can engage her, do so by all means. If questionable documents are involved, you'll do no better than employing her. That's my advice to you and Sammy."

"I value your opinion, sir."

Harpe's gaze pierced Jesse, his cunning obvious. "Is your father guilty, Mr. Caine?"

"No, sir."

Harpe nodded. "Then Sammy Cohen's your man. Stick with him. And engage Elizabeth Pendleton if she'll hire out for you."

Harpe knocked ashes from the pipe and cast a surreptitious glance over Jesse's shoulder where paying clients waited beyond the closed door. He stood and offered his hand again.

"Do tell Sammy we miss him."

Jesse left Harpe's building and walked Boston's streets. He thought about Elizabeth Pendleton and her insufferable brother. Necessity offered little choice but to rely on Harpe's opinion and pursue her. Despite her barbed manner, she'd struck a chord. Not simply her exotic beauty—because she was indeed beautiful—but because she could extricate a failing man from his tomb. Her disconcerting manner and ill-mannered brother were small penalties if she agreed to help. He was surprised when the memory of her alluring features persisted, and he found himself attracted to more than her reputation.

Just because she's pretty woman...

He hailed a carriage to Cambridge and found himself at her door again in a matter of minutes, hesitant to enter another contest of wills. Elias Pendleton answered his knock immediately, his appearance more disheveled than the previous day. A grimy hand pushed the bundle of documents through the partially open door.

"My sister asked me to return these. She's not disposed to travel south, nor does she wish to speak with you again."

Chocolate-scented tobacco wafted from the hallway. Tempted to bull his way past the scornful face to plead his case again, Jesse said, "I'll gladly pay whatever fee she requires."

"It's not a question of money, Mr. Caine," Elias said smugly. "She doesn't like you."

The door closed with a resounding click. Tempted to kick it until the boy or woman reappeared, he turned and trudged back to his hotel. A reputable pub attached itself to the side of the building, and against his better judgment he went inside and ordered a whiskey, then another.

He'd traveled a thousand miles and came close to being murdered. The abrupt refusal he'd endured was unacceptable. His father was worthy of more than an casual dismissal by a haughty abolitionist.

His balance almost failed him as he walked from the tavern. The short walk cleared his head somewhat and he found him nearing the frame house again just as Elizabeth Pendleton opened the door and stepped onto the porch. Surprised to see him, she started back inside but changed her mind when he called to her.

"I must speak to you again."

She hesitantly stepped forward to face him. "I thought I made my position clear, Mr. Caine." She inspected the street for an ally if one was needed. "My work does not include travel, especially to a slave state."

Jesse leaned closer to her, suddenly aware the whiskey's residue polluted the air between them. "Slavery has nothing to do with my father's plight. We have no other alternatives but to engage your assistance."

Elizabeth tilted her head away. "I don't intend to stand in the street and argue with you, Mr. Caine. I fully understand your situation," she said, her tone softening, "but I have no desire or inclination to leave Boston. Good day to you."

"Miss Pendleton..."

She limped past him and Jesse stood nailed in place by defeat. He resisted the urge to follow her and renew his pleading. He'd lost the battle, and whatever happened to his father now would not be affected by whatever skills she might have possessed.

Chapter Fifteen

March 17
Late Afternoon
Aboard 'The Lorelei Queen'

The ship's two masts dipped and swayed at the far end of wharf, a westerly breeze from the sea ruffling Boston Harbor. Struggling to catch his breath, Jesse ran up the gangplank and dropped his luggage on deck. Fortunate to have found the last berth on a vessel sailing for Savannah, there was no reason to linger in the extraordinary city. He surveyed the veteran ship's lines, a serviceable brig that carried mail to Charleston, Savannah, and down the Florida coast. She guaranteed he'd walk ashore in Savannah within the week if wind and weather cooperated.

He handed his ticket to a bearded seaman, who added his name to the passenger manifest. His cabin, small but clean, seemed little recompense for the inbound voyage that almost cost his life. Elizabeth Pendleton had proven a conceited harpy and waste of time despite her charms, and he hoped Samuel Cohen had devised another defense in his absence. Or that Kerrigan located the two swindlers.

Jesse hung his coat on a hook. The aroma of sugary tobacco wafted from his coat and he cursed the eccentric woman. Intriguing as she appeared, the woman cared nothing about his father's plight and had dismissed his plea for help. More convinced than ever that his father's fate was connected to the mountain of documents, Jesse's and Cohen's gamble had nonetheless failed. Unable to dispute the written evidence, the thick folio at the courthouse ensured a guilty verdict.

Jesse stored his valise in the cabin's single closet and wedged the folio onto the top shelf. Sitting on his bunk, the weight of the voyage descended on him. He studied the deck under his feet. He'd almost died and the woman counted only as loss, a waste of time he could ill afford. Trapped for a week in another closet-sized cabin, he was marooned in the mid-Atlantic, isolated and unable to assist Cohen or comfort his father. False documents waited for a jury's inspection, while his father breathed the poisonous air in the buried cell. If shipwrecked, it would all be a forgotten footnote in a few years. Too damn much, he thought. Finding no remedy to the conundrum, he resisted the temptation to lie back and tempt sleep. Instead, he went on deck and surveyed his fellow passengers, wondering which one might seek for a second opportunity to kill him.

As the *Lorelei Queen* weighed anchor in Boston harbor, Elizabeth Pendleton shifted on the high stool behind her desk. She was only partially aware that the last of the alleged receipts on the desk awaited her final inspection. She'd required less than a week to expose them as clumsy forgeries, a junior partner's attempts to defraud his company. Poor efforts, all of them, she saw, the work of a greedy amateur lacking skill or cleverness. Her client would be overjoyed with the money he recouped, minus her fee and the agreed-upon bonus.

Despite her sense of accomplishment, her thoughts wandered back to Jesse Caine. His bronzed image lingered, the scarred face hopeful as he'd thrust the strangely scented documents at her. Battered into a shambles, his appearance had repelled her even as his plea sparked a note of sincerity.

She tossed a receipt aside. Why am I obsessing about him, she wondered? Her eyes and whatever common sense she possessed told her he was a common ruffian, despite a reference letter from an attorney whom she knew only by reputation, an ex-Boston pugilist practicing law in the distant South. Experience indicated both were to be avoided.

She tried to concentrate on a poorly forged receipt, but the memory of the oddly fragrant papers returned. She'd only briefly inspected them, but a hint of the aroma lingered in the stuffy room like stale flowers. The scent intrigued her, as did the battered face. Claims of innocence were nothing new to her, but he'd indicated there were many such documents. Large masses of possible forgeries always intrigued her, and she wished she'd inspected the papers more closely. Something indefinable had reached out to her from Jesse Caine's folio.

Elizabeth shoved aside the receipt and bit her lip. She'd been short with him for good reasons. Why obsess about a man she'd seen only once? He was reasonably well dressed, but his face hinted he was a brawler, a dweller of rougher streets. But had she judged him too quickly? He claimed an attack onboard ship, and beneath the bruises his features had hinted at an exotic origin she did not recognize. She picked up the receipt a third time only to lay it aside after a moment, angry with her musings.

Most likely, the bruises resulted from a drunken brawl, she reasoned, but the face seemed an honest one, if such wonders existed. He'd traveled a thousand miles to meet with her, an arduous voyage in her mind's eye. An act of desperation by a man who professed to love his father. Challenging her beliefs had added nothing to his case and done nothing to win her over, but his reaction was natural enough, given her abruptness.

She slipped from the stool and retrieved a cigarillo from the jar, recalling the soft accent. Why should a stranger mean anything to her?

He likely considered her little more than an oddly-dressed eccentric, a forlorn remedy, and she'd pushed him away like so many others who appeared at her door, both for business and possible pleasure. Desperation too often entered the room on two legs. Half were dull suitors at best, the others liars and criminals desperate to believe she possessed spiritual insight to free the guilty. She lit the thin cigar and frowned at the receipts scattered across her desk.

"Damnation," she said aloud.

Shocked she'd uttered the obscenity, she gave a half-smile. Swearing was a luxury forbidden her sex, but perfectly attuned to her confusion. A flush rose to her face.

Georgia, for God's sake.

An enclave of slaves, a city without friends or acquaintances. All to help a man with a battered interesting face whom she'd rejected out of hand, one she now remembered as strangely attractive. What in God's name was she thinking? She drew on the cigarillo and looked wistfully out the smudged window. Chained to her desk, the drab winter had seemed an endless procession of work, but it sustained and excited her in a way she could never explain. Fantasies were for adolescent schoolgirls and she was no longer a frivolous girl. She sighed heavily and slid onto the high stool. Relegating Jesse Caine's interesting face to her lackluster past, she arranged the receipts into orderly piles. There was always her work.

Chapter Sixteen

Jesse rode from the empty house after a cold breakfast, gladly enduring Aristotle's unyielding gait. He regarded the familiar streets with reborn appreciation. The houses seemed shuttered against his return, but the earth did not roll and toss, or challenge his breakfast. He'd suffered enough ships and the sea for a lifetime.

Boston and Cambridge had provided no respite, an attempt on his life tossed into the bad bargain. Looking back, Elizabeth Pendleton and her haughty brother had seemed adversaries in a foreign land, and her refusal left both father and son at an empty well. He was back where he began, but he looked at spring's emergence, grateful for the beauty around him. If he'd accomplished nothing else he'd returned home reborn, confident his father was innocent.

He recalled the woman's lovely face, an enigma who dismissed him as a whip-wielding slaveholder. Scornful and enticing in the same instant, her arrogance and summary dismissal returned his thoughts to reality. Cursing, he kicked Aristotle into a trot toward the jail.

John Dew's underfed deputy preceded him down the steps into the abyss. Jesse wished he could stall the descent, providing time to explain his failed quest. Carefully chosen words were needed to soften the truth. No matter the outcome, he'd returned clean, reborn in his faith in his father's innocence. The seconds in which he'd fought for his life above the waves had generated a new bonding with the sick man in the cell.

His father sat on the bunk, back against the stone wall, arms wrapped around knees as though hoarding body heat and withdrawing into himself. He stood and forced a smile, drawing back when he saw Jesse's discolored face.

"What in God's name happened?"

"Someone tried to murder me on the ship."

"Murder you?"

"A stranger attacked me. He made no attempt to rob me, which says someone hired him to kill me."

"What happened to him?"

"He's dead."

"Did you kill him?"

"He washed overboard in a storm," Jesse said without elaborating.

His father hung his head. "With you gone, the thieves would have had a clear road. Did you report the attack to the sheriff?"

"What could he do?" Jesse scoffed. "He'd see it as a fairy tale I concocted to help you."

"Do you believe me now?"

"What?"

"Do you believe I'm innocent?"

Jesse looked at his boot tops as though his doubts were written on the cell walls. "How did you know?"

"Because I'm your father."

Ambrose sat down heavily and ignored Jesse's look of shock. "And the woman in Boston?"

Jesse dolefully shook his head and looked at his father, feeling as though a burden had been lifted from him. Whatever happened they were father and son again with nothing between them. Any remaining doubts were gone, washed overboard with the killer.

"I take it the news isn't what I want to hear," his father said.

"A peculiar woman," Jesse said, at a loss to describe her dismissive manner. What purpose would it serve to describe her disdain for him and their situation? Recounting her attitude offered nothing to help them. "I'm afraid we'll need to look in other directions."

"She was not competent?"

Jesse shrugged. "I have no idea. She simply declined to help."

Ambrose Caine suddenly sat forward, his voice suffused with rage. "I am not guilty, Jesse. I am *not*!"

"I know that. I'll find other avenues."

Ambrose Caine stifled a sob. "I can't believe anyone would believe I'd do such a thing."

"I saw the evidence," Jesse said. Jesse met the surprised gaze without flinching. "Cohen let me examine the documents. Every piece appears to be in your handwriting. According to Cohen, they're collecting more proof." Jesse fixed his father with a direct gaze. "They're all forgeries, damn it," Jesse said. "I know you never set hand to them. The damned woman might have helped us, but she has prejudices we can't overcome." Jesse said. It sounded churlish to blame her, but his father deserved a better defense, and Elizabeth Pendleton had dismissed him like a street beggar who'd wandered into her parlor.

Jesse sat on the bed and put his arm around the narrow shoulders. With no clever words to lessen the pain, he embraced the crestfallen figure. Defeat, it seemed, ruled the week for the Caines.

Chapter Seventeen

March 26
Downtown
Late Morning

Fletcher Tyree stood beneath the tobacco shop's striped awning with three friends. All four lighted fresh cigars and extolled the merits of their purchases, satisfied faces wreathed in smoke. Fletcher brushed ashes from his checked trousers, pleased with his reflection in the shop window. Turning back he paused in mid-sentence, the morning's pleasure quashed as a familiar figure and young woman emerged from a restaurant half a block away.

Victoria Danford—with Jesse Caine on her arm.

Tyree's companions turned and dragged their eyes over Victoria. Grinning, they looked at one another, then back to Tyree.

Two men nudged one another, leering. "My, my," one said.

"Miss Danford has a reputation to uphold," another said archly. "She's no business being seen in public with Caine."

Fletcher Tyree stared until one of his companions elbowed him. "I see you've not lost your good taste, Colonel." The men continued their inspection of Victoria, smiles broadening as they gave vent to their fantasies and drew at the Cubans. A rangy man with a lacquered cane leaned over and whispered to Tyree, "She's a delightful piece of quim, a welcome addition to any one of our beds. With the wife absent, of course."

The men chuckled. The cheroot's pleasure dissipated, Fletcher turned back to them with a diffident smile. "Yes, most certainly."

"Got you tongue-tied, has she, Fletcher?" said the taller man. He gently shoved Tyree in Victoria's direction. "Go to it, man. You're the only widower among us, and Caine's no competition for you in his current state." The man nudged him again. "Go gauge your prospects, you randy old lion."

Chuckling at Tyree's discomfort, the three watched him stride toward Jesse and Victoria with a confidence he did not feel. Fletcher hoped to avoid Jesse until the trial, but the inevitable had happened. He strolled toward them, appearing nothing more than a wealthy bachelor testing his possibilities. Sweat coated the band of his top hat. He doffed it and forced a smile.

"Victoria. Jesse." Mindful of his composure, he looked at Jesse's bruised face. "Are you injured?"

"A mishap," Jesse replied carefully with a strained smile. "No damage done."

At a loss, Fletcher twisted the gold ring around his finger and contrived a smile for Victoria before turning back to Jesse. "I'm anxious your father's situation will soon be resolved. The lost money will affect the entire city."

"As I explained to Miss Danford, I'd hoped to disprove the evidence, but the attempt proved useless."

Fletcher concealed his relief. "I'm sorry your trip proved fruitless, but a jury will be believe what it sees with its own eyes."

"That's why I need your help," Jesse said.

Fletcher Tyree removed a handkerchief and wiped his hatband. "I'm among those who lost a great deal of money, Jesse. Ambrose will have to pay the price for his folly."

Jesse stared at him. "You believe the charges?"

"The law must take its course."

"So you will not assist him?"

Tyree replaced his hat. "I saw the evidence and I know your father's handwriting. Perhaps your mother's desertion unhinged him more than you realized."

Victoria remained silent and looked at each man in turn as Tyree cleared his throat.

"Financially, this affair's come close to ruining me, to say nothing of destroying plans for the canal."

Jesse tensed. "So you're convinced he's guilty?"

Tyree tossed the cheroot into the gutter. "I wish him no ill, but the evidence can't be refuted. He defrauded us, plain and simple. "

"And the two men who sold the bonds?" Jesse asked. "As my father's friend and partner, I'd think you'd feel responsible to find them and help prove him innocent."

Tyree's face darkened. "It's more than a matter of dollar and cents. You and your father were never a part of this city. You live here and we tolerated you because you were trusted."

Taken aback, Jesse said, "None of that matters, not now."

"I suggest you talk with the sheriff," Tyree snapped. "Apprehending criminals is his profession, not mine." He tipped his hat, and strode back to his friends.

At a loss, Jesse turned to Victoria who had not uttered a word during the exchange. Surprised by her reticence, he imagined her shock at hearing accusations from a man of Tyree's standing. Given her outspoken nature, she'd shown good judgment to keep quiet.

"The Colonel believes he knows more than others," she said.

Surprised by her candor, Jesse said nothing as she arranged her hat and scanned the street for her carriage. Tightening the bonnet strings beneath her chin, she turned back to him. "Thank you for a lovely lunch, Jesse. I do hope your father's not inconvenienced much longer."

'Inconvenienced' seemed a weak term for his father's imprisonment. More than ever, he needed her reassurance.

"I thought we might spend the afternoon together," he said. "We haven't seen much of each other."

She laid a gloved hand lightly on his cheek. "Not today, my love. Mother has so many things for me to do." She kissed him lightly and waved to Aaron who waited a block away. "Another day perhaps."

The carriage rattled up the street and halted beside them. Aaron leapt down and opened the door for Victoria who stepped inside and gave Jesse a reassuring smile, her eyes lingering on his face for a brief moment, her expression unreadable. Without speaking she sat back and tapped on the compartment roof. Aaron snapped the reins across the team's backs and the coach disappeared around the corner.

Shaken by his encounter with Jesse, Fletcher Tyree glared across the desk at his son and tried to contain his temper.

"You want to enlighten me about your flawed plan?"

Randall crossed his legs with a nonchalance he did not feel. Startled by his father's outburst he'd absorbed the revelation that Jesse Caine had returned alive from Boston. Anxious to allay his father's fears in spite of his own confusion he managed a nonchalant shrug.

"Your paid assassin obviously failed," Fletcher said. "Your extreme methods have endangered both of us."

"I have no idea what happened," Randall replied with rare candor. "I paid our man well with the promise of more when he completed the job, so I doubt Caine survived without a valid reason." With reluctance bordering on admiration, he said, "I'm left to believe he somehow bested our man."

Distressed at the blasé response, Fletcher recalled Caine's damaged face. Something sure as hell went wrong, he thought.

"And if Caine discovers you hired someone to kill him?"

Randall looked blankly at him, considering a possibility that had never occurred to him.

"Well?" his father asked.

"If he possessed evidence, the sheriff would already be at my door."

"And this woman he sought out in Boston? This so-called expert?"

Randall lifted his palms to the ceiling. "She obviously rebuffed him. Most likely, she offered nothing to help him. To my knowledge, the courts have little interest in handwriting disputes."

"How reassuring," his father huffed. "Given your wealth of legal knowledge, you've put my mind at ease." He pushed himself from the chair and wheezed in disgust as he walked to the window. Unwilling to look at his son, he raised the sash and yelled at a gangly slave in the garden below.

"Damn it, Joseph! What's required for you to properly tend boxwoods? If I find them butchered and dying from the heat, you'll find yourself on the block!" He slammed the window shut and sat down.

Randall hardly moved as he watched his father's growing agitation. He languidly waved a hand. "If our man met his fate on the voyage, it's not the disaster you seem to believe. His death severs another link to us."

"And your forger?"

Tyree's smile returned. "Our helper is well hidden."

No longer persuaded by bland promises, Fletcher removed a cheroot from the humidor and regained control of his emotions. Hopefully, whatever Caine had sought in Boston had proved a false expectation. He rolled the moist tube between his thumb and forefinger and reassessed the odds facing them, avoiding his son's doleful scrutiny. He applied a match to the tip and savored the cheroot's bite, wishing its pleasure vanquished the uncertainties swirling around him. The confident figure seated across from him believed himself clever, but age confirmed little else if not a finely honed sense of survival. He'd lived long enough to know life offered no airtight designs. Someone or something could emerge from the shadows to disrupt the most calculated plan. Strangers. Competition. Poor luck. Bad timing. Old enemies and new ones. Plans had the nasty habit of being foiled by fickle miscues and overconfidence. The unexpected ruled, fortunes gained and lost on the whims of chance. He fingered the signet ring and forced himself to meet his son's amused eyes.

"No matter what happened, I worry about Caine. Cohen's a tenacious little bastard. Too many snakes tangled around our feet."

Randall shrugged. "Both brothers are most likely dead, but our forger is secure and we retain the services of a valuable associate. Caine found no help in Boston, so nothing's changed." He lifted his palms toward the rococo ceiling again in a final benediction, relishing his father's distress. "The odds continue in our favor, dear father."

His father inhaled a lungful of smoke. "None of this is progressing as planned."

"There are always remedies."

"Remedies," his father scoffed. "Your solutions cost people their heads."

Randall's features hardened. "You must admit such applications are effective. We've more money than most of our friends ever imagined." He placed his right hand on his father's desk. "I'll do whatever's required, and if young Caine gets in the way, he'll find himself posted in the City Market."

No!"

Fletcher jabbed the cheroot into the ashtray with such force that it tipped over, spilling ashes onto the leather blotter. "No, and no again! We don't need people conjuring up links back to us. Even the dullest pry into killings, justified or not. Since your man failed on the ship, you need to avoid Caine now. If he has any sense, he'll guess the reason behind the attempt. Once Ambrose Caine's found guilty, the matter will be quietly put to rest."

Randall loosened his cravat and scratched his neck. He leaned back and propped a boot heel on the desk, resuming his inspection of the ceiling. "Your wait-and-see strategy works admirably, but we are not brokering a shipment of cotton. We crossed the Rubicon when we began our little venture. There's no going back, and I'll do what's necessary, with or without your consent."

His father lunged forward to sweep the boot off the desk. A crystal inkwell flew across the room and crashed against the baseboard with an explosion of black ink. A lovely antique, he thought, and now a ruined antique inkstand.

Fletcher stared at the stained wall and river of black ink as it crawled toward the Persian rug. Panicked, he strode to the disaster and folded the carpet's edge away from the encroaching tide, yelling for a servant as he glared at his son's amusement.

"You bring a calamity each time you enter this room," he grated.

Chapter Eighteen

March 28
Just Past Daybreak
The Caine House

The image shifted as he stood in a meadow, watching the solitary figure that beckoned to him beside the bonfire, the sculptured face and bare chest decorated with black war stripes. He stepped forward and fell into a pit, tumbling headlong into its depths, wind rushing past his ears. Skeletal hands reached from the shaft's dirt walls, tearing at his clothing. From the depths below he heard a rhythmic pounding. The drumbeats grew louder and he fell faster and faster until the noise abruptly stopped.

Jesse sat up, legs tangled in clammy bed sheets. Early sunlight smudged the room's heavy drapes, the silence ringing with the dream until he fell back onto the pillows. He bolted upright when the hammering began again like thunder trying to escape the empty house.

He donned a robe and picked up the loaded pistol from the table. Pausing at the top of the stairs he saw a slender shadow on the front porch. He opened the door, and Robert, the sallow-faced clerk from Cohen's office, recoiled at the sight of the pistol.

"I've a note from Samuel Cohen," he stammered.

Jesse laid the weapon on the table beside the door. "Sorry."

Robert thrust the envelope at him. "Mr. Cohen said you're to come right away. 'Urgent' was his last word before he shoved me out the door."

The clerk retreated down the steps, and Jesse opened the envelope. The note revealed nothing other than the urgency to come at once. Good news or disaster, Jesse wondered? He quickly dressed and saddled Aristotle. Searching his sleep-addled mind, he tried to summon a valid reason requiring his presence before breakfast.

Five minutes later, Jesse walked into Cohen's office that blazed with its customary heat. Cohen beamed and came around the desk and took Jesse's cape without a word, enjoying his perplexed expression. Indicating the wingchair he crossed the room to warm his hands at the fireplace until he faced Jesse, his face abruptly falling.

"Who attacked you?" he asked.

"A stranger aboard ship. Someone wanted me out of the way."

"Was he apprehended?"

Jesse shook his head. "He went overboard in a storm."

"We should have anticipated this at some point."

Jesse recalled the terrified face as black-green water covered it forever. "It was all for nothing," he said. "Your expert declined to help us."

Cohen's grinned conspiratorially. "She arrived from Boston late yesterday."

Jesse blinked. "Elizabeth Pendleton?"

"And her brother. They've taken rooms at Mrs. Watkins boarding house," Cohen continued. "The brother accompanied her as a chaperon. Their lodging's temporary, I'm afraid. The old woman doesn't take well to outsiders, and claims she committed the rooms to a pair of corset drummers. I suggested Miss Pendleton consider taking a room in your home if you're agreeable."

Jesse did not move. Elizabeth Pendleton and her brother. In Savannah. A flash of anger rose at the memory of her rejection in Cambridge.

"Are you agreeable?" Cohen asked. "To have stay her at your home?"

"What?" Jesse managed.

"Under your roof."

What had changed her mind, Jesse wondered? "Yes, of course."

Cohen returned to the desk. "She now claims the evidence you brought intrigued her. That she's willing to consider employment. For a fee, of course."

So Cohen knew about the pilfered documents, Jesse thought. He was willing to accept the consequences if they brought Elizabeth Pendleton to Savannah.

"I believe she detected something amiss in whatever you showed her." Cohen's face contained a hint of disappointment as he met Jesse's eyes. "And what exactly did she see? I need to know before becoming a party to this. She'll be here in half an hour, and I'm due an explanation."

With only the truth remaining as an option, Jesse confessed to taking pages from the courthouse. He opened his folio and placed them on Cohen's desk. "I also took documents from my father's office for comparison. I had to satisfy for myself."

Jesse described the attack aboard ship and his meeting with Thaddeus Harpe. Cohen listened without interrupting, his annoyance gradually subsiding. "You violated a confidence, one that might have cost me my practice," he said. He exhaled and shook his head, resigned and conciliatory. "I doubt I'd have acted differently had I found myself in your shoes."

"My father's life is involved. I can offer nothing but an apology."

Cohen drummed his fingertips on the table. He'd slip the documents back into the file after the Pendleton woman examined them. Even attain a fresh batch if Brewster retained his nerve and remained compliant. Jesse had increased the risks if things went awry, but risks came with a criminal practice, although few ever endangered his livelihood. He sat back and indicated a door across the room.

"I'll clear my cloakroom for her if we come to terms. There's a sizeable window, and I'll provide whatever she needs, keeping her out of sight as long as possible. In all likelihood, the entire city will know of her arrival with forty-eight hours, but there's no reason to tempt fate."

They arranged the two files on his desk and marked them in chronological order. Jesse had sweated through his shirt, and his initial elation sank as spiced ink wafted from the purloined papers. The cloves reeked like sweet poison, every page written, signed, or annotated in his father's ink and hand. The scent and heat threatened to overpower him as Cohen placed two documents side by side. The signatures appeared identical, but Cohen turned one page over and added a faint pencil mark on the back. He selected another document from Ambrose Caine's office and added a similar mark.

"We know both these were signed by your father. I'll mix them with those entered as evidence by the prosecution. She'll examine them without knowing which documents are genuine. Then we'll know if she's capable."

"You don't fully trust her?"

Cohen regarded him with an intensity reserved for wayward witnesses. "I've never worked with her," he said, "or with falsified documents in a courtroom for that matter," he added cryptically. "I require assurances other than Thaddeus Harpe's recommendation. I don't want undue zeal or conceit to flavor her conclusions or mine. My reputation's at stake along with your father's freedom."

A knock interrupted them, and Robert ushered Elizabeth and Elias Pendleton into the office. She glanced at Jesse, who smiled at her, taken aback again by her exotic beauty. Elias, freshly pressed and stylishly dressed to impress, ignored Jesse and shook Cohen's hand. His tailored frock coat and white silk neck stock contrasted sharply with his sister's unadorned black walking dress. Despite Cohen's announcement of her arrival, her entry into the office lighted the room, a vision that might vanish when he found himself alone in his bed, awakening from another dream.

Cohen indicated two chairs and noted her limp. She ignored Jesse's offer of the wingchair and took her seat in one of the wooden rockers. She waited for one of them to speak, examining the furnishings.

"Miss Pendleton, I am Samuel Cohen. Welcome to Savannah."

"This is my brother, Elias." Elizabeth indicated the sallow youth.

Removing a woolen shawl, she gathered her dress about her and carefully arranged the folds. Except for a fringe of white lace at the collar and cuffs, she appeared to care little about prevailing fashions. Jesse and Cohen took their seats and waited expectantly. She briefly searched Jesse's face for remnants of his altercation before she turned to Cohen.

"As I told Mr. Caine in Boston, I do not relish traveling in the South. I'm not accustomed to traveling to distant cities to undertake employment, especially those that countenance slavery." She looked sharply at Cohen.

"Do you own slaves, sir?"

"Only myself, chained to this table," Cohen replied lightly in attempt to lighten the tension. "Those two young men you passed in the outer office might admit to slavery."

"I made an exception to Mr. Caine's request from professional curiosity." When Jesse and Cohen made no reply, she stated her terms with crisp New England certainty.

"My fee is the same charged your acquaintance, Mr. Harpe. Plus travel expenses with an additional twenty percent if my conclusions are accepted by the court. Except for lodging and meals, all payments are due at completion."

Her stipulations stated, she waited as Cohen glanced at Jesse, who appeared far removed from the issue of money, unable to look away from her. Did her arrival signal a portent of salvation or failure, he wondered? She appeared more exotic than he remembered: olive skin, the midnight hair, the hint of sugary tobacco in the over-heated office. Slightly embarrassed when Cohen coughed, he signaled his agreement.

She looked at Jesse, her glance unfathomable before turning back to Cohen. "I'll require ample lighting and certain tools for my work. And I'll broach no questions or interruptions while I work." She paused and looked at both men as though daring opposition, a suggestion of pride in her conditions. "My analysis is more detailed and time-consuming than either of you imagine."

"Your terms are agreeable." Cohen pointed to the small door to his left. "You may use the space there. I'll procure whatever you require." He sat back. "When can you begin, Miss Pendleton?"

"As quickly as Elias and I find lodging."

A sheen of perspiration moistened on her upper lip in the overheated office, and Jesse restrained the urge to tenderly wipe it away. "There are several Africans at the boarding house, slaves, where we're staying," she said. "The owner's an unpleasant woman, and I won't stay under her roof another night."

"I have spare rooms at my home," Jesse said. "It's minutes away, and you're both welcome as my guests."

Elias, slumped in his chair, shrugged.

"Very well, then. I'd like to spend the remainder of the morning discussing the evidence against Mr. Caine's father," Elizabeth said. "I'll begin my analysis tomorrow."

"Can we eat now?" Elias interrupted. "I assume there are decent restaurants within walking distance."

"One of my clerks can direct you to the best inn in the area," Cohen said. "It has a very acceptable dining room."

"You go ahead," Elizabeth said to Elias. "I'll manage something later and collect our belongings from the boarding house."

After he left, Cohen and Jesse recounted events leading to Ambrose Caine's arrest. Cohen arranged two stacks on his desk; one included the documents Jesse had taken, plus the two he'd marked. "It may be possible to acquire more." He shot Jesse a look. "Unofficially, of course." He indicated a second group. "These are verified as being in Mr. Caine's hand. As you know, Miss Pendleton, guilt or innocence is not the primary issue here. We need prove nothing. The state has the burden of guilt."

"I want him absolved of any crime," Jesse interjected.

"First, we need to get him out of that pestilent hole," Cohen shot back.

Elizabeth Pendleton arched her eyebrows. "I fully understand the law. If a chance of reasonable doubt exists. If so, you'll have your verdict of 'not guilty.'"

She half-rose from her chair and spread the pages on Cohen's table, her fingertips lingering on them as though they were gifts. She wrinkled her nose. "What *is* that peculiar odor?"

Jesse pulled his chair closer to her, as if providing a better view of the documents. The ink and her scent were a heady mixture of cloves, feminine soap, and something exotic and personal. He glanced sideways at her flawless complexion.

"My father's hobby," he explained. "He mixes his own spiced ink."

Squinting slightly, she bent closer to the first document, then the second one. Her face inches above the paper, her sleek hair fell forward and partially obscuring her face, reminding Jesse of the first time he saw her. She shifted her attention from one document to the next, her concentration absolute. Jesse and Cohen might as well have abided on the moon as she retreated into her closed world of analysis until she straightened.

"Do you detect anything?" Jesse asked.

"Impossible without closer inspection."

"We'll provide whatever you require," Cohen said.

She made a list. Pulling the shawl around her shoulders despite the heat she got to her feet.

"Perhaps I can offer you lunch or a late breakfast," Jesse said.

She hesitated as though debating his offer. "Alright. I need fresh food after the ship's fare. And I thank you for offering your house. Elias and I will try not be in your way."

Jesse inclined his head. His spirits rose at the thought of sharing the same roof with her. Cohen missed nothing and gave Jesse a barely discernible wink as he escorted them to the door. Outside, a chill persisted, the last breaths of winter dying hard in the afternoon shade. Jesse draped his cape around her shoulders as they walked through Orleans Square.

Victoria had consumed the last few years of Jesse's life, but he could not take his eyes from the exotic creature who walked beside him. They strolled through the square as though she inspected the curiosities as though in a foreign land. The slight breeze conducted a symphony of swaying moss above their heads, and she made no attempt to conceal her limp. She remained silent, contrasting the surrounding houses to staid mansions decorating Beacon Hill. More intrigued than ever by her striking features and raven black hair, Jesse allowed her quiet comparison, and it dawned on him they must look like brother and sister to passing strangers. Elizabeth lightly trailed her fingers across white and pink blooms of a large shrub alongside an empty park bench.

"I've never seen these flowers," she said.

"They're imported, a breed of rhododendron called azaleas," he explained, relieved to find common ground. His father dabbled as an amateur horticulturist and had subjected him to a lengthy discourse on the new imports. "They were introduced to Savannah from Charleston, and they're capable of defying our heat and uncertain winters."

The Jameson Inn offered a passable dining room, and they found a table by the window. Jesse noted a momentary look of consternation as she scanned the unfamiliar menu, low country fare a challenge to her Boston tastes. They ate with little conversation, Jesse stealing glances at her. He waited until a waitress refilled her coffee cup before he asked the question that intrigued him.

He studied her and imagined heat wafting from her bare arms across the table. He looked down at her hands. Her fingernails were blushing pearl, each perfectly symmetrical as though her beauty extended to its furthermost limits.

"I have to ask. Why did you change your mind?"

Elizabeth looked down. She owed him an explanation and decided on a half-truth. "We had our differences in Boston," she admitted, "but your documents intrigued me." She kept her voice level, hoping to conceal her attraction to him.

Seeing her a second time provided the sharpest jolt since his father's ordeal began. Her manner was more subdued, a welcome change from the harridan he'd faced in Boston.

"Whatever your reasons, I'm grateful. My father *is* innocent, Miss Pendleton, no matter what you may hear. We need only discredit the documents."

Elizabeth's bluntness surfaced again. "You're his son," she admonished. "I'd expect nothing less."

Jesse no longer retained doubts after the attack aboard ship. He sipped his coffee, surprised at the impulse to confide in her. "I wasn't always the loyal son. I'm a Doubting Thomas by nature, Miss Pendleton. My mother deserted us for another man, and the city never lets me forget my mixed blood." Surprised at his candor, he confessed his doubts aloud for the first time. "I trusted no one after she left. When charges were brought against my father, I saw only a second desertion at first. Then when Cohen showed me the evidence, my doubts doubled and you became our only hope." He absently rubbed the side of his face, the soreness gone. "The attack on the ship brought me back to my senses." He watched her closely, relieved when she appeared not to judge him.

"You've every right to suspect foul play," she said.

"Whoever tried to kill me knows I'm his last line of defense. If they'd succeeded, he'd have rotted in jail alone."

"And the documents are the only proof linking him to the crime?"

"Two anonymous strangers peddled the notes in his name. He never met with any of the victims, and the two men have since vanished. You're our last hope, Miss Pendleton."

Her indigo eyes settled on him with the same obstinacy he'd endured in Boston. "I want you to know something, Mr. Caine."

"Jesse, please." He wanted to hear her say his name.

"I am not a bought witness," she continued. "I will report what I see, no matter the fee or consequences. I won't raise your expectations and then crush them."

"All we require is your honest opinion."

Elizabeth held his eyes. "Just so we understand one another."

Jesse paid the check and they walked back to Cohen's office. Patrick Kerrigan sat on the front steps, twisting his hat in his hands. He frowned at Elizabeth as they approached, his craggy face unreadable. Jesse introduced him to Elizabeth and the Irishman asked for moment alone with Jesse.

He led Jesse from the entrance and glanced back at her with a slight shake of his head. "I warned you."

"She's here to help."

"This is not about her."

Jesse's heart fell. "What's happened?"

"You've been posted. In City Market."

"Who?"

"Jacob Belden."

"The banker?"

Kerrigan nodded. "The time's past for promises to your father. You've no choice but to face him."

Jesse ran a hand over his face. Damn! It was what he most feared. Not the danger it presented, but another pitfall that threatened his father. He recalled Belden's threats in Sanderson's office. He had no intention of confronting the blustering fool.

"Let me escort Miss Pendleton to her boarding house and I'll go see for myself."

"I'll come with you. He's likely returned home, but he may loiter at the Market to see if you appear." Kerrigan grinned crookedly. "If a banker can be accused of loitering."

They escorted Elizabeth to the boarding house. She returned his cape and Kerrigan hailed the first carriage they saw.

Chapter Nineteen

Savannah City Market

Eight blocks from the boarding house the coach rolled to a stop. Jesse peered from the window at the swarm of buyers and sellers who strolled through the market place. Kerrigan frowned at the sprawl of rough booths and lean-to sheds.

"Looks like a shanty town," he said. "Should've rebuilt the old market after it burned down." He opened the carriage door and ordered the coach driver to wait.

Jesse barely noticed the rickety booths and knock-together stands. Overlapping voices surrounded him, promising all manner of goods, a harried cosmos of traders and shoppers. Ringed by sheltering oaks, the bustling market embraced sellers, buyers, farmers, fishermen, loafers, thieves, and friends who haggled and traded barbs. Slaves and free blacks mingled, the atmosphere seasoned with excesses of vegetables and flowers and human sweat. Caribbean spices and uncured tobacco. Last night's catch of silvery fish and barrels of oysters. Incense of the low country. Jesse averted his eyes from an elevated platform where slaves were auctioned on Saturdays. Two old men sat at the edge and dangled their legs off the makeshift stage, smoking long-stemmed pipes, oblivious to the line of chains and posts behind them. Somewhere at the edge of the crowd a blacksmith's hammer added a tang of brimstone to the air.

Followed by Kerrigan, Jesse ignored Negro women in calico who balanced woven baskets of vegetables and fruits on bandanna-wrapped heads. Syrupy Gullah and rapid Geechee dialects lilted above the din as free black men and women tempted buyers with clever rhymes and verse. Other sullen black slaves trailed in their white owners' wake, barefoot beasts of burden who shouldered their masters' purchases and coveted what they saw.

The crowd fell silent as Jesse made his way through the throng. Trailed by Kerrigan he angled toward an ancient oak that dominated the heart of the teeming market. The wounded tree trunk bloomed with rusted nails and chipped bark. Rain-curled notices of slave sales, land auctions, horse races, and political meeting festooned the impromptu billboard. Nailed in the center of them, a single sheet of ivory-white paper flapped in the gentle breeze. Elbows prodded neighbors and the onlookers fell silent as Jesse read the posting.

To Mr. Jesse M. Caine
I hereby declare Mr. Caine and his
father to be thieves and cowards.
Given that the senior Mr. Caine is
rightfully incarcerated in the city jail
at present, I hereby await the reply
of his son, Mr. Jesse M. Caine,
freely offering him satisfaction at
his earliest convenience.

Jacob T. R. Belden, Esq.

Jesse ripped away the notice and dropped it to the ground. Seething, he pushed onlookers aside and bulled his way to the carriage, his reputation reduced to a common criminal in the most public of places. He yanked open the carriage door and climbed inside. Kerrigan followed and banged his fist on the interior roof.

"The Cotton Exchange," he yelled to the driver.

The coach rattled away and he knuckled Jesse's knee. "Most bankers are pompous fools," he said, "but Belden's left you no choice."

Jesse stared out the window as the coach jolted onto Bay Street. "How can I remain in this city when he labels me a thief and coward?"

"I warned you," Kerrigan reminded him. His own life, free of words or promises, progressed without such encumbrances. Fools and enemies insulted him only once. Neither spoke again until the carriage slowed outside the Exchange buildings above the river. Kerrigan pounded on the roof and they rolled to a stop.

"Come inside," he said. "We need to talk."

The burly hand urged him out the door, Belden's posting bitter as quinine. Kerrigan paid the driver, and started up the steps as they heard raised voices.

An expensive brougham bowled down Bay Street toward them, men trotting behind it like anxious petitioners. The voices swelled as the matched pair of gray horses slowed and the driver yanked hard at the reins at the foot of the steps where Jesse and Kerrigan stood. The team skidded to a halt, heads blowing hard.

Features contorted, Jacob Belden leapt out, a polished wooden box clutched beneath one arm.

"You can't avoid me, Caine!" He glanced around at the expectant band of onlookers and held the brass-hinged case aloft. "Name your seconds, sir!"

Jesse peered down at the sweaty rotund face and the milling crowd. The moment he'd dreaded stood before him in the form of the corpulent figure. He forced his voice to remain calm.

"I won't fight you."

"Then you're doubly a blackguard, a half-breed thief and coward!" Belden shouted.

The crowd pressed closer, smelling blood, those at the back standing on tiptoes, sensing the potential for mayhem. Belden dined on their mood, gathering courage from the press of eager faces. He took a half-step closer to Jesse and squinted at Kerrigan. "This has nothing to do with you."

"Neither my father nor I cheated you," Jesse said.

"You stole over half my fortune," Belden sputtered. "A lifetime of work."

"No," Jesse kept his voice even. "We stole nothing."

Belden's face grew redder. He glanced down the sidewalk. "This is as good a place as any," he muttered half to himself. He turned back to Jesse. "We'll finish this here and now."

He opened the hinged box. A matched pair of long-barreled pistols slept in their velvet-lined bed. Holding the case above his head Belden pivoted left and right to display the gleaming brace of weapons to the crowd before he turned back to Jesse, holding them out as though making an offering.

"You have first choice."

"No. I won't fight you."

Belden's face grew redder. "You refuse to act the part of a gentleman?"

"I have no quarrel with you, Belden."

"No reason?" Belden seethed. He slipped one pistol from its nest, snapped the case closed, and tossed it onto the carriage floor. Hands trembling, he pressed a percussion cap on the barrel vent, raised the pistol, and fired point blank.

Splinters erupted from the door behind Jesse's head and something bit the back of his neck. A veil of white smoke drifted away among the stunned silence.

Lips quivering, Belden stared at him. "The devil's luck."

He dropped the weapon in the street, reached inside the coach, and lifted the second pistol from the box. The crowd edged away as Belden jammed another cap into place and fired again.

The lead ball pierced the right side of Jesse's cape and flattened against a steel door hinge. Belden and the crowd gawked at the specter who remained upright.

Jesse bounded down the steps and yanked the weapon from Belden's grasp. He smashed the walnut stock against the steel-rimmed coach wheel and picked up the first pistol. He swung the heavy octagon barrel against the rim until the engraved lock and hammer snapped off. Breathing hard, Jesse reached past a stunned Belden and pulled the case from the carriage floor . He dumped the powder flask and cleaning tools into the muddy street, and tossed the lacquered box at its open-mouthed owner who flinched and dropped it. Hemmed against a carriage wheel, Belden gaped at Jesse who marched up the steps without looking back at him again.

Kerrigan grinned at the crowd and opened the door with a flourish as they disappeared inside the building. He led Jesse past desks that guarded rows of glass-fronted offices until he found an empty room. Pushing Jesse inside, he closed the door and burst into laughter.

"My God, Caine! You provided a spectacle. The newspapers will have the loveliest time for weeks." He caught his breath, grinning. "You should have beaten the pompous ass to death with his own pistols."

Jesse, not trusting his voice, dropped into a chair.

Kerrigan pointed at his neck. "You're bleeding."

Jesse reached behind his head and touched his neck stock. His fingers came away sticky with blood.

Kerrigan gently tilted his head forward. "Fat little bastard of a banker," he rasped, inspecting Jesse's bloodied collar. "You can have him arrested, you know. Bring him up on charges for attacking an unarmed man."

Jesse winced as Kerrigan removed a small jagged splinter of wood. "A waste of time," he grunted. "The sheriff can't afford to accommodate the Caine family."

Blunt fingers plucked smaller splinters from his neck. Satisfied, Kerrigan wiped a bloody hand on his trousers and pressed Jesse's handkerchief against the wound.

"Then it's time you consider my offer," he said. "Most likely, the next incident won't involve a scared old man with a pistol. Most likely someone will just shoot you, or you'll find yourself with a sword in your hand."

Jesse held the handkerchief in place, remembering the gaping pistol muzzle pointed at his head. Only Belden's trembling hand had allowed him to walk away with his life. Words forced upon him by his father had not protected either of them; a promise proved no talisman against a bullet. Challenged again, the next outcome promised more than scratches, and he no longer trusted his resolve to walk away. If he picked up a sword, he would join Charlie Rushton alongside the long-dead Revolutionary heroes.

The bleeding stopped. Jesse removed the handkerchief and looked at the bloody stain before tossing the cloth into a waste basket. "What's your friend's name?"

"You don't know him. He's a Frenchman."

"I can pay him," Jesse said, wondering where he'd find the money.

"It won't be a question of money."

"Then arrange a meeting."

Chapter Twenty

Same Afternoon

Jesse walked back to Cohen's office. He held a fresh handkerchief against his neck, wincing as the scene on the steps replayed itself. The promise to his father would come to nothing if it got him killed, he thought. Stolen money meant reprisals and more attempts on his life. Try as he might to justify his response to Belden, only the fat banker's poor aim had saved his life. Kerrigan was right. The odds dictated he would find himself facing another cheated investor, next time with a sword in his hand. That, or be forced from the city. No choice remained but to meet with Kerrigan's friend if the man was agreeable.

Jesse dined with Elizabeth and Elias that night. Small lamps around the inn's dining room imparted an intimacy to the meal. Other diners' conversations were muted as the three of them sat at a corner table, the objects of curiosity.

Elizabeth Pendleton studied her plate, and Jesse wondered if she'd rethought her decision. Her features softened in the candlelight and he longed to take her hand, risking a rejection. Worn full length, her hair cascaded to her shoulders, glossy black by the candlelight. Flaunting current styles, the loose hair framed her face, and he again imagined her by a campfire in a roadside Gypsy camp. Had she admitted to a legacy of painted wagons in the dark woods of some eastern European country, he'd easily accept the admission. The woman had come unbidden into his life, unattainable, a treasure beyond his reach. She caught him staring.

"You were kind to offer us your home," she said. "The house is most comfortable. A far cry from Cambridge."

"It's not up to Boston's standards, but it has permanence in a city that attracts hurricanes and bouts of Yellow Jack. My father built it with brick after the last one, determined to leave me something of value." Jesse shrugged and managed a smile. "If he's convicted, good intentions will turn to dust."

He told her everything: Dew's arrival during dinner. Tyree's taunts. The confrontation in Sanderson's office. His father's deteriorating health. She listened without offering judgment as though an unspoken code had unraveled between them. Uncertainties about her ability continued to plague him, the discipline's details beyond his comprehension. Could minute differences between two written hands be

111

explained to a jury's satisfaction? Cohen required undeniable proof to sway a jury and admitted she represented a possibility for acquittal, not a guarantee. Harpe might be satisfied with her triumphs, but Ambrose Caine's life rested with a Savannah jury predisposed to believe his guilt. Jesse, though enamored with her, reserved judgment of her capabilities. The mountain of evidence appeared irrefutable, but he would have to trust her.

Across the table, Elias fidgeted with his silverware. He picked at his food, increasingly impatient with his sister's questions about documents and familiar explanations of her methods. He pushed back his chair and stood.

"I leave the details of my sister's work to her," he said to Jesse. "Since she insisted I travel with her, I assume there are more interesting diversions than loops and whorls and paper thickness." He leaned over and gave Elizabeth a chaste kiss on her forehead, cutting her short when she started to protest. "I'll have no trouble finding my way back to Mr. Caine's house. The city's founders seemed enraptured with mind-numbing symmetry. I can easily maneuver on my own."

Elizabeth's gaze followed him out the door, her lips compressed until she turned back to Jesse. "I'd hoped the voyage and new surroundings might cure his restlessness. He spends too much time with wastrels in Boston, some from the best families who can afford their amusements."

"Is he employed?"

She shook her head. "When our parents died, I indulged him with my small inheritance. He enrolled at the university, but study bored him. He has no means of support other than my earnings."

"How did you come to this work?"

"Handwriting fascinated me from childhood." Elizabeth's eyes sparked. "I read and studied everything I could find, some works going back over three hundred years. As a child I compared people's writing. I picked up old letters and bits of paper, anything I could find, trying to see how words and characters differed. I measured what I believed could be compared. Used my eyes. Deduced." She slowed her explanation. "My work is not a trick or sleight of hand, Mr. Caine. It's a new science."

Jesse, surprised by her fervor, watched as she traced lines on the tablecloth with her index finger as if unconsciously composing words as she continued.

"It supports us in a reasonable fashion, but I worry about Elias. He passes his time in taverns, never returning home some nights. I should insist he leave the house and find his own lodgings, but I fear what will happen if he's left to find his way."

"Savannah offers its share of temptations, I'm afraid," Jesse said. He sipped his coffee and sought to repay her openness with his own. He looked more closely at her and it seemed more stones fell away from the wall she'd constructed to keep him at arm's length. He leaned forward, hoping to explain what she faced. "Since you're amongst us now, you should understand how Savannah conducts itself." He gave a sardonic smile. "You'll find our city regards herself as Athens by the Sea."

Elizabeth looked at him quizzically. "By what standards?"

"Her own. She's an exquisite painting marred by pretention. She has unparalleled beauty, but the eye's eventually drawn back to the flaws."

"Which are?"

He wondered how to reveal the shards of his broken love affair with a city that viewed him an outcast and spurned his love since boyhood. He picked up three forks and aligned them on the cloth. He wanted her to comprehend what she faced.

"You could say we're three cities." Jesse lifted the first fork and placed it parallel to his plate. "This represents our gentry, a class of its own making. The city's original settlers were debtors and others in dire straits, most from good families who were granted reprieves by the Crown if they joined Oglethorpe's venture. Savannah began with the promise of forgiveness, but over the years it lost that virtue, granting little acceptance to who weren't native-born. The city grew into a gentleman with a fine watch who won't give you the time, closing its borders to a world not of its liking." He managed an amused smile. "I always suspected a few arrivals were impressed sailors who slipped off the ship when the old boy wasn't looking. Most developed short memories about their beginnings. I have acquaintances among them, but friendship halts at their front door."

Jesse gave a wry grin and Elizabeth looked at him, nonplussed. "Then you weren't born here?"

"No, and that oversight in geography keeps us below Savannah's standards. My father's moderately successful, but I'll inherit no fortune. As a young man from Tennessee's hill country, he married an Indian woman, a Shawnee princess. After I came along, they carried me over the mountains into Georgia. My father's lack of foresight in not being born here consigns us to the second rank. We rarely find ourselves invited inside their homes. Imagine if they discovered a silver spoon missing." He smiled despairingly. "Now with my father in prison, we're seen as more than thieves."

Elizabeth looked closer. That was the answer to his coloring and sharp cheekbones, she thought. "Then you're one-half Indian."

"Half-breed's the more common term. Does it bother you?"

113

"Why should it?"

"It matters to some."

"There's prejudice and small minds in every city," she reminded him.

"Savannah excels in punishing its outcasts."

"That's harsh, even by Boston standards."

Jesse gave a harsh laugh. "Savannah is not Boston. Too many Tories crouched behind our closed doors during the Revolution, ready to wave little Union Jacks when British soldiers marched through the streets."

Elizabeth raised her chin. "Definitely not Boston," she smiled.

"I apologize for making a speech," Jesse said, "but you must realize many old families were gutted by the fraud. Their greed and gullibility were exposed like fishes' innards." He recalled his encounter with Wilford and Moore and the Middletons, the confrontation with Belden and Sanderson. "Loyalty's become meager fare."

"Friendships often dissolve into air when money's involved."

To Jesse it seemed they'd always been intimates who discussed their personal lives.

"And the rest of the city?" she asked after a moment.

"The rest?" He picked up the second fork and aligned it beside the first. "Shopkeepers, businessmen, printers, sailors, fishermen. People like me. I grew up pressing my face against the city's shining windows, peering at what they denied me. But without the masses, the city will cease to exist." He sat back, his coffee cold. "Those are our unwritten decrees, Miss Pendleton. We may seem provincial after Boston, but we're a kingdom of our own making."

"And your third fork," she asked?

"The slaves. They may as well exist on the moon."

"But they *do* exist," she insisted. "Slavery's a fever in the South. It keeps you chained to cotton. If you'd admitted to owning contraband, I would not be sitting here." She drew a breath and lowered her voice. "As you know, I'm passionate on the subject, but I'll not let it interfere with my work."

Delighted with her candor, Jesse turned to safer ground. "Your family?"

"My father was English," Elizabeth Pendleton said, "my mother an Italian immigrant. She died giving birth to Elias." She gave a cheerless smile. "My father was a doctor, a good one. He lost a prominent patient others thought he should have saved. It ruined his practice, and he killed himself a year later. Elias and I lived with friends who took us in. Now there's only the two of us."

"Then we're both orphans of a sort."

"Foreigners," she smiled.

Jesse glanced around them and caught the stares of several occupants. Elizabeth Pendleton was a stranger, and people expected to see him with Victoria. He had no doubt they would set tongues wagging.

"I deceived myself into thinking you might be a Gypsy," he said.

Elizabeth laughed. "A Gypsy?"

"I apologize," he smiled.

"Because I smoke in front of strangers?" she teased. "Nothing that exotic, Mr. Caine. My mother came from the Tuscan hill country, nothing more exotic." She changed the subject. "Your bruises are almost healed. Did you discover who attacked you on the ship?"

Jesse shook his head. She may as well know what she'd stepped into. "There was another incident today," he said. "A cheated investor fired two pistol shots at me."

Elizabeth sat back, eyes wide. "Was he arrested?"

Jesse took a small measure of delight in her shock. "You forget the inner kingdom. Their status guarantees a wide range of privilege, especially when it concerns a depleted pocketbook. My assailant merely exercised his rights."

"A duel?"

"Of sorts." He momentarily relived standing in front of Belden. "I refused his invitation and served as his target."

She could only stare at him over the cup's rim as he continued.

"Both my father's two brothers were killed in duels when I was only a boy," Jesse said. "I swore not to become embroiled in so-called affairs of honor."

"Like your father, I'd think less of you if you succumbed to temptation," she said. "I admire men who step away from imagined insults."

Step away, Jesse thought, wishing matters were that simple. Aware of the vast disparity between the worlds of men and women, he said nothing. He'd always seen his father as faultless, the unquestionable arbiter of right and wrong with no reason to doubt him. Would his own faults appear less egregious if he knew his father's frailties and failures? Or was it better not knowing Ambrose Caine as a man with flaws and disappointments collected over a lifetime? Sons, he decided, were better served keeping their fathers on pedestals. Even if it meant looking down a pistol muzzle.

"Surely you see the fallacy of judgment outside the law?"

"It's not always that simple."

"I imagine we'll disagree on that point, Mr. Caine."

"I didn't imagine the pistol shots," Jesse said. "Principles come at a high cost. I'm no plaster saint, Miss Pendleton. I don't intend to be killed because people believe my father's a thief." Anxious to retain their unexpected bond, he said, "Most of those who were swindled are high-ranking citizens who believe we cheated them. Regardless of what I think of them, they're not villains, but they'll come after us with little mercy."

"I cannot abide dueling. It's damnable and barbaric." She drew a deep breath. "I apologize for my language. Sometimes my passions run away with me." She looked at him, pleased again at what she saw.

"I feel I should make amends for my behavior in Boston," she said. "I had no right to blindly judge you. You've been most kind to Elias and me."

"And I apologize for there being no cook or housekeeper in the house," Jesse said. "Both left us when the authorities took my father away."

Elizabeth waved her hand. "I've kept house without servants my entire life. I'll gladly earn my keep."

Despite their confessions and her apology, Jesse remained uncertain why she now sat in front of him. No matter, he thought. He offered his hand across the table.

"Then we have an agreement. I won't fight duels, and you'll assume whatever household tasks are needed. Agreed?"

Elizabeth Pendleton took his hand. "I'm called Lizzie."

"Lizzie." He smiled. "And I'm Jesse."

He continued to hold her hand a moment longer, the warmth lingering as they rose to leave.

Jesse awoke to angry voices. He pushed himself upright in bed and dismissed the sounds as remnants of a dream until the voice rose. He found his watch on the bedside table and held the face to the window.

Half past three in the morning.

Outside his closed door, Lizzie's voice swelled, indistinct, but angry as she hurled words at Elias. Unable to make out her brother's drunken responses, he waited until her footsteps faded past his door. A final burst of irate words, more footsteps, and Elias's door banged shut.

He started to go to her but fell back. Sibling disagreements were none of his business, but he did not need her concentration dissipated. Despite Lizzie Pendleton's charms, he comprehended little of her work or value other than Harpe's praise, her abilities outside his known world. An alluring but unproven ally, she'd become an oasis in the desert, but whatever skills she might possess meant life or death in the days to come. He needed her wits intact. A querulous brother did nothing to aid her faculties.

He thumped his pillow and turned over. The house became quiet again, and he remained awake another hour, rethinking about his feelings.

His attraction to Lizzie aside, she represented his father's best hope.

Chapter Twenty-One

March 30
Morning
Samuel Cohen's Office

As if by an overnight sleight of hand, Cohen had acquired a tall wooden contrivance and an elevated bookkeeper's stool, the bizarre arrangement flanked by two lamps and a mismatched pair of tables cluttered with small bottles and unfamiliar implements.

Jesse, perspiring in the constricted space, bent close to four promissory notes spread across the elevated desk. He and Cohen peered over Lizzie's shoulder, both men in their shirtsleeves. Lizzie, dressed in a long black skirt and white blouse, watched as Jesse picked up a note and scrutinized the handwriting. The spice caught in his throat.

"I know my father's handwriting," he said, his spirits spiraling downwards.

"There'll be variations if written by a different hand," she explained, aware of his warm breath on her neck. She put down a heavy magnifying glass and pointed at the documents. "Differences will be clearly discernible if one knows where to look." She gestured at the pages without looking up at Jesse. "If someone other than your father wrote these."

Had she already discovered something and hesitated to tell him, Jesse wondered? His confidence in his father wavered until he caught himself.

No. The time for doubt had long passed.

Whether she discovered discrepancies or not, he would never abandon his father again. Others might believe whatever they wished, but Jesse's doubts blew away on the *Abraham Reed's* ravaged deck.

He gestured at the documents. "My handwriting changes," he challenged, reluctantly assuming the devil's advocate role. "If I'm rushed, or writing in a cramped space, there're changes. How can you be sure that didn't happen if my father wrote these?"

Cohen picked up the page. "And if such differences are minute, can a layman be convinced?"

Lizzie sat back and observed at them in turn with a slight smile, accustomed to doubters.

"That's why I traveled from Boston, gentlemen. If differences indeed exist, they *can* be illustrated to the uninitiated. They occur whenever someone attempts to duplicate another's handwriting, no matter how skilled." She turned back to Jesse. "I assure you—"

"You must first convince *me*, Miss Pendleton," Cohen said, addressing her as though she sat on the witness stand. He picked up a page. "Twelve strangers will presuppose guilt based on what they've heard. I know you by reputation, but little of your methods and the persuasiveness of your conclusions. I'll need to convince judge and jury if Ambrose Caine is to walk from the courtroom a free man."

Lizzie looked intently at him as if he were the forger. She brushed away strands of wayward hair from her face and drew a long breath.

"As you're no doubt aware, Mr. Cohen, several courts in New England *have* validated my conclusions. I deal only in comparative analysis, not presumptions or vague conclusions. Visual evidence of two separate hands can clearly be shown. I am not among those who believe in the false science of personality detection disclosed by handwriting. That's not what we're about here." She lifted the page from Cohen's fingers and smoothed it on the desktop as if comforting a favorite pet.

"This nonsense of personality identification began several hundred years ago," she said. "Aldoisio and Demelles claimed handwriting revealed an individual's character. Sir Walter Scott and other notables were led to believe similar fallacies." She made a face as though a foul odor had crept into the room. "I do not believe personality traits or criminal tendencies can be revealed through handwriting."

"Yet there are numerous advocates of the theory," Cohen persisted. "They claim success by pointing out examples."

Lizzie waved away the assertion. "A matter of hindsight, nothing more. It's a false science, one I abhor. My work deals solely with comparing the actual versus the false. Hard evidence, not parlor tricks, Mr. Cohen. I can clearly demonstrate what my research reveals."

"But can't a forger simply copy what he sees?" Jesse asked.

Lizzie drew another deep breath. "The key lies in close study. Let's begin with Mr. Caine's signature. Fortunately for us, he appears a careful man with good handwriting. His signature's always legible. Had he been careless or scribbled like other busy people, it's far easier for someone to simulate his writing. Such people are a forger's best ally."

Lizzie showed no hesitation in her analysis and Jesse's hopes rose again.

"In this instance, a clear signature like Mr. Caine's has two advantages," she continued. "First, it is far more difficult to emulate. Second, given the quantity of documents, the forger had to duplicate the signature many times. A point in our favor."

"And the sheer volume of documents?" Cohen pressed.

Lizzie nodded. "Overwhelming at first glance, but more to our advantage in the end. The forger must restrain his own hand over and over. Endlessly, in fact, to sustain the fraud. Suppress it line after line. In other words, the forger must repeatedly attempt to assume the victim's writing characteristics when he puts pen to paper."

Cohen interrupted again. "But if a forger's work is perfect, how will you know?"

She cut him off. "The perfect forger doesn't exist. Too many nuances to successfully duplicate."

Jesse picked up the largest glass and peered closer at his father's signature on a promissory note. Lizzie took the magnifier from him. Their hands brushed, and she cleared her throat, holding the glass close above the signature for him, the cloistered room suddenly warm. Her hip pressed against him as she squinted through the glass, her cheek close to his. Flushed, she quickly straightened and she ran her fingers over the paper again, avoiding his eyes.

"A forger must duplicate the writer's stroke without hesitating or lifting the quill. If they do either, a blot or break or strikeover appears. Therefore, there's always a hesitancy in attempting to keep the writing instrument moving naturally. Inconsistencies in thickness also appear in inked lines of text. Small blots and variations in pressure. Differences then become obvious." She met Jesse's eyes. "That's especially true in trying to copy your father's handwriting." Her certainty growing, she looked from Jesse to Cohen. "It's simply not possible to duplicate the confidence and consistency of another's signature and writing. If the falsifier attempts to write with a flourish, the variation becomes more apparent."

She warmed to her task, scanning the scattering of documents as though anticipating a sumptuous meal. "I look for anomalies, gentlemen. Divergence, *not* similarity. Letters' size, height, spacing, pressure. The quill point's indentation on the paper itself. The size of loops and whorls of certain letters. They all come into play. Even periods and commas are revealing." She glanced down appreciatively at the documents, her eyes bright with anticipation. "The forger in this instance appears extraordinarily competent, if he exists."

"And the matter of the ink?" Cohen asked. "It's color and odor are distinctive. The prosecution will hammer this point, and the jury will grasp its significance immediately."

Cohen's argument speared Jesse. "Employing his own ink would be a clever touch to strengthen authenticity," he admitted, "but it's not proof of guilt. Anyone could have used it." He cast about for other explanations but found none.

"We must leave that to Mr. Cohen's devices." Lizzie turned to Jesse. "Who had access to the ink? Can you supply a list of people?"

His father kept several large bottles of the hand-mixed formula at his office and their home. Almost anyone might easily have taken a small amount. Guests. Friends. Workers. Even the cook or housekeeper. Jesse shook his head.

"The list's too long," he said.

"Then we'll assume someone stole a quantity," Cohen said, "or duplicated it."

"Proving duplication is beyond my capabilities," Lizzie said.

Cohen handed her a separate sheaf of papers and shot Jesse a look over her head. "The prosecution will include what's on this desk in evidence." He handed her a separate sheaf of documents. "Jesse collected these from his home. You saw most of them earlier in Boston. Use them for comparison."

A wry smile. "I'll inspect all the documents, Mr. Cohen. The truth's in the details."

"Time's short," Cohen warned. "I'm filing motions to delay the trial, but my options are limited. How long will you require?"

She indicated the stack and shook her head. "I'll start today, but if a forger exists, much depends on his ability as well as mine."

Annoyed by her insistent reservations, Jesse indicated the documents as though contaminated, scattering them across the desk. "My father's innocent," he said with more vehemence than intended. "These are forgeries."

"Then I'll prove it," Lizzie said, "if you'll allow me to continue my work." Concealed by the desk, her leg brushed his again.

"You *must* be absolutely certain," Cohen reminded her. "A jury cannot doubt your conclusions. They must clearly *see* the differences in order to believe you."

"I'll provide proof if it exists."

Jesse and Cohen left her to her work and closed the door. Jesse settled himself across from Cohen, who offered him a cigar from a rarely opened humidor. Jesse declined, studying the closed door. Cohen pulled at the damaged eyebrow and squeezed his eye closed as he explained trial procedure. Jesse tried to concentrate, but as Cohen outlined the court's mandates, the warm touch of Elizabeth's leg persisted as though she still stood beside him. Accidental contact, he wondered, or something more. Desire rose thick and insistent in his throat, the distraction palpable despite the gravity of Cohen's words.

"Let's hope she's as good as Harpe claims," he heard Cohen say.

"You doubt her?"

"Unless we find the two swindlers, she's your only hope."

Chapter Twenty-Two

Same Day
Samuel Cohen's Office

Jesse and Cohen spent the day discussing strategies for the trial if Lizzie's conclusions inclined in Ambrose Caine's favor. Jesse understood only the barest fundamentals of her methods, and could only hope her abilities matched her sincerity. At the same time Cohen, acutely aware twelve diverse individuals must be convinced, reminded Jesse that juries were normally composed of men steeped in lies, rumors, and laziness despite the court's admonition to remain unbiased. Her conclusions might appear unfathomable or outlandish to smaller minds. Details confused jurors, Cohen explained. They preferred simple answers and emotional arguments; dead bodies and bloody weapons were preferred over academic arguments. Handwriting comparisons constituted wild cards, he said, but may not constitute a winning hand. He could only hope for rational minds in the jury box, else a frail man might easily fall prey to confused jurors.

"I'm certain she'll do her utmost," Cohen summarized as if reading Jesse's thoughts.

A knock interrupted him, and Robert peered around the office door. "Someone to see Mr. Caine." He glanced at Cohen. "A Mr. Patrick Kerrigan. He... he smells like the docks, sir."

"Show him in, Robert."

Unshaven and clad in heavy boots and a stained jacket, Kerrigan strode into the room and glanced first at Jesse, then at the office's expensive appointments. Jesse stood and indicated Cohen.

"Pat, this is Samuel Cohen."

Kerrigan removed his floppy hat. "I know Mr. Cohen by reputation," he said as they tested one another's grip.

Kerrigan cast a glance at Jesse and eased his bulk onto one of the spindly rockers, afraid to fully test its construction.

"I thought it best to come straightaway," he said to Jesse. "I found a stevedore who believes he saw two men who might be the swindlers. Even better, he knows them."

Jesse's heart jumped. "Will he talk with me?"

"I bought him several drinks. He's waiting at the Mermaid's Promise."

Cohen waved a hand. "Go now."

Ten minutes later, Jesse and Kerrigan ducked through the tavern's doorway. Deserted, only Rose looked up at them, pausing as she sharpened a slender stiletto on a whetstone, caressing the blade over the gritty surface in faint whispers. Kerrigan pointed at her as a warning as they walked past, and she busied herself with the knife, forgetting she'd seen them.

At the back, a single candle illuminated a grimy storage room that smelled of damp decay. Littered with empty crates and bottles, rows of dusty shelves surrounded a rickety table where a plump man half rose from his chair as Kerrigan closed the door.

Several decades older than Kerrigan, an unkempt pointed gray beard partially hid the jowly face, jutting forward like a ship's prow. A hedge of black eyebrows almost hid two small eyes. His skin was tanned to leather, lined with valleys of heavy labor. A sharp sourness clung to a pullover shirt and patched wool trousers held up by brown suspenders, the galluses stretched over an ample stomach.

Kerrigan plopped his hat on the table, raising a billow of dust as he and Jesse sat down. The man sneezed without turning his head. He wiped his nose with one hand and did not offer to shake hands, much to Jesse's relief.

"Doherty, this is Jesse Caine."

Sniffing loudly, he ignored Jesse and lifted his mug to Kerrigan. "Can I have another?"

Kerrigan tilted back his chair and called to Rose. The man scrutinized Jesse until the barkeep shoved a fresh tankard in front of him. She closed the door on her way out, and Doherty took a long swallow. Kerrigan accentuated his Galway accent and indicated Jesse "Tell him what ye told me."

Doherty took a second swallow and exhaled heavily, his breath dredged off the river bottom. He cut his eyes to Kerrigan and jerked a blunt thumb at Jesse, his voice raspy with phlegm.

"Heard about him and his father," he said. "His kind won't live on hog and hominy like us, not if they stole the city blind. If the big ship owners was to close up, most of us is out of work." He fingered the pewter tankard and appraised Jesse's tailored coat. "Now he's down here in an all-fire hurry, lookin' for help. I can get my throat cut just being seen with him."

A bone-handle knife suddenly appeared in Kerrigan's hand and he grabbed Doherty's left wrist. The blade tip pressed into the back of the hand and drew blood. Doherty yelped and Kerrigan inclined his head as though admonishing a child, his Gallic accent more pronounced as though lending weight to his words.

"I appreciate your concerns, but ye ain't no judge and jury, bucko, and if it's knives ye fear, you need to remember this one," he grated. "Your opinions ain't going to earn you no money or keep your darlin' throat safe."

Doherty yanked back his hand. Kerrigan laid the knife on the table and pulled a gold coin from his pocket. He placed it next to the blade and kept a finger atop the money as Doherty wrapped a dirty rag around the cut.

Kerrigan snatched the rag away. "Tell him, or you'll never spend this."

Doherty rubbed at the trickle of blood and pointed at the coin. "That ain't but half the shiners you promised."

Kerrigan picked up the knife. "Tell him if you want to keep your fingers."

Doherty tucked his bleeding hand in his lap and shot a look at the closed door, lowering his voice. "I seen Mr. Harris Coley about a month ago. He owns them big marine warehouses. I been on his work gangs a dozen times, so I knows him straight away. Almost walked right past the other two that was talking to him, all three rightly dressed like gentlemen. I didn't recognize the two at first, but then I saw who they was." Doherty took a drink. "Dressed like they was didn't make no sense to me, so's I turns around and strolled back kind of casual like, just to be sure it was them, you know."

"Get on with it, dammit," Kerrigan said.

Doherty sniffed loudly. "Dressed to the nines, they was, blabbing with Mr. Coley like they was old friends, me never getting so much as a howdy-do."

"Doherty!" Kerrigan whispered sharply. "Tell him who you saw before I forget you're a Dubliner."

Doherty, his moment in the sun was cut short, frowned and said, "The older one was Alvin Mincey. He's the slick one. Big man with a crazy eye, but talks like a gentleman when there's money in it. Big Hat Mincey they calls him, 'cause he once killed a man for his hat."

Mincey, Jesse thought. The clouded eye glaring down at him as he dangled over the ship's rail. The name on the *Abraham Reed* manifest.

"I seen 'em all whispering. Mr. Coley, Alvin and his little brother, Edgar, though he ain't little. Must weigh out at three hundred if he's a pound. Both them Minceys are bigger than country hogs, but real talkers. Smooth as grease. Anyways, they was showing Mr. Coley some papers. I heard them say something about the canal and money to be made, but they looked my way so's I kept walking since it weren't none of my business, you see."

"Where are they now?" Jesse asked.

Doherty gave a grunt. "Not around here no more. They're hill people. Live up in North Carolina, around Asheville. Ain't laid eyes on either since the day I seen 'em talking with Mr. Coley."

Kerrigan sheathed the knife and dropped another coin on the table. "Go on about your way." Doherty snatched up the money and wheezed out of his chair, adjusting his grease-stained suspenders as he moved beyond Kerrigan's reach.

"Ain't never talked to either of you," he said. "And tell Rosie to keep her fat mouth shut. I don't fancy bleeding out in some alley."

He slipped out and Jesse turned to Kerrigan. "One of the Minceys tried to kill me on the ship," he said. "Big man with a milky eye, but he didn't weigh three hundred pounds."

Kerrigan tugged on the floppy hat. "Which leaves baby brother Edgar. Most likely he's broken the traces and run for the stable. They're slick, like Doherty said, but neither's clever enough to think up a scheme like this. If I can find Edgar and convince him to sing a song for us, your attorney friend can begin earning his money."

Ten minutes later Randall Tyree emerged from the League's entrance, a sword case beneath one arm. His hair was wet, face damp with sweat. He spotted Jesse and Kerrigan and blocked the sidewalk until they halted in front of him. Ignoring the Irishman, he smiled at Jesse with mock good humor.

"Jesse Caine," he said. "You've been well-hidden since our conversation at the hotel. As I explained to friends just now, I fully understand your reluctance to be seen in public." He shifted the leather case under his arm. "I take it the morning at Oyster Point proved instructive. Your friend hardly made the ride worthwhile."

Kerrigan touched Jesse's arm, but he pulled away. "Then why kill him? A wound should have satisfied your delicate pride."

"Injured dogs bite. It's better to put them out of their misery."

"Charlie Rushton was not an animal to be put down for your amusement," Jesse grated.

"Our disagreement concerned the two of us. It was settled in a manner agreeable to gentlemen, though the outcome was not to his satisfaction."

"You appear to fill your calendar with such matters."

Tyree laughed and shook his head. "You'd have me appeal to the law to redress slurs or the laying on of hands? The courts are too busy with other matters to deal with affairs of honor."

"In Charlie's case, an elegant justification for murder," Jesse said.

Tyree's eyes widened. "Murder?" He pursed his lips as though considering the possibility. "If you like, but you must admit it's an effective remedy."

"Someone will change your mind one day."

Tyree's smile dimmed. "If courage ever darkens your doorway, I'm at your disposal."

Kerrigan leaned close to Jesse's ear. "Not now," he whispered.

Randall leaned closer. "If your friend's advising you to consider your words, I'd heed his advice unless you seek a remedy."

"He does not," Kerrigan interjected. He steered Jesse past Tyree, whose smile returned as he watched them walk away.

"Good day to you both," he called.

"I'll ask you not to interfere in my affairs," Jesse said as they crossed the street.

"If you want the bastard dead, either murder him, or meet him on equal terms. Otherwise, he'll kill you."

"I can take care of myself," Jesse seethed.

Kerrigan stepped in front of him and Jesse stopped short, Kerrigan's eyes cruel. "Can you really? Your skills are such you can best the finest swordsman in the city? If not, you're a damned fool."

Jesse did not respond, and they walked without speaking until they reached Cohen's office. Kerrigan's warning represented the unvarnished truth. How long could he rein his temper? Getting killed assured his father's slow death in his cell, but there were limits until Lizzie or the missing Edgar Mincey ended the nightmare. Either way, he had to find a way to survive.

"Have you spoken with this friend of yours?"

"I have."

"Is he highly skilled?"

Kerrigan gave an enigmatic smile. "I'll leave that judgment to you. I've no use for gentlemen's toys."

His father detested the archaic code that cost him two brothers, but Jesse found himself oddly driven by an instinct that survived the Stone Age and the deepest reaches of his mother's forest. Allowing Randall Tyree or another victim to kill him achieved nothing, but somewhere a dam had burst and pushed him over the lip? The image of his father huddled in his cell returned, replaced by a clearer view of their world.

He never intended me to die on my knees, he thought.

Chapter Twenty-Three

March 31
The Caine House

Lizzie left the house early the next morning and walked to Cohen's, letting herself into the office with a key he'd given her. Determined to bolster her arguments, she'd cloistered herself in the dingy cloakroom and ignored Cohen when he arrived.

Jesse dressed and ate a breakfast of three day-old bread smeared with jam and butter. He locked the backdoor and entered the carriage house. Both horses greeted him at their stall doors, the interior smelling of fresh straw, leather, and horses. Jesse led Aristotle from his stall and heaved the saddle onto the horse's back, his thoughts drifting as sunlight angled through the open doors, creating a swirling universe of dust motes. He tossed the stirrups over the saddle and thought about Lizzie, tightening the belly cinch until he recalled his encounters with Randall Tyree and his father.

The Colonel had been Ambrose Caine's friend and partner for twenty years. The more he replayed the scene outside the tobacco shop, the less sense his actions seemed. The old man was wealthy, poised to become wealthier with the canal's success. He claimed he'd lost a hundred thousand dollars in the swindle, money Randall stood to inherit. Only now, he appeared more interested in assigning guilt than recouping his loss, while Randall took special pleasure in goading Jesse.

It made no sense that neither mentioned the losses nor made efforts to help in recouping them. Cohen's profession, skilled at unraveling motives, might uncover a plausible answer. Leading the stallion into the alley Jesse mounted and allowed the horse's rough gait to divert his thoughts.

Jesse and Cohen spent the morning discussing the Tyrees' behavior and whereabouts of the surviving Mincey. Elizabeth remained cloistered behind the closed door.

Cohen looked at the door. "She issued orders not to be disturbed unless the building caught fire." He sniffed the air with an amused parody of concern. "As long as she uses the ashtray, I don't worry about her setting us aflame."

"I appear to be getting my money's worth," Jesse said.

Quiet reigned inside the oversized closet, and for three hours he and Cohen explored defense options and how to find Edgar Mincey.

When Lizzie failed to appear for lunch, or request so much as a glass of water, a small line of concern creased Cohen's forehead.

"You don't think she perished while we sat here?" he asked.

"Either that, or turned into to a very small mouse," Jesse said.

"I think you've created a believer in your father's cause," Cohen said. "She arrived before me or the clerks this morning. If there's something to discover, she'll drive herself to prove forgery."

At that instant, Lizzie opened the door. She limped to Cohen's desk, beaming at Jesse, her long dress flowing around her legs. Jesse could not take his eyes from her and wondered if she was aware of her allure. Her face suffused with confidence, she barely concealing her delight as she placed three documents on Cohen's desk. She placed her forefinger on the first.

She looked at Cohen. "You indicated *all* the documents were the forger's work." She tapped the first one.

"But, in fact, I compared this document to one Mr. Caine brought to Boston. He assured me his father wrote it."

She picked up the second page and slid it in front of Cohen. "This one was among the documents you said were forgeries; design notations for a canal lock." She aligned the third page beside the first two. "*This* page was also included among the evidence." Lizzie tapped each in turn, unable to suppress a look of satisfaction.

"These first is unquestionably in the senior Mr. Caine's handwriting," she said. "The only difference from the other two documents is a faint pencil mark on the back. I suspect you placed the mark yourself."

Cohen kept his face neutral as she continued.

"No such markings appear on two other documents I believe are forgeries," she said.

Elated, Cohen leaned back and inclined his head. After a moment, he smiled until his pleasure extended into a wide grin.

"You've unmasked me," he said to her. "I freely admit adding the marked document. Your discovery confirms the criminals mixed Ambrose Caine's actual work among the forgeries. A clever misdirection we've now uncovered. The fact you discovered the addition only increases my faith in your abilities."

Cohen rubbed the space between his separated eyebrow, then grasped her hand. "Miss Pendleton, you are indeed a ray of light." His amused grimace resembled a predator catching the first scent of prey. "You may think lowly of my subterfuge, but recent changes in the law strengthen our case. The courts have ruled that *outside* original documents *may* now be entered by the defense for comparison purposes."

"You doubted me," she said, unable to mask her irritation.

Cohen shrugged. "You validated your credentials. It means you are indeed a genius." He graced her with another smile, but Lizzie's expression remained unchanged as though he only confirmed the obvious.

Jesse's hopes rose again. "And my father?"

Cohen picked up the original document. "We can now prove the prosecution's evidence includes real and forged documents. Why would your father consort with a forger when he could simply create the required documents himself? And why didn't he disappear? Why remain in the city after the fraud? As the saying goes, the swindlers may have hoisted themselves by their own petard."

"And Edgar Mincey?" Jesse asked.

"If we locate him, it strengthens our chances beyond Miss Pendleton's detective work."

Jesse left Cohen's office and rode to Caldwell Printing Company. He'd rarely set foot inside their door since his father's arrest, but the exigencies of funds to help his father required his presence if they'd have him. At the end of Abercorn Street, he slowed Aristotle as he neared his employer's offices, surprised when he saw the venerable old building's shutters were closed and latched shut as though expecting a hurricane. A large sheet of paper hung limp on the entrance door. He dismounted and walked up the steps, knowing the door was locked before he tried the handle. The sheriff's notice informed him the firm had been closed by court order; customers and creditors would be duly informed of the company's pending disposition.

At dinner at his favorite inn, Jesse lowered his voice as he sat across the table from Lizzie and Elias. "My employer has closed its doors," he said. "It seems the owner invested heavily in the fraudulent bonds. Not just his funds but the firm's capital as well. There's a good chance he'll find himself sitting in jail alongside my father."

"What will you do?" Lizzie asked.

"Fall back on my resources, such as they are. They'll have to suffice unless the court impounds them."

"That's a small concern," she said.

Jesse forced a smile. "Sooner or later, it'll become more than that."

Elias smirked and dropped his fork with a clatter. "So now you have no money to pay us."

"To pay *me*," Lizzie corrected him. "Instead of your nightly forays, you might rethink your lifestyle and seek employment."

"I didn't ask your advice," Elias retorted.

She leaned toward him, an edge in her voice. "There's more to life than your pleasures."

"Certainly more than *your* fascination with paper and ink," Elias retorted. "Spending days bent over dry paper is not my definition of living. I require far more than that."

"My work supports you and your rakehell antics." Lizzie, her voice rising, glanced at Jesse if suddenly remembering his presence.

"There're alternatives to your patronage," Elias replied defiantly.

Lizzie sat back and folded her arms. "I'd be delighted to hear them."

"I met a gentleman last night. His family's wealthy and respected."

"I imagine the friendship bloomed in a tavern or dram shop."

Elias patted his lips with his napkin and smiled. "It seems we have much in common. He shares my interest in fencing, and he's the best swordsman in Savannah."

Jesse knew the answer even as he asked. "His name?"

"Randall Tyree. You're acquainted, I believe."

"You'd do well to avoid him." Jesse painfully recalled Charles Rushton's lifeblood on the leaves. "He only plays the part of a gentleman. His father controls the purse strings. He's not what he seems."

Elias twisted in his chair and faced Jesse with a sardonic grin. "Oh, I know your father's connection to the Tyrees. There's far more to the crime than you revealed to my sister."

"Elias," Elizabeth scolded.

"You've been led astray," Elias replied. "Your parlor tricks may fail you this time."

The dining room hushed and attentive, Jesse ignored the faces turned their way. "Your sister's here to help my father, not judge him," he said. "And you'd do well to avoid Randall Tyree."

Elias stood, shoved his chair under the table, and marched out without looking back. Jesse watched him disappear and wondered if he'd been as foolish at his age. Tempted to go after him, he stopped when Lizzie placed her hand on his arm.

"Let him go," she sighed. "He's an overgrown boy. It does no good to argue with him." She looked at Jesse to reassure him. "His temper won't affect my work."

No turning back for either us, Jesse thought. *Not now.*

"Let me take you home," he said.

Jesse sat up in bed for the second night, awakened again by raised voices. He listened as Lizzie tried to calm her brother, his shouts overriding her, the words slurred by drunkenness. Footsteps stumbled down the stairs and the front door slammed. Faint sobs came from Lizzie's bedroom until the house fell silent again. Jesse squinted at his watch on the bedside table.

Three A.M.

At this rate, he thought, a full night's sleep will become a luxury. He slipped on a dressing gown and walked to her room. Tapping lightly on the door, he heard the pad of bare footsteps. The door opened several inches and blue eyes peered at him, the long lashes wet. Jesse could not keep his eyes from straying to the thin cotton gown that clung to her breasts and thighs.

"What can I do?" he asked.

Elizabeth sniffed loudly and shook her head. "Just another skirmish in an ongoing war." She opened the door another inch, her bare arm pebbled with the night air. "I'm sorry we woke you."

"I'm a light sleeper," he lied.

A single lamp in the room backlit her tousled hair and outlined her naked body beneath the thin material, leaving her face in shadow. Unsure how to comfort her, he looked down at her toes curled on the cold wooden floor and fervently hoped she wouldn't leave him standing in the hall.

Lizzie's hand lingered against the frame. The awkward stillness became long seconds. The cold deepened in the hallway, and she gave a slight shiver and rested her head on the doorjamb.

"We're your guests," she said. "Elias's behavior is unacceptable." She fell silent again and looked at him in the darkened hall, her eyes alight in the darkness. "This is not what I want."

Jesse made an effort to slow his breathing, controlling the urge to enfold her in his arms. Instead, he hesitated, his old companion of doubt raising its head. If he misread her, he risked the prospect of losing her forever.

"Go back to bed, Lizzie," he managed. "The house is cold."

She hesitated another second and quietly pushed the door shut. Jesse did not move. He stared at the paneled door as she returned to bed. A thousand emotions coursed through him. He stared at the offending door and listened to his breathing until his emotions overcame him.

What the hell.

He softly knuckled the door and turned the doorknob. Lizzie rose from the bed and the lit the bedside lamp, the room assuming a golden glow. For a few silent seconds they faced one another across the room.

"Do you want me to leave?" he asked.

She met his eyes and bit her lip.

"No."

Jesse closed the door with his heel, crossed the room, and enveloped her shivering body in a single movement, tossing aside everything but his need for her. Every puritanical admonition vanished as he watched her slip the nightgown over her head and pull back the rumpled covers of her bed. Rendered speechless by her nakedness, he quickly shed his nightshirt and slipped beneath the heavy comforter beside her. She shaped her body against his, and he kissed her, tasting what he'd longed for since their first meeting in her strange parlor.

They pulled apart for a moment and faced each other on their sides. Neither spoke as she twisted beneath him, gripping his hips between her thighs. Jesse groaned and time stopped, unmeasured. They joined effortlessly with no restraint or shame, the room filled with cries and murmurs of longing.

When they finally pushed apart, Jesse struggled for breath, amazed at her ardor and flesh that smelled delightfully of damp rich heat and perspiration and unabashed pleasure. Sweating, he kicked the comforter aside and kissed her shoulder, her tawny skin salty beneath his lips. The faint light lit her face, a vein throbbing at her temple, slowing with the beat of her heart. A fan of windswept black hair fanned across her pillow. Jesse submerged his face in the silken mass, reveling in its scent. He uttered her name several times, the words muffled.

Lizzie yanked the cover over them, shivering as she clung to him. She threw her arms wide across the pillows and flung a bare leg over his, the expanse of smooth flesh drawing his eyes and a smile.

"My god," she said with a throaty laugh. "I think I'm drunk." She turned back to him and grasped him more tightly as though drowning, laughing again. "The rumors of Southern passion are not overdone," she murmured, "or is it your forest blood?"

"Only you."

"How gallant," she teased. "At least my infirmity didn't slacken your ardor."

He raised the cover and surveyed her bare legs. She made no attempt to cover herself, turning slightly to compare their bodies, their bronzed bodies marking them as exiles.

"I see only two lovely legs, along with a menu of other charms."

In the lamp's faint light, her eyes followed his hand, and she studied their nakedness in the dim light before rising. She withdrew a cigarillo from a small box in her suitcase, motioning him to follow her. Naked, she pushed open the French doors and walked onto the small balcony outside the bedroom, lighting the dainty cigar. He followed her, kissing her bare shoulders until she smiled.

"I feel we're phantoms," she said dreamily, looking through bare branches at the night sky, "dismissed from the living world."

"Dismissed or cast out?"

She laughed and drew lightly at the cigarillo, blowing a thin stream of smoke into the night. Jesse wrapped his arms around her nude waist and buried his face in her tousled hair. How had his world tumbled off its axis in a matter of mere weeks, he wondered? Whatever the fates had decided would be his future, he'd found this exotic creature.

They stood without speaking until the feel of her nakedness propelled his hands and found her breasts again. With a groan he flicked cigarillo over the baluster and they stumbled back to the bed. Jesse, liberated from weeks of misery, lost himself between her long legs, prolonging the ecstasy until they pulled apart, both struggling for breath. After a few minutes he rose on one elbow and looked at her with a certainty he'd never imagined. He needed her now as surely as air and water. Her warm thigh pressed against his leg, she leaned over and blew out the lamp as they sprawled on their backs.

"Do you think we can hide this from Cohen?" he asked the darkness.

"I don't think much is hidden from your friend." She turned and ran her hands through Jesse's hair, taking pleasure in the wetness of his scalp.

"I don't want to hide anything," Jesse said.

Lizzie sat up in bed, the blanket slipping below her breasts as she peered down at him. "Am I the only woman in your life?"

Victoria's face intruded, but the image vanished like wind-blown smoke. So much had changed. A week earlier, he'd seen her as the most desirable element in his life. Whatever had existed between them now lay scattered among tangled bedclothes.

"There was someone once," he said.

"Tell me about her."

Cloaked by darkness, Jesse told her about Victoria and her talent on stage. The more he talked, the more his bewilderment grew. He told her about Victoria and her reaction to his father's imprisonment, then the doubts of his father's innocence. About Charlie Rushton's death. The verbal skirmishes with Randall Tyree. Everything except his decision to meet with Kerrigan's friend.

"I'm content with that for now," she said, "but you'll find my jealousy's a ravenous monster if you lie to me, Jesse Caine."

"Monsters are supposed to have green eyes," he teased. "Yours are blue."

"Keep your wits about you," she said as if divining the truth about the danger Randall posed. She slipped closer and buried her face in his chest. "I'm frightened for Elias. His attraction to fencing only heightens my fear of what could happen to him. And you." She touched Jesse's cheek and kissed him softly.

"Promise me I won't lose you," she whispered, the words as urgent as her body's demands moments earlier.

Another promise, he thought. He closed his eyes, and Lizzie held him tightly when he did not reply. After a few minutes, her arms relaxed and she mumbled indistinctly. He realized she'd drifted off to sleep, her breath steady on his neck. Relieved of the need to confess his decision to take Kerrigan's advice, he gently extricated himself from her grasp and lay on his back, staring at the ceiling. Despite her plea, he did not plan to die like a newborn lamb led to the killing pens. He'd make amends later, make her understand more than pride drove his decision. Or had he only rationalized his actions, he wondered? The decision had undoubtedly entwined around self-preservation, but the sensation was new to him, a deeper stirring.

With Lizzie's sleeping body pressed against him, he stared out the window at morning's first timid glow. The soft light outlined her features, and he marveled at a single night's power to alter his life if he managed to retain it.

He slipped from bed and looked down at her face, realizing he'd added another element of risk to his life.

Chapter Twenty-Four

April 1
Next Morning

Jesse rapped softly on Lizzie's door. She opened it, her face glowing with an unrepentant smile. An embroidered cloth handbag dangled from her wrist, and her frilly light blue dress conformed to the current day's fashion. She now appeared every inch a well-bred lady, as opposed to the exotic creature he'd encountered in Boston. He pulled her close and kissed her.

"Good morning," he whispered.

Lizzie looked down the door at Elias's closed door. She leaned back and met his gaze without embarrassment. "Well, it *is* a good morning," she said, returning his kiss. "Not as pleasurable as last night, but a nice beginning to my day."

"No regrets?"

"None." She kissed him again, her lips lingering.

"I left your bed before dawn," Jesse said. "I never heard Elias come home, but I didn't want to embarrass you if he returned. The rooms are too close." He smiled, the day ahead endurable by her nearness.

She did not blush or look away as he stared at her, the night's memories palpable in her eyes. She took his arm. "We have work to do," she said brightly. "Mr. Cohen is expecting us."

"Do you ride?"

"Of course."

The morning greeted them with a chilled sting. Jesse swung open the carriage house doors, liberating the rich smell of horses and leather. The boy he paid to muck the stables took his money without hesitation and did a credible job. Jesse absently wondered if the street lad knew his present condition. He and his father had never owned carriages, instead building stalls for the two horses. Ears thrust forward, the animals leaned their heads over waist-high doors in anticipation.

Lizzie limped to Mercury. Any thought of her infirmity had vanquished in the previous night's delights. The gray gently shook its head as she stroked the warm muzzle, and Jesse wondered again if such a beautiful woman admitted to any flaws.

She smoothed the mottled gray's face. "Beautiful animal. May I ride this one?"

"My father's favorite," Jesse said. "He's called Mercury, a totally unsuitable name. He's well-behaved and will appreciate the exercise."

He stroked Aristotle's flank, and the horse stamped a hind foot, anxious to be released from the stall. Jesse slapped the muscled neck.

"This one has a head of his own."

"I would tame him," Lizzie said.

"I have no doubt."

"Then let's proceed by all means."

"I apologize there's no sidesaddle," Jesse said.

"I can manage unless you plan on galloping to Samuel's office."

Jesse saddled both horses and shortened Mercury's near-side stirrup. He hoisted Lizzie sidesaddle onto Mercury's back. She settled onto the English saddle and hooked one foot in the stirrup, her other leg bent around the low pommel covered by her voluminous skirt. Bundled in a light woolen coat, a silk scarf covered her neck, and she smiled down at Jesse from her perch. He mounted Aristotle and led the way from the alley.

Lizzie enjoyed the short ride, inspecting the city's squares and trees festooned with weeping Spanish moss, so different from Boston and Cambridge's stark streets. They rode side by side, passing few people and enjoying the new unspoken closeness. As they neared Cohen's office, she glanced both ways, leaned from the saddle, and kissed Jesse. When he reached to kiss her again, she reluctantly pushed him away.

"We must remember to show decorum," she said with mock sternness. "We cannot shock the good attorney, even on April Fool's Day."

Leaving their horse tied to a railing, she surprised herself remembering the date in light of what had occurred and what awaited them in the coming days. Jesse ushered her into Cohen's office where the usual wall of warmth struck them at the door. Cohen stood and graced her with a smile. He preempted Jesse, helping her out of her coat, his brusque manner tempered by a welcomed infusion of femininity in the drab surroundings. Taking her coat and scarf, he gestured at her cloister.

"May we have a review of your progress?"

The three crowded into the small room, and Lizzie slipped onto the elevated stool. Selecting pages from the stack of documents she spread them across the desk, assembling them with a professional demeanor.

"If I may, I'll explain my approach in more detail."

She selected six pages and aligned them across the desk. Jesse leaned forward, his thoughts wandering to the previous night's delights. Not for the first time he wondered why she didn't pile her hair into a chignon, secretly glad she left it loose. A wisp of hair curled behind her ear like weightless silk, the down on her neck enticing. He inhaled her scent as he tried to concentrate, wondering if Cohen had tumbled to the change in their demeanor.

"I won't bore you with every nuance," she said, aware of Jesse's nearness. She failed to suppress a smile as she felt his breath, "but I've discovered discrepancies." She cleared her throat, picked up an investment agreement, and laid it beside a letter in Ambrose Caine's hand.

"First, I must warn you both. Our forger is excellent, a master at what he attempts despite inevitable failings to disguise his hand." She leaned closer and briefly surveyed each document with a hint of satisfaction before sitting back and looking at each man in turn. "These are not clumsy attempts. It required several hours before I was certain of the discrepancies."

"If he's skilled as you say, can I expect to convince a jury?" Cohen pressed.

Jesse leaned closer, his breath warm on the nape of her neck.

Trying to ignore Jesse's presence, she looked at Cohen.

"What?"

"Miss Pendleton, I asked if I can reasonably be expected to sway a jury?" Cohen said.

"Blind men can be made to see, Mr. Cohen."

Jesse rescued her. "You're certain they're forgeries?"

"Yes. Proving forgery to laymen is challenging but I believe there's ample proof. In this instance, however, a jury of prejudiced skeptics may prove more difficult."

Cohen grimaced and absentmindedly cracked his disfigured knuckles. "A high wall but scalable if I'm given the tools. Jurors take the easier path if an effort's required on their part."

"There'll always be skeptics," Lizzie admitted. "It's a new science." She touched the nearest document. "And frankly, I rarely see this ability. Nevertheless, the missteps are discernible when one looks closely." She faced Cohen. "As I explained to Mr. Harpe, my task is to uncover the deviations. Yours is to create reasonable doubt."

"We may have to provide magnifying glasses for the judge and jurors," Cohen sighed. "A novel approach."

Jesse looked again. "Show me what you see."

"First, the paper's too thick for tracing." She rubbed a document between her thumb and forefinger. "Therefore, the forger had to simulate Mr. Caine's writing. That's a challenge for any forger, no matter how accomplished. Look closely."

Lizzie handed both a magnifying glass and picked up a dry quill. Cohen bent closer as she pointed the tip at the word *specifications*. The improvised stylus touched the letter *f*.

"Take your time and look carefully. The formation of the letter wavers." She placed a letter beside the document. "Now look at your father's actual hand. The same letter is graceful and flows without hesitation." Her animation increased as she moved the pen across the same letter farther down the page. "And here again. The width of the letter is thicker in every instance where the forger wrote slower in an attempt to replicate the letter."

Cohen glanced at Jesse above her lowered head. She saw the glance and picked up another document.

"Only one example," Cohen said. "I'll require far more."

"There are many more," Lizzie said. "The inconsistencies may seem small, but they're obvious when repeated." She moved to another word and focused her glass above a paragraph before she looked up.

"Look at this page. The letters *h* and *r* have been retouched where additional strokes were added to conform to the original letters. You can clearly see the additions. And the capital letters are awkward —too labored, sometimes wavering and oversized." She pointed to another line of text. "And the slope of these words. Rushed near the end." Her excitement built as she impatiently brushed hair from her face, looking back and forth at the two men. "Look at the words. The size and proportion suddenly changes at the end of sentences, as though the forger became impatient and revealed his own handwriting." She selected three sheets from Ambrose Caine's correspondence.

"You never see carelessness or impatience in Mr. Caine's penmanship," she said. "It's an engineer's careful script. An occasional flourish here and there, but even those are restrained. Blotted pools of ink and hurried words are non-existent in his precise world."

"Interesting," Cohen said, "but I see them because I *want* to see them. Will a jury be so accommodating, I wonder. Will tired men in a sweltering courtroom have the patience to stare through a magnifying glass?"

"None so egregious, but there are numerous missteps, apparent to anyone willing to look closely. The sheer number of variations is our strength in identifying the fakes."

"The ink," Cohen persisted. She sat on the witness stand now, and Cohen hammered at her, probing for errors and failings. "The ink *is* consistent on every page. A strong element in the prosecution's favor. Can it be proven false?"

Lizzie gave a knowing shrug. "Our problem is its distinctiveness. Most likely, it's Mr. Caine's own ink. As I said earlier, I'm not a chemist. Examining inks is another science. Hanschritt in Germany has done good work, but I know little about his treatises."

"What else?" Cohen pressed his elbows hard against the desk's surface.

Lizzie pointed to several sentences. "The periods and commas. They're inconsistent in size and pressure."

Cohen caught Jesse's eye again. "Periods. You give me a large stone to roll, Miss Pendleton."

She smiled patiently. "Your reputation precedes you, sir, but I won't mislead you. I can point out inconsistencies, but your challenge is greater. A jury will tend to see only the similarities. Your task is to clearly *prove* that discrepancies exist."

An argument sounded from the anteroom accompanied by heavy footsteps. Elias, disheveled and unshaven, flung open the office door and tottered into the room, looking at his surroundings as though seeing them for the first time, depositing a trail of mud on the patterned rug. The two clerks hovered in the anteroom doorway and looked fearfully at Cohen, who waved them back to work. Hair matted and waistcoat stained he leaned a shoulder against Lizzie's doorframe, waved a hand, and shook his head with a sardonic smile.

"The defense at work," he slurred.

Lizzie pushed past Cohen. "Where have you been?"

"The City Hotel."

"All night? Do they never close?" Lizzie asked the air above her head.

Elias raised his eyebrows in mock horror. "I hope not." He grinned crookedly at her distress. "But I did not partake of the owner's hospitality for the entire evening. Randall provided a bed in his home last night." Glassy-eyed and amused, he belched behind his hand, a rank addition to the confined space. He grimaced as though he'd swallowed something unpleasant. "It was most comfortable," he managed.

Lizzie, face flushed, started to speak when Elias raised his hand.

"No!" he blurted. "I won't be lectured this early in the day."

"Tyree and his friends may seem good drinking companions," Jesse interjected, "but there's little else to recommend them."

"You are wrong, sir." Elias drew himself erect and tugged at his waistcoat. "They've offered membership in their fencing association. I plan to sharpen my skills under Randall's tutelage."

Jesse spoke to him as he might a younger brother. "You should reconsider."

"I can see why you'd object." Elias absently rubbed a cheek as if making certain it remained attached to his face. "Randall told me of your cowardice."

"Elias!" Lizzie cried.

Elias met Lizzie's stare. "It's true. Randall called him out, and he walked away. Ask him."

"Jesse's right," Cohen said. "Randall Tyree's a notorious duelist with little else than his family name. He subsists off his father's generosity."

"Your opinion is not required, sir," Elias replied stiffly.

"Your manners, Elias," Lizzie reminded him. "We're guests here."

Elias grinned triumphantly at Lizzie. "That's no longer true in my case. Randall's offered a room in his house."

"A shorter walk to City Hotel," Cohen mumbled to Jesse.

Elias either did not hear the aside or ignored it as he leaned closer to Lizzie. "If you remain in Caine's home without my presence, you'll need to think about your reputation. This is a small town in more ways than one."

"You and Lizzie are both welcome," Jesse said. "There's no call to desert your sister."

"Were I you, sir, I'd concern myself with more than my comings and goings," Elias said. "Such as your affairs with Randall."

Elias muttered something unintelligible and lurched from the doorway. He tramped through Cohen's office, swore at the two clerks, and slammed the front door, the brass bell falling to floor with a distressed clang.

Jesse stared at the mud-tracked carpet, chagrined by the slur on his courage. Drunk or sober, Elias Pendleton had driven home a truth. Randall Tyree loomed larger by the day, a pariah provoking him from the shadows. If he was to save himself and remain alive to help his father, Kerrigan's friend provided a small window of hope.

Chapter Twenty-Five

Same Day
The Randall Tyree House

The elegance of the three-story house shamed its neighbors. Randall paused a moment on the sidewalk and admired the Georgian style, a parenthesis of opposing steps sweeping upwards from the sidewalk to the front door. Four majestic windows flanked the door and overlooked President Street, the red brick edifice a testimonial to respectability in the city's heart. Engulfed by ageless pin oaks the house remained one of Randall's pleasures—ownership made doubly appealing since its acquisition cost him nothing. Purchased by his father in a weak moment, the old man had secured it at a good price, but now regretted deeding title to his sole heir.

The notion of gain coupled with his father's chagrin lightened his mood, and Randall took the front steps two at a time. He paused in the spacious foyer for a moment, admiring the attention to detail that defined the workmanship. An imposing winding staircase led to the second floor. Wide-planked floors extended into the parlor on his left, arched casement windows facing the street, the space supremely bare of overwrought furniture one endured in flamboyant homes. No paintings or mirrors marred the walls, no tables cluttered with useless personal artifacts or family treasures. Only a brown settee and two high-backed chairs shared space with a writing desk and glass-front secretary, the grouping attended by a sideboard of glasses and liquor bottles. A single wall exhibited the sole point of interest in the room. Polished wooden pegs had been carefully bored into the plaster to support rows of swords and rapiers, the display an embodiment of their owner's pride.

Randall started up the staircase and halted in mid-step. A cloud of smoke rose above a chair in the parlor. The old man's singular breach in carefully cultivated tastes, the cheap Burmese leaf left an acrid stench, one that lingered for days after rare visits. Head buried in the wing chair, Fletcher Tyree pretended to ignore his son's entrance, engrossed in inspecting an epée in his lap.

Randall crossed the room and lifted the sword from his hands, waving at the smoke.

"I prefer no one handle these but me."

He wiped away smudges from his latest purchase with a handkerchief and resettled the rapier on two pegs. Satisfied with the blade's alignment, he turned back to his father.

"Surely you can afford better tobacco," he grimaced.

Fletcher Tyree ignored the remark and gestured at the swords. "Tools of your chosen trade. Toledo steel, most of them. Stylish playthings but useless in battle."

He gazed around the sparse room with distaste. Narrow shelves lined the other walls, the ledges displaying marching ranks of lead toy soldiers. Legions of brightly-painted red and blue warriors. Cannons. Caissons. Prancing horses. Multihued flags and pennants. Carefully arranged beneath the shelves and in every corner, tall clear jars of every shape were filled with glass marbles. The containers dominated the room like colorful sentinels. Smaller jars adorned the desk, sideboard, and interior of the secretary, stark contradictions to the wintry display of naked steel.

Fletcher looked around and flapped a hand at the containers. "You could do much more with this wonderful space."

Randall said nothing. His father had only explored the house once after purchasing it for him. Content to fill the same chair when he rarely visited, he had never ventured into other rooms where battalions of soldiers marched across identical shelving above similar jars. Randall walked to the sideboard and poured two fingers of Calvados into a plump snifter. He lifted the bottle toward his father, who waved away the coarse Normandy liquor, its rawness beneath his selective palate.

"Filling rooms with your childhood indicates a certain flaw in your maturity," Fletcher said as his son assumed the identical chair across from him. "The entire house looks like a toy emporium occupied by a weapons dealer." Pleased with the analogy he allowed himself a small grin as his son sipped the strong apple brandy.

Randall cared little for his father's opinions. His collections never failed to charm female visitors who mistakenly believed they could control any man who collected toys. He surveyed the room's contents, took another sip of the rough brandy, and waited for the visit's purpose to be revealed. An unsettled silence descended as though the two men were strangers in a public carriage, eying one another with barely concealed misgivings. Randall broke the impasse.

"You rarely grace my door."

Fletcher's temptation to flee the cold setting grew by the minute, but he tapped the cigar against an ashtray. "I heard you confronted Caine again."

Randall, stricken by the old man's wintry voice as though it pained him to speak to his sole offspring, looked at the frowning face. He crossed his legs, smoothing the fine woolen material stretched over his knee.

142

"You'd have been proud of my restraint," he said. "I didn't pursue the occasion if that's what you're inferring. I remained the consummate gentleman, although Caine seemed tempted to accommodate me."

Fletcher uttered a derisive sound.

"The meeting was purely accidental," Randall assured him as his father continued tapping the cigar against the edge of the ashtray. "But not as unfortunate as you might believe." Randall studied the gloomy figure who glanced at the front door as if it led to a refuge from their enterprise.

"In fact," Randall soothed, "Caine's fear works to our advantage."

He stood and removed a cigar from a plain wooden humidor. Lighting the tip he kept his smile in place, troubled by the older man's fidgeting.

He needs shoring up, Randall thought. I've made every decision, while he hesitated to do what's required. He may not fully recognize the consequences if we fail, but I don't plan to spend the rest of my years in prison. He can bumble around his little museum and let me handle Caine and whatever arises. He exhaled a stream of smoke and continued in a more conciliatory tone, considering the cigar's smoldering tip.

"This handwriting specialist Caine brought from Boston," he began. "Her brother frequents the City Hotel to over-indulge in our city's liquid inducements, despite his tender age." Randall took pleasure in his father's impatient expression. "He also enjoys the finer elements of fencing. A piece of luck for us."

Fletcher Tyree waved a hand. "Better, I hope, than your questionable luck at the gaming tables."

Annoyed at his father's dismissal, Randall abruptly leaned forward in his chair.

"It's not luck I have in mind."

The flush of perspiration on his father's face pleased him. He rose and tossed the half-finished cigar at the cold fireplace. If the older man's timidity presaged panic, they both faced consequences he preferred not to consider. Randall regained his chair and lowered his voice.

"The brother's not well disposed toward Caine," he explained in a placating tone. "Or Cohen, or even his sister for that matter. He appears to resent her success since he possesses none of his own. I invited him to stay here with me, and he's agreed. He's an arrogant twit, but he may prove a source of useful information."

Fletcher drew hard at his cheroot, assessing the pros and cons of his son's impromptu invitation. He recognized the value of keeping his enemies close though he knew it bore risks. But forewarned paid dividends if disaster crept too close, he thought, and a rich man did not acquire a fortune without understanding winners determined the final arbiter of right and wrong. A pretense of friendship offered the guarantee of no surprises.

"Is he agreeable?" Fletcher asked.

"Very much so. His presence here assures the odds remain in our favor."

"Then do what you must to keep him close."

"I expect him momentarily."

Fletcher rose and looked around the room a last time with a heavy sigh.

"I'll leave him to you then, but consult me before you confront Caine again."

"As always, dear father."

Chapter Twenty-Six

April 2
Early Morning
The Caine House

Kerrigan sat beside Jesse on the Caines' back steps. Both men were bundled against the unrelenting morning chill. The day promised fair weather, veins of thin stratus clouds scattered across blue skies. The twin carriage house doors stood open, both horses peering over stall doors at the sound of voices. Blowing warm air into cupped their hands the two men looked into the stable. Kerrigan scuffed the brick steps with his boot toe, wiped his mouth, and frowned at the horses.

"A cart or wagon would have suited me just as well," he said.

"Will your friend help me?"

"We'll have to ask him."

"But he can teach me?"

"If you're serious," Kerrigan eyed the horses as if reconsidering his offer. "He's not a man to be trifled with."

"Hard?'

"Harder than most."

"How do you know him?"

Kerrigan spit into the yard. "From a long time ago." He frowned into the eyes of the dark bay who tossed its head, anxious for release from the stall.

"I knew him before I came to America. A Frenchman, down to his toes. A little daft to some." He spat over the steps again. "We served together in the Emperor's army. Me, a dirt-eatin' infantryman, him a fancy cavalryman of the hussars. But don't be misled by pretty pictures you've seen."

Surprised, Jesse studied the craggy profile. "You fought in Napoleon's army?"

"Irish Legion." Kerrigan inspected the surrounding rooftops, a hint of arrogance in his tone. "Wild Geese, we was called." He smiled at memories proud and terrible. "My family bolted from Ireland for good during Bonnie Prince Charlie's problems back in '45. Grandfather, father, uncles. We all crossed the Channel and followed the French drum." Kerrigan scratched an armpit. "The British loved to hang or shoot a captured rogue Irishman. Great sport for the bastards."

"I never took you for a soldier."

"Enjoyable as it was, killing their lordships is not something to brag on. Not in Savannah. Too many old Tories still about."

"What's your friend's name?"

"Lobeau." The knowing grin again. "Marcel Etienne Lobeau."

"My god," Jesse said with a half-laugh. "How'd he come to be in America?"

"A story best left for him if he wishes to tell it."

"When can I meet him?"

Kerrigan studied the two horses as if making a decision. "Now. This morning, if you like. An hour's ride, then some rowing to his Island. "

"Where?"

"A scrub island on a nothing creek," Kerrigan smirked with a hint of jealousy. "No one ever claimed it, so he named it after himself."

"I should tell Lizzie—"

Kerrigan snatched off his floppy hat and shook his head, running his hand through his mass of curly hair. "Lizzie, is it now."

Jesse ignored him but thought better of telling Lizzie what he planned. Cohen would look after her for the day.

"You can ride my father's horse," Jesse said.

"Better to walk if we had time. The beasts are four-legged dragons, all of 'em."

An hour later they reined at the edge of Skidaway River. The winding channel, part of the lowlands' endless rivers and streams, ran broader and deeper than most tidewater creeks, flowing with the tides past miles of unnamed islands inhabited by ospreys and herds of wild hogs. A small tin-roofed shed constructed of driftwood and odd bits of lumber sat a few yards away from the water's edge, its front steps sagging.

An old Negro appeared and took the horses' reins without speaking. Jesse was to find the man either a mute or uncaring about his customers, never offering a welcome or greeting. He pointed, gestured and shrugged, never moved to words. Barefoot, he wore a faded red plaid shirt and faded gray trousers above knobby ankles. Dark parchment skin stretched over his ridged features, a skeletal face cratered with smallpox scars and topped by a shiny dome ringed with a Roman emperor's fringe of bristly white hair. He avoided looking too closely at them, aware of his diminished status.

Two horses nibbled straw in a rundown livery near a row of weather-beaten bateaus, each boat stacked on its stern against the wall of a second shed. Kerrigan handed several coins to the old man who thanked him in a soft Gullah dialect that revealed his Georgia coast roots. With surprising strength, he manhandled one of the flat-bottomed boats to the ground. He tossed in heavy wooden oars and started back to the shed when Kerrigan yelled at him.

"Uncle, you can damn well earn your money."

The old man hesitated, then shoved the boat across the muddy bank Kerrigan stepped into the bateau and Jesse pushed off, facing Kerrigan who set the oars into rusted metal locks. Using his river skills, he maneuvered the bateau into the current as the impassive black face watched them disappear down river.

The incoming tidal flow propelled the boat swiftly up river and Kerrigan kept the bow centered in the current. Mud flats and tan marsh grass marked their passage, low tide blocking what lay beyond the palisade of reeds. Jesse picked up a tin ladle and bailed water from the worn floorboards. Kerrigan settled into a gentle cadence, the prow following the tide's urgings. A bird flying overhead would have seen only the solitary boat and shallow creeks that bled off the river into dead-end mazes.

A half an hour passed in scenic silence until Kerrigan plunged the outboard oar into the current and heaved at it with a grunt. The bateau reluctantly swung into the seemingly impenetrable barrier of reeds. Two startled white egrets burst from the marsh. A sliver of water appeared on either side of the boat. The man-made opening closed behind the stern, leaving no evidence of their entry.

The current in the creek remained strong as marsh surrounded them and took them deeper into the reedy wilderness, drifting past glistening mud flats that reeked of spoiled eggs. The marsh pressed closer until only the tops of pencil-thin reeds remained visible. Hemmed against the banks, one side of the bateau scraped against an exposed oyster rake jutting from the marsh. Kerrigan lifted the oars and allowed the current to take the boat. Jesse peered over the side, surprised to see the creek measured a full fathom deep.

Another minute passed without either man speaking, as though voices would break a covenant imposed by water and wilderness. Without warning, the creek abruptly widened into a lagoon of sapphire water barely twenty-five yards wide. An undersized dock jutted from the far shore, the rough structure barely visible through a maze of overhanging limbs and moss. Kerrigan pulled toward the makeshift dock, and Jesse saw a small boat hidden beneath the tree line. Beyond, a single path led from the dock through a wall of scrub pines and oaks.

The boat bumped the planks and Jesse picked up the bowline.

"Wait," Kerrigan said.

He stepped past Jesse and looped the bow line around a piling, keeping his hand against Jesse's chest.

"Lobeau! It's Kerrigan!"

"*Wait*," he warned again as Jesse stirred.

Barking exploded from the woods. Two huge mastiffs loped to the dock, howls echoing across the deserted marshland. Kerrigan yelled at them and shoved the boat several yards away from the tiny pier. The dogs loped onto the dock, teeth bared, braced to leap into the boat until a pair of boots thumped along the path. A small puppet of a man appeared and half-heartedly kicked at the frantic dogs.

"*Tais-toi!* Quiet!"

Jesse tried not to show his disappointment. Their rescuer seemed an emaciated store clerk burdened down by a well-oiled pistol and short-barreled musket. More disconcerting than his firearms, the diminutive figure strode onto the dock and halted above the boat, wearing a faded military jacket and scarlet trousers frayed at the cuffs. Embroidered gold stripes disappeared down the outer seams into outdated hussar boots. His thin upper lip supported a groomed black moustache, supporting sharply waxed tips that curled upward toward hawkish eyes. The first signs of thinning black hair covered the encroaching baldness of age, long strands pomaded and gleaming in the sunlight and gathered in back into a single oiled tube knot over his collar.

"Kerrigan, *mon ami!*"

The figure smiled, un-cocked the musket, and laid it carefully on the dock. He stuffed the large caliber pistol into his belt and lowered one hand toward the dogs who settled around his feet with guttural growls. Kerrigan secured the boat's stern and jumped to the dock to embrace the Frenchman. Jesse joined him, wary of the dogs that were waist-high and sniffed his boots until they lost interest and settled again beside their master.

Kerrigan pulled away from the little man.

"Jesse, this is Etienne Lobeau. Etienne, my friend, *Monsieur* Jesse Caine." His voice turned serious. "We've come to beg your help, my old friend."

Lobeau glanced sharply at him, the smile fading. Creases appeared around the half-lidded eyes as though Jesse represented a careless recruit on parade. He did not offer his hand, and Jesse experienced a sense of dread, the innocuous little man a creature to avoid. Appearing older than Kerrigan, he carried himself with the assurance of someone who long ago consumed his allotted ration of pity or fear.

He nodded and the three of them started up the footpath followed by the panting dogs as Jesse's uneasiness grew. What could an aging former soldier offer against Randall Tyree? His life and father's future dangled by a hair if Tyree or another disgruntled investor called him out.

A cabin emerged several hundred feet from the dock. A thin spiral of smoke curled from a stone chimney. Sawn logs were neatly chinked with gray tabby complemented by a perfectly pitched cedar shake roof. A forest of ground-level tree stumps produced an unobstructed view around the structure, creating what the military labeled an open killing ground.

The dogs loped ahead and settled to the ground by the cabin door, ignoring Jesse and Kerrigan. A fat raccoon ambled round the side of the cabin and stood on its hind legs, black-edged bandit eyes scrutinizing the new arrivals. Lobeau tied a thin leather leash around its neck, clicked his tongue, and the raccoon waddled into the cabin ahead of him.

Jesse stopped inside the doorway, stunned by the single room's opulence. The floor had been constructed of puncheon planks locked in place by flush wooden pegs, covered by a woven woolen rug. A few pieces of gilded and elaborately carved Empire furniture completed a tasteful arrangement, flanked by a 17th century walnut cabinet of crystal wine glasses. Jesse could only compare the elegance to the hunting lodge of some minor nobleman.

Lobeau arranged three matched chairs around a handsome table next to the fireplace. He tied the raccoon's leash to his own chair and selected a bottle from a tall wine rack. Arranging long-stemmed glasses, he uncorked the long-necked bottle and poured red wine. The former hussar settled in his chair and stretched his legs full length, crossing his ankles. He scratched the raccoon's back and drank deeply, heedless of the early hour.

"So," he said to Kerrigan, his accent pronounced, "you find time to visit an old friend when you require a favor."

Kerrigan removed his hat and hung it on the back of his chair. "I know, I know. I'm a *bâtard* for not coming more," he said. "Old soldiers like us need to drink and tell lies. Remember dead friends and enemies." He grinned and raised his glass. "A poultice for guilty souls."

"*Salut.*" Lobeau raised his own in acknowledgement. Jesse hesitated to lift his own to an unimaginable past.

Lobeau swiped his wet moustache and inspected his glass. Restless, the raccoon chattered and tugged at its leash beneath his chair. Lobeau murmured a command in French, and the animal and cabin fell silent. Kerrigan gave Jesse an imperceptible nod as Lobeau stared into the glass, content to wait.

Jesse, at a loss, wondered at his situation, sitting inside a lavish cabin while an outlandishly dressed stranger waited for him to explain himself. How was he expected to ask a stranger for assistance in killing a man? He forced himself to meet Lobeau's eyes and delayed his reason for intruding on his host's seclusion.

"How did you come to America?" Jesse asked.

Lobeau looked at Kerrigan who shrugged. "I told him nothing."

The Frenchman contemplated an answer inside his wine glass, fingering the stem. "Americans," he said. "So careful not to appear inquisitive."

Fearing he'd broken a protocol Kerrigan failed to mention, he watched Lobeau caress the crystal, fingertips caressing the surface. After a moment he seemed to relax and a furtive smile lifted the corners of their host's mouth.

"I am a thief," he said almost to himself. "If robbing Prussians can be called thievery."

"I call it the devil's luck," Kerrigan said. A fleeting look passed between the two men before Kerrigan inclined his head at Jesse. "Tell him," he said to Lobeau. "He can be trusted."

Lobeau poured his empty glass half-full, stretched his boots in front of him again, and held the wine to the light. A mass of scars disfigured the back of his right hand, and Jesse noticed an angry ridge on the left side of his neck.

"Victory waited a hundred yards ahead of us," he said. "The British on the ridge were making a final stand when the Prussians appeared on our right flank and in our rear. Thousands of the *cochons* poured out of the woods and ended it for us." The room and its elegant furnishings disappeared before the former hussar's eyes. "What the world calls Waterloo was over, and we ran for our lives." He blinked and found Jesse again. "The world called it a cleansing, but they weren't there. There was nothing clean about it."

Jesse tried to imagine him on horseback, filthy and bloodied from the terrible fighting. Lobeau gave a resigned sigh and took a long clay pipe from the sideboard behind him.

"I became separated from my regiment in the forest outside Plancenoit, a dirty little Belgian village clogged with our dead and theirs." He lighted the pipe and exhaled, submerged again in the sights and sounds. After a second, he remembered Jesse and cleared his throat.

"I forget my manners," he said abruptly. "Are you hungry?" Both shook their heads, and Lobeau scratched the raccoon's ears.

"By sheer good fortune, I stumbled across a Prussian paymaster's wagon driven by two fat old hogs. God knows why they were wandering alone in the woods. Lost lambs was my guess. Naturally, I killed them both."

He wiped his mouth with a linen handkerchief and refilled all three glasses. He took a generous swallow and sat back with a contented air, holding up four fingers with a faint smile.

"Four bound chests of gold coins," he said. "I pulled them off the wagon into a ravine." He gave a Gallic shrug. "Loaded my pockets and *sabretache* with as much as I could carry and buried the chests among the trees." He sucked hard at the pipe.

"When I reached the main road to *La Belle Alliance*, the panic was on everyone, the roads were choked with dying and terrified men. Prussian cavalry sabered every Frenchman they could ride down. My mount gave out and I found an abandoned officer's horse." He frowned at the memory. "Two days later I was in Paris as our enemies approached the doomed city."

Kerrigan downed his wine and poured another full measure, heedless of the early hour. He held his glass high. "He's probably the richest man in Savannah," he said to Jesse, "maybe all Georgia," Envy clouded his countenance, and he grinned crookedly at Lobeau. "A lot of money, *n'est pas?*"

Lobeau knocked the pipe into his palm and did not return the smile. He walked to the door and tossed the ashes outside, gazing toward the river as though his collection of riches was too high a price for exile on a backwater Georgia island. The raccoon hopped into his vacated chair until Lobeau returned to the table, clicked his tongue, and gently nudged the animal to the floor.

"I slipped back into Belgium several months later and retrieved the rest," he continued, "but wine loosened my tongue in too many taverns, and my good fortune found its way to Prussian ears. The bastards put a price on my head, and I ran." He shrugged. "I am going back, though," he said wistfully. "Soon."

"Before you leave this Garden of Eden," Kerrigan said, "my friend has need of your skills." Kerrigan sat forward on the edge of his chair and looked at Jesse with a gleam of pride. "Lobeau was the fencing master in his regiment. Seven years, the *maître d'armes* as we called 'em. His position allowed him to reply to insults to the regiment's reputation, some frivolous, some uttered in earnest, others to provoke him and earn a reputation." He turned to his friend. "How many died because of bad manners?"

"In affairs of honor? Fifteen. Possibly more. Who remembers after so many years?"

"All by the sword," Kerrigan said to Jesse.

Lobeau said nothing, his victims' faces dimmed by time.

Kerrigan turned to him, "*Monsieur* Caine may soon be forced to defend himself against a man of some skill." He recounted the scandal and Jesse's confrontations with Belden and Randall Tyree. Lobeau listened without interrupting until Kerrigan sat back.

"Have you experience with the sword?" Lobeau asked Jesse.

"No."

Kerrigan shot a glance at Jesse. "He's half Indian, Etienne." He winked at Jesse. "A *demi-sauvage* in your parlance."

Lobeau nodded. "I see it in his face, his eyes. The eyes of a *chasseur*." He looked back at Kerrigan. "And I am expected to provide instruction?"

"I'll pay you," Jesse said.

"I have no need of your money." He swept one arm around the cabin. "Worse, no place to spend it."

"There's no one else who can help him," Kerrigan said.

Lobeau stood and motioned Jesse from his chair. "Stand up."

Jesse got to his feet and the diminutive Frenchman stepped back, assessing him with a practiced eye.

"Tall," Lobeau said. "That's to his advantage."

He opened a brass-bound chest near the rear door. Inside, rows of cloth bags lay carefully wrapped like family heirlooms. Lobeau removed a covering and revealed a simple blade, its tip protected by a metal button. He turned back to Jesse.

"Does your enemy prefer the epée or saber?"

Enemy.

For the first time Jesse understood what he had agreed to undertake, his gaze on the naked blade. Hidden from prying eyes on an unknown island, he'd placed himself in the hands of a thief and killer. A single word and Kerrigan would row him back to sanity, away from the lethal little man. But running solved nothing. His only salvation stood before him in polished boots.

"The epée," he said.

Lobeau nodded. "Then we'll forego the heavy plastron. You'll be in no danger other than an occasional touch on the chest." He picked up two leather masks, the eye openings covered by a fine mesh. "Not up to the finest fencing salons in Paris, but they will suffice." The slender blade at his side, he looked closely at Jesse.

"Have you ever killed a man?"

"Never."

Lobeau handed him the other epée. "Time to learn."

Chapter Twenty-Seven

April 3
Afternoon
Savannah City Jail

Jesse's arm and back throbbed as he descended into the prison depths behind the deputy, footsteps muffled by damp stones. Each foray into the catacombs left him more determined to free his father, to let him taste sunlight again. Age and collapsing lungs were devouring him, gnawing flesh to the bone, an innocent tortured by uncertainty and the sameness of days.

The jailer unlocked the cell door, and Jesse spent the next hour explaining Lizzie's methods to his father. He kept his voice low, the jailer only a few yards away. Jesse did not tell him about Lobeau, sparing him the disappointment of another confession.

That night, he found solace in Lizzie's arms. There was unspoken recognition that two of society's outcasts had found their way into one another's souls and bodies. Jesse could think of little else but the taste of her skin and glory of her body as she shifted and groaned atop him. Finally satiated and gasping, she rolled off his heaving body and they collapsed on their backs. The house, empty and silent now after absorbing their cries, enfolded them in a blanket of complicit contentment. Jesse raised a corner of the sheet and wiped his face, listening to Lizzie's labored breathing.

"My god," he murmured.

She nestled closer. "Where do you go when you leave me?"

"Kerrigan and I are looking for answers," he said.

He said nothing about Lobeau or the hidden island, and Lizzie found the answer sufficient from a man who cared nothing for her deformity. She looked at him to ask what he'd discovered, but his jumbled thoughts had given way to the day's final exertion, and Lizzie saw he was asleep.

When Lizzie left for Cohen's office next morning, the blanket of guilt resettled onto Jesse's shoulders. He hurriedly dressed and rode to the boat landing, carrying his secret like a verdict. Kerrigan waited on a stump, impatiently digging his boot heel into the ground, ignoring the old black man who tended his horse.

The keeper took Aristotle's reins and watched as they shoved the encrusted bateau over mud and broken shells into the river. Jesse climbed into the bow seat and Kerrigan allowed the incoming current to bully the boat away from shore. Without speaking he dipped the oars into the water and steadied the shallow craft as the tide propelled it down river.

Huddled in the bow, clouds hid the sun and the morning chill found the back of Jesse's neck. He pulled up his cape collar to fend off the insistent moisture that bored into his bones. His boots touched the canvas sack beneath his seat containing two bottles of his father's French brandy. Removing them from the cabinet had seemed a betrayal to his father.

Kerrigan tugged his hat brim lower, his face reddened by cold and the oars' bulk. He said nothing as glassy water swept past the boat's gunwales, a trail of bubbles marking their course. Jesse shivered and wondered what in hell happened to spring. A vaporous layer of fog clung to the water's surface, deepening the cold and brushing the Irishman's face as he pulled harder at the oars. The spring tide ran faster than the previous day, and the bateau veered toward the screened inlet. Kerrigan forced the prow into the invisible gap and the reeds swallowed them.

The creek unwound slowly at Jesse's back. The sky dimmed to blue-gray, the overcast consuming their shadow. He massaged his right wrist and saw Lobeau and the dogs on the dock. Every muscle tightened in Jesse's legs and shoulders. The little Frenchman had proven the ultimate taskmaster, caring nothing about the state of Jesse's body, pronouncing fatigue an unacceptable malady.

Jesse pulled the cape about him and thought of Lizzie snug in Cohen's sanctuary. Warmth held a new lure, one removed from the ordeal in the chilled clearing behind the cabin. Suddenly envious of the overheated office, he watched slate-colored clouds scud closer to the treetops like dirty gray rags wrinkling the horizon. The overcast edged lower as though anxious to punish the dreary island. Lobeau, arms folded, watched his approach. No uniform today, he wore only a long-sleeved shirt buttoned to the neck, scornful of the weather. His face aglow, he watched the boat with a starving man's anticipation. The word Jesse had quickly come to hate sprang to his ears, a command hurled without pity.

Again—again—again!

The prow bumped the dock, and Kerrigan stepped past Jesse to secure the bowline around a piling. The trio walked to the cabin, the dogs loping behind them. Kerrigan muttered something to Lobeau and the two men laughed. Inside the cabin Lobeau waited impatiently as Jesse removed his cape and coat, shivering slightly as he remembered the last lesson. Two blunted epées and leather face masks waited beside the back door.

"Actually, I'm glad Kerrigan brought you to me," Lobeau said as they walked outside. "I keep my hand in, fencing shadows and frightening the air. An old habit that keeps the rust from my bones."

He tightened the mask's straps around Jesse's head and donned his own. He strode away, sword in hand, swinging the blade in graceful arcs. Ignoring Jesse, he paced the perimeter, steel slicing the moist air. Jesse gave an involuntary shudder, seeing what Lobeau's adversaries beheld the instant before they left the earth. He'd decided not to judge his teacher's past. Nothing was gained in judging his teacher, and whatever blood Lobeau once spilled most likely provided sufficient afflictions within his soul.

Kerrigan seated himself on the bench beside the door and crossed his legs, steam rising from the mug of coffee in one fist. He stretched his other arm across the back, content to enjoy a morning's entertainment at Jesse's expense.

"Better you than me," he called to him.

"We begin," Lobeau said. He positioned Jesse's body with a few gestures, gave a slight bow, and touched his blade to Jesse's.

Soreness slowed his reflexes, then gradually fled his arms and legs as Lobeau led him through basic movements. The morning air revived him and reverberated with abrupt commands and the clash of steel in the quiet glade. Jesse's agony reasserted itself and gradually leached into his protesting muscles as Lobeau barked a stream of orders.

Your feet! Position your feet!

Watch only my eyes!

Thrust. Parry.

Again!

Again!

The relentless commands pursued Jesse across the open space. No matter how hard he strove to anticipate Lobeau's movements, the Frenchman remained a killing second ahead of him. His blunted epée effortlessly parried Jesse's attacks and ripostes, finding his chest with firm touches. The smaller man skated on dainty feet, unencumbered by his boots, feet precisely positioned for every attack and parry. A fresh torrent of attacks assailed Jesse as the pace increased, Lobeau's touches harder until Jesse feared the blunted tip would pierce his chest.

The sword tip painfully jabbed into Jesse's forearm, ripping the shirt sleeve. Frustrated, he lunged clumsily and met only air, his humiliated gasp audible beneath the sodden leather mask. He heard Kerrigan's laughter as he pursued Lobeau, intent on revenge, yearning to strike a single blow. His tormentor, face hidden beneath the mask, easily danced aside until Jesse's face burned with frustration. After a full minute of careless attacks, Lobeau struck Jesse's throbbing chest in rapid succession, each of the three blows harder than the last. Jesse stepped away and threw up his arms.

"Enough," he gasped.

Lobeau stripped off his own mask and glared at him. "That accomplished nothing! If anger rules your mind, you will die."

Jesse bent forward from the waist and pulled off his own mask, dizzy, his lungs ablaze. Sweat dripped from his chin.

"Courage is not enough," Lobeau said. "You must become skilled."

Jesse straightened and flung the mask at the cabin door. "That's why I'm here!"

Lobeau walked to the door and retrieved the mask. "We begin again," he said. "Control your anger if you want to live."

Jesse donned the repulsive mask, disgusted by the brew of sour sweat and wet leather. Despite his body's protests, the anger receded and he slowly absorbed the rhythm of thrust, counter, and riposte.

Lobeau reduced his pace and Jesse mirrored his movements. He easily flicked away Jesse's thrusts but graced him with a nod when the blade once brushed his arm. As if to smother the minor triumph, he launched a series of rapid attacks. Jesse stumbled back, lost again as Kerrigan grinned and clapped derisively.

Another ten minutes passed and Lobeau whipped off his mask.

"*Ça suffit, assez,*" he said. "Enough. You are making stupid mistakes again. We eat, then begin again."

Jesse stripped off the clammy mask and greedily inhaled the moist air. Inside, Lobeau set the small table with fine china. He opened a bottle of Jesse's brandy and poured three glasses as he prepared a meal, moving around the cast iron stove with the same dexterity with which he danced over the packed earth. Grateful for the chair beneath him, Jesse wiped his face with a towel and sipped the brandy.

Lobeau fried bacon, assembled three omelets, and placed a basket of hard bread on the table, his movements quick and sure as a fastidious bachelor who lived alone. The morning had warmed, and Lobeau scattered the few glowing remnants in the fire. He filled fresh glasses with wine and settled to his food, taking no further notice of his guests as he ate. His jaws moved without pause, face bent close to his plate, eating with the deliberation of someone who'd known hunger on too many fields of despair.

An overcast covered the sky as a storm approached, pushing pale gray overcast ahead of pregnant rain clouds. The room darkened and thunder shook the floorboards. Fat raindrops pummeled the wooden roof. The windows flashed white with lightning, and the rain's intensity increased until it roared against the roof as though seeking entry. The planked floor shuddered again as thunder passed over the island.

Lobeau took no notice of the storm, his fork moving with mechanical fervor. Scraping his plate clean with a scrap of bread he collected the delicate plates and eased them into a wooden tub of water by the sink pump. Opening the rear door, he squinted into the storm, heedless of the rain that lashed his face. He frowned at the clearing that held an inch of water, a squat city of marooned stumps.

"*Merde.*"

Peals of thunder browbeat the woods, hammering leaves from trees. Cold rain swept over the island in spite of the calendar, a condition only the low country seemed capable of inspiring.

Lobeau wiped his moustache and returned to the table. "I've seen such storms before," he said. "This one will remain with us until morning. You do not want to risk the river, so you will be my guests tonight."

Kerrigan grinned and made circles with his palm across the tabletop. "Two bottles of gentlemen's brandy and a wall of good French wine. More than enough to see us through the night." He grinned at Jesse. "Not to worry. Your lady friend will find someone to comfort her."

Jesse remembered Lizzie for the first time since arriving. Wishing he'd confessed his absences but afraid of the repercussions, he could do nothing now but wait out the weather. She had no idea where he spent the night—or if he'd spend it alone. Can't be helped, he thought.

Lobeau poured more brandy and it slowly seeped into Jesse's aching muscles. He poured a third glassful and allowed the golden heat to do its work. A draft of wind found its way into the cabin, and Lobeau relit the fire. Jesse stretched his legs under the table, relishing the pleasant lassitude. The warmth lulled him into amiable submission, and they quickly finished the first bottle of brandy.

Twilight arrived beneath the rain's onslaught. Lobeau and Kerrigan repeatedly refilled their glasses and relived their days on foot and horseback as the storm raged outside. Kerrigan inspected the first empty bottle and glanced at Lobeau who uncorked the second. Jesse held out his glass for refills and listened as the two men relived a past beyond his understanding. The second bottle disappeared faster than the first, and the war assumed the high point in men's soldiers' lives. Past battles were refought, and Jesse's head whirled. The cabin walls wavered and he later remembered Lobeau opening a bottle of Burgundy, showing no ill effects from the brandy. Kerrigan half-closed his eyes as he topped their glasses. The fencing master swiped at his moustache with a flourish. He leaned toward Kerrigan and clasped his forearm.

"You served honorably," he said. "A friend of France."

Kerrigan grinned, reliving past memories. "We killed a lot of men, you and I. Their lordships and all them what supported the bastards against the Emperor."

"We were patriots," Lobeau said. "Innocents. At least in the beginning."

Kerrigan laughed. "The only innocents I remember were German and Polish milkmaids whose innocence we stole on cold nights."

"We killed France's enemies," Lobeau said, his voice revealing the liquor and wine for the first time. He gripped Kerrigan's arm harder. "But we never betrayed the Emperor. Or one another, old friend." He drained his wine. "We never became animals like some we knew."

"Unless it saved our hides," Kerrigan laughed.

Lobeau gazed into the fireplace. "But we stayed comrades, you and I. Remained honest *soldats*, even in those last terrible days." His eyes deadened with memory. "You remember near the end? At Montereau? On the stone bridge?"

Kerrigan nodded at the memory.

"Your fellows cleared the way," Lobeau said. "We were halfway across when a Bavarian traitor shot my captain." A look of disgust twisted his face. "They were supposed to be allies, but they turned against us at the end, the whole lot of them. You and my fellows cut them down, even their wounded. Remember?"

Kerrigan belched and gave a brutal grin. "No prisoners that day. Did the same during the retreat back into France." His eyes narrowed, the alcohol slowed his words. "Bayoneted everyone who stood in our way."

"Soldiers' work," Lobeau said. "We survived, That was all that mattered."

The alcohol made Jesse drowsy as the two soldiers swapped tales, an innocent among wolves. They had been professionals who accepted war as a way of life. He'd listened to soldiers' tales from his father's friends, but Kerrigan and Lobeau evidenced no remorse. Kerrigan's accounts grew more boisterous, a torrent of lurid reminiscences. Their world seemed less significant after the war, a worrisome place populated by lesser men.

Forgotten amongst the memories, Jesse stumbled from the table. He pulled a blanket from Lobeau's bed and dragged it to the fireplace, ignored by the two veterans. Before closing his eyes, he heard Lobeau lower his voice:

"A comrade I trusted," he said to Kerrigan. "That was all that mattered."

Jesse curled up before the dwindling fire fully clothed, asleep in less than a minute.

The fireplace smelled of wet ashes, the rain having moved across the island during the night. Sunlight inched across the floor and touched Jesse's eyelids. He opened them, squinted, and frowned. Kerrigan, head tipped back, snored in his chair. Sore and tangled in the blanket, Jesse turned his back to the malicious sun, his mouth tarred with moist sandpaper. Something brushed his face and he opened one eye. The small paw touched his cheek again, the raccoon inspecting his nose. Jesse pushed the animal away. A foot kicked his boot sole and he turned to find a sword blade inches from his face as Lobeau stared down at him

"*Debout!* Time to continue your education."

The sun edged above the windowsill, and Jesse guessed the time an hour past dawn. Lobeau, dressed in fresh clothes, looked as though he'd slept twelve hours. The boot kicked him again.

"There's coffee. And whiskey if you require it."

Jesse's entire body ached like a single contained bruise, mocking his pounding head. The raccoon watched him struggle to the stove and pour a cup of coffee. Lobeau strode out the back door without waiting for him, the swords in one hand. Jesse gulped down the coffee and followed him outside, the raccoon at his heels.

Head throbbing, Jesse pulled on the nauseating mask. He gagged at the sweat-stiffened leather, bile in his throat as his stomach threatened to empty itself, led by the coffee. He listlessly swung the sword from side to side, his watery arm mocking him from shoulder to fingertips. Most of the rainwater had drained away, leaving the leafy ground waterlogged.

Lobeau showed no mercy. He drove him across the slippery ground, barraging Jesse with corrections and criticism. Shoes caked with mud and leaves, Jesse twice lost his footing, his legs quickly tiring as Lobeau came at him.

Attack!

Parry!

Too slow!

Faster! Again!

Always the same commands, Jesse thought as he retreated and fought off Lobeau's relentless onslaught. Survival lay in repetition and anticipation. The assaults continued for fifteen minutes. Each second produced a new agony in his limbs until Lobeau held up his hand and allowed five minutes rest. Awakened by the voices Kerrigan walked outside, frowning at the morning sun. A cup of coffee laced with whiskey gripped in one hand, he shoved the raccoon aside and collapsed on the bench.

The lesson continued and consumed the morning, brief pauses filled with critiques. Lobeau exhibited a teacher's patient skills, and Jesse slowly responded to the commands. Lobeau uttered a single note of praise at a skillful riposte, small payment for Jesse's torturous exertions. Noon approached and Lobeau lifted his hand, stripping off his mask. Jesse trudged after the little Frenchman and watched him wipe both swords with an oily rag, inspecting the blades from hilt to tip. He placed them inside the two soft bags and laid them inside the chest before turning to Jesse.

"*Meilleur*," he said. "Better. You make progress, but far more is needed. Tomorrow we concentrate on the killing strokes." He scanned Jesse's exhausted face for a reaction. "In the end, only they matter."

Kerrigan said little on the return trip. Lobeau's rebukes replayed in Jesse's ears, each word magnifying his mistakes and blunders. Was he the ultimate fool, he wondered, asking help from a man whose skills he could never emulate? If he never bested Lobeau, how could he meet Randall Tyree on equal terms? He stared unseeing at the reeds that slipped past the boat until they exited the creek into the river, its beauty offended by Lobeau's parting words—"*killing strokes.*"

At the landing, Jesse paid the old negro man an extra dollar for feeding the horses. On the muddy road, Kerrigan found his voice again and endured the rented animal's canter with an infantryman's dislike of horses, extolling Lobeau's talents. Jesse imagined the coming night with Lizzie, wondering where he'd find the energy to satisfy her demands on his aching body. After a few miles Kerrigan seemed to read his mind and asked about Lizzie.

"Is she a paid impostor relying on tricks?"

"She's competent," Jesse said, He started to say more and stopped. Loose talk by Kerrigan in a besotted moment might undermine Cohen in the courtroom.

"What makes you believe she can save your father?" Kerrigan persisted. "A jury will believe what it sees. Can she conjure up innocence from scribbles on paper?"

Jesse recalled her detailed explanations. A judge might well agree with Kerrigan, and a jury indeed needed patience to see small differences between words and letters.

"We'll see," Jesse said.

His thighs chafed against the leather saddle skirt as a reminder of the clearing's torments. With practice, he might stand a sinner's chance. Whatever the outcome, Etienne Lobeau embodied his single hope if Randall Tyree called him out.

Chapter Twenty-Eight

Same Day
The Caine House

Jesse bid Kerrigan farewell near the carriage house where rainwater stood in the yard and dripped from tree limbs. His arms and legs protested as he picked up a curry brush. The brush strokes proved therapeutic, however, soothing man and horse. Latching the stall door, he trudged up the back steps. Slapping at his grimy coat sleeves, he caught a scent of himself. Two days since he'd bathed.

Empty rooms greeted him. If only his father and Lizzie were there to hear the back door open and come down the stairs to greet him. Even the cook and housekeeper's prattle would be welcomed in the silence. Passing through the front hall, he saw a small pink envelope beneath the front door. Jasmine perfume wafted from the paper as he opened it and he recognized Victoria's handwriting.

Dearest Jesse,
I've missed you these past few days. I know you have little
time for me in the midst of your tragedy, but it seems ages
since we last talked. Please call on me.
Victoria

The sight of her name produced a flare of guilt and regret. Lizzie had all but erased her from his life. He reread the note and pocketed it. How long since he'd thought about her? He'd consigned Victoria from the light to the shadows, and the realization pricked his conscience until he recalled her distant manner when they encountered Fletcher Tyree. Still, she'd once filled his thoughts and he owed her the courtesy of one last call.

Upstairs, he stripped off rumpled clothes and bathed, remembering he needed to hire a washerwoman despite Lizzie overseeing the house. So many things had changed since Dew's arrival in the middle of the night. He opened his watch. Three o'clock. Time enough before going to Cohen's office. He finished dressing and re-saddled Aristotle.

Victoria met him at the door, a painted fan in one hand. Wayward strands of carefully-arranged blond hair framed her slender face. She gave him a brittle smile, flourishing the ivory panels in rapid strokes as he followed her into the sitting room. She suddenly turned and kissed him, her lips lingering. One hand slipped around his neck and she brought her lips close to his ear.

162

"Mother's shopping," she whispered. "The house is ours for several hours."

Surprised, he started to speak, but she pulled away and sat on the red velvet settee, primly adjusting her skirts as though she'd never spoken. Fanning briskly, her gaze darted about as though other visitors waited their turn, the implied invitation seemingly forgotten. Jesse noticed a new sideboard, the waxed top laden with polished silverware. The curved convex surfaces reflected her watercolors arranged on the dining room wall. Her mother's two cats begged for her attention, but she swatted them away with the fan without speaking.

Baffled by her behavior, Jesse said, "It's been awhile."

"Yes. Ages and ages." She dropped the fan on the couch and plucked at a loose pillow thread, the kiss forgotten.

"I received your note," he said.

Victoria frowned and blinked as though he'd broken some rule of etiquette before snatching up the fan with an exasperated sound.

"Of course, the note." She reopened the fan. "Silly me. I walked to your house to deliver it myself."

Jesse's confusion intensified. He'd never known her to walk more than three blocks in any direction. Assuming the role of a mere pedestrian had always been beneath her station in life, forcing her to share the sidewalk with lesser beings.

"I wondered why you haven't called on me," she pouted. "I've not seen you since your disagreement with Colonel Tyree."

"Samuel Cohen and I are building a defense for my father."

A blur of the fan. "Working with the woman from Boston?"

Jesse caught himself before his anger and guilt erupted. "She's part of our defense."

Victoria lifted her chin. "I would have thought she offered little, not understanding Savannah's ways."

Jesse, unable to make sense of her logic, said, "I'm only concerned with her capabilities."

Victoria made a small sound. "Is she wealthy?"

"Not to my knowledge."

"You have faith in her?"

"I have little choice."

Had someone previously pointed out Lizzie to her on the street, he wondered? If so, he imagined her emotions ran the gamut from jealousy to resentment. Beautiful women did not relish competition, and an attractive woman like Victoria competed for the admiration of every man who entered her territory; she marked it like a wary lioness without surrendering ground to another woman. Clouds passed over the house,

163

and the room darkened. She turned up the lamp wick and they sat without speaking. Jesse glanced at the foyer, escape beckoning.

They got to their feet and faced one another, their intimacy drained though one of her plays had ended. She smiled sadly and touched his cheek.

"Be careful, Jesse."

He squeezed her hand and let himself out without looking back.

A carriage pulled up at the front gate, Aaron on the driver's seat. The slave hopped from the driver's box and assisted Martha Danford from the coach. The widow motioned him away and took Jesse's arm. Without her accustomed effusive greeting, she led him several yards from the gate.

With a glance at the house, she said, "Jesse, how is your father?"

"As well as can be expected."

She looked past him at the house again, his reply unnoted. "Have you talked with Victoria?"

"We talked," he said, aware how tightly she clutched his arm. "She seems distracted. Is she well?"

Martha Danford suddenly pulled away and wrapped her arms around her ample bosom. Drawing a deep breath, she faced him, her features drawn.

"I've detected nothing amiss with her physical health," she said. "She recently auditioned for the lead in 'A Midsummer Night's Dream,' but they passed over her for a new actress. It was a devastating blow to her."

"Her reputation's well deserved," Jesse said. "I'm sure there'll be another role soon."

Martha Danford looked imploringly at him, her voice quavering. "It's more than the theater. She's enamored with new possessions." She gazed at the house. "Not that I don't appreciate the finer things we've acquired. I tried talking with her, but she's only wants to discuss our trip to Europe. She's planning a voyage this summer."

Jesse saw no gain in admitting the end of their relationship. Victoria was a beautiful figment of his past, alluring as ever, but Lizzie's entry into his life reduced Victoria to a troubled friend, nothing more. She'd changed somehow, possibly hurt by his distance. She would always remain in his life, but she'd changed and the transformation troubled him.

"Being passed over for the part must have been a blow," he said, "but I imagine she's dealing with it in her own way."

Her mother patted his hand. "I'm certain you're right," she said. "We speak freely, you and I. About everything. I'm sure it's only a passing phase." She looked imploringly at him. "I know you've many things on your mind, Jesse, but she needs you just now."

She kissed him lightly on the cheek and walked to the house. Jesse nodded to Aaron and mounted Aristotle, determined to keep his mind clear. Victoria vexed him, another riddle to resolve. One problem at a time, he thought.

The short ride to Cohen's office lifted his spirits. Tree leaves and shrubs glistened, washed clean after the morning rain. The morning grew warmer, and he put aside Victoria's behavior, appreciating the reprieve of fresh air. Savannah had donned her spring face in spite of the fickle weather, basking in the amnesty before summer's onslaught. Days such as this made him forget the city's shortcomings.

He walked past Cohen's two associates; heads down, they barely acknowledged his entry. The inner office sat empty. Lizzie sat bent over her desk, a study in concentration as she peered at a certificate through the largest magnifying glass Jesse had ever seen. His heart jumped as she looked up, surprised.

"Good morning," he said carefully.

She rose and quickly walked past him. She closed the door to Cohen's office, wheeled, and slipped her arms around his neck. Her sinuous body pressed into his, and she kissed him hungrily before she pulled away to search his face.

"Where were you last night?"

"Kerrigan and I attended matters away from the city." Guilty at the half-lie, Jesse added to it. "Storms washed out the roads and we had to find lodging." Explaining Lobeau and his visit to Victoria's risked a worse fate, and dire consequences he didn't want to consider at the moment. At least not now.

He pulled her closer. "I'm sorry for not getting word to you."

Her knowing eyes roamed his face as if seeking more answers. "Did business detain you this morning as well?"

Balancing two women presented a challenge he'd never faced, one at an end now. "There was another matter I had to attend," he heard himself say.

She sensed his unease and stepped back. "When you didn't come home last night, what was I supposed to think? It wasn't like you."

Jesse fervently wished Cohen would appear to rescue him.

"I'm sorry."

"What's happened you don't wish to tell me?"

Jesse recovered his courage. Admit half a truth, he thought. "I received a note from Victoria Danford. I went to her house this morning."

Lizzie stiffened and resumed her seat behind the desk, brushing hair from her face. She picked up the magnifier and tapped the edge against the paper without looking through the lens or looking at him. She started to speak but it emerged as a small sob. Jesse came round the desk, but she turned away and refused to look at him.

"What else have you kept from me?" she said.

Determined not to lose her, Jesse gently pulled her to him, her body tense with anger and confusion.

"Victoria's somehow slipping away," he said, unable to explain what he'd heard. "Her mother cannot explain her behavior, and I visited her as a friend, nothing more. This has nothing to do with me."

Lizzie leaned her head back and peered at him. "You didn't sleep with her?"

Jesse, fearing the consequences, restrained a small grin. "No."

She came back into his arms and he held her, neither speaking. The only sounds came from the anteroom where the clerks' muted conversation seeped into the confined space. She took his face in her hands.

"I believe you. This time."

"There's no one else," Jesse said. "No games or lies. I love you, Elizabeth Pendleton."

The admission came out before he uttered the admission aloud. He locked his hands behind her back and kissed her.

"Can you leave for the day and come home with me? Aristotle can easily carry two."

"If you'll tell me where you spent the night."

Jesse's stomach constricted. Tempted, he weighed telling her the truth, knowing her aversion to dueling. She'd traveled to a strange city to help him. Admitting the truth about Lobeau would likely destroy what they'd unexpectedly discovered in one another. He started to confess but his courage failed him.

"It's something I had to do. I can only apologize and ask you to trust me."

Uneasy about his evasion, she said, "And this woman, Victoria? You're not playing me for the fool?"

"My thoughts of her ended the night you invited me into your bed."

She turned away and set her work on the floor next to her desk. She picked up her purse and took his hand.

"Are you certain Aristotle can carry two?"

Chapter Twenty-Nine

April 7
Morning
The Fletcher Tyree House

Randall abhorred the room where he sat. He hated the memories it evoked, and he detested everything it contained.

His father sat across from him, backlit by the arched window. Only the muted voices of slaves laboring in the garden below defied the room's temporary calm. Randall studied the agitated face, determined to keep his own neutral, suppressing a perverse contentment at the older man's discomfort. Randall had, in fact, insisted on an immediate meeting. "A necessity," he'd told him, "minor complications." He'd chosen the words carefully, taking delight in knowing they'd elicit anxiety.

The scheme had begun as Randall's brainchild. Its audacity surprised him but he immediately grasped the opportunity. Now pitfalls were appearing, discovery pursing them like clever hounds.

Curious how the rich believe life continued in a straight line without affecting their plans or dreams, Fletcher thought. Maybe self-imposed delusions were the most debilitating disadvantage to having wealth. It dimmed reality, an ever dangerous condition.

Neither spoke, and Randall remained content to wait for his father to reveal his latest fear.

"Is it falling apart?" Fletcher Tyree asked.

Randall raised his hands in a placating gesture. "All's progressing as planned," he said. "The Pendleton boy's an excellent source of information. We hold all the cards." His humorless smile sought to pacify. "No need to worry yourself. I plan to be very careful, dear father. The thought of hemp rope around my neck distresses me as well."

His father glared at him. "Then why this urgent meeting? I was under the impression we mapped our course some time ago."

Randall nodded. "With both Minceys eliminated, any trail leading back to us is wiped clean."

"Then what's happened?"

"Certain things have changed." Randall took perverse satisfaction in the flash of apprehension that crossed his father's face.

"The Pendleton woman goes to Cohen's office every morning," he said. "No one outside of Caine and Cohen has seen her work, but her brother claims she had success up north, and she doesn't seem inclined to go away." Randall grinned. "If nothing else, I must admit there's a rough beauty about her. Rumor says she's sleeping with young Caine."

Fletcher flicked his fingers as if annoyed by a fly. "Their dalliance doesn't concern me. You assured me she was a charlatan. What's changed your mind?"

Randall allowed a small frown. "Pendleton's a worthless donkey, useful but expensive, given my liquor bill. Spends most of his time at the League or City Hotel bar, but sees his sister on occasion. When he's sober he claims she's making progress with our documents. If she uncovers the truth, we'll need to act quickly."

Fletcher Tyree began shaking his head before his son finished. "You assured me the documents were perfect."

"Our colleague's talents are superb," Randall assured him. "I don't believe we'll require a remedy, but we can't afford disruptions." He stroked his father's need for reassurance. "In any event, everyone believes Ambrose Caine is guilty. Arguing about a few documents won't change anyone's mind."

Randall patted his coat and frowned. He opened his father's inlaid humidor desk and removed a cheroot. Running the noxious cigar beneath his nose, he winced at the pungent foreign leaf. He removed a small gold cylinder from his pocket, unscrewed the top, and withdrew a wooden match; the phosphorous-tipped Lucifers were relatively new toys. He ran the bulbous tip beneath the desk ledge and lit the cigar, wincing as the coarse tobacco scorched his tongue. He made a face at the offending tube.

"I'm prepared for any eventuality," he said, turning his face away from the noxious smoke, "unpleasant as such measures may appear to you. That's why I asked for this meeting." He gave an acerbic smile. "We should always be working in concert."

The older Tyree grunted. "You'll do whatever pleases you no matter what I say. If you're as smart as you pretend, you'll let the court do its duty and put the woman in her place."

A maid timidly knocked on the door.

"What?" Fletcher called.

A roughly dressed man brushed past her. Randall met him halfway across the room and shook his hand, motioning him to a vacant chair in front of the desk. His father's displeasure evident, he ignored the man and glared at his son.

"Why is he here?"

"You'd prefer the three of us met at the Excelsior Room for all Savannah to observe?" Randall asked.

Their guest ignored the exchange and peered over the Colonel's shoulder at the sideboard where sterling cups encircled a crystal decanter. He arranged a smile, his tone solicitous as he removed his hat.

"Colonel, as a valued business partner, do you think I might have a whiskey?"

Randall walked to the sideboard and half-filled a cup. He handed the drink to the man, and the whiskey disappeared in a single gulp.

The man wiped his lips appreciatively with one finger and held the goblet in his lap with a bemused stare at his host, his voice cold.

"You may not like my kind, Colonel, but I'm at your service." He hefted the empty cup, turning it, testing its weight and value. "For a fair price, I can resolve whatever concerns you." Indifferent to Fletcher Tyree's obvious distaste, he reluctantly placed the cup on the desk. "I removed our fat associate in North Carolina, the one with the loose mouth. Randall tells me his one-eyed brother's died as well, although I cannot take credit for hurrying him toward his reward." He picked up the cup again and turned it over to inspect the maker's mark. "And you've no need to worry about young Caine. He's lost as ever, but should he become a problem, your son won't need my help." He handed the cup to Randall who refilled it. "Likewise, the woman from Boston can disappear if she disturbs your sleep." Sighing, he slowly savored the whiskey. "You only need enlarge my purse."

Randall stepped behind the desk and clapped his father on the shoulder. He removed the offending cheroot from his mouth and gave their guest a furtive wink. "He's right, dear father. No need for alarm." He made a face and laid the cheroot in the ashtray, glad to be rid of it.

"As I've already explained, we're safe as long as we do what's required. Even though you insist on hearing the sheriff at your door, no one's going to the gallows. We'll reap our reward if we keep our heads."

The shabbily-dressed man drained the cup. "Wise advice, Colonel. Stay the course, and we're all rich."

Chapter Thirty

Same Day
The Caine House

Lizzie insisted that she prepare dinner for Jesse and Cohen. In the kitchen she laughed as she searched for pots and pans, ignoring the men's teasing suggestions. Jesse watched her limp from cabinet to cabinet, enthralled by her beauty as she performed the most mundane tasks.

He removed brown butcher paper from a fresh flounder wrapped in ice and placed the fish on a wooden chopping block. Lizzie skinned the ugly mottled fish and dusted its delicate white flesh with flour. Arranging it in a shallow buttered pan, she squeezed lemon juice over the carcass, added several more pats of salted butter, and slipped the pan into the oven.

Jesse and Cohen left her to her work and retired to the dining room table, arranging cutlery and napkins to form three place settings. Jesse uncorked a bottle of Riesling and stepped back to inspect the table with a pang of regret. The night lacked only his father's presence at the head of the table, but the fourth chair sat empty. Nothing to be done about it tonight, he thought. Dinner, wine, and close companions would have to suffice in his absence, the reality precariously balanced against despair and his clandestine trips to the Frenchman's island.

Cohen glanced at Lizzie in the kitchen and lowered his voice. "You've acquired a most attractive cook," he murmured.

"I'm sure we're the talk of the town."

"I don't judge friends."

"Bring a lady friend and join us one night," Jesse suggested. "If she's not scandalized dining with us."

Cohen filled stemmed glasses and sampled the wine. "Maybe I shall." He poured three glasses almost full and continued with a lightness that surprised Jesse. "Perhaps I'll find a nice gentile girl if women of my persuasion continue to refuse my obvious charms." He placed the bottle in a silver wine coaster and lifted his glass toward Jesse. They toasted, and Cohen looked at Lizzie again. "As a bachelor, I envy you."

Jesse lighted candles and doused the lamp wicks around the room, the slender tapers imparting a convivial glow. He glanced at the front door where Dew's sudden arrival had altered two worlds. During dinner, they discussed Lizzie's work and the city's latest news. Cohen surprised Jesse again by assuming the role of an urbane dinner companion, knowledgeable about light gossip and the city's business matters. Jesse masked his thoughts with a forced smile, unable to take his eyes from the vacant chair. The next morning promised another visit to the jail and Lobeau's island. Worse, the river trip meant deceiving Lizzie again.

Time to end the charade, he decided.

As though affirming his uncanny ability, Cohen seemed to decipher his thinking, "Are you leaving us again tomorrow?"

Jesse drew a breath. "I'll be gone much of the day, but—"

He faltered, recalling another confession at the same table. The memory led back to Tyree and Charlie Rushton facing one another beside the deserted marsh. He wouldn't stand like a stone statue when another fool like Belden used him for target practice, but Randall Tyree distained pistols. He would leave him little choice except to swallow his insults or concede to swords. By meeting with Lobeau he'd drawn the line between being a plaster saint and defending himself despite the odds. Gathering his courage again, he looked across the table at Cohen, unable to meet Lizzie's eyes beside him.

"I'm taking fencing lessons," he said.

Cohen's fork froze in midair and Lizzie's body stiffened.

"Kerrigan's introduced me to a man trained in the art. An exile of sorts." Jesse kept his voice level as though details mattered. "He lives on an island near Skidaway River."

Lizzie folded her hands in her lap. "So you didn't travel on business."

Jesse held out his hand to her. She hesitated but took it, her fingers limp. "The situation's left me no choice."

"How often have you seen this man?" Cohen asked.

"Three times."

Lizzie, her disappointment obvious, asked, "Who is he?"

"A Frenchman named Lobeau. An ex-fencing master in Napoleon's army. I'm learning how to defend myself without attracting attention."

Cohen propped his elbows on the table. "And you believe he'll prepare you to face Randall Tyree?"

"I have to try."

Lizzie withdrew her hand and looked at Jesse. "This is—"

A knock on the front door cut her short. The memory of another interrupted confession overtook Jesse as he rose.

An impatient Elias stood on the front steps. Two horses sat at the front gate in the darkened street behind him, a slender rider barely discernible on one of them. Jesse looked closer and recognized Randall Tyree in the moonlight. His expression hidden, the apparition doffed his hat. Jesse turned back to Elias as Lizzie and Cohen joined him in the doorway.

"No need to knock, Elias," he said. "You're always welcome."

"I came for the last of my things." Whiskey fumes wafted into the hall.

"Come in and join us for dinner," Lizzie said.

Elias leaned past Jesse and gave her a chaste kiss. "I dined earlier at Randall's club."

Jesse stepped aside, and Elias bounded past Lizzie up the stairs. She joined Jesse in the doorway and looked at the shadowy silhouette in the street.

"Miss Pendleton," Randall called, his voice solicitous. "I regret disturbing your dinner. Your brother tells me you're making progress with your work. I congratulate you." His horse shifted beneath him and pawed the ground, gnawing at its bit until Tyree jerked the reins. "It's a gallant effort on your part, but we have the criminal behind bars."

Elias came down the stairs with a small satchel. He kissed Lizzie again and brushed past Jesse and Cohen.

Randall leaned forward in the saddle as Elias mounted. "Enjoy your dinner, Miss Pendleton," he said, "but please don't let me detain you. I know more intimate matters occupy you and Jesse."

Jesse stepped onto the porch, but Cohen restrained him.

"How kind of you to be concerned with matters that don't concern you, Mr. Tyree," Lizzie called. "You must have little else to occupy your mind."

Tyree laughed and the two figures trotted into the night.

Jesse listened to the fading hoof beats. They returned to the dining room and he became more convinced that providence appeared determined to mar his life by conveying a succession of catastrophes to his door.

"*That's* my brother's new friend?" Lizzie asked.

"Randall Tyree's a dangerous man," Cohen said. "You must persuade Elias to break away from him."

"He talks of nothing but fencing and this man whenever I see him." She looked unseeing at her half-finished dinner. "When he's not in his company, he lives in a barroom."

She sought a target for her grief and turned to Jesse. "You seem intent on joining their ranks." Anger built behind her eyes. "I wonder if you're man enough to walk away from a meaningless insult."

"I'd think less of myself," Jesse retorted.

"Dead men can't think," Cohen said.

"As a man, you must see my position."

"Don't be a fool."

Tired of recriminations, Jesse lashed back. "You can afford denial and ethics. Courtroom arguments won't protect me. I'm trying to survive."

"Then you're throwing away your life for some foolish Southern notion of honor," Lizzie said.

A quiet settled over the room as they stood behind their chairs and looked at one another. A certainty overcame Jesse, anger too long ignored, the remnants passed down by his mother. A gift or curse, he wondered? Raised by his father to believe a man's principles distinguished his worth, a baser force slapped aside such niceties. The perpetual war of conscience and desire, of principles and need. Standing in the candlelit dining room, he could not return to his former self, despite Lizzie's anger and Cohen's arguments.

"My intentions don't include getting killed," he said. "Or allowing my father to die in prison."

"Both of you will die if you persist in this!" Lizzie burst out.

Exasperated, he turned to her. "That's precisely what I'm trying to prevent."

"Lizzie's right," Cohen said. "You won't survive an encounter with Randall Tyree." He gripped the back of his chair harder. "We're close to formulating a viable defense for your father, but it means nothing if you're killed. Your death will only finish what the jail began."

Lizzie closed her eyes as though shutting out the possibility. "You have me, and there's a chance your father will be freed. Think beyond your pride."

"My pride?" Jesse exclaimed. "Do you believe this is about pride?"

"Behaving like Charles Rushton is not the answer," Cohen insisted.

Jesse exploded. "Charlie has nothing to do with my decision," he declared. "There's an end to anyone's endurance. I won't be killed like a lamb."

Lizzie fled the table. Jesse heard her footsteps on the stairs and let her go.

Cohen's voice pulled him back. "I understand your anger, but if this concerns your pride, you need to place boundaries on your temper."

When Jesse did not reply, Cohen saw the futility of arguing against willful blindness. He donned his coat and bid him goodnight, softly closing the front door behind him.

Jesse surveyed the half-filled glasses. He splashed wine into his own and marshaled his convictions. No middle ground appeared and his frustration mounted. Lizzie stood with Cohen, criticizing him through a prism of principles Jesse could no longer afford. Too exhausted to clear away the dinner's remains, he blew out the candles and climbed the stairs to Lizzie's room, carrying the wine bottle and two glasses. Uncertain what he'd say, he tried her door and found it locked. He called to her but his voice died in the empty hallway. Unable to endure another argument or defend his decision, he trudged to his room. He placed the bottle on the night table and stared at the wine, knowing it promised a temporary resolution to Lizzie's locked door. His thoughts raced ahead to the clearing behind the cabin. He picked up the bottle and set it down abruptly.

No, he reasoned. Better to face Lobeau with a clear mind. Without undressing, he fell back on the bed and lost himself to sleep inside the hushed house.

Chapter Thirty-One

April 8
Early Morning
The Caine House

Jesse awakened and found Lizzie had left at first light. A two-wheeled cart clattered outside his window. Filled with the day's fruits and vegetables, the pushcart's owner hawked his wares to housewives along Charlton Street. Dressing, he listened to the rickety conveyance rattle past the house, the peddler plaintively calling to closed doors and windows. He planned to rendezvous with Kerrigan at the riverfront and ride together to the river landing.

Sunlight sprayed across the dirt and cobblestone streets, slowly dissipating a thin layer of warm fog. Despite the sun's efforts, a doleful gray overcast reasserted itself before Jesse reached the river, the bleak canopy reflecting his dread of the coming day.

Kerrigan stood in the shade next to steps leading down to the wharf. He stepped from the shadows, hands buried in his coat pockets and shook his head as Jesse reined Aristotle, warily eying the horse. Kerrigan spat into the street and the stallion jerked away.

"Can't go today," he said. "Too much lost time. I get nothing but what's earned down here."

Jesse grinned at him. "You only want to avoid another horse ride."

"Can you handle the boat? Find the creek?"

"I think so."

Kerrigan glanced down at the river. "Four bloody ships due today. I'll have to earn what little they pay me with a day's sweat, but you'll be fine. Rowing loosens the muscles."

Jesse paid the wizened black man and they pushed the bateau into the river. Settled on the center seat he fumbled awkwardly with the oars as the black face observed the bateau slide into the river. After a few minutes, Jesse found a steady rhythm. The incoming tide was weaker but he managed to keep the boat in the channel, letting the current propel him down river, the tide doing most of the work.

Perched on one spindly leg a pristine white egret warily eyed his efforts from the muddy shallows. Perched on a spindly leg, the bird edged forward, careful not to frighten its prey, stiletto beak poised to strike until the head turned to follow the boat as it drifted past. Only the cries of curious seagulls accompanied his passage as he counted off familiar landmarks and found the telltale curve in the reeds. He backed oars and swung the bow into the creek. The marsh quickly closed behind him, and he allowed the tide to propel him through the familiar channel. The heat and humidity exerted their unpleasant existence, and sweat soaked through his clothing. The oars trailed in the water beside the boat, bumping the sides. The reeds pressed closer and the flow propelled him farther from the river until he entered the lagoon. He swung the bow toward the dock and bumped against a piling. The waiting dogs met his arrival with only a few desultory barks before the bandy-legged figure strode onto the dock, and Jesse tossed him a line.

"Kerrigan?" Lobeau asked in a flat tone.

"Working today."

Jesse jumped to the dock and they walked up the path, the dogs sniffing his footprints. The epées waited on the bench behind the cabin, the masks' empty eyes inspecting him. He stripped his coat, removed his boots, and pulled on supple shoes he'd remembered to bring. The raccoon hopped onto the bench and sniffed his coat.

Jesse indicated the inquisitive animal who pawed at the pile. "Is he my second today?"

"He will suffice," Lobeau said dryly. He donned his mask and walked into the open space, sword in hand, rolling his shoulders. Jesse adjusted his mask and faced him with the usual moment of trepidation.

The next fifteen minutes devoured him.

His arms and legs refused to settle into familiar patterns as Lobeau's attacks came faster, each movement more complex and indefensible. He slipped past Jesse's parries as though he'd learned or remembered nothing. Stung repeatedly by Lobeau's blunted tip, Jesse dodged away, feeling as though he'd never touched an epée. Determined not to give Lobeau the satisfaction of humbling him, he charged at him, finding only empty air. The glade rang with the blows, the Frenchman's normal rush of instructions and critiques lost in the relentless attacks.

Unable to keep him at bay, a lassitude overtook Jesse. Sweat soaked the stiff leather shield and ran into his eyes, and Lobeau seemed to time each blink to find his chest. Not benign taps but painful prods. Desperate to fend off the attacks, all thoughts of counter thrusts vanished.

The blunt tip vigorously rammed against his bruised chest again and Jesse gasped with pain. Lobeau stepped back and lowered the epée with a curt gesture for Jesse to do the same. He stripped off his mask and walked past him, leaving Jesse to stare at his back.

"We must talk," he called from the cabin.

Bent forward, hands on his knees, Jesse struggled for breath. Straightening with a slight groan, he pulled off the rancid mask and wiped his face with a sweaty sleeve. He touched his bruised chest and winced. The raccoon chattered and cocked its head at him as though confirming his shortcomings. Jesse slung his mask at the bench and the animal jumped down and preceded Jesse inside.

Lobeau waited with an open wine bottle. He poured two glasses full and corked the bottle. Jesse collapsed in a chair and took a grateful swallow. Birds settled in the trees, songs mocking the one-sided struggle that had just ended behind the cabin. Massaging his aching wrist, the rented boat tempted him. A short walk and he'd never see his torturer again.

Lobeau watched him, judging his anger and humiliation. He took a swallow of his wine and sat back, tapping a finger on the tabletop.

"*Je vous prie de m'excuser*. I apologize for handling you so roughly," he said. "It was necessary to—how do you say—hold a mirror in front of you."

Jesse regained his breath. "You did nothing wrong. I need to learn."

Lobeau waved him off. Running his hand through thinning black hair, he fixed Jesse with pitiless eyes. "Kerrigan is your friend," he began. "You trust him and that's good." He sipped the burgundy. "Trust only your friends. Other people show you only part of themselves. Kerrigan's a good man, but he did you no favor bringing you here."

Lobeau swept his hand over the table as though momentarily wiping away what he'd said. Jesse started to speak, but Lobeau cut him short.

"You have a measure of talent," he said, the teacher explaining the obvious to a slow student. "But competence is not enough." Better to be honest than have another dead man on his conscience, Lobeau thought.

"I told you my history, that I was fencing master of my regiment, defending its reputation. My position was no different from those in other regiments. But do you know why I survived? Why I lived to find myself on this forsaken island, telling you this tale?"

Jesse said, "You were the most capable."

Lobeau suddenly sat forward. "*Non!* Most *feared*. Feared before I even saw my adversaries. The code allows a scratch to end quarrels. To satisfy one's honor. I considered the decree silly and ignored it." He rubbed the scar on the side of his neck. "I gained my reputation by thrusting home in every instance. Never an exception. Not one survived, and many saw me as a cruel man, but I lived while others died."

Repelled, Jesse managed a nod. "I think I understand."

Lobeau slammed the table with his palm, toppling both glasses. "You understand nothing!"

He shoved his chair back and strode to the water basin. Wetting a cloth he wiped the table clean and righted the glasses, inspecting them as he regained his temper. "Better you avoid this man Tyree or find another way to dispose of him," he said. "If he's deserving of his reputation, he will kill you."

At a loss about how to respond to Lobeau's death sentence, Jesse said nothing. The dogs barked at something in the woods, and an aura hovered about Lobeau. Jesse guessed his long-dead victims never interrupted his sleep. The realization revealed the Frenchman's bond with Randall Tyree; Both killed without remorse.

I'm not like them, he thought.

Lobeau pressed a forefinger into his forearm and Jesse resisted the urge to pull away. "Kerrigan asked how many men I killed," Lobeau said. "I told him fifteen or twenty. I don't remember the exact number, but I left none with a wound." He refilled his glass.

"Defense and mercy will not keep you alive," he said. "Today I demonstrated what is required. You must have an element of *élan*, not simply skill, but also a desire to see your opponent fall. I doubt you possess that will, *Monsieur* Caine."

Jesse wanted to refute the little Frenchman's words, but nothing came.

Lobeau suppressed a smile, his expression quizzical. "I would like to observe this man who tempts you to throw your life away," he said. "To confirm the reason you fear him."

Jesse bristled. "I don't fear him."

"If he's as competent as Kerrigan claims, you should be very afraid."

Jesse remembered how Randall Tyree had toyed with Charlie Rushton. Charlie's child-like cry and blood on the leaves. Wounding Charlie would have ended the charade, Randall entertained no thought of mercy. Like Lobeau, killing assured his survival and reputation. Much as he wanted to live, Lobeau could not instill a bloodlust where none existed.

"We are finished today," Lobeau said. "Go home and think about what I've said."

They walked to the dock, and Jesse took his seat at the oars. Lobeau untied the bow rope and tossed it into the boat. Lobeau shoved the bateau away with his boot and watched Jesse disappear among the reeds.

The tide had rotated, rushing back to the sea. Jesse pulled hard against the outgoing current, missing Kerrigan's strong back. Lobeau's words returned and he rowed harder, trying to distance himself from the warning. A one-man fishing skiff steered past him in the opposite direction, drying nets draped over the boat's worn sides. Pungent fishing odors reached Jesse as gulls swooped and trailed in the larger boat's wake, devouring unwanted catch the fisherman tossed overboard. The stranger looked up and raised a hand, and for the briefest second Jesse longed for the fisherman's simpler life. He returned the greeting as the other boat's wake gently slapped the bateau's side. He redoubled his efforts against the current, the sun hot on his exposed neck. Lobeau's counsel refused to fade, a schoolmaster's lesson wasted on a hopeless pupil. Jesse tried to envision burying his blade in Tyree's body, but the image refused to materialize. Lobeau knew his mind: He'd hesitate and die.

Amid the passing beauty, Jesse's thoughts returned to Lizzie. She'd refused her bed the previous night. Jesse could not deny her fear that he'd attempt to affirm his manhood on some desolate piece of ground. Drained by the pull of heavy oars and newfound admiration of Kerrigan's strength, he rounded the final bend. The old caretaker stood at the water's edge. Jesse pulled hard at one oar and swung the flat-bottomed craft toward the hostile world that awaited him.

Chapter Thirty-Two

Jesse paid the old man and mounted Aristotle. Tiers of falling moss enclosed the road and formed a gray-lined cave, hoarding the day's heat. His bruised chest throbbed with each off-canter hoof beat. The empty road offered no answers. Lobeau's words refused to fade, assailing him like barbed arrows.

Thrust home... the killing stroke... no one left alive.

Enduring the horse's awkward gait he cast off the morning until Lobeau's prophecies faded to a manageable memory. Openings in overhead limbs splayed sunlight across the weedy road until ramshackle houses appeared at the city's outskirts. He slowly emerged from his chrysalis. He'd find a way to survive and make Lizzie understand.

He dismounted at Cohen's office and brushed at his coat as though he could wipe away the morning. He looped the reins over the hitching post and looked down the deserted street. The city remained inside, avoiding the heat as if someone had opened heaven's oven door. Inside, the two clerks acknowledged him as he walked into Cohen's empty office, the door to Lizzie's alcove open. Bent to her work she did not notice him until he rested his aching body against her doorframe.

"Am I allowed in your dungeon?" he asked.

She straightened, her expression trapped between surprise and uncertainty. She laid the magnifying glass on the desk without responding, and Jesse feared the worst.

He rested a hand on her desk. "I apologize for wearing two faces," he began. "It's not what I wanted. You're here to help me, and I've not been honest. You mean so much—"

She came around the desk and buried her face in his chest, arms locked around his back.

"I'm not as strong as you believe," she said. "I can't endure losing you and Elias." She leaned back, tears in her eyes.

"What's happened?"

"Elias's temper got out of hand," she said. "He's asked if he might return to your house."

"An argument?"

"There was a comment made about me at the City Hotel. Tyree laughed at the remark, and Elias shoved him. They argued and—"

"Elias must leave his house," Jesse said. "Where is he now?"

"I don't know. He takes his meals at several taverns."

"I'll find him and bring him home."

Lizzie grasped his hand. "I can't believe this would go any further."

Jesse pushed the door closed and kissed the top of her head. She raised her chin, and the kiss grew more urgent, her supple body molded to his. She clutched at him with a new desperation, and they heard voices from the anteroom. Lizzie pulled away as Cohen opened the door.

"Ah, you're back," Cohen said.

Jesse held out his hand. "I apologize for my remarks last night. You were a guest. Nothing personal was intended."

They shook and Cohen went to his desk. "You must know we both fear for you," he said.

Lizzie took a seat in front of the desk. "I'll abide by Jesse's decision," she said. Both looked at her. "If he's forced to defend himself, I'll try to keep good sense on his side."

Knowing her abhorrence to dueling, Jesse found yet another reason to love her. He looked at Cohen.

"Another problem has arisen. Elias quarreled with Randall Tyree," he said. "We need to stop him before the matter goes further."

"No challenge's been issued?"

"None we're aware of," Jesse said.

Cohen swore under his breath. "I'll have Robert and Charles look for him."

"Thank you," Lizzie said as Cohen went into the outer area to speak with the clerks.

When he returned she gathered herself and went to the work table. She reemerged a moment later with a sheaf of documents. "There's something I must show you."

She stood behind Cohen's desk and arranged the paper in two rows. Selecting a page from the first stack, she held it toward the desk lamp, her face suffused with discovery.

"Watermarks," she said triumphantly.

Jesse and Cohen blankly looked at one another.

"I could not find a single authentic page where your father did not use this brand of watermarked paper," she said. "The forger, however, used whatever came to hand without checking for the watermark."

Cohen took the page from her and held it closer to the light, while she withdrew another page from the second stack and handed it to him. "No watermark," Lizzie said. She picked up more sheets. "None here— nor here." Lizzie lifted a letter from Ambrose Caine's office and elatedly pointed to a faintly embossed mark. "This is missing from every forged document and letter of guarantee."

She turned to Jesse with exhilaration and pride. "Every true document bears this singular brand. Even his correspondence."

"And Mr. Caine's ink?" Cohen asked. "Have you an answer for it?"

She shook her head. "I can only surmise someone stole a quantity." She looked at Jesse. "How many people had access to his office and house?"

"Too many, I fear," Jesse said. "Friends, business associates, guests. They all knew about the ink and anyone could have taken a supply."

Cohen glared at the documents as though they'd won a point.

"There's something else," she said. She selected a page from the stack in question. "As you know, I don't subscribe to theories that a person's qualities can be determined by his handwriting, but our forger's hand is materializing through the fog. We see his presence in ways he never contemplated." She centered one of Ambrose Caine's documents.

"Look closely." A fingernail slowly underlined a sentence as she glanced at Jesse. "Your father's an engineer, meticulous in everything he undertakes. See how evenly spaced his handwriting appears, how uniformly words and letters are formed."

Jesse and Cohen bent closer as Lizzie skimmed her nail along multiple lines. She then placed a questionable page beside the document.

"As I made comparisons, it struck me the forger's words are not always evenly spaced. It's very obvious in several instances." She pointed "Here and here again. Even the placement of periods and commas is telling."

Cohen massaged the segregated eyebrow at the mention of periods again. "Small points in our favor," he said, "but time's running short, and placement of periods and watermarks may not be sufficient. We'll require far more to gain the jurors' attention."

Jesse guessed the reason for Cohen's pessimism. "What's happened?"

"The trial date's set. One week from today. Unless we apprehend the two men, everything rests on Lizzie's findings."

Seven days.

The surviving Mincey brother had gone to ground, and whereabouts of the stolen money remained a mystery. Without hard facts to dislodge judge and jury prejudices, Lizzie's work might well fall on deaf ears and neuter Cohen's courtroom skills. Robert knocked on the door and handed Jesse a note. His opened it and the world lurched again.

"My father's doctor asks that I come to the jail right away."

The afternoon was slipping away when Jesse arrived at the jail. The deputy led him on the now familiar trek underground, keys jangling on his belt in the stairwell. Jesse followed the uniform's back, stone walls mute witnesses to their passage as the man unlocked the final door. Somewhere in the building's depths, a piercing wail erupted and abruptly halted as if presaging disaster, leaving only echoes of the jailer's keys and his hobnailed boots.

Jesse's father was stretched full-length on the thin mattress, a stick figure beneath the soiled blanket. The covering rose and fell with shallow movements. Above him a black-coated figure pressed one ear to the frail chest. He acknowledged Jesse with a curt nod, motioned him outside, and opened a black leather satchel. The deputy left the cell door ajar and leaned against the wall a few yards away.

The doctor started to speak when his father opened his eyes and managed a feeble smile. "I regret bringing you back so soon," his father whispered hoarsely to the doctor. His fevered eyes found Jesse. "Knowing him these many years, I trust his judgment, but it's not as serious as he portends." A smile turned into a sodden cough that forced itself from his lungs. "I'll mend quickly enough when I'm permitted to leave these luxurious quarters."

Jesse said, "Just do as he advises, and we'll have you home soon."

Ambrose Caine struggled onto one elbow. Jesse observed the movement's painful effort as though glass shards had invaded his joints.

"Is Cohen making progress?" Ambrose asked Jesse.

The doctor closed his bag. "I'll be just outside if you need me."

Jesse waited until he joined the jailer and lowered his voice, recounting Lizzie's discoveries. His father listened to the revelations without hope. The minutiae and complexities of her work appeared small weapons against the mass of evidence. Jesse said nothing of the trial date, seeing no reason to have an ill man count the days until he was led into a courtroom.

Ambrose eased back onto the pillow, a different pain in his voice. "People *must* see I had no hand in this matter. I don't want the stigma of a thief as my epitaph." He arched his back and struggled for air as though speaking robbed what little breath lingered in corrupted lungs.

Jesse took hold of the skeletal fingers with hope he did not feel. "We'll uncover the truth. Kerrigan's helping, so all's not lost by any means," he said with contrived fervor.

His father closed his eyes, his breathing more shallow. His head lolled to one side and Jesse pulled the blanket over his chest. At a loss as to how to mend what remained of his father's hope and body, he remained kneeling by the bedside until the doctor placed his hand on his father's forehead, then checked his pulse. After a few minutes, he motioned Jesse outside and warned the jailer of his prisoner's condition.

"He's asleep, but I'll need to be called immediately if his condition worsens."

To Jesse's surprise, the man said, "I'll watch him."

Outside on the jail's steps, the doctor donned his hat and faced Jesse. "His condition's worsening. He never had the strongest heart, and I fear he now suffers from consumption as well." He waved a hand at the gray stones. "This will kill him if he's not released soon."

Time now joined the ranks of Jesse's enemies, an implacable adversary he could delay but not defeat.

Chapter Thirty-Three

April 9
Late Morning
Skidaway Landing

The small sailing skiff's prow buried itself into coffee-colored mud in mid-afternoon. The stooped black caretaker recognized the boat's sole occupant and waded out to pull the small craft ashore as its occupant collapsed the sail. Dressed in somber black, the slight figure jumped to the shore. The African nodded at his monthly visitor who returned the greeting. The apparition appeared from the river at regular intervals, rented a horse, and returned later in the day laden with provisions, vanishing again as quietly as a river spirit. The old man could not understand half what the ghost said, but he paid in gold.

Lobeau adjusted his cloak. He pointed to the two horses that nibbled feed behind the bateaus stacked on their sterns like muddy gray soldiers awaiting inspection. The caretaker brought out one of the horses, its roan coat surprisingly sleek despite the crude pen and animal's age. Lobeau dropped a gleaming coin into the creased pink palm, then saddled the animal with an ex-cavalryman's practiced movements as the old man watched.

Lobeau nimbly swung into the saddle and assessed the gunmetal sky with a soldier's eye. Clouds blotted the sun, but the weather held, and an hour later, he tugged at the reins as the docile horse halted on Bay Street. The river's stench had inched its way up the bluff. He never liked expanses of water, and endured his island exile only from necessity. Across the broad river, channel buoys clanged lonely greetings as wind stirred the water's surface.

Few people glanced at the black-garbed sprite who dismounted and secured the reins to an iron railing. The sky grew danker and raindrops dotted his outdated bicorn. He adjusted the hat, bounding down the steps to the wharf before the sky rebelled in all its fury. Hunched against a quickening breeze and the dock's stench, he stopped a stevedore and asked Kerrigan's whereabouts. The man pointed to a small brigantine half-hidden by stacks of wooden crates.

Lobeau heard the curses before he spied the imposing figure on the ship's deck. Hands on hips, Kerrigan ignored the incoming storm and shouted at the operator of a massive davit lifting the last crate from the deck of a towering five-mast barque. Kerrigan spotted the figure in black and jumped to the wharf.

"Lobeau!"

Kerrigan surveyed the sky as an army of purple clouds threatened the docks. Fixing Lobeau with a quizzical look, he steered the Frenchman toward the nearest tavern door. Fat drops bombarded the wharf like a drum roll as they reached the door.

"Get inside unless you favor drowning."

The Top Sail rivaled its worst competitors, besting only a few. Reeking of sour bodies and planked floors softened by spilled alcohol, the windowless cupboard served sailors who cared little about gentler amenities. A length of sawn lumber was balanced atop two barrels; three scarred tables kept the makeshift bar company. Kerrigan pulled out a chair for Lobeau and held up two fingers to the barkeep, but Lobeau waved the man away.

Kerrigan pointed at himself and a flagon of rum quickly appeared in front of him. "You don't come to town much," he said.

"I came to find you."

"A problem?"

Lobeau removed the old bicorn, palmed rain from it, and arranged it on the table. "I can no longer help your friend."

Kerrigan took a swallow and flung one arm across the back of the chair with a quizzical frown. "He needs you, Etienne. He's no other place to turn."

Lobeau shrugged, and a look passed between them. "He does not possess the instinct to survive. You understand me when I say he will think too long about what must be done. He will waver and die."

Kerrigan shrugged, "That may be, but sooner or later, he must fight." He drained the rum, licked his lips, and raised a finger toward the barkeep. "He'll have no say in what happens. I want to give him a chance to live."

"Then he must run. Leave the city. Begin his life again elsewhere."

"He can't. His father's dying in prison."

"Then it's a question of *when* he dies," Lobeau said. "If what you say about his enemy is true, your friend stands as much chance as a child with a wooden sword." He waited until the bartender placed the tankard in front of Kerrigan. "I might form a different opinion if I observed this Tyree. You are acquainted with him?"

Kerrigan shook his head and took a drink. "A gentleman above my station. Too high-toned for the likes of a river rat."

"This man involves himself in many affairs?"

"The next is scheduled today.

Lobeau frowned. "*Monsieur* Caine?"

"No. The brother of the woman Caine brought to Savannah. They're meeting at dusk near the old British redoubt."

"I know the place. A bad business that cost many French lives during your revolution."

"There's a Jew's cemetery's near the trenches. Walled off from prying eyes."

Lobeau inclined his head without taking his eyes from the tabletop. "Then I will delay my decision until after I observe this man." he said. He pulled a heavy watch from his vest and flicked open the engraved cover. Looking around, he frowned at their surroundings. "We have several hours to pass the time. Is there decent wine in this excuse for a *taverne*?"

Lobeau and Kerrigan walked westward along Bay Street toward the burial ground as the sun began its descent toward the horizon. A breeze from the river followed them, carrying the tang of low tide. From a distance the disparities in the two men made them appear father and son. They paralleled the river for several blocks and turned onto West Broad, leaving the waterfront at their backs. Eroded ramparts rose on their right, the old redoubt's round-shouldered berms once protective barriers for British defenders. Divine intervention proved stronger than muskets and cannonballs, and the British survived the attack along with the Jewish cemetery's stout walls.

Kerrigan placed his hand on Lobeau's back and pointed. Jesse and Cohen crossed the street ahead of them.

"Jesse!" Kerrigan called. "That's his attorney with him," he muttered to Lobeau.

"Bound for the gentlemen's affair?" Kerrigan asked with a rogue smile.

"We're come to stop it," Jesse said. He turned to Cohen. "Samuel, this is Etienne Lobeau, the friend who's advising me."

Lobeau bowed. Cohen said nothing.

Kerrigan wagged his head. "Too late. Blood's in the game now."

"A game for fools," Cohen said.

Lobeau's head snapped up but he said nothing.

"Miss Pendleton knows nothing about this," Jesse said. "Her brother issued the challenge to Tyree without informing her."

Jesse and Cohen disliked Elias, and only the fact he was Lizzie's brother drew them to the graveyard. Jesse glanced at Lobeau and assumed he was there at Kerrigan's invitation to observe Randall Tyree. A group of men walked past them and cast glances at the somberly dressed Frenchman.

Jesse and his companions walked along a weedy path that sloped from the street, ending at a walled enclosure. A hundred yards to the west of the ancient cemetery a persistent layer of impenetrable fog covered a forlorn swamp of rot and diseased water. A set of blackened cast iron doors stood open, facing the bog. Past the gates the burial ground bore no semblance to its counterpart that flaunted Revolutionary heroes, offering only a modest sanctuary and quiet haven for Jewish dead. Measuring a hundred feet square, the acreage had been granted by Oglethorpe to the first Sheftal family. Plain slabs of stone and marble adorned with Hebrew inscriptions honored the deceased, some topped with small rocks of remembrance. Inside the enclave, onlookers clustered along the northern wall, reminding Jesse of condemned men awaiting the firing squad. One broke away and closed the gate.

Randall Tyree was clad in his favored white shirt. A dour man in a black morning coat buttoned to the chin stood at his elbow, and Jesse recognized Harper Jerrard, Randall's perennial second. Randall caught sight of Jesse and broke away with a slight smile as though recognizing a friend. He inspected his companions and allowed his eyes to linger on the shorter man dressed in black who stared back at him.

Tyree bowed, his face flushed with barely concealed anticipation. "Welcome, gentlemen. Partaking in the day's entertainment?"

"Miss Pendleton asks you to walk away from this," Jesse said as though Lizzie was privy to the challenge. "She said you cannot offend her."

Randall Tyree drew back with mock seriousness. "I did not offend *her*. Indeed, it seems I offended her brother." He turned to Cohen. "As an officer of the courts, surely you see the difference, counselor."

A few yards away Jesse spied Elias talking with his seconds. He turned as Jesse touched his arm. "Your sister would not want you here," Jesse said. "You know her well enough to realize she can't be offended by the likes of Randall Tyree." Elias started to walk away, but Jesse stepped in front of him, ignoring glares from the two seconds.

"Please, Elias. There's nothing to be gained here.'

"You've no right to interfere."

Jesse led him to the nearest wall and stepped closer. "This is madness. He'll kill you without a second thought."

His face pale, hesitation stole into Elias's eyes. He dug at the ground with his boot toe without looking up. "I insulted him in front of his friends. I can't—"

"You can. You have only to apologize."

Elias chewed his lower lip and glanced at Tyree, who stood with his back to him. "He laughed when his friends insulted Lizzie. I don't want this, but he left me no choice."

Jesse stepped closer. "Dammit, there's always a choice. We'll walk out the gate together."

Charlie had rejected his similar plea, and the only remedy that would save Elias's life waited twenty paces away. "Say it was a rash act and offer an apology. No blame falls on you, and you can return to Boston if you like. Do it for Lizzie's sake. She'll only think more of you if you walk away."

A spark lighted Elias's eyes and he straightened his back.

"Tell her we'll discuss this tonight."

"Don't do this, Elias."

Harper Jerrard motioned to Elias who pulled away from Jesse and walked to the sullen figure, surveying the gravestones as though aware of life's finality for the first time. He stopped in front of Jerrard and Tyree. Searching the ground at his feet, he nodded mutely at Jerrard's instructions. Randall Tyree cocked his head at him as though their meeting meant nothing more than another fencing lesson. The seconds examined the swords and Elias shed his coat. Jesse started forward, but Kerrigan grasped his arm and shook his head. Elias followed Tyree to a grassy patch next to the eastern wall, an unhindered lane bordered by gravestones.

A chill crept over cold stone and brick walls. Tyree's blade tip toyed with the spring grass as though searching for something lost. He assumed his position on one side of Jerrard, twisting his neck inside his shirt collar. He measured the crowd's mood, nodding to friends as Jerrard took his accustomed place at center stage, prolonging the moment in the manner he knew pleased Randall. He raised his arms, brought the two swords together, and stepped back.

Tyree danced away. He darted backward as if fleeing a pursuer, drawing a ripple of uncomfortable laughter from several onlookers. He grinned and waved his epée above his head in a parody of confusion. Elias gave an uncertain smile and made several half-hearted thrusts, as though the late afternoon represented nothing more than a humorous diversion for his friends. His smile in place, Tyree stretched his arms wide, raised his eyebrows, and lunged.

Elias groaned and collapsed like a severed marionette, sinking to the ground as though sucked dry of bone and muscle. A small coin of blood appeared on his shirt and spread into a blossoming red flower. Tyree glanced at him and walked to his seconds.

Jesse rushed to the still figure as one of the seconds retrieved Elias's sword, its grip barely warm. Cohen joined them and started to speak when Jerrard stepped in front of the attorney.

"You have no business here," he said.

"You should be proud," Cohen said. "Elias Pendleton was little more than a boy."

"A boy who could not control his tongue." Jerrard inched closer. "You are defending Ambrose Caine, are you not, sir?"

"I am," Cohen said.

"Ambrose Caine is a thief," Jerrard declared loudly, playing to the crowd. "Accepting his stolen money makes you a thief as well." He drew himself up. "Anyone defending Caine is a poltroon not worthy to call himself a gentleman."

"Go away," Cohen said. "I don't converse with fools in public."

Stung, Jerrard faced Jesse. "Two thieves and one coward." He grinned at the hushed crowd, the faces eager for two spectacles in the space of a single day.

"Coward," Jerrard proclaimed more loudly.

Jesse stepped close to him. "Samuel Cohen labeled you a fool," he said, "but I doubt to have sufficient brains to attain such an elevated status."

Jesse caught Jerrard's intended slap in mid-air. He tightened his grip on Jerrard's wrist. Jerrard's eyes widened in surprise and he choked off a cry of pain. Jesse released him and gripped his coat lapels in both hands. Knuckles pressed against his windpipe, Jerrard staggered back. Jesse looked into the startled eyes.

"You want satisfaction? All right. I choose bare knuckles. Here in front of God and your friends." He shoved Jerrard back another step, fists jammed beneath his chin. "Strip your coat and shirt."

Unable to rein his anger, Jesse heard Cohen and Kerrigan from a distance. Spellbound, the crowd watched Jerrard clutch at Jesse's hands. Jesse's knuckles gouged deeper into the soft flesh, his pleasure mounting until Cohen pried his hands away. Jerrard fell to his knees. Jesse hesitated, then walked through the gates followed by Cohen.

Randall Tyree watched Jesse stride from the cemetery. He ignored Jerrard's distress, and wiped his blade clean with a fresh handkerchief, surprised by Jesse's assault. Handing his sword to a second, he slipped on his coat and followed the crowd through the gate, considering how he might exploit his temper.

Kerrigan and Lobeau remained among the gravestones in the empty cemetery. "I underestimated *Monsieur* Caine," Lobeau said with a hint of amusement. "I would not care to fight him with my bare hands."

"And his chances against Tyree?"

Lobeau walked to one of the stones and looked down at the inscription as though measuring the slab for himself. Tyree's confidence had reminded him of other assured faces now rotting in countries trampled by the Emperor's armies. The muted daylight slowly admitted

190

defeat, giving way to the impending night, and for the first time since the frigid retreat from Russia, Lobeau recoiled from the encroaching night. He longed for his dogs and a fire and the sanctuary of his river island. He'd killed enough men to last several lifetimes. In a surreal moment he'd witnessed another senseless death in a Hebrew graveyard in a strange land fate imposed on him. He studied the crushed grass at his feet.

"This man Tyree has skill," he said. "In our day, it would have been sufficient in one of the lesser regiments."

"And Jesse Caine?"

Lobeau studied the pool of congealed blood beside the wall.

"Fists are not blades, *mon ami*."

Chapter Thirty-Four

April 10
City Colonial Cemetery

Lizzie looked down at the newly-turned earth, Jesse beside of her. Cohen waited a few discreet feet away, hat in hand. A flawless spring sky ridiculed Lizzie's somber mourning clothes as she knelt beside the mound of earth, fistfuls of newly-turned dirt clenched in both hands. Jesse merged his pain with hers, glancing at the nearby plot where wilted flowers still covered Charlie's grave. He scanned the grounds for Kerrigan without expecting to see him. He suspected he attended few funerals. Elias Pendleton had meant nothing to him, and the Irishman would not choose to spend a morning above a stranger's grave. Lizzie swallowed a sob and smoothed the earthen mound.

"I could not bear a voyage to Boston with his remains." She looked up at the grove of young trees shading the grounds, green buds decorating the bare limbs as sunlight touched them. "This is such a lovely spot," she said. "He'll be content here."

Standing, she brushed the loamy coastal soil from her gloves. She kissed her fingertips and bent to touch the grave a final time as Cohen murmured a few words of Hebrew.

Two condoned murders, Jesse thought, looking back at Charlie's grave. Randall Tyree had assumed the role of the city's angel of death, wounded honor's appointed executioner. He wrapped his arm around Lizzie who laid her head against him.

"I feel responsible," he said. "Elias would be alive if you'd not come here."

Lizzie pressed harder against his shoulder. "No," she said softly. "You couldn't have saved him. Elias was determined to find an early destiny. I lost him long ago." She raised her head and looked at him. "I cannot understand this man Tyree. He pretended to be my brother's friend. Could he not have simply wounded him?"

Jesse recalled Lobeau's creed, a view mirrored by Tyree. "That's not who he is."

He led her from the gravesite, Cohen at their side. She looked back, her tears dampening the front of her somber dress. Jesse pulled her against him again as they walked in step.

"I know it's hard to understand, but Elias's temperament could not endure a slur, real or imagined," he said. "To your brother's way of thinking, Tyree left him no alternative."

Her tears started again. "My God," she sobbed, "he had to know words from such a creature meant little to me."

"I told him your feelings. In his defense, Elias acted as a man. Some insults are not turned aside by offering the other cheek."

She wiped a sleeve across her face. "Did this have anything to do with my work?"

Jesse looked at Cohen and wondered if he harbored the same suspicion. Had they been missing a piece all along? Elias had been a penniless outsider. Why had Randall taken him under his wing? They had shared nothing other than a preoccupation with fencing and pleasures of the City Hotel. Jesse could only surmise he pretended friendship to gain insight into Lizzie's progress.

Sharing Jesse's thoughts, Cohen said, "I'm uncertain of Tyree's motives as well. All this appears misaligned, yet somehow connected. Both Tyrees lost a great deal of money." He scrutinized the protestant stone crosses and elaborate burial vaults as if they held answers. "I'm convinced the scheme involved a local presence. Someone with ready access to your father's papers. Those who were cheated are all prosperous Savannahians. An outsider wouldn't know whom to approach, or who possessed sufficient capital to invest."

"The Tyrees," Jesse said.

"They're one possibility, but we have no proof. Still, they had keys to every door," Cohen said. "The canal documents. Information about the project. A simple matter to inflate projected returns and shift blame onto your father. They needed only a forger to complete the ruse."

"The Colonel lost money in the fraud," Jesse reminded him.

"So he claims."

"And the forger?" Lizzie asked.

Cohen's mouth tightened. "Ah, the missing piece. We need to produce him. Otherwise, we have a Herculean task, even with your discoveries. Remember, a jury of men will be trapped in a stuffy courtroom, eager for simple answers and anxious to return home for dinner." He turned to her. "Without meaning to frighten you, I worry about your safety now."

Jesse took her hand, hating the words even as he spoke them. "Do you want to leave? Return to Boston?"

"Running away accomplishes nothing," she said. "I'll finish what I started."

At Cohen's office, Lizzie walked straight to her desk. She quietly closed the door, removed her gloves, and climbed onto the stool, spreading her mourning dress about her. For a moment, she stared at the neat piles of paper. Tears welled up again, and she wept bitterly, her hand over her mouth to stifle the sound. When she finally caught her breath and wiped her cheeks, she dried her hands on the voluminous skirt. She picked up the largest magnifying glass and pulled a sheet of annotated drawings from the pile, anger overwhelming her grief. If there was any way she could bring her brother's killer to justice, she would be God's instrument.

Jesse followed Cohen from his office into the anteroom, where the two clerks heads buried their heads in their work. Cohen ordered them out of the office for the remainder of the day. Taken aback by the unexpected reprieve, they snatched up their coats and hurried out before he changed his mind.

Seated at his desk again and assured of privacy, Cohen gestured at Lizzie's door. "You're to be envied."

"No matter what she says, I caused Elias's death," Jesse said.

Cohen rubbed a hand in slow circles atop his desk. "Nothing of the sort. Elias was one of those people destined to make a lifetime of questionable decisions, the last one disastrous as it turned out."

"What you said at the cemetery. Do you believe his death's connected to the Tyrees and Lizzie's work?"

Cohen looked at Lizzie's door, deliberating. "Too many coincidences to ignore," he said. "The attempt on your life. The Colonel's lack of concern. Now Elias's death. If one looks closely, they appear to be erasing their trail."

"You suspect both of them?"

Cohen sat back and folded his hands over his lean stomach. "I've seen what Randall Tyree is capable of. He and the Colonel have done nothing to aid your father. Fletcher Tyree's a callous old man who lives alone in a house surrounded by his wealth. I don't pretend to understand him, but money's at the heart of all this misery. Loyalty and friendships are many times discarded when opportunity includes a fortune."

"We need to confront them," Jesse said. "If they believe we've uncovered evidence, they may make a mistake."

"Or kill you and Lizzie," Cohen said. "You'd hand them an engraved invitation to remove you both." Time spent in a courtroom with men like Randall Tyree left him aware of their boundless capacity for death and mayhem. He aimed a finger at Jesse. "Push a man like Randall too far, and he'll gladly accommodate your fencing fantasies."

When Jesse fell silent, Cohen smiled. "I didn't tell Lizzie about the encounter with Jerrard. Bare knuckles, indeed."

Chagrined, Jesse said, "Randall will opt for swords, but that doesn't assure he'll best me."

"Don't be a fool," Cohen said. "I watched him kill Elias Pendleton, and you witnessed poor Charles Rushton's death at his hands. Unless your Frenchman conjures up the patron saint of fencing, you stand no chance. I know nothing of this former soldier's skills, but I can't believe he'll create a master swordsman in the space of a few weeks."

Tyree's deft thrust at the plantation reappeared with sharp clarity. Jesse imagined himself beneath the same canopy of trees, sword in hand, a grinning Tyree circling him. Cohen saw what would happen, but he had no answer except to have Jesse turn away. Trapped in a netherworld between honor and revenge, Jesse faced the proverbial Gordian Knot with no choice but to continue with Lobeau and prepare for worst.

Chapter Thirty-Five

Same Day
The Fletcher Tyree House

"You *had* to kill him?"

Fletcher Tyree frowned at his son without expecting an answer. The afternoon was late, and he was too tired to press the point. The question assumed rhetorical proportions in light of the fact the boy's body occupied an undertaker's parlor. Randall's latest feat had already gone the rounds, much of the talk whispered behind closed doors as though people had grown weary of death as an entertainment. Drained, Fletcher thrust his disgust aside and thought about the Van Dyke. Due within the week, the painting's expected arrival was a balm. The anticipation of bearing it into the room where he sat reduced all other matters to distractions that failed to dampen his eagerness. He leaned back in his chair and basked in the anticipation of the arrival, picking with his thumbnail at the leather writing pad, subduing the temptation to turn and imagine the painting gracing the wall behind him.

His enthusiasm gradually faded as the day's events returned. He forced himself to regard the confident face seated across the desk. Another man, younger than most by all indication, had died by his son's hand. More distressing, someone linked to the venture he once considered iron-tight. He dug harder at the desk pad until his nail punctured the Moroccan leather. He stared at the damage and rekindled his anger. Immense wealth lay at their fingertips, but quietly taking possession of the money had careened off track due to a conceited fetish for dueling. Unexpected death tempted questions and complications, the city's funeral homes experiencing a windfall.

"Our original design did not include enriching every undertaker in town," Fletcher said.

Wearied by the harping criticism, Randall watched the older man's features shift from doubt to fear. Boyhood memories surfaced as though yesterday was a blink. The years had changed nothing; he sat in front of the elaborate desk while his father berated him. He'd endured endless hours awaiting the sentences of heavy-handed slaps or the barber's leather strap he feared most. Any violation or disobedience assured pain and humiliation. He now forced his body to remain motionless in the chair, suppressing the impulse to circle the room, smashing every object within reach, reveling in his father's cries of astonishment. Regaining control of his fantasy, he buried the impulse and sought simplicity for his father.

"The Pendleton boy was unplanned. A complication," he said. "A humorous remark about his sister got out of hand, and the little bastard shoved me in front of friends. What choice did I have?"

"If you wanted him removed, why not employ your friend?"

Randall waved a hand. "An unnecessary expense. There were witnesses to the insult, so why tempt investigation of a murder?"

His father winced at the word as Randall continued. "They all saw the provocation and will stand in my favor if need be." Randall kept his voice level. "No reason to panic, dear father."

"And young Caine?" Fletcher Tyree persisted. "This boy's sister lives at his house. People may see a connection."

Randall sighed. Even the cleverest and wealthiest men like his father evidenced a strange malady, an emotional shortcoming. The flaw surfaced as an inability to accept the truth if it proved inconvenient. Age appeared to exacerbate the hazardous trait, and the man sitting in front of him had grown older before his eyes, his comfortable world threatened.

"Disposing of Pendleton poses no danger to us," he said. "In any event, he was estranged from his sister, which lessened his value to us. Nothing more was gained by my continued association with him." Randall kept his tone light to placate his father. "Worse, he depleted my liquor cabinet at an alarming pace."

"And this handwriting diviner who's sleeping with Caine? What of her?"

"My guess is she'll return to Boston, the grieving sister."

"She might have done so sooner if you hadn't killed her brother. "

Randall drew another tolerant breath, weary of pointing out the obvious. "There's an ancient parallel," he said. "An Italian mercenary in the 1300s said, 'Kill them all and let God sort them out.' An overly pragmatic approach, but had I only scratched the boy, she'd have tended him while continuing her work. Odds are, she'll now leave our fair city."

His father opened the humidor and looked into the box. Empty. He held his hand out to his son, who produced a cigar and match. Fletcher applied the flame and squinted at his son through the smoke.

"You have a serpent's heart."

"And a knave resides in yours," Randall snapped. Years of resentment welled up. "I got rid of gratitude long ago. You gave me whatever I wanted because it made you feel good. I don't owe you a damn thing."

His father flushed. "You'd think differently if it disappeared."

"I'd live."

The exchange lay heavy in the silence that followed, venom neither could mend nor retract. Fletcher employed the silence to study his son. Even at a young age, the boy had exhibited more cunning than intelligence, his propensity for violence more prevalent as he grew older. After his wife's death, Fletcher recognized a larger void in Randall's spirit, as though his mother had taken part of him with her to the grave. The moral deficit grew, twisting itself from unpleasantness into something far more dangerous. When time permitted, Fletcher had made efforts to correct the boy's failings, but the years had passed too quickly, and he'd decided to overlook the faults, wanting his son near him as the years advanced. While Randall's extreme measures removed impediments with practical certainty, his decisions edged them closer to ruin. "None of that matters now," Fletcher said. "Too many people are dying around us. The man in North Carolina. His brother on Caine's ship. Now young Pendleton. Too much points at us if there's a mistake. Disposing of people never formed part of our plan. I retain a few principles even if you've misplaced yours."

Distracted by the assault, Randall did not allow his feelings to show on his face. He checked the empty humidor and wondered why were so many wealthy men parsimonious in small matters such as cigars. He lighted one of his own, mutely conceding his father's point about people dying around them. A collection of bodies increased the risk of blind luck raising its arbitrary head. He considered his father's reasoning and found himself in partial agreement despite the hand-wringing. Everything was progressing as planned, but violent death lingered in people's minds. Even the dullest had the maudlin habit of remembering what they viewed as tragedies, mulling them over and occasionally connecting dots. Much as he detested conceding the point, they needed to be careful as Ambrose Caine's trial approached. No matter his father's timidity, loose ends were dangerous. He inhaled deeply and sent a stream of smoke toward the desk, closing his eyes in thought. Who else stood in their way? Jesse Caine flailed about, and their forger remained invisible. If Caine challenged him, no blame attached to him or his father. Samuel Cohen had a keen mind and represented a legal threat, but he was hired help with no vested interest other than his fee. That left only the woman from Boston. Randall knew little about handwriting detection, but if she possessed the skills claimed by her brother, she could tip the scales of a vacillating jury. And with the elder Caine free, the authorities would begin their search again.

He drew at the cigar and considered the threat. In all likelihood, the woman from Boston embodied a forlorn hope, nothing more. The odds still favored them, no matter her claims, and if she stood in their way, she became expendable. His worries dampened, he envisioned the coming years of leisure: Membership at the finest gambling establishments. Travel abroad with female companionship of his choice. Satisfied, he started to speak when he heard voices. He pushed himself from the chair and walked to the window. A dozen slaves labored in the garden below. Absently calculating their value on the block he returned to his chair, his father worrying the strip of torn leather, his concerns unsatisfied.

"You and I made a decision when we began this ball," Randall told him. "We might be pirates, but we're egalitarian pirates. We lifted purses only from those who could afford the loss and chose to dance with the devil, adjusting what you call morals. We did nothing more than thatching our desires to opportunity, different as they may be. We were both fully aware what we were doing."

Pleased when his father remained silent, he smiled at the downcast face. "Rest easy, dear father. The dance is almost over."

Chapter Thirty-Six

April 11
Mid-Morning
Samuel Cohen's Office

Lizzie stopped counting her hours behind the closed door. Time dampened her grief and narrowed her world to the confined space. She sat back on the high stool, arched her back, and promised herself that her deepest grieving was at an end. She'd always revere his memory but Elias could not be returned to life. Life went on. She looked at a document, the words and letters of old friends. She ran her fingers lightly over the page, the ridges and indentations of pen and ink comforting in their familiarity. She loved the mysteries of her work, but Jesse had provided meaning to her life, a new beginning in the eccentric city.

With Elias gone, her family was dissolved in its entirety. She remained sole heir to very little. The small house and a modest amount of money, but the Pendleton line ended with Elias's death. She'd suppressed the briefest temptation to bolt back to Cambridge and the familiar, but Jesse stood as a bulwark in her life now. Jesse and the demands of her investigation proved an ally and strange comfort, absorbing much of her grief. Without them, the days and nights would have been intolerable. Ambrose Caine faced trial in matter of days, and her will to free him provided the blessing of diversion.

Relieved when Jesse tapped on the door, she shoved aside her work and joined him for lunch. Moss-weighed limbs formed a botanical cavern as they walked through the succession of squares. She drank in the points of dappled sunlight speckling the sidewalk as though spring was attempting to make amends for her sorrow.

Stepping from the sidewalk to cross the street, she stumbled, and her ankle boot submerged beneath a patch of glutinous mud. Jesse tugged her foot free without the laced boot that disappeared beneath the mire. He picked her up and carried her across the street, setting her on the boardwalk. She looked back at her footwear's final resting place.

"One shoe on and one shoe off, as the nursery rhyme says," she said, surprised at her capacity to feel amusement again. She leaned against Jesse and lifted her muddied foot above the rough boards, grimacing at the ruined stocking until she laughed.

"A delightful way to enliven my appetite. The perfect lady."

"Very stylish," Jesse said, relieved to hear her laugh. He led her limping to the nearest lady's shop, a trail of sodden footprints behind her. She pretended to ignore amused stares and he waited outside until she reappeared and raised the hem of her skirt to expose new cotton stockings and fashionable black boots.

"Whole again," she said. She hooked her arm in his when a voice called to him.

"Jesse!"

Victoria Danford waved a white-gloved hand and rushed toward them, a lacy pink parasol in her other hand. Her pleated gown of yellow silk glowed with newly-bought intensity, its high waist tightly pinched. She stopped squarely in front of them and snapped the umbrella closed, teardrop-shaped gold earrings dangling like gold commas beneath lustrous golden curls. Her face flushed and oblivious to Lizzie, she took Jesse's arm as he swept off his hat.

"You've been avoiding me," she said.

"There hasn't been much time for visits." Ill at ease, he watched the two women appraise one another with judgmental expressions women fashioned only for one another.

"Victoria," he managed, "this is Miss Elizabeth Pendleton. Lizzie, Miss Victoria Danford."

The two women touched fingers and Victoria cocked her head at Lizzie. "Pendleton? I don't believe I know any Pendletons."

Jesse could not help but compare them: a dark-skinned beauty with vestiges of a Tuscany vineyard, and blond goddess with hints of the fjords. Victoria ignored Lizzie as though she'd evaporated from the sidewalk. Eyes aglow, she tightened her grip on his arm. She started to speak again but stopped, searching the street as though someone might be watching them. The awkward silence lengthened until Lizzie glanced at Jesse. He started to speak when Victoria pulled him closer with an intimacy that embarrassed him, beaming as she pushed aside a wisp of wayward hair and gazed up at him.

"You must visit me," she gushed. "I have so many wonderful things to show you."

Jesse risked a glance at Lizzie, who stared at the spectacle in yellow. "We'd love to come," he stammered.

Victoria's words tumbled faster, ignoring his discomfort. "Mother will make tea for us. I found the most delightful Ceylon variety, a new blend. You know how foolish I can be, but the flavor and aroma are simply exquisite. You must come and sample it. Men of your breeding appreciate finer things."

Before he could reply, she removed a glove and presented an oversized concoction of bright stones on her ring finger.

"It arrived yesterday from one of New York's finest jewelers." She cast a quick glance at Lizzie, disappointed when she failed to inspect the stones more closely.

Anxious to escape and unable to frame a response, Jesse said, "We'll try to visit. Just now I'm expected at Samuel Cohen's office."

Wide-eyed, Victoria gave a high-pitched laugh. "Of course. I have business meeting to attend to as well. There are papers I must sign to complete the sale of Aaron. Fortunately, we acquired him at such a reasonable price."

"He's your slave?" Lizzie asked.

Victoria momentarily looked perplexed. "Of course."

"Did he consent to being owned by you?"

Victoria's brow constricted and Jesse headed off the storm before it broke.

"Did you get the part in the play?" he quickly interjected.

"I'm no longer concerned about such things," Victoria's smile brightened. "There are more important matters now. I can't concern myself with the theater's poor judgment in new actresses." She looked at Lizzie again as though seeing her for the first time.

"Jesse, do tell me your companion's name again."

Jesse extricated his arm from her grasp and placed it around Lizzie's waist. "Victoria, this is Elizabeth Pendleton. She's working with Samuel Cohen to prove the evidence against my father are forgeries."

Victoria blinked. After a few seconds she leaned toward Jesse again and lowered her voice as though Jesse had not spoken.

"The city's abuzz with talk of the latest duel," she said. "A young man named Elias Pendleton. Randall killed him in a duel, poor boy." She looked at Lizzie. "Were you related?"

Thrust into a strange game without rules, Jesse said, "He was Miss Pendleton's brother." At a loss, he replaced his hat, not risking a glance at Lizzie. "Now you must excuse us if you will, Victoria."

"They offered me the role of Queen Gertrude in *Hamlet*," Victoria blurted, "but I refused it," she added with a note of pride, her eyes ablaze. "They'll see their new actress is not up to my standards. They stole what's rightfully mine."

Head raised, she walked around them with a swish of silk, leaving the lush fragrant scent of lavender in her wake. Jesse and Lizzie watched her divide an oncoming crowd of men like a ship's figurehead, smiling acknowledgment to bowing admirers.

Lizzie stared after her. "Is she always so peculiar?"

"I can only tell you she's not herself. Did you detect alcohol or spirits of any kind? Some other stimulant?"

"None." Lizzie's eyes followed her until she turned a corner. Jesse took her arm to go but she stopped him. "I never met her before today, but there's something strangely familiar about her."

Chapter Thirty-Seven

April 12
Morning
The Randall Tyree House

Randall Tyree took no pleasure in sunlight that spilled through his living room windows. He craned his head against the panes and surveyed the length of West York. His house commanded the street, the tree-shaded avenue more than suitable to complement the structure. The tableau seemed arranged for his enjoyment, but he took no pleasure in the setting today. The sun did nothing to brighten his mood, and he did not look up when plum-colored clouds obscured the rays.

He walked to a small sideboard, poured a large brandy from a crystal decanter, and returned to the window to await the coach that would inevitably appear. Glass in hand, he fully expected its arrival although he'd warned his visitor to stay away. A moment later, a liveried slave deftly maneuvered the coach to the curb. Victoria Danford stepped down, the hem of a yellow gown gathered in both hands above her ankles. He admired her grace in spite of his mood, but a garish ballroom gown in mid-afternoon? It was as though she desired every eye on the block to witness her arrival. Randall could not hear her instructions to the driver but showed no surprised when the slave climbed onto the driver's seat and propped a boot on the driver's board, signaling his mistress's intent to visit.

Randall made no movement toward the front door. His annoyance building, he watched her gracefully ascend the coiled steps. In spite of his irritation, he admired her grace, wondering why so many attractive women lacked common judgment in significant matters. Whorehouses offered simpler options—and more variety—without the tedious task of attempting to balance beauty with brains.

He finished his drink and stepped away from the window, waiting until she rapped the brass knocker, the echo hollow in the hallway. He slowly walked to the sideboard and replaced the glass before returning to open the door. Victoria walked past him and he quickly closed the door. Smiling, she swept into the parlor, stopped, and whirled to face him. Her smile faltered as she saw his annoyance.

"You appear upset, Randall. Did you not receive my note?"

"Obviously I did since I replied to it," he snapped. "I asked you to come after dark."

"Why should anyone be curious about my coming here? They'll merely believe you're courting me again. Or have you forgotten our delightful fling?"

"Does Caine know about us?"

"Why would he? I just talked with him and the woman from Boston. He has no reason to believe we're other than casual acquaintances." She inclined her head to one side and smiled coyly. "But *I* have the most delightful memories of New Orleans." Enjoying his discomfort, she twisted the barb.

"He'd be shocked to learn we were lovers."

"Better you keep it that way."

He indicated to a chair away from the window, and she raised her right hand as she sat. "You haven't seen my new ring," she said. Distressed when he showed no interest, she rotated her wrist and admired the purchase in a singsong voice. "An emerald attended by a court of little diamonds. I required a bauble to brighten my day."

"I'm more interested in your conversation with Caine."

Exasperated, she dropped her hand and surveyed the room, dismayed as usual by the hodgepodge of children's toys and rows of dreadful swords. She'd stayed overnight in the house only three times, their brief affair limited to sweaty liaisons in his bedroom and luxurious New Orleans hotels on occasion. But this *room*. She made no effort to hide her disapproval. So strange, she thought. Devoid of a gentleman's taste and civility despite his wealth. She decided the room contained nothing of real value. She'd once heard the Colonel express the same sentiment, glad an experienced man of his position sustained her opinion.

Perched demurely on the edge of the chair, she said, "You're not yourself today."

Randall sat down and watched as she rearranged folds of glossy silk and admired the ring again. Forearms on his knees, he leaned close. "You talked with Caine?"

"He believes our documents are forgeries," she said.

"The woman told you that?"

"No, Jesse told me. You don't listen to me."

"And you believe him?

"You assured me no one would detect differences in the writing," she said. "I used the ink your father provided." She pouted with disappointment honed by the stage. "You even used the word *perfect*. How could she know?"

Randall folded back in the chair. "*How* doesn't matter."

Victoria lifted her hand toward the window to admire the light's play on the emerald before her eyes widened.

"What if someone believes her, Randall? You said we'd remain hidden. I don't want to go to jail." Panic edged her voice, reminding him of his father's timidity.

"It's unlikely people will take her seriously," Randall said. "She's only a woman. "

Victoria's sensuous mouth firmed. "*I'm* only a woman, and they believed my work."

Randall waved his arm.

"It suited your purposes, so don't patronize me, Randall."

A corner of his confidence crumbled. He stared at her, anger and confusion rearranging her features. He thought back to the beginning when he'd discovered her cleverness. In a playful moment he'd asked her to forge a note from his father to Charbonneau, the New Orleans casino owner. She'd looked at a letter from his father's office and copied the handwriting with amazing clarity. Half-dressed in the middle of his bed she'd teased him by making him choose between her reproduction and the actual letter. He could not. The ploy had bought him time with the gambler. Her talent astounded him and she'd succumbed to his praise at the same moment her usefulness came into focus. It had started as a game. They'd laughed at their success and her startling skill. Randall could never explain her talent. Some trick of nature endowed her with mimicry. Her skills with the watercolor brush and acting ability seamlessly morphed onto the written page. The discovery had been a godsend, the missing piece of a plan that lacked only her bizarre ability.

Dismayed now by the birth of fear in her eyes, he abruptly leaned forward and clutched a handful of yellow silk in his fist, pleased when she recoiled.

"You were well paid for your work."

Victoria snatched the material from him. "Randall! You forget yourself." She smoothed the fabric. "I need more, another payment."

Another payment.

Randall's burgeoning sense of uneasiness rose full blown, his trust in her flaking away like summers of sun-baked paint. The ring consumed her again, her revelation about the woman dismissed or forgotten.

She refocused on him, her tone clipped and more confident.

"I *need* the money," she said. "There's a marvelous house on Abercorn. My mother desires it, and I intend to buy it before the week's out."

"Victoria—"

"Of course, you and your father will be invited to our first party. We'll invite all our friends." She smiled warmly at him. "It'll be glorious."

Randall admired the sudden flush of excitement, one he knew well from their uninhibited romps in New Orleans and nights in his bedroom. An emotion approaching sadness touched him as he foresaw the future. He composed a cold smile.

"Of course," he said. "The money's well earned."

He got to his feet and went to a small writing desk. His back to her, he pressed a concealed lever. A small drawer within the woodwork sprung open, and he counted out a sheaf of bills. He handed the money to her.

"Forgive my earlier abruptness. That should keep the seller happy until you negotiate a mortgage." He coerced another smile. "Go buy your new house."

Victoria tucked the bills inside her bodice, and he followed her to the door, her face radiant again. "I have so many new things that will look wonderful in the house. When this awful matter with Jesse and his father is over, you'll be our first guest."

Aaron sprung from the driver's seat to open the carriage door, and Tyree glanced up and down the street as she slipped inside. Hoping his neighbors had more important tasks than gazing out their midday windows, he experienced a stab of remorse as a yellow sleeve waved from the coach window. He returned the wave, and Aaron snapped his whip above the horses' heads.

He closed the door and poured a drink, his tremulous hand wrinkling the brandy's surface. He glared at the glass and waited until his hand obeyed his will before he lifted whiskey to his lips. He sat down and replayed the disquieting scene.

Why did the simplest part of a machine fail, he mused? In the beginning, she'd played the role of a somewhat delighted accomplice, pleased to earn the money and his admiration. In Randall's experience, people took your money and demanded more only when you showed weakness or chose them poorly. Victoria began without guile, wishing only to fulfill some fantasy: With the right trappings, she and her mother would enter Savannah's tightly wrapped society. At least that had been his estimation. He wondered now if he'd underestimated her from the beginning. The finely-tuned mechanism he'd nurtured appeared to have more gears and wheels than he initially imagined. A rare error in judgment on his part. His instrument emitted a grinding as greed raced past the reality of their situation. If her avarice trumped the potential consequences, they were all in danger.

A knock interrupted his thoughts. He put down the glass and went to the kitchen, opening the door. A rush of sweaty clothes brushed past him. Randall relocked the rear door and they sat in opposing chairs in the parlor, away from the windows.

"I saw our little helper's carriage out front," the new arrival said. "Brand new rig with a blackie up top. Coming up in the world, is she?"

Randall retrieved his glass and emptied the contents in a single swallow.

"So it seems."

"I waited out back until she left."

"At least you had the good sense not to be seen."

He shot Randall a humorless smile. "Despite your father's doubts, my kind knows the back door."

Randall filled a second glass and handed it to him, refreshing his own. He resisted the urge to gulp it down as he firmed his decision.

The new arrival took a swallow and held the glass toward the window with an appreciative smile, inspecting the contents. "Mother's milk." The grin fell away when his host did not respond.

"You've found trouble," the man said. "Not a good sign."

Vaguely appalled the man's clothing transferred a layer of grime onto the velvet-covered chair, Randall managed a shrug. He'd discovered his guest by a stroke of luck, discerning an innate intelligence with an alley cat's instinct for survival. In other circumstances, Randall might never have spoken to him, but he'd needed a blunt weapon, one who remained malleable so long as money flowed into his pockets. The reek of work clothes grew stronger, and he offered the guest a cigar to appease his olfactory senses. He waited until the tip glowed and the man's eyes narrowed in pleasure.

"As you surmised, an issue has arisen," Randall said, pleased when smoke overpowered the scent of hard labor.

"An issue."

"Miss Danford, to be precise."

The man raised an eyebrow. "You mean she's become a problem."

"She's moving away from reality."

The man spat a shred of tobacco onto the floor. "Forget the fancy damn words. Just say what you mean."

Randall bristled, then relaxed. He'd calculated the risks, but hesitated again until the man pointed the cigar at his face.

"There's always answers for them what forgets their place."

Randall abandoned any lingering reluctance in face of the man's outspoken verdict. "It would benefit both of us."

His visitor poured another drink and resumed his seat, amused at the tiny fracture in Randall's smugness.

"You're behind on what's already owed me. That's why I'm sitting here drinking your whiskey."

"My father controls the purse strings," Randall reminded him.

"Your problem, not mine. My money?"

Randall lifted his palms. "Miss Danford temporarily depleted my reserves just now. She demanded money to buy a new house."

The man smiled and revealed surprisingly white teeth. "A house? And you gave her my money?" He looked around the room and wondered where Tyree hid his money. He gestured at the marbles and shelves of soldiers. "How do you intend to pay me? With children's play pretties? Or perhaps the paymaster of your little army will produce what's owed me."

"You'll be paid."

The man puffed appreciatively at the cigar and licked his lips. "Add another five hundred if you want your new problem to go away." When Randall paused, the man downed his drink. "Dirty work's expensive. You and the Colonel can afford it."

Randall inclined his head in agreement. Survival trumped money. "There's also the Pendleton woman," he said. "I'll pay double when both women no longer trouble us."

The man placed his empty glass on the floor by his chair and shook his head. "I draw the line at killing one woman."

Randall sat back, surprised at the creature's reluctance to enlarge his purse. The refusal made the woman from Boston his personal problem. If he wanted to ensure she never saw the inside of a courtroom, another solution would be required.

"Agreed," he said. "Just so our forger is removed."

"And if something happens to you? No one will believe you owed the likes of me."

Randall saw the logic, much as it displeased him. He'd repeatedly reminded his father they needed the man's coarser talents. For awhile longer at any rate. Randall smiled. In the end, a quiet reckoning in some out-of-the-way venue would dissolve their association.

"Will an IOU calm your fears?"

"Cash is better, but you're a gentleman." The man grinned. "No need to fear you or your father not keeping your word, is there?"

"Of course not."

"Better, though, if you'd not paid our actress anything."

"Given her state of mind, I had no choice." Randall sat at the desk. "The money bought time to resolve the issue."

He removed a sheet of embossed stationary, dipped his quill in the well, and penned an IOU, signing it with a flourish. To further allay Kerrigan's fears, he creased the paper and held a candle beneath a soft red stick, dripping sealing wax onto the fold. He pressed the family seal into the wax and blew on it, the delay allowing him to confirm what must be done. He handed the folded note to the man who slipped it into his coat pocket. Randall rose and walked him to the kitchen door, indicating an end to their meeting.

"If you find the money I gave her, keep it as a bonus," he said. An expensive gesture but he also knew the man would never admit to finding it. Another pang of remorse overtook him, but he brushed it away. "Make it appear a robbery. Help yourself to anything else in the house, but be careful how you dispose of anything. Savannah's a small city."

"And the woman from Boston?" The man looked at the display on the far wall. "You can't use one of your fancy swords."

"She's my concern. Her death won't concern anyone but Caine." Randall started to open the door and stopped. "But let's increase the odds in our favor, shall we? A disaster at Mr. Cohen's office could be most beneficial. If a fire should occur, there'll be a bonus for you. Just be careful and make it appear an accident."

"You're telling a blacksmith how to shoe a horse."

"Finish this now," Randall said. "The time's past for loose ends."

The man nodded and Randall let him out.

Chapter Thirty-Eight

Same Night
Coach and Six Tavern

"Damn all hell!"

The outburst drew quizzical looks from Robert's friends. The youthful law clerk chastised himself for swearing aloud but the outburst had sufficient cause. Cursing again, he found his hat and coat and started for the tavern door before he caught the publican's accusatory stare. Abashed, he mumbled an apology and slid money onto the bar to pay for his drinks before he stepped into the night.

Head down, he hurried from the Barnard Street Inn and wove his way through unlit streets to Cohen's office. As senior clerk, his responsibility included assembling assigned precedents, leaving the marked volumes on Cohen's desk for inspection the following morning. It required no more than fifteen minutes to mark them before he left each day, but the lure of ale and female company had overwhelmed his routine. The lapse, in his opinion, was completely understandable, given the amount of work heaped on him and his co-worker.

A light drizzle fell and the clerk jammed his new top hat more tightly atop his head, attempting to protect it with both hands. The pose made him appear somewhat ridiculous as he broke into an awkward sprint, but the hat was worth humiliation. His splurge on new haberdashery would be ruined if rain penetrated the silk. He quickened his pace as larger drops fell from overhanging limbs. He'd considered coming in early next morning to pull the citations, gambling on Cohen's late arrival, but changed his mind. Not worth the risk, he decided. Savannah offered few openings for law clerks, and he couldn't risk Cohen's displeasure. The office was only four blocks from the tavern; he'd be back in a matter of minutes.

Turning the corner Robert pictured the five volumes stacked beside his desk. He's been careful to place them in plain sight as a reminder—then promptly forgot about them. He needed to make a final check to be sure he'd marked all of them, but the night could be salvaged if he hurried.

Back at the inn in less than an hour, he thought.

He mounted the office steps two at a time, anticipating the remainder of the evening. Reaching for his key, he wondered if he could cajole friends into the next round of drinks. The rain fell harder and cascaded from the eaves onto his back. He hurriedly removed the hat and held it against his chest, aiming the key toward the lock. He blinked and stopped. The front door stood open.

I locked it before I left.

The rain poured into the street behind him, his hand inches from the doorknob. He tentatively pushed the door open and peered into the anteroom that appeared empty. His sleeve snagged something and he noticed the door lock dangled by a single screw, the stout wooden jamb splintered. Tempted to find a constable, he looked into the darkness until the murky interior proved irresistible and he stepped inside.

His desk occupied the far corner of the sable-black room. Nothing appeared out of place. Tiptoeing across the space and feeling slightly foolish, Robert made out the five volumes stacked beside the desk. As his eyes adjusted he saw Cohen's open door, a door he *always* closed and locked before he left. A light flared inside the office and sputtered out. Robert froze in the doorway. A shadow moved. Another match quavered and he crept into the office, his brain screaming at him to run.

A tower of flames suddenly erupted next to Cohen's table. A second fire leapt up, then another, illuminating the other door where the woman worked. A figure crouched by her door, shoving paper into a pile. A match flared and Robert heard himself yell.

The silhouette straightened and spun in his direction. Backlit by the flames, the massive shape crossed the office with surprising speed. Robert staggered back, unable to make out the intruder's face. He took another step back, and the recesses of his mind registered a flicker of recognition. The way the figure moved. An unpleasant odor. He turned and made it halfway to the door before lightning exploded behind his eyes.

His head thumped rhythm with dull pain's cadence. A strong arm held him in a seated position, the seat of his trousers soaked through, his clothes clinging to his body A light rain still fell, and a confusing maze of boots encircled him.

Why was he sitting in a wet street, he wondered?

More pain collected at the end of his left arm. He lifted his hand in front of his face, surprised to see the palm and fingers wrapped in a thick bandage. The crowd moved closer and he winced as the pain flared again. Disoriented, he ran his other hand over his scalp to find his lank blond hair soaked. He touched the bandaged hand and winced again.

"My hat," he mumbled.

Cohen squatted beside him and lifted a flask to his lips. He swallowed a mouthful of good brandy and coughed.

Cohen squeezed his shoulder. "Robert, can you hear me?"

The brandy caught in his throat and threatened to reappear in the street. He blinked rainwater from his eyes and twisted his head toward the office. Men stood in line along the steps and passed buckets hand-to-hand past the damaged door. A sheeted waterfall ran down the steps, tendrils of gray smoke drifting from the interior. He ran his bare hand through his wet hair and recalled the fire and hulking figure.

My God, the intruder had been immense!

Cohen thumped his shoulder. "You were fortunate. A constable saw the open door and smelled smoke. He dragged you out of the flames and found help. Your hand's burned but not seriously. "

The stench of charred wet wood grew stronger as the crowd broke the circle around him. Cohen ignored the remaining gawkers and helped the clerk to his feet. The rain petered out, and Cohen offered the flask again. Robert unscrewed the top and drank deeply before he returned the pewter container.

"Are we ruined?" he asked.

"Most likely but for your timely return."

"I forgot to mark the precedents," Robert confessed.

Cohen laughed. "As they say, it's an ill wind that blows no good." His arm around the slender waist, he smiled at the confused face. "You saved the office."

Robert, surprised by his boldness, asked, "Perhaps another swallow of your brandy?"

Cohen turned the flask upside down. "Empty," he said.

"I'm sorry." Then, "How much damage was done?"

"The floor will have to be replaced," Cohen said, "and the remains of my table will make fine kindling next winter."

"And Miss Pendleton's work?"

Cohen lowered his voice. "We lost some papers and books, but nothing of consequence. She removed much of the critical evidence to Mr. Caine's home several days ago." He lowered his voice.

"Keep that information to yourself," he said to the wide-eyed clerk. "If asked about the fire, you're to say nothing about what was lost."

Relieved the attractive woman's labors had survived, Robert gritted his teeth as fresh pain gnawed his wounded hand. His hand throbbed in unison with his head, and anger mixed with the pain as he realized how close he'd come to being killed. Assaulted and left to die in a burning building! His head grew light at the thought, but he kept his feet. The brandy spun his brain round. Ignoring Cohen's warning, his outburst turned heads in the crowd.

"We'll see the bounder pays and buys me a new hat!"

Chapter Thirty-Nine

Next Day
April 13
Cohen's Office

The rasp of saws greeted Jesse as he stepped inside Cohen's office. The room stank of charcoal and blackened wood. Pungent layers of ripe golden sawdust dusted the scarred flooring where Cohen's table once stood. Two workmen pried up a charred plank, while a third sawed new boards. Cohen stood over Robert at the fireplace, one hand on the clerk's back. The clerk, his bandaged hand at his side, knelt at the grate and shoveled ashes into a coal bucket with his uninjured hand. The window stood open in reluctant homage to the noise and heat.

Cohen saw Jesse and stepped over a pile of lumber. Oblivious to the carpenters who hammered new flooring into gaping holes, he motioned Jesse to an undamaged rocker.

"The other was lost," he said.

Jesse yelled over the hammering, "What the devil happened?"

"A fire last night," Cohen said.

He waved Robert and the carpenters outside and Jesse stripped off his coat. Cohen waited until the clerk closed the office door.

"Someone tried to burn us out," he said. "Robert returned after hours before the fire spread." Cohen said. "He surprised the perpetrator who knocked his head about."

"Is he all right?"

"Other than a headache and scorched hand, he's fine."

"An unhappy former client?"

"Or someone connected to your father's case."

"Which means we may be closer than we thought," Jesse said. He looked at the window and cold fireplace. "At least you've conceded summer's arrival."

Cohen gave him a puzzled look as though he'd spoken in Persian.

Jesse looked at the second closed door. "I take it she's in her cave?"

"She was already here when I arrived. As usual."

Lizzie tapped an ash from her cigarillo and heard voices in the office. The morning chill had abated, leaving the confined space warm but comfortable. She stabbed out the slender cigarillo and waved away the slight haze of blue smoke, nibbling the feathered end of a quill as she inspected the sheets of paper spread before her. Words and letters might not be the only keys that proved forgery, she thought with mounting excitement. She laid the quill aside, closed her eyes, and held a page's upper edge beneath her nose. The placed it to one side and tried to compose what she'd say to Jesse and Cohen. Picking up the quill again, she twirled it lightly between her fingers and subdued the desire for another smoke. Bewildered at first by her discovery, she slipped off the high stool and wondered whether they'd believe her.

Both men worked in shirtsleeves. The single window behind them was open, Cohen's concession to the stench of burned wood. She smiled at Jesse and perched on the edge of the arm of the high-backed chair that smelled of smoke.

Cohen sensed her excitement and reached across the desk for the document she held, but she placed the page in her lap.

"You found something?" Cohen asked.

"Something unexpected."

"I'm not sure we can survive another shock today," Jesse smiled.

Lizzie looked at him with a hint of sadness. "This one is different."

Apprehension momentarily restrained her excitement. Secluded for hours since Elias's death, she'd inhabited a cloistered world during daylight hours. Only once had she allowed Jesse or Cohen to glimpse the journal where she catalogued her findings, the columns noted for Cohen's benefit. On more than one occasion, Jesse had sat across from her and watched her make notes, unaware of his presence.

She drew a deep breath and looked at Jesse. He momentarily feared that she'd reversed her beliefs, a new discovery putting his father's innocence in doubt.

"When you introduced me to Victoria, I told you I experienced a premonition of sorts," she said. "I searched my memory, but you were right. I never met her before yesterday."

"Now?"

"Her perfume."

Lizzie held the page's lower edge between her thumb and forefinger and hesitated, uncertain of the consequences of what she would show them. Both men sensed her indecision but allowed her time to gather herself. Did the discovery grasp at straws, a desperate gambit to prove her work? Just as quickly as the thought arose, she dismissed it. Certain no sane person could doubt with her conclusions, she looked at Jesse and pushed the document across the desk to Cohen as though it carried a pox.

"Victoria's perfume." She attempted to keep her voice free of triumph. "Your father's ink pervades the paper, but I found another scent. Victoria's perfume's is present on every forged document."

Cohen looked at her as though facing a witness who'd contradicted earlier testimony. He picked up the document and inhaled the edge several times.

"It's most prevalent on the upper right corner. Where I believe she picked up the pages."

Lizzie turned to Jesse. "When I asked about her perfume's distinctiveness, you told me she had it made for her in Paris." She drew a deep breath, certain now of her conclusions. "I believe she's part of the conspiracy. How else to explain the scent's presence on forged documents?"

Cohen sniffed the page again and handed to Jesse. "The scent's faint, but it's there at the upper corner."

"I missed it earlier, overwhelmed by Mr. Caine's ink," Lizzie said. "It's most prevalent on the page you hold, but I have a dozen more. I believe she's our forger."

Jesse closed his eyes and inhaled, a shock stealing over his face. Overwhelmed by the accusation, he stared at Lizzie. It made no sense. No evidence linked Victoria to the Tyrees, nothing to implicate her as part of a forgery.

Jesse handed the page back to Cohen. Did Lizzie grasp at the perfumed pages like a drowning swimmer, he wondered, anxious to prove her contentions? The possibility of jealousy raised its head, but he immediately dismissed it, Lizzie's dedication too strong. Whatever the reason for the accusations, however, Victoria's involvement seemed implausible. He could not conceive of a compelling reason she would betray him and his father.

Cohen steepled his fingers, his eyes on Lizzie's as though she sat in the witness chair. "The scent is present," Cohen admitted, "but circumstantial to our defense."

Her elation dashed, Lizzie's mouth tightened. "I'm not the attorney. I can only point out what I discover."

Baffled by her revelation and certainty, Jesse said, "Lizzie, she's no forger. Why get involved in the scheme?"

"Money," Lizzie replied. "Money's compelled every forger I've uncovered."

"Jesse has a point," Cohen said. "I need proof and motive before entering her perfume as evidence."

Jesse walked the window as though he could distance himself from the consequences. He stared into the street, trapped in his disbelief. He turned back to her.

"It makes no sense. Money drives people to extremes, but she and her mother are financially secure. They purchased a new carriage, a slave, and have an option on a sizeable mansion."

Cohen looked up, his eyes suddenly alight. "Mansion?"

Jesse sensed blood in the water but continued. "Her father died with a sizeable estate, so that's not unusual."

"Actually, it is," Cohen said. "Franklin Danford suffered severe reversals shortly before his death. I represented his creditors in several instances. He was an honest man and paid his debts, but died leaving few assets to his wife and daughter. Few people had any inkling of his circumstances." For the first time since placing the scented document on his desk, Cohen smiled at Lizzie.

"I know," he said, "because I represented his estate."

Cohen stood and rummaged through a file cabinet until he withdrew a large thin envelope. Thumbing its contents, he withdrew a single sheet and placed it before Jesse.

"A list of his estate's assets." He ran a finger down a column. "Less than five hundred dollars remained. Franklin Danford died almost insolvent. Not exactly the stuff of slaves, carriages, and expensive jewelry. I'd assumed they were subsisting on her earnings at the theater."

"Motive," Jesse said with sorrow.

Cohen considered the consequences of Lizzie's discovery. "I don't want to minimize your discovery," he said, "but motive and proof are separate issues. A judge and jury has to connect them."

Jesse picked up the document. "Victoria will have to explain this and the purchases."

Cohen tugged a battered ear lobe. "Accusing her could be a mistake." he said. "Let's say you confront her. To fully work to our advantage, Lizzie's finding must be a surprise at the trial, one that strengthens our allegations of forged documents. If she's alerted beforehand, we've provided time for her to concoct a story. Or worse, she panics and other evidence vanishes."

Jesse folded his hands in his lap and slowly shook his head. Despite Cohen's caution, he saw no alternative but to face her with the truth. Given her state of mind, a chance existed she might admit to some degree of complicity. Any admission changed the game. With the trial only days away, no trace of the stolen funds or remaining Mincey brother had surfaced. As it now stood, Lizzie's handwriting analysis and the perfumed paper bore the full weight of convincing twelve jurors. Threatening Victoria entailed a gamble, but the clock had become an implacable enemy.

"We've run out of alternatives," he said to Cohen.

"Do you honestly think she'll incriminate herself?"

Lizzie looked at Jesse and back to Cohen. "She might."

"You haven't talked with her," Jesse said. "She's moving in and out of reality."

He paced back to the window and watched people begin their mundane day, affected by little more than a spouse's slight at their breakfast table, a job they hated, or their children's school grades. Cohen's fear might prove true. Victoria might undo Lizzie's work if she panicked, but what alternatives were left to them? He gave Lizzie what he hoped was a reassuring smile.

"You've accomplished wonders. Now we must make it work to our advantage."

Cohen exhaled noisily and shook his head at Jesse. "I've given you advice, but I can't make you accept it. If she's become unstable, the results may not be what you desire."

"What choice do I have?"

"You have the choice of heeding your lawyer's advice," Cohen said. "Allow a night to pass before you act."

Jesse stood and Lizzie joined him. "All right," he said. "One night."

Chapter Forty

April 14
1:00 AM
The Danford House

A single church bell peeled twice, announcing the darkest morning hour. The killer slowed along the sidewalk and looked up at the heavens. The skies obliged his plan, solid clouds hiding the full moon. A block away, a single streetlight cast a pool of feeble yellow light that failed to reach him. He checked both ends of the empty street and quickly stepped over the low picket fence and ran him into the house's shadows. The dwelling next door showed no lights, and his dark cap and clothes blended into the night. A late stroller would need to look directly at him to discern the motionless shape pressed against the clapboard exterior. Experience taught him never to trust in luck, so he kept his back against the wall a full minute as he listened for dogs or warning shouts.

When no alarm disrupted the night, he edged sideways along the house. At the rear corner, he made out a ramshackle hut fifty feet away, a black carriage in front. The acrid aroma of stabled horses behind the shed clogged the night air. He'd checked the house earlier in the day and remembered the modest hut housed the Danford's slave. He waited another thirty seconds to be certain the shed door remained closed. No light appeared in the single window and he moved to the rear porch.

Gripping the porch railing, he gingerly tested his weight on the first step, then the second and third. Invisible beneath the overhang, he made out tubs, mops, and buckets. He picked his way through the clutter and stepped to the door. He tried the handle.

Locked.

The man removed a stiff bent wire from his jacket pocket. He inserted the hooked tip into the lock, relieved when he felt no key on the other side of the lock. He jiggled the wire. His practiced fingers found the old tumblers in less than a minute. A twist produced a soundless release and the lock retracted with a soft click. He stepped inside a kitchen and eased the door closed.

The residues of cooked vegetables and bacon drippings filled the kitchen air. Shelves were lined with jars, dishes, pots and pans. A chopping block occupied the center of the room, a dishtowel draped over one edge of an enameled basin. Ahead, dim light illuminated a carpeted hallway flanked by closed doors.

The man drew a knife from its sheath and started forward. Light glinted off the razored metal and he hefted its weight, returning it to the scabbard.

No call for that, he thought.

Something brushed against his trouser legs. He reached for the knife and saw two cats eying him curiously. When he did not move they trotted away, stopping to groom themselves until they lost interest in him and disappeared at the far end of the hall.

The man went to the first door on his right, eased it open, and stepped inside. A mirrored dresser. Bookcase. Chest of drawers. An empty bed. He turned to leave and his arm knocked over a lamp with a muffled thump. The stench of kerosene permeated the room. He froze and when nothing disturbed the house's stillness he moved the second door.

Almost identical to the first bedroom, the interior bore the sickly sweet smell of lavender. A ghostly figure sat up on the bed and looked directly at him.

Victoria swung her legs over the opposite side of the bed with a startled cry. Mouth agape, she leaned forward, her hands clenched on the coverlet. The man stared at the disarray of golden curls, pale skin shimmering in the darkness. Her white gossamer nightgown seemed to glow with a light of its own. Only the bed's width separated her from the massive figure that stood in the doorway.

Victoria's voice broke. "Go away. There's no money in the house."

When the man did not move, she picked up a cut-glass jar from her dresser and hurled it at him. The container shattered against the wall. She bounded across the bed and tried to slip past him. The bedclothes tangled her feet and she stumbled into his arms. He jerked her toward the bed, his coarse wool sleeve rough against her skin. He spun her around to face him and Victoria smelled the river.

Her bare feet kicked the man's shins, small hands flailing at his face. Massive hands tightened around her throat and she thrust her fingers at his eyes. He held her at arm's length as though she were a child's doll, his leathery voice soothing.

"Shhhhh, now, it'll be over in a second."

Victoria's scream never emerged as the callused hands choked off her breath. A pair of dirty thumbs pressed into her windpipe. They stumbled against the bed, Victoria clutching at the coverlet as her feet lifted from the floor. The man crushed her larynx and her world dissolved, the pain purged forever.

The two cats sat and watched as her arms dropped to her sides, the blanket still clutched in one hand as though signaling the end of a ritual dance. The man suspended her in mid-air a few seconds longer, then gently lowered her lifeless body to the floor. He chastely arranged the frilled nightgown, her outstretched slender arms and bare feet pallid against the dark blue rug.

A purse sat on the dresser. He removed Randall's roll of bills and tossed the cloth bag aside. Grimacing at the overpowering fragrance of lavender perfume he glanced inside the dresser drawers and saw nothing more of value. When he looked back at the body, a glint caught his eye. He knelt and raised a lifeless warm hand, slipping a large ring into his pocket.

Breathing heavily, he walked to the front of the house and entered the parlor. A carriage rattled in the street and he crouched. When it continued past the house, he looked into the dining room where an array of serving silver beckoned from a sideboard. He stuffed two large ladles in his belt and buttoned his jacket over them. In the hall Victoria's bedroom door stood open. He looked inside a final time at the white nightgown on the rug. Averting his eyes, Kerrigan reverently closed the bedroom door and let himself out the back door.

Chapter Forty-One

Same Day
Mid-Morning
Danford House

Jesse lifted the saddle from its resting place, then changed his mind and replaced it on the carriage house railing. Tired down to his boot heels, he'd spent the past days on horseback fending off Lobeau, or hunched in a rowboat. He wiped his face with a bare hand, already sweating in the humidity. Animated by her success, Lizzie had hurriedly kissed him and left the house at daybreak, infected with her latest discovery.

He would walk to Victoria's house despite his exhaustion. Cohen's warning rang in his ears, but he'd had time to think. The right words would be required when Victoria opened the door, but another day has passed. Still, how to accuse her of forgery and deceit? He turned onto Liberty Street, focused on the bricks under his feet, considering his options if she rebuffed the accusations.

The Danford carriage stood in front of the house. Aaron dozed on the driver's seat, the horses' heads lowered. His face glistening like wet coal as the escalating morning heat, a faded top hat tilted forward to provide a scrap of shade. Without opening his eyes, he tugged at his high collar and twisted his neck. He heard Jesse's footsteps, looked up, and touched his hat brim.

"Mr. Caine, suh."

"Good morning, Aaron."

The slave planted a frayed but clean boot against the footboard. He pulled a handkerchief from his coat pocket and swiped it across his broad face.

"Is Miss Victoria home?" Jesse asked.

"Don't know, suh," Aaron removed his hat and swabbed the headband. "Her mother tol' me to come get her. I knocked on the door, but she don't answer."

Jesse looked at the house. "Where's Mrs. Danford?"

"She down at her sister's on Drayton Street, the ol' house by the bakery." Aaron centered the hat on his head. "She done spent the night there and sent me back here to fetch Miss Victoria."

"How long you been sitting out here?"

Aaron pursed his lips and patted his vest pocket with an exaggerated gesture. "Don't own no gold watch, so I don't rightly know. An hour, mebbe?"

"You going to sit here until she comes out?" Jesse teased.

Aaron grinned and placed his other boot on the footrest. "Her mother say Miss Victoria got a trunk full of ol' clothes for her niece, and I was to come get it. I figure mebbe Miss Victoria dressin' and be down directly. Can't rightly go in the house by myself."

Jesse beckoned him down from the coach. "Well, come sit in the shade, and I'll see if she's in there."

Aaron jumped down and tethered the horses with a halter weight, dropping the lead sphere to the ground. He patted the jaw of a horse and followed Jesse through the gate, taking a seat on the porch steps out of the sun.

Jesse tugged the door's brass bell pull, his uneasiness rising when no footsteps sounded in the hall. The whirring chime rang again, the sound assuming a desperate familiarity. He peered through the door's glass panel. Behind him, the slave fanned his face with his hat, content to be out of the sun and let Jesse solve the mystery.

Jesse tried the handle and the door opened. A rush of kerosene fumes flowed past him onto the porch. He moved inside and the odor grew stronger the constricted hall.

"Victoria?"

The two orange tabbies bounded down the hall in tandem, tails high. He stooped and absently rubbed their heads, looking into the empty parlor. Only the twin purring broke the quiet as the cats performed figure eights between his legs, concerned about missing a meal. The kerosene fumes grew stronger as he walked toward the kitchen, the cats trotting in front of him in anticipation. The far bedroom door stood open, and the odor grew stronger. Just inside the doorway, the remains of a broken lamp sat in a damp pool on the carpet. He walked into the empty kitchen. Familiar dishes, all neatly stacked. Nothing out of place. The back door stood slightly ajar and Jesse closed it. He turned back to the second bedroom and lightly rapped on the door. He waited, heard no sound, and stepped inside as the cats rushed between his legs.

"Victoria?"

An open steamer trunk rested near a four-poster bed, sheets and coverlet in disarray. He took another step and saw a bare leg and delicate toes pointed at the ceiling. The cats sniffed at the naked ankle as Jesse knelt by the body.

Clothed in a white nightgown on a blue rug, Victoria's arms were sprawled akimbo, her eyes half-open as though awakening from a confused dream she could not understand. Her right hand clutched the downy coverlet as if she'd given up trying to pull it from the bed. An open purse lay a few feet away, contents strewn across the floor.

Jesse placed two fingers against her discolored neck. Except for the deep bruises, she appeared she might sit up any second, shocked to find him in her bedroom. He touched her bare arm, the skin cool as the shaded room. Unlike her orderly stage deaths, her mouth hung open and a streak of saliva had dried along one cheek, an ugly conclusion to a vibrant life.

Jesse looked away. After a moment, he gathered himself and closed her eyelids with a feathery touch. So alive when he and Lizzie had talked with her. Now murdered in her own bedroom. He straightened and walked into the hall, followed by the cats who darted to the kitchen again.

"Aaron!"

The slave opened the front door and warily scanned the hall. Jesse motioned to him. He walked slowly, eyes darting from side to side until he stood beside Jesse, who moved to one side. Aaron stared at the naked foot.

"Lord Jesus, Mr. Caine," he whispered.

Jesse said, "Go to the jail and find the sheriff. Bring him here."

Aaron ran down the hallway, boots thudding on the bare wood floor as if the corpse pursued him. Jesse closed the front door and watched the carriage lurch away. For a long moment, he watched the retreating coach until he imagined the watch in his pocket ticking away irretrievable seconds. With Victoria dead, his hopes had risen, but the options narrowed, time his most dangerous adversary now.

He walked back to the bedroom and looked beyond the sprawled body. Aware that minutes were enemies, he rapidly surveyed the room.

Bed. Closet. The ornamental dresser. Where would she have chosen to hide things?

He stepped over the body and sat on the padded dresser bench. The dresser mirror held a display of old playbills inserted around its edges, and Jesse saw one for *Othello* where he'd first seen her on stage. He stared at the frayed program for a moment, unable to connect the memory to the corpse sprawled on the floor behind him. He tried a drawer that rattled loosely but did not budge. How much time did he have?

He rapidly walked to the kitchen, imagining his watch discarding precious minutes. He found a small knife and avoided looking at the front door as he slipped back into the bedroom. A few seconds later, the knife popped the dresser lock, and he slid open the middle drawer.

Glass jewelry and baubles. An ornate necklace. A scattering of earrings. The left drawer revealed more inexpensive jewelry, colored gauzes, and a profusion of ribbons. He ran his hand beneath the cloth.

Nothing.

The other drawer yielded more female trimmings. He rummaged through them, then impulsively ran his hand deeper and touched something solid. He removed the fistful of ribbons and placed the collection on the dresser top. Crusted quills. Scribbled pages. Miscellaneous correspondence from his father's office. Blank pages.

Heart pounding, he picked up several sheets of paper and rubbed the edges between his thumb and forefinger, coating his fingertips with lavender. Only a few pages evidenced the now familiar watermark; others bore no telltale markings. Three pages were filled with attempts at his father's signature. Others included repetitive words and half-finished phrases, many hastily scratched out or discontinued mid-sentence. Sweat coursed down his spine.

How long since Aaron had left?

The deserted house vibrated like thin glass waiting to be shattered by boots in the hall. Jesse sat looking down at what lay before him, unable to rouse himself from the silken bench. He stared at the tools of a forger. He thrust his hand back into the drawer and found a small bottle of his father's ink, undeniable proof the road had turned in his favor.

He dug past the cloth strips again and touched glass, recognizing the distinctive shape. He removed it and opened his fist to reveal an elliptical glass frame surrounded by a tiny beaded gold decoration. Behind the glass Randall Tyree stared up at him. He blinked at the assured half-smile and closed his fist around another the miniature, another link in the conspiracy. He turned the portrait over and read the neatly printed inscription on the back of the ivory:

"From R to V"
Edmund Desaix, Artist, New Orleans, 1834

Jesse stared at the inscription. The image clarified many things, including his status as a fool. Evidence of his blindness sat in his palm and littered the dresser. Ink. The miniature. Attempted forgeries.

Victoria and Randall Tyree. Lovers and partners.

He recalled Charlie Rushton's blood glistening on dead leaves. Elias Pendleton's lifeless figure in the cemetery. He looked at one of Victoria's small detailed watercolors on her bedroom wall. Her talent obviously had extended beyond the stage and easel, trading paintbrushes for a traitorous quill. A trail through the wilderness now beckoned, sufficient to free a sick man who coughed away his life in a dank cell. Despite his elation, skepticism raised its head as Cohen's warnings returned. Could they connect Victoria to the Tyrees?

He picked up the items, expecting footsteps on the front porch any second. Leave now, he thought. But disappearing before Dew arrived might cast suspicion on him. Forcing himself from the bench, he left the dresser drawers open, slipped the forged papers inside his shirt, and concealed the ink bottle beneath his coat. He considered leaving everything for the sheriff, but the authorities would only accuse him of planting false evidence. He weighed the miniature in his palm for a moment and tossed it onto the dresser.

Let the bastard explain it.

Stepping over Victoria's body, he noticed the indentation on her finger; the ring was missing. Everything in the room pointed to theft and a murder—or a robbery gone awry. But other than the ring and open purse, the room remained undisturbed. No frenzied rummaging through drawers, the trunk, or her closet. No signs the murderer had ransacked the house.

Jesse knelt again and laid his hand on the cold arm, reluctant to leave the body. Only days before, he'd sought to capture her love and support. He recalled the confrontation with the Colonel. Her odd detachment. Her mother's fears. Lizzie's reaction to her bizarre behavior. Sorrow and anguish unlocked an empty vault between his gut and his heart, a feeling remembered from his mother's desertion. Taught that forgiveness required the burial of wrongdoing, he recoiled from the trimmings of nobility, the wound too raw.

He stared at the dresser where Tyree's painted image mocked him. Tyree and Victoria. Blinded by his faith in her, he'd missed the obvious.

Whoever killed her prowled the city at will. Jesse doubted either Tyree risked being caught at a murder scene. That left the second Mincey brother. From Kerrigan's description, the huge swindler could easily overpower a woman. Failure to find him had cost Victoria her life, finding little honor among thieves. Jesse went to the door and looked down the hall. He needed to make a decision. In all likelihood, the Tyrees had hired the Minceys to sell the notes and eliminate threats, engaging two murderers as casually as hiring gardeners or shipwrights. Jesse needed to find Kerrigan and convince him to double his search for Edgar Mincey.

Jesse looked back at the body of the woman he once loved and eased the door closed. In the end, death found her alone in a darkened room. Victoria approved an implement who simply outlived her usefulness to Tyree. Jesse walked to the front porch to await John Dew and his deputy. The folly of such beliefs struck Jesse with full force, and he swore vehemently at the counterfeit notion. The Tyrees had allowed nothing to threaten them, Victoria an implement who simply outlived its usefulness.

Chapter Forty-Two

Same Day
Johnson Square

Jesse walked the city streets until dusk. The evidence concealed beneath his clothes gnawed at his skin like small animals. Victoria had traded his love for money and died as a result, so they were back to Edgar Mincey and Lizzie's conclusions that would appear suspect at best to men in the jury box. He'd never know if Victoria entered the scheme out of love for Randall Tyree, or simply grasped at money that would somehow fulfill her dreams. She'd used him, and the prospect of telling Lizzie and Cohen added to his despair.

He stayed to the backstreets, attempting to sort through what he'd found beneath the clutter of colorful ribbons. A flurry of showers chased him into a storefront doorway and he waited until the clouds dissipated. Would the city ever see three days of uninterrupted sunshine, he wondered? A mist persisted and he crossed the street to Johnson Square, brushing at his shoulders and hat. Sunlight banished the misting rain and fell across the sidewalk like blotches of spilled paint. Leaves dripped rainwater onto rust-colored bricks, humidity thickening the air like a quilt of damp wool.

Kerrigan sat on an empty bench in the square. An open whiskey bottle rested between his boots. Cracking walnuts, he tossed nut meats to an excited flock of pigeons cooing around his feet. He looked up when Jesse sat beside him. The air reeked of cheap whiskey, overpowering jasmine shrubs behind them. Jesse sensed the Irishman tottered on the brink of being dangerously drunk. Kerrigan hoisted the bottle and poured whiskey down his throat. An oily slick of sweat greased his forehead. One hand filled with unshelled walnuts he carefully returned the bottle to the brick sidewalk with a hollow clink. Thick fingers crushed more corrugated hulls and blunt beaks attacked the feast scattered around their benefactor. English sparrows skirted the larger birds and stole smaller crumbs. Across the square two old men bent over a chessboard. Church bells tolled the quarter hour before Kerrigan broke the impasse.

"Damn hot," he muttered, not meeting Jesse's eyes.

"You heard about Victoria Danford?" Jesse said.

"I heard."

"I found her body."

Kerrigan's head came up. "You found her?"

"Her mother spent the night away. She's alone."

An obelisk in the center of the square pointed its shadow at them, the stone needle the only decoration amid surrounding trees. Jesse started to relate his discovery to Kerrigan but let the thought die. He would talk with Cohen first.

A shock of damp curly black hair fell onto Kerrigan's forehead. He sat forward and brushed it away. "I know you had feelings for her." The words slurred and Jesse realized he'd never seen him drunk.

"Her purse was emptied, and a ring was taken," he said. "Her mother claims some silver's also gone missing, but she's too addled to make much sense."

Kerrigan picked up the bottle and emptied it in a single gulp. "Death's a bastard, especially when it finds a beautiful woman. Slips in like a shadow or kicks in the door." He cradled the empty bottle in his lap. "Either way, she's dead. Best not to dwell on it."

Jesse hoped her killer never found peace. She'd proven a better actress than her stage performances, but who'd murdered her? And why? A random burglary gone awry, or had she threatened to expose the swindlers, asking for more money to ensure her silence? No, he reasoned, that would have incriminated her along with her conspirators. The reality suggested her erratic behavior posed a liability.

"God damn whoever did this," he whispered.

Kerrigan glowered at the begging birds and brushed husks from his trousers. "Not likely. Your God takes no notice of our little disasters, but damns us all to hell if we break *his* rules." Eyes dulled, he wiped both hands on his trouser legs, raising the bottle before he remembered it was empty.

"My ol' granny would've claimed damnation will follow whoever killed her," he said, gingerly returning the bottle to the sidewalk, "but I don't believe that." He looked toward the river bluff where an ocean and Ireland beckoned. He blinked. What was done was done and he might live to see the North Sea again. He closed his eyes and imagined a ship's deck tilt beneath the bench as though already at sea, green countryside rising beyond the unnamed ship's bow, island fog hiding toy villages and rolling hills divided by poverty and low stone walls.

He opened his eyes and squinted into the glare. "The old lady stayed on her knees her whole life, suffering cold stone floors," he said. "Confessed everything to some bored priest in a smelly confessional, hoping her guilty admissions kept hell's doors closed. Maybe God welcomed the old girl with a bag of gold and glass of good Dublin stout." The whiskey wore off and he felt tired to the bone. "Who the hell knows what God plans for us?"

"You don't believe evil is punished? That's there's nothing beyond all this?"

Kerrigan kicked at the boldest pigeons that fluttered away. "Meat for the worms, nothin' more. If there's a heaven, it's likely a damn lonely place." He managed a half-smile. "Won't be many there I know."

Laughter and unintelligible words drifted from the two chess players engrossed in their game across the square.

"She died for a few dollars." Jesse said. "There has to be a reckoning for that."

Kerrigan shot him a crooked grin. "Then you ain't lived long enough, bucko. People like you wake up worrying about your breakfast menu, not if you'll survive the day." He found a walnut meat on his jacket and popped it into his mouth, his jaws methodically working around it. "You've no fear you'll end up crippled or a street beggar when your employer's seen enough of you. Your money keeps you safe."

Jesse looked sideways at him. "Tell that to my father."

Kerrigan grunted. "Makes my point. Nothing's certain in the end, but there's fewer sharp edges with money filling your pocket." Kerrigan spat a piece of shell toward the birds and looked across the square without seeing the two old men. "Whoever did in the pretty actress had little to lose. He'll sleep warm tonight and let tomorrow take care of itself." He found another meat on his jacket and popped it into his mouth, Jesse forgotten in the memory of the fragile figure on the floor. Still looking across the square, Kerrigan stretched his arms across the back of the bench. "You need your wits if you want to survive."

"I offered to help the sheriff." Jesse said. "The bastard laughed at me."

Kerrigan snorted. "You ain't well-liked these days, in case it's escaped your notice."

"There's more," Jesse said, the urge to confess his discovery overpowering. "Victoria was a forger. She forged all the documents. I found them."

Kerrigan studied his boots. When he did not raise his head or reply, Jesse wondered if he'd heard him.

"I discovered evidence before the sheriff arrived."

The shaggy head did not move. "What else did you find?"

"False documents. My father's ink. More than enough to prove he's innocent. Someone planned all this, then disposed of her."

Kerrigan slid his right hand behind his back and fumbled for his bandanna. In the same instant he pulled the knife from its scabbard and slipped it beneath his thigh. He wiped his face with the cloth. The whiskey's numbness left him, a gift that had saved him more than once.

"You find proof who else might be involved?"

"I believe she and Randall Tyree were partners, but there had to be others."

One of the two elderly players gave a yell and raised his arms in triumph. Kerrigan watched them fold up the chess board and waited until they ambled across the street, leaving the square deserted. He reached under his trouser leg and grasped the knife handle.

"Lizzie can prove forgery," Jesse said.

"Maybe and maybe not."

"I need you to find Edgar Mincey, Pat." Jesse, his back to Kerrigan, rested his forearms on his knees. "You're my last hope."

Kerrigan scanned the empty square again. With a sudden movement, he released he knife and retrieved the bottle, flinging it at the monument. Glass shattered against granite.

"Don't know what they was thinking when they built their fancy parks," he spat, eyes locked on the stone monument. "Nothing more than a goddamn patch of pretty bushes for rich men and their ladies. Left good land barren as an old maid." He withdrew his hand from the knife and sat back. "Maybe they wanted reminders of heathen England. Sooner or later, they'll fill it with statues and gee-jaws. Carve a crook's name on a stone." He spit toward the obelisk. "Most likely Randall Tyree's greedy old Da."

Jesse looked at him and an unfamiliar distance settled over them. Kerrigan continued to stare at the obelisk as though tempted charge across the Square and topple it. A couple walked past and stared at the unlikely pair. Kerrigan's unseeing eyes followed them until he blinked, returning from an abyss.

"Mincey and the money's long gone," he said. He laid a hand on Jesse's back. "If what you say is true, the actress planned the entire game with the Minceys. She likely got greedy and Edgar killed her."

Jesse stood and waited for Kerrigan to join him, but his friend only stared at the peaked stone until Jesse walked away with a curious sense of loss.

Chapter Forty-Three

April 14
Morning
Savannah City Jail

The jail's exterior walls shunned the sun's warmth. Cool to the touch like hardened scales of a long-dead reptile, it would have repelled Jesse had he been compelled to run a hand over the granite surfaces.

The cell key rattled in the cell lock and a bony hand pushed back a soiled blanket at the sound. Ambrose Caine emitted an involuntary groan and forced himself upright. He smiled weakly at Jesse, blinking as though grateful at being rescued from a disturbing dream. The blanket remained wrapped around his hunched shoulders as he stood and wrapped his arms around his son before he stepped back to look at him.

"What news?" he asked.

Jesse sat on the familiar stool and steeled himself.

"First, how are you?"

"A little better." His father indicated the deputy. "Luther brought me cornbread muffins and peach preserves this morning." The deputy pretended to study the cells at the far end of the passageway. "They'd have gone down easier with better coffee, but beggars can't be choosers," Ambrose said loudly enough for his jailer to hear him.

"You need to know what's happened," Jesse said. "Someone murdered Victoria Danford last night. Strangled her."

Luther stepped to the cell door. "The actress? I saw her on stage last month."

Jesse nodded. Visibly shaken, Ambrose Caine sat down heavily. "My god, I'm sorry, Jesse. I know you were close."

Jesse lowered his voice and turned his back to the deputy who retreated to his wall. "There's more. Someone tried to burn down Cohen's office last night. We were lucky they failed." He removed the ink bottle and attempted forgeries from his folio.

"I found these in Victoria's house. Forged notes and documents. She was our forger."

Hands trembling, his father examined the pages. Jesse recounted the discovery of her body and the cache of evidence. "I also found a miniature portrait of Randall Tyree inscribed to her and bearing last year's date."

"You suspect Victoria and Randall Tyree?"

"The two of them and the Colonel."

Ambrose slumped. "She and Fletcher Tyree. My friend and partner."

"The portrait and her forgeries connect them," Jesse said.

"What does Cohen say?"

"I'm on my way to see him."

They talked a few minutes longer about Victoria's murder before Luther led Jesse up the stairs. Jesse stopped him at the top.

"Thank you for the extra food," Jesse said.

The deputy swiped a hand over his balding head and opened the door without looking at him. "Don't know nothin' about muffins," he mumbled.

"We heard the news of Victoria Danford's death," Cohen said. "I'm sorry, Jesse."

Jesse found Lizzie's hand. "I discovered her body."

She stared but before she could speak, he opened the folio and removed the papers and ink bottle, placing them on Cohen's desk. "I found these before the sheriff arrived."

Lizzie and Cohen shuffled through the paper. "Many came from your father's office," Lizzie said, holding up several pages, "but these are attempts to copy his handwriting and signature." Picking up the bottle, she sniffed the stopper. "Certainly his ink." She looked at Cohen with a look of vindication.

"I also found a miniature of Randall Tyree inscribed to her in New Orleans less than two years ago."

Lizzie at him. "You never knew?"

Abashed, Jesse shook his head.

Cohen indicated the papers. "Did anyone see you remove these?"

"No."

"Then a jury will have only your word you discovered them in her room."

Jesse, angry he'd overlooked so much, started to speak.

Cohen held up one hand and walked to the door. The two clerks looked up apprehensively, but Cohen only closed the door and resumed his chair. "Best not to tempt fate," he said, looking at the door. "Both are loyal, but law offices grow large ears."

"I can't believe Victoria jeopardized my father's life," Jesse said.

"We talked with her yesterday," Lizzie said. "She appeared unsettled. Now I believe we know the reason."

Cohen slowly shook his head. "It confirms our suspicions, but—" He hesitated and searched for a way to adjust Jesse's expectations. Sitting back, he looked at the orderly rows of law books on the far wall, considering the case he'd place before a jury.

"Surely this strengthens our case," Jesse insisted.

"She's spent a great deal of money," Lizzie added. "That could tie her to Tyree."

Cohen waved his hand as though clearing the air. "The miniature in itself proves nothing. The prosecution will allow paper and ink that came from your father's office, but their concession will prove nothing," he said, preparing Jesse for the courtroom's harsh realities. "The prosecution will accuse you of planting everything in her room, saying they were never in Victoria's possession before your arrival. The portrait reveals them only as lovers, not accomplices in a crime. Connecting them to a conspiracy will be a long reach."

"And if I'd left them on the dresser," Jesse said, "Dew would claim I planted them."

"Exactly."

"But, dammit, I *found* them in her room. She was part of it."

Cohen leaned forward. "It may be enough to create reasonable doubt in the jury's mind, but think about it, Jesse. A popular young actress murdered in her own bedroom. Now we claim she was a forger and a criminal. It'll appear a desperate accusation, placing blame on a dead woman who can't defend herself." He gestured dismissively at the ink and papers. "We can't connect the Tyrees without more evidence."

"The fact I found evidence in her home should count for something."

"*Should* and *fair* are words attorneys avoid in a courtroom," Cohen said.

Jesse stood and paced the office. He touched Lizzie's shoulder and tried to clear his thoughts. Every avenue closed the moment it opened, he thought. What Cohen said made sense. 'Fair' was a nonsense word in legal matters.

"I talked with Kerrigan," he said, regaining his chair. "He's had no luck finding Edgar Mincey. He believes Mincey most likely murdered Victoria, but there's no proof."

"With the trial only a few days away," Cohen said, "we need more than suppositions. Tell Kerrigan to redouble his efforts. Threaten his friends if he has to. We'll cover any expense required to find Mincey. In the meantime I'll assemble my arguments to show Miss Pendleton's discoveries prove the documents are forgeries."

Lizzie looked at Jesse. "It's late. I think we should leave and let Samuel do his job."

They sat close to one another on the couch, both windows open to the cool night air. Lizzie removed her shoes and curled close to Jesse, her bare calves tucked beneath her. She laid her head on his chest, and when he didn't speak, she pulled him closer.

"You've had a long day." She gave a half-laugh. "I'm sorry. I imagine I just uttered the year's most obvious statement."

Jesse wrapped his arm around her. "No, no. It's more than Victoria's death. I'm trying to find what else I've missed. It's like dying of thirst with a lake right in front of us."

"I wish we lived a hundred years in the future," Lizzie said. "When my work is accepted and its appearance in a courtroom is commonplace. When I'm not seen as a witch and half-baked spiritualist."

Jesse pressed his face into her hair. "We're all captives of the time we live in. Victoria and Elias died because criminals selected my father as a scapegoat. Neither picked their time, yet they're both dead, and my father's dying in prison."

"If Randall discarded them so easily, you're in danger too."

Jesse recalled Lobeau's warning. Jesse tried to warn him he could not match Randall's ruthlessness. He had killed Charlie Rushton without remorse, a casual dalliance after a leisurely morning ride to the dead plantation. Then Elias for reasons Lizzie may have correctly guessed. Like the ex-fencing master, Randall in some way required death to complete him.

"Victoria Danford was murdered to protect him," Lizzie said. "He won't hesitate to kill you."

"Randall won't dispose of me in the dark of night. He'll prefer the role of avenging angel to those who lost money. No blame attaches to him if he kills me in a duel."

"Then don't give him what he wants," Lizzie pleaded. "I can't return to an empty house in Boston without you."

"I don't intend to let him kill me."

"Stay with me then," she whispered, a new hunger in her voice.

He kissed her and the kiss turned urgent. Their hands moved to each other's clothes. Jesse needed her, and her fervor matched his, one another's refuge from the sadness and frustration that had engulfed them since Elias's death. Her mouth tasted of honey and bittersweet chocolate. He found her damp breasts beneath the loose chemise; a light perfume paired with her scent and she moaned as he unhooked laces and buttons. He pressed her into the cushions, slipping off her skirt. Half naked and gasping, she stood and picked up her clothes.

"Your bed's a far better place to continue this discussion."

Jesse stood on a hilltop open to the sky. Legions of birds circled soundlessly overhead, pointed black wingtips silhouetted against a crimson sky. He walked down the hill into a dense fog and found himself on a bridge. Surprised that no water or ravine appeared beneath the structure, he stopped as Randall Tyree immerged from the mist on the far side. Behind him, the fog coalesced into Victoria and Elias. The ghostly shapes motioned him forward. Tyree, sword in hand, waited, unmoving. Jesse took a step and realized he had no weapon. Lobeau materialized from the mist in full uniform beside Tyree, his face remorseful. Jesse stumbled backward and found himself in his father's cell. A skeletal arm fell from beneath the blanket, rotted skin sloughing from the white bones. One finger crooked and beckoned to him. Panicked, he lurched away and—

Jesse bolted upright, sweating. He hated dreams. They served no purpose other than ruining a night's sleep. Swallowing his dissipating fear, Jesse replayed the eerie foray, the night terror slow to recede. Beside him, Lizzie mumbled and turned in her sleep. He lifted a corner of the sheet and wiped perspiration from his face and neck. Shivering, he eased from bed, pulled on his nightshirt, and slipped downstairs without lighting a lamp. In the kitchen, he pumped tepid water into a small basin at the sink. Eyes squeezed shut, he submerged his face and held his breath until the images faded. Dreams were nonsense, meaningless scraps of the mind, senseless mirages, and unless you struggled to find a connection, soon forgotten. But the ghostly figures beckoning to him swam too near the truth, and his fear resurfaced.

It won't happen like that.

Soft footsteps padded down the stairs, and Lizzie appeared with a lamp in the doorway, her white nightgown luminous in the muted glow.

He wiped his face with a dish towel and ran a hand through his damp hair. "A bad dream."

"I was frightened when I found an empty bed."

He walked to her and wrapped his arms around her. "I won't leave you, now or ever."

"Come back to bed."

She took his hand and led him up the stairs. Buried beneath the covers, she wrapped him in her arms and held him. Captives of one another's needs Jesse drifted into a dreamless sleep.

Chapter Forty-Four

April 15
Mid-Morning
Samuel Cohen's Office

Cohen placed his hand atop a small stack of papers and wrinkled his nose at the overlay of burned wood and fresh paint. "The more I study Lizzie's work, the more I respect her skills," he said. "If one looks closely, the discrepancies become clear as rainwater to anyone with an open mind."

"Let's hope a jury recognizes rainwater when they see her conclusions," Jesse said.

"I'll do my utmost to sharpen their vision." Cohen shoved aside the pile of documents. "Where is she this morning?"

Jesse frowned at the fireplace where flames gleefully rose. "She's playing the role of housekeeper before she visits Elias's grave," Jesse said.

"She's earned a day away." Cohen looked at her small office. "Besides, this place stinks like Lucifer's outhouse."

Jesse unbuttoned his collar, seeking relief from the heat. "If the discrepancies she uncovered are as obvious as you claim, a jury will have to consider them."

Head down, Samuel Cohen placed his elbows on the desktop and rubbed his palms together. He slowly wagged his head back and forth. "If it were only as simple as men believing their eyes, your father walks away a free man after an hour's deliberation."

"Combined with the evidence I found..."

Cohen's slapped the stack of documents, patience at an end. "What you found adds nothing! I keep telling you that!"

He sat back, exhaled heavily, and lightly tapped his fingertips together. "My apologies," he said, sitting forward again. "Let me explain the workings of a courtroom to you. Juries for the most part are comprised of the blind, the biased, and the ignorant, anxious to return to their businesses and wives. Maybe even their children. They prefer confident eyewitnesses, weeping confessions, and bloody axes, any solution requiring a minimum of thought on their part. Requiring them to inspect words and punctuation marks through a magnifying lens, then accept a woman's explanations..." He shrugged.

"I thought we brought her to Savannah for just that purpose," Jesse argued.

"I don't doubt her conclusions," Cohen said." I firmly believe her discoveries, but I warned you in the beginning she represented slim hope. I see the differences as plainly as I see you, but I hoped for something more substantial before we go to trial. A living suspect remains our best weapon that I can dismantle on the witness stand."

"Victoria's murder and what I found in her room *must* count in our favor," Jesse persisted. "I'll gladly swear to finding the ink and paper in her room."

"We discussed this. Your word against the prosecution's claims," he said. "Your discoveries might raise an eyebrow or two, but little else in my opinion."

Cohen's arguments remained undeniable. The previous night's dream returned with alarming clarity, the shapes beckoning him toward Randall Tyree. Was a guilty verdict a foregone conclusion before the courtroom doors opened? He glared at the offending fireplace and went to the door. Stopping, he turned to Cohen and slapped the doorframe.

"Mincey's the key," he said. "If Kerrigan finds him, we'll beat the truth out of him."

"A bloodied witness?" Cohen shook his head. "Even if you gained a confession, he might recant his story on the witness stand. Deny every word." Cohen rubbed his eyes with his thumbs. "Such as they are, Lizzie's documents are our strongest defense unless he turns up, and he's compliant to our needs." He pointed to the stack of documents that showed wear, the edges smudged and curled. The dog-eared papers seemed a single flimsy barrier between Ambrose Caine's freedom and death.

"I'll try to make the jurors see the obvious," Cohen promised.

"Where does the road bend, Samuel?"

Cohen frowned and walked to the fireplace. He scattered dwindling embers that angrily flared and died. "The attempt to destroy my office proves the Tyrees are alarmed." he said. "They're frightened of Lizzie's work and may yet make a mistake. We need patience."

"Time's run out, Samuel. Waiting's not an option."

"It's Victoria's murder that concerns me," Cohen insisted. "If they'll kill a woman, you stand no chance if you're seen as an obstacle."

Jesse's smile tightened. "In which case, I'll stay close to Kerrigan. He's watching my back. We're returning to the island this afternoon." He reached for doorknob and Cohen placed his hand against the door.

"You mustn't persist in this fantasy of confronting Tyree. Lizzie needs you alive."

When Jesse didn't reply, Cohen removed his hand. Jesse walked out.

Chapter Forty-Five

Same Afternoon
Skidaway Landing

Buffeted by the strong current, the boat quickly surrendered to the river's urgings. The pocked African face watched as Kerrigan pulled hard against the tide, the opposing flow trying to sweep them toward the Atlantic. Spring had briefly triumphed over winter's last ditch attempts to prolong its dominance, and he quickly broke a sweat as he shrugged out of his jacket. Only the cries of river birds and the oar locks' steady rattle broke the tranquility.

Jesse faced him from the bow, wondering where his silent friend's thoughts took him as Kerrigan bent his back to the oars. "You heard about the fire at Cohen's office?" he asked.

"A poor job. Most likely a sneak thief or former client."

"All our work could have been lost in a single night."

Kerrigan shrugged and Jesse fell silent again. Distracted by what awaited him on the island, he allowed the river's murmurings to fill the void. Did he lack the will to 'thrust home' as Lobeau termed it? The familiar barricades of tan reeds slid past them, the pencil-thin shoots interspersed with green as spring promised renewed life. A prim white egret stood motionless on one leg in the muddy shallows. It interrupted its search for prey and lifted its elegant head to watch the boat drift by. Was it the same creature he'd seen on his last trip from the island? The snow white feathers contrasted with russet-brown mud, the winged hunter the only sign of life along the desolate shore.

Kerrigan's strength defied the river's energy and they made steady headway against the current. Dark green water slapped at the bow, mirroring the lush islands, and Jesse sensed this was their final voyage to the forlorn cabin. Lobeau had done his best but Jesse knew he'd spoken the truth: He'd never equal Tyree's skill and casual willingness to take a life.

The prow veered into the creek and the reeds swallowed them yet again. Kerrigan struggled with the oars as the outgoing current rushed from the constricted channel. The narrow banks were taller as the tide receded and left little room to maneuver. Kerrigan dug a single oar into the flow to force the light craft forward.

Lobeau waited on the dock in shirtsleeves, the dogs crouched at his feet. Kerrigan shipped the mud-caked oars and Jesse cast the bow line to Lobeau, who secured it to a piling. He seized Jesse by the hand and pulled him onto the dock with surprising strength.

"Do you have a dram for an old Mick and thirsty oarsman?" It was the first words Kerrigan had spoken since Jesse mentioned the fire.

Inside the cabin, Lobeau poured three drinks. The dogs sniffed Jesse's boots, lost interest, and trotted outside at Lobeau's command. The raccoon pawed the two cloth bags and leather masks on the table by the rear door, anxious for the day's entertainment. Kerrigan tossed back the brandy and poured a second that quickly disappeared. He turned to Lobeau as though Jesse was not in the room.

"You saw Tyree," he said. "Can he survive?"

Lobeau walked to the table without replying. He rolled his shirtsleeves to his elbows. He removed the training epées from their jackets and stepped outside. Jesse donned his mask, surprised when Lobeau left his mask on the table.

Kerrigan, a third brandy in hand, settled on the bench next to the door.

Taking deep breaths, Lobeau inspected the sky and rotated his shoulders. The wordless overture completed, he stepped back and smoothed his moustache, his eyes on Jesse's mask. He snapped his blade side to side in menacing arcs, the air sliced with ominous hisses. Jesse started to speak when he lunged.

The blunted tip struck the center of his chest. Taken aback by the unexpected attack, he retreated, stumbling as Lobeau pursued him. The master feinted and struck the same spot. Jesse blinked away the pain, his anger rising at the ferocity of the attacks. Lobeau circled to his left, his face impassive. Jesse had never seen him without the mask, recoiling from the hungry look of a predator. The movements grew more deft and complex, mechanical and certain in their preciseness, each executed with the smoothness of an oiled unfeeling machine.

Snake-like, Lobeau's sword arm swept aside Jesse's attack again and slashed his left arm. The strike ripped Jesse's sleeve and numbed his arm to his fingertips. Lobeau lowered his blade and faced him. Jesse sprang but found only air. Lobeau pivoted and slashed him across the back, the blow a whip crack in the still air. Kerrigan uttered an amused laugh, grinning at his bewilderment.

Provoked by shame and the laughter, Jesse's woodland blood begged for reprisal. Lobeau stopped again, his epée performing teasing circles at the earth, tempting another rush. His back burning, Jesse lunged. Lobeau swept away the thrust and found Jesse's sternum again. Enduring the blow, his Shawnee blood forced away the pain and he charged Lobeau. The Frenchman knocked his blade aside and turned his back, emulating Tyree's disdain as he'd mocked Charlie Rushton's final moments.

Jesse rushed after him, intent on nothing but striking a blow. Lobeau spun and parried Jesse's carelessness. The rounded tip slammed into Jesse's throbbing sternum. Uttering a declaration of disgust, Lobeau lowered his blade.

"Enough," he said. "No more."

Jesse swept off the mask, tempted to strike the unguarded face, thinking of nothing but retaliation. Gasping, he controlled the impulse and said, "No, I can continue."

"No, you cannot," Lobeau exclaimed. "You are dead a dozen times, and a dozen more deaths would follow if you enjoyed multiple lives." He walked away, Jesse staring after him.

"I'm learning!" he yelled at Lobeau's back.

Lobeau walked into the cabin and laid his sword on the table. He did not look up when Jesse appeared beside him, his shirt wet the skin. He jerked the epée from his hand and tossed it on the table with a clatter.

"No more," he proclaimed again. "Not today. Not ever."

"I can learn." Jesse forced the ragged words.

Lobeau turned on him. "There is nothing more you *can* learn. I told you what is required. Some things cannot be taught. I watched this man Tyree kill the boy at the Jews' old cemetery. No hesitation. No mercy. He knows what he's about and will kill you without a thought. I will not tempt you to face him."

Kerrigan entered the cabin, pulled off his jacket, and flung it over the back of a chair. Lobeau looked through the open doorway as a flurry of wind rustled the trees. A curtain of swollen clouds approached the cabin.

Kerrigan topped his glass with brandy and sat down heavily as Lobeau closed the door. "He'll face Tyree sooner or later, Etienne." He emptied half the glass. "Without your help, he's got no choice but to murder him."

Lobeau shrugged. "*C'est tant mieux.* Maybe that's for the best. At least murder allows him to live."

Jesse listened to the conversation as if murdering Tyree signified a feasible alternative. "Joining my father in jail solves nothing," he said.

Kerrigan ignored him. "He's learned from you!" Kerrigan said to Lobeau. "With more instruction, he'll at least stand a chance against Tyree."

Lobeau placed his hands flat on the table and leaned toward Kerrigan's chair. "No, he will not, *mon ami*," he said. "You know what is required. You saw for yourself just now. My intention was to dissuade him from fighting this man."

Kerrigan slammed the heavy glass on the table, splashing brandy on Lobeau's sleeve.

"God dammit, Etienne! You agreed to help. He can't—"

Lobeau wiped his hand and stared down his former comrade. "*Non.* I cannot work miracles. This man will kill him if *Monsieur* Caine persists in his fantasies."

Kerrigan's hand swiped the spilled whiskey from the table. "I brought him here for your help."

Lobeau straightened and walked to the window. He crossed his arms, his reply barely audible, "I wash my hands of him."

Jesse's hopes evaporated in the six words, dismissed as someone already dead. His anger boiled over.

"Randall Tyree is not you," Jesse said to his back. "I'll take my chances if you'll help me."

When Lobeau did not turn or respond, Kerrigan placed his empty glass on the table and heaved his bulk from the chair. He yanked on his coat and started for the door.

"It's over," he said.

Jesse shot a final glance at Lobeau and followed Kerrigan to the dock. Kerrigan settled behind the oars and Jesse jumped into the boat, rocking the shallow craft as the overcast darkened the water. Lobeau appeared on the dock above them and looked down. He waited until Jesse looked up, then tossed a sharpened epée to him, sister to the practice epée. Jesse caught the hilt in mid-air.

"Take it," Lobeau said, his face impassive. "You may as well die with something familiar in your hand."

Kerrigan refused to look at Lobeau and stabbed the dock with an oar as the tide took them across the small lagoon. After a minute, the reeds blocked Jesse's view of the solitary figure on the dock.

Lobeau filled a glass from the half-empty decanter. In the clearing rain swept across the open ground. After a minute he donned a cape and walked back to the dock. The bateau had vanished. His cape soaked, he ignored the rain and gazed at the few muddy bubbles left by the boat's wake. The dogs joined him, puzzled why their master endured the rain. They shook water from their coats and heard a small exclamation.

"*Bon chance,*" Lobeau said to the deserted patch of water.

He trudged back to the cabin, sadly acknowledging what lay ahead for his pupil, pride a willing executioner for the unprepared. Only the Virgin Mary produces miracles for innocents, he thought, not a scarred old fencing master. He spread the sodden cape over Kerrigan's chair and saw a folded slip of paper on the floor. He picked it up, glanced toward the door, and tossed the note on the table. He started to walk away and halted. If the paper represented something important, he'd be forced to return it as quickly as possible. Resigned, he pulled up the chair, unfolded the note, and saw Randall Tyree's signature.

Lizzie folded herself into Jesse's favorite chair and took pleasure in her muscles' small aches, looking around the room with satisfied contentment. Jesse would be home in another hour, and though her traitorous leg rebelled from the day's labors, she'd discovered a curious satisfaction looking after his home. Surprised, she imagined herself a dutiful wife. She yawned and stretched her arms above her head, the thought adding to her pleasure.

Limping from room to room during the morning and afternoon, she'd speculated about the history of the house and its former occupant, touching the few remaining feminine objects. Ignoring tinges of guilt, she'd opened closet doors and inspected the contents as though she'd reverted to a naughty child looking for adult secrets. After days confined to her tiny office lifting nothing heavier than a magnifying glass, exploring the house offered a reprieve from her sterile world of paper. The pleasant fatigue reasserted itself and she burrowed deeper into the chair's cushions.

The mantle clock's chimes pulled her from the depths. She sat up with no idea of how long she'd dozed. The windows were dark, and she pushed herself upright, sleep fading, her mood buoyed by the thought of Jesse's return. She changed clothes and found an oversized straw shopping basket in the kitchen. She could saddle Mercury, but the thought of walking in the cool of the evening overcame the temptation to ride. She locked the front door and closed the ornamental iron gate behind her.

There's still time remaining to find what I need at City Market, she thought. The last fishermen arrived at dusk and laid out their afternoon catch by torchlight for those who dined late. With luck, she thought, I'll find a fresh flounder, corn, and okra, Jesse's favorites.

With the basket hooked over her arm, she headed toward the river, the streets and sidewalks almost deserted. The last twilight slipped into deeper shadows as she planning the meal. Limping north along Bull Street, her aches disappeared at the pleasures promised by the coming night. Grateful for the cool air, she set her imagination free in anticipation. The street's moonless corridor stretched in front of her until she picked up her skirt hem and crossed the street, angling east toward the Market. The streets grew darker as she moved away from the larger houses, few dwellings showing light. She slowed her step, careful where she stepped on the rough sidewalk.

She paid no attention to another set of footsteps behind her. Did the heavy footfalls mimic her limp, keeping pace with her? She dismissed the sounds as echoes off the nearby buildings. The steps grew louder, footfalls more distinct. She halted in mid-stride and turned.

A motionless figure in dark clothing stood six feet away, the face cloaked by the night. One arm raised and a flared yellow brilliance lit the face behind the explosion. The sound arrived an instant after a painful fist knocked her backward. She fell heavily into the muddy street, bewildered why she'd lost her grip on the basket.

Chapter Forty-Six

Dusk
Same Day
Skidaway River

A fresh line of squalls appeared as they rowed away from the island. Jesse lowered his head and saw Kerrigan scowl as rain pounded their backs. The tide had reached its zenith and ran in full flood. The bateau raced past the fading shoreline, fat raindrops beating the water around them as Jesse's thoughts strayed back to the island.

Darkness found them still on the river, low rain clouds preempting the dusk. Kerrigan deftly maneuvered the boat, racing the rain, oars stabbing the water like ancestral enemies. The wind picked up and the flat hull skimmed past scrub and marsh, both men's thoughts replaced by the downpour's noise. Jesse kept his eyes inside the boat, Lobeau's warnings repeating with each oar stroke. He touched the tender bruises on his chest and massaged his arm where the blade had ripped his sleeve, Lobeau's warnings more painful than the collection of welts.

The rain halted as suddenly as it began. His ears readjusted to the river's sighs and he saw the old black man waiting on shore. Intimate of the river's sounds, he'd saddled their horses when he'd heard the oars a quarter mile from the landing. Kerrigan beached the small craft in the dark. Without a glance at Jesse or the old man, Kerrigan snatched the reins from the caretaker and awkwardly swung into the saddle. Jesse paid the African, then helped him slide the boat to the lean-to. By the time he mounted Aristotle, the roadway was empty. Abandoned to his thoughts, he rode beneath the canopy of moss-draped limbs. The waterfalls of Spanish moss seemed to reach for him as Lobeau's words replayed in his head, a Gregorian chant of defeat, the warning attended by mournful songs of night birds.

When Charlton Street appeared, Jesse wanted only to banish the day by Lizzie's side. He started to turn Aristotle's head toward the rear of the house and pulled up short. Robert sat on the front steps, turning a new hat in his hands. He slowly stood as Jesse dismounted and opened the front gate. The parlor light behind the fidgeting clerk lighted his face and Jesse saw tears.

"Robert?

The clerk opened his mouth, raised the hat, and let it fall to his side. He wiped his free hand on his trousers, his voice breaking. "We've been looking for you, Mister Caine. I think she's dead. Miss Pendleton's dead."

Jesse stared at him as Cohen stepped from the house and brushed by the bewildered clerk.

"She's alive," he said to Jesse. "Someone shot her, but she's alive. They took her to the Catholic hospital."

Jesse blinked. "Shot?"

"A passerby found her in the street."

Jesse ran to Aristotle. *Damn them all. If she died, someone would die and rot in hell, no matter what happened to him.*

Bent low over Aristotle's neck, he spurred up Abercorn Street followed by Cohen, whose horse strained to keep pace. Hoof beats reverberated against houses along the street, horseshoes sparking on cobblestones, scattering shards of stone as Jesse quickly outdistanced Cohen's mare.

Aristotle sensed Jesse's urgency. The animal strained at Jesse's frantic pressure against its flanks. St. Bonaventure Hospital materialized ahead, rows of lighted windows punctuating the gloom. Jesse jumped from the saddle at the one-story building and rushed inside.

A white-robed nun looked up near the door. Startled, she hesitantly got to her feet as he stumbled past her and halted at the juncture of two hallways. Frail pools of lamplight dimmed both passages, small square drears of misery concealed behind closed doors. Repelled by the unseen death and sickness, he looked back and forth between the two Stygian corridors.

The nun's starched habit whispered along bare floor behind Jesse. She gently touched his arm, and he spun around.

"The woman who was shot," he managed.

The nun fingered an oversized gold crucifix on a chain around her neck, her serene face, framed by a canopied white hood. "Are you Mr. Caine?"

Jesse nodded, fear choking off words.

"She was calling your name when they brought her to us." She guided him to the right corridor. "I'm Sister Mary Katherine. I'll take you to her."

Moving with surprising grace despite the constrictive habit, she led him along plastered walls past closed doors. Despite the faint light the corridor shone with scrubbed care. Glancing right and left, he ignored groans and night whispers behind the closed doors. Midway down the hall, Sister Mary Katherine stopped at a partially open door and motioned him inside an intensely lit room. Half a dozen oil lamps burned brightly, shadows in sharp relief cast on the walls.

An older nun leaned over a mound of bloody bandages and frowned at his intrusion. A smaller gold crucifix dangled from her neck above the still figure on the bed. A damp cloth in one hand, she wiped

Lizzie's contorted face Jesse barely recognized. Beside her, a third sister held a bloody sheet high above Lizzie's prone body, a lantern steady in her other hand. Beside them, a shirt-sleeved doctor, vest streaked with blood, uttered a curse and mumbled an apology. He wiped a sleeve across his face and bent closer to the destruction beneath the sheet.

Jesse walked to the bedside. Strands of hair matted Lizzie's pillow like damp black seaweed. Eyes clenched shut with a wedge of thick leather clamped between her teeth, her head rolled back and forth in pain. She emitted high-pitched keening as the doctor probed deeper. Jesse looked away. Feeling slightly sick, Jesse allowed the Sister to lead him from the bedside. She shut the door behind them and faced him, her white habit a beacon of benevolence.

"Doctor Barrow removed the ball and is trying to stop the bleeding," she said. "You can't do anything except get in his way."

Jesse's eyes pleaded for her to help Lizzie. Lizzie wailed again, and he leaned on the door frame.

"Is she going to die?"

Sister Mary Katherine's dark brown eyes softened. She looked at the closed door and quickly crossed herself. "Her fate's in God's hands. I've seen worse wounds, but she suffered a serious injury. The bullet missed her heart by less than two inches."

Lizzie. Shot down in the street.

The world had stumbled again, he thought despairingly. His rage returned and he suppressed a strangled cry, the black hole of his youth returning. He'd been fated to die, not her. He arranged it alongside his other wounds, bonding the anger until he caught his breath.

"I'll stay the night," he said.

The nun led him back to the foyer where Cohen waited beside her desk.

"How is she?" he asked.

Jesse collapsed into a chair. "They're trying to stop the bleeding. The doctor's too busy to tell me anything."

Cohen sat beside him and slapped his thigh with a rare outburst of profanity. "Damn the bastards. God damn them all to hell."

Sister Mary Katherine sat down, turned a page in the patient ledger and pretended not to hear the blasphemy. She didn't know many Jews although the city abounded with them. The profane lawyer was clearly of the Hebrew persuasion, but appeared a close friend of Mr. Caine. With a life in the balance, she decided to overlook his religious shortcomings.

Jesse gazed down the corridor. "Wasn't money enough for them?"

"Not if they're caught," Cohen grated. "Greed erases mercy. Too many people see a pot of gold and believe it's worth any risk." He laid a gentle hand on Jesse's back. "Sometimes they get away with it, but the law eventually makes them pay."

Jesse remembered the bloody sheets only yards down the corridor. He'd worn a civilized cloak his entire life, but now rational words seemed dirty clothes, lame excuses for what innocent people suffered. The veneer of civilization peeled away.

"I want them dead," he whispered.

Unable to fashion an argument in the face of Jesse's grief, Cohen and the nun locked eyes and tried to assemble a reply.

"As an attorney, I only contend with the wreckage left in people's wake," Cohen said, attempting to divert Jesse from the corridor's bleak tunnel. "Sometimes they're contrite and beg for forgiveness, claiming they never meant harm. The worst of them kill without remorse, tossing away lives like yesterday's newspaper. In the end they all pay at heaven's gate."

Jesse cared nothing about legalities and courtrooms. Lizzie could die any second. There was only the present. "Lizzie discovered the truth," he said. "Elias may have uttered a careless word, I don't know, but the Tyrees found out."

"We can't prove they're involved," Cohen warned. "Not yet."

Jesse jumped up and leaned against the entrance door with a guttural cry, an echo of brutal ancestors. Startled by the tormented howl, Sister Mary Katherine's hand sprung to the elaborate cross on her habit.

"You can't..." Cohen began, but Jesse struck the wall, bloodying his knuckles.

The willowy nun flowed around the desk and placed her hand on his arm, her eyes pleading with Cohen.

"Why don't you lie down, Mr. Caine," she said. "I'll pray with you if you like."

Cohen joined her. "I'll stay here until the doctor comes out."

Jesse, at a loss, trudged after the nun to a spare room at the end of the corridor. He collapsed on a narrow bed and didn't resist when Sister Mary Katherine eased off his boots and quietly closed the door. The single window admitted a smear of moonlight. He lay back and listened to the void. Lizzie suffered the torments of ruined flesh only doors away, and he could do nothing to take away her pain. His breathing slowed, and he heard a rush of light footsteps filter past his door. He dismissed the possibility Lizzie had died, but the bright blood and pale figure rose each time he closed his eyes. Sleep overtook him and he eventually drifted away, the comforting presence of vengeance snug beside him in the narrow bed.

The click of the door handle awakened him instantly. Disoriented, Jesse sat up. An ethereal figure in white stood in the doorway, dawn's light from the window suffusing Sister Mary Katherine's robe.

"Is she dead?" he blurted.

Only then did Jesse see her smile. "No, Mr. Caine. Amazingly, she's awake and asking for you. I can't believe it, but she remembers you came last night."

Jesse pulled on his boots and rushed past her. The nun caught up to him outside Lizzie's room, her hand on the doorknob as his fears erupted again.

"The doctor says she's the healthiest young woman he's examined in months," she said, her relief evident. "She'll need weeks of rest, but he sees no reason she cannot fully recover unless there's infection." Her smile widened. "Given my prayers last night, I can't see that happening."

Jesse's voice broke. "Can I see her?"

"The doctor's given her a compound to ease the pain. Five minutes and I'll come get you."

Lizzie's pale features seemed to melt in the pristine white pillow that framed her head, her eyes closed. The sheet covered a mountain of bandages that rose and fell with every breath; red stains discolored the wrapped edges. He crept to her, afraid she'd awaken to pain. He eased a chair from the wall and lightly laid his hand atop hers. Anger and guilt flared. Unable to settle upon a single feeling he stared at her wan features. So far from home, he thought. She'd lost her brother, and now death lay beside her because she'd tried to help him.

He gently squeezed her fingers. Her eyelids fluttered and she blinked through half-open eyes. She stared at the ceiling, and the laudanum's compassionate haze pulled a childlike voice from her.

"Jesse?"

"Welcome back," he whispered.

"I didn't..."

"Not now. You're going to be all right."

A faint groan. "It hurts."

Cohen tiptoed into the room and her half-lidded eyes found him.

"I was shot," she murmured, her eyes wide in child-like astonishment, her hand clammy.

Jesse leaned closer. "I know. We'll find who did it."

Lizzie tightened her fingers around Jesse's. Her strength surprised her and she suddenly swayed her head from side to side, the pillow wet beneath her spray of damp hair. She licked her lips, gathering strength as the drug's embrace held her. Eyelids fluttering, she resisted the urge to drift away. Forcing a sharp intake of memory, she dug her nails into the back of Jesse's hand.

"I know who shot me," she gasped.

Cohen knelt beside the bed.

"Tyree," she whispered fiercely. "Randall Tyree shot me."

Tyree, Jesse thought. Tyree from the beginning.

Jesse heard Sister Mary Katherine's approach and bent closer to Lizzie's ear.

"We'll find him," he promised. He gently brushed strands of hair from her forehead. "The only important thing now is to obey the Sisters."

Jesse got to his feet. Lizzie had fallen asleep and he eased his hand from her limp fingers placing her hand gently on the sheet. Cohen followed him from the room where Sister Mary Katherine waited in the hall. She promised to send word if Lizzie's condition changed. She gently pushed them outside and closed the door, leaving them in the morning's first light, houses and buildings around them a montage of grays and pinks in the dawn.

"If I hadn't brought her to Savannah, she'd be safe in Boston," he said to Cohen.

"I promise you Tyree will stand trial," Cohen said. "The sheriff will have no choice but to issue a warrant for his arrest. Then we'll ask for a postponement of the trial until Lizzie's recovery. For the first time since this began, your father stands a chance."

Jesse barely heard him. He studied the intersection of the dirt and cobblestone streets. A silver-white crescent of quarter moon shared his elation that Lizzie lived, but only poor aim had spared her life. Charlie and Elias had failed some other arbitrary test of fate. He mounted a drowsing Aristotle. Good fortune was a fraud, he realized; surviving required human input. He looked down at Cohen.

"Warrants and trials no longer interest me."

Cohen grabbed the reins. "Nothing foolish, Jesse" he warned. "Tyree will face justice."

"Your law isn't justice. Not any longer."

Cohen tightened his grip. "Listen to me. I admit there can be gaps in the law, but ignoring it places us alongside the Tyrees." Jesse looked past him at the hospital, and Cohen saw he'd stopped listening. He thumped Jesse's booted knee with a ruined fist. "We'll make him pay, I swear it."

Jesse yanked the reins free. "I'll see you at your office in an hour."

Chapter Forty-Seven

April 16
The Caine House

Jesse sat alone at the dining room table, fighting the lack of sleep. The madness of the past few hours sat beside him like a nightmare revisited. He rubbed his eyes with the heels of his hands, recalling his argument with Lizzie and Cohen, and his father's nightmare that had begun at the same table. Face buried in his hands he imagined the acrid smell of disaster if such a thing existed.

I've spent my life denying my blood, trading away my heritage for a society that claimed civilized behavior rose above the dictates of passion, that claimed savages lived by nature's impulses, placing little or no value on human life. The lie lay exposed on bloody sheets only blocks away. Fine clothes and soaring church spires had only masked a different form of barbarity. But no more.

The attack on Lizzie wrecked their pretenses. Half his being admitted to his father's heritage, but he'd unlocked his Shawnee blood from a discarded past. He closed his eyes and again saw the lone figure of his dreams standing by the log fire in the clearing. In his mind he walked closer until he saw the face was his own. If he'd tipped into madness, it was a cleansing insanity.

He bathed and dressed within the new certainty. Pausing at the liquor cabinet in the parlor, he removed a glass and bottle of brandy and carried them into the dining room. He removed the cork.

No. He needed his wits, feeling as though he'd awakened from a deep sleep.

He jammed the cork into the bottle and walked from the house. Inside the carriage house, he scooped oats into two feed troughs for the horses. He brushed Aristotle, the rhythmic strokes firming his intentions. He saddled the horse and looked around the interior. A roughhewn workbench rested against one wall. Tools, looped rope, bridles, and harnesses hung from nails and hooks. A heavy hammer sat atop the bench; he dropped it into his saddlebag and scooped up a handful of rusty nails.

The ride into the city's heart carried Jesse past azaleas and struggling vines of honeysuckle that gloried in the moist heat. He recalled Lizzie's admiration of the flowers during her first day in the city before the memory of their stroll dissolved into desperation as she uttered Tyree's name. He looked away from the white and pink blossoms, afraid they might dispel the new sovereignty, the awareness more insistent as he neared Cohen's office. Samuel was a good man, he thought, but law was an invention created by men who considered themselves enlightened. They codified laws and bound their edicts into books until no room remained for justice unfettered by words. His mother's people had understood the need for retribution, a far older concept than codified laws on musty pages. Whatever her weaknesses, she'd instilled a knowledge where courtrooms did not exist.

The clerks inside the anteroom were nowhere in sight, and Cohen's refurbished office smelled of fresh wood and paint with only a faint residue of charred wood. Cohen sat at the temporary desk dressed in a silk vest and buttoned frock coat, his face reflecting the few hours of sleep he'd managed in the hospital chair. His exhaustion intensified when he looked up. Jesse pulled a chair closer to the desk and Cohen shook his head as though denying the request before Jesse uttered the words.

"I need a large sheet of paper," Jesse said. "The largest you have."

Cohen continued shaking his head. "If you persist in calling out Randall Tyree, I'll resign from your father's defense. I'll not take part in seeing you killed."

Jesse got to his feet and walked to the door.

Cohen threw up his arms and shouted at his back. "Damn your eyes! Sit down and close the door!"

Jesse slammed the door shut and resumed his chair. Unable to suppress a tight smile, he said, "Don't count me dead yet. I received excellent instruction." The words sounded boastful, but he no longer cared. As his mother's son, he'd run out of options.

"You're hell-bound to face Tyree," Cohen declared, his anger resurfacing. He shoved a heavy volume across the desk toward Jesse.

"There's your revenge," he said, tapping the book. "The sane recourse for men with courage to accept it. The law punishes the Randall Tyrees of this world."

Jesse looked away from the black and brown book as if it might seduce him. "Charlie, Elias, and now Lizzie," he said. "I can't afford to gamble on the law. Chances are my father won't survive jail, and you admitted juries are made up of men willing to flee the inconveniences of truth." He held Cohen's gaze. "I need your promise that Lizzie will be protected if I fail."

Cohen rose and reverently replaced the volume on the bookshelf. He placed both hands flat on the desk.

"The Old Book says He will have His vengeance."

"An eye for an eye," Jesse retorted. "Your religion confirms it."

"Your beliefs offer a turned cheek to the wicked, letting God administer the ultimate justice."

"God's a busy man," Jesse said. "I'll give Him a day off."

"I won't presume to call that blasphemy."

Jesse regretted his friend's wounded look, but there was no going back. "You and Lizzie are my father's only chance. I need to protect you."

"Think this through," Cohen said with a tenacity reserved for closing arguments. "If Lizzie survives and your father is cleared, what's gained if Tyree kills you? Do you want revenge so badly you'll gamble their future happiness?"

"Maybe Tyree and I are the same."

"You're not Randall Tyree. Don't coarsen yourself with such comparisons. You don't think like him, and you never will." He took a handkerchief from his trouser pocket and wiped his face. Pocketing the handkerchief he tried another tact.

"I've defended many men who lived to regret their vengeance. You've witnessed what happened when emotion ruled Charlie Rushton and Elias Pendleton. What's gained if you end up face down in the grass with your life draining away? It changes nothing." He perched on the edge of the desk and looked down at his broken hands, kneading the misshapen knuckles as though trying to reshape the damage.

"You know I fought professionally in my younger years. I know the urge to strike back. Twice, I almost killed a man in the ring from nothing more than a blood lust that overtook me. I thank Jehovah I walked away from it. If I'd succumbed to my rages in the ring, I'd most likely have ended up dead in some Boston alley."

Jesse looked up at him. "And if you stood in my shoes today? If Lizzie loved you and Tyree tried to murder her?"

Cohen stood. "I can't honestly answer that, but I'd hope to rise above the temptation."

The most illiterate beggar could see Cohen's logic and reject why Jesse sat in his office. But he saw only unspeakable consequences if Randall Tyree walked away a free man.

"May I have the paper?" Jesse asked.

Cohen experienced a rare failure of his persuasive skills. Logic and diversion were his stock and trade, but such sane approaches applied to rational men and women who chose to save their lives, not toss them aside. He studied Jesse's tormented face and the years of legal training and rational thought momentarily slipped away. The familiar blood lust threatened to crawl from the pit where he'd buried it after retiring from the ring. Chewing his lower lip, he recognized how easy it became to surrender to the pleasure it brought. As a boy, his father had read from the Torah, and in only a few instances did he remember men who willingly walked to their death, and only then for the glory of their god. His rational being wanted no part of Jesse's madness, but pen and paper existed elsewhere if he refused. Emptied of clever arguments, he could not desert his client and friend. He resumed his chair and pushed a quill and inkstand across the desk, instruments that might represent a death warrant. He opened a drawer and removed a large sheet of vellum.

"I take it you don't require the words."

Jesse stared at the blank page without hearing him. Once he posted Tyree, his life, whatever remained of it, would be altered forever, one way or the other.

He picked up the quill, dipped it in the inkwell, and began to write.

Randall Tyree

I hereby accuse you of attempted MURDER and the deceitful FRAUD perpetrated on the good citizens of Savannah. In doing so you have cloaked yourself in the mantle of a damned COWARD. If you care to assume the role of a man, I will await your pleasure tomorrow morning in the Jewish Cemetery at 10:00AM so all may witness justice administered to a common thief and murderer.

Jesse Caine

Cohen took the proclamation and read it. He pushed the paper back at Jesse. "Don't ask me to act as your second in this folly."

"Will you at least accompany me to the City Exchange?"

"You plan to post Tyree there?"

Jesse blew lightly on the ink and carefully rolled the vellum into a loose tube.

"On the front door."

Cohen brought his horse from the rear of the building, and they rode together toward the river. Catcalls assaulted them from several well-dressed men, the loudest hecklers yelling threats as they neared the building. Cohen reached across to Jesse as they started to dismount.

"You're convinced you must do this?"

Jesse handed him the reins and stepped down. He unbuckled his saddle bag flap and removed the hammer and nails. Several couples paused when Jesse marched up the steps to the massive door and unfurled the paper over the center panel. Smoothing it with the flat of his hand, he placed at nail at the upper right corner. More passersby stopped as he hammered the thick paper into place, driving home the three other nails.

The blows resounded like musket shots throughout the cavernous building, the hammering rising to the third floor. Jesse imagined heads suddenly raised from desks like alarmed wildebeests at a waterhole. He stepped back and pounded the center of the door with a final blow.

The echoes inside died away, replaced by footsteps on marble floors. The twin doors swung inward and John Sanderson gaped at Jesse, then the posting. A crowd gathered behind him and riders dismounted as people watched the scene.

"What in god's name do you think you're doing?" Sanderson sputtered.

"Redressing wrongs that are far past due." Jesse gestured at the posting with the hammer. "I advise you to leave this in place."

Sanderson read the document again as the crowd surged forward. Recovering a modicum of his dignity, Sanderson drew himself up. "Who's going to pay for defacing this door?"

"Send the bill to the Tyrees," Jesse said.

He strode past the astonished faces and Cohen handed him the reins.

"Madness," he said, his voice intended only for Jesse's ears.

Ambrose Caine coughed and looked up from the book on his lap, life's light faint in his eyes. A bloody rag in one hand, he patted Jesse's knee as his son sat beside him. Shaken by the blood on his chin and several days of gray stubble, Jesse gathered his courage.

"I finished reading *Robinson Crusoe*," the frail figure declared, cracked lips nearly devoid of color as he smiled. "It gave me hope for rescue. Even Mr. Defoe allowed his castaway to survive his ordeal."

Jesse had spent the last hour debating whether to tell him he'd posted Tyree. In the end, he determined not to die with a lie in his mouth. If he never walked from the old walled cemetery, his father deserved the truth.

He began slowly. "Randall Tyree tried to kill Elizabeth Pendleton last night."

"This will never end," Ambrose said. "Will she live?"

"She'll survive, though she's grievously wounded."

"Fletcher Tyree," Ambrose whispered, "a murderer."

Jesse grasped one of his father's frail hands and risked thirty years of trust. "I posted Randall this morning," he said. Ambrose slowly removed his hand and looked past Jesse at the cell wall. Jesse waited for the condemnation but his father remained silent, avoiding his eyes. Little remained of their lives of a few weeks earlier. Jesse might have shattered his father's faith in him, but there was no turning back. If he knew the names of his mother's Shawnee gods, he'd invoke them to make his father understand and allow Lizzie to live.

Chapter Forty-Eight

Same Day
Early Evening
The Randall Tyree House

Randall leaned against the window frame and studied the red bricks along West York Street, the symmetrical patterns dissolving in the twilight. The house's interior remained silent as though sharing his contentment. After all the unexpected complications he'd soon enjoy the rewards though unforeseen adjustments had been required. His father remained unconvinced of their safety, but removing impediments had required a resolve the old man lacked. Now fate delivered Jesse Caine into his hands.

He looked at the wall of blades. He checked his pocket watch, expecting his father momentarily. As though anticipating his thoughts, a closed carriage rattled around the corner, iron-rimmed wheels clattering across the bricks. The team halted at the curb and Fletcher Tyree stepped down. Randall studied him from the window and recognized that his movements were stiff with anger. The agitated figure aimed a finger at the driver, and Randall suppressed a smile as he imagined the harangue. A few seconds later the caped figure brushed by him and flung off the cloak without a word.

Flushed, Fletcher Tyree walked into the parlor and looked around the severe setting. His eyes fell on a knee-high vase of marbles, and he crossed the room in four strides. He kicked over the container, scattering marbles and broken glass across the bare floor like frenzied insects. He raised a fist toward a shelf of toy soldiers and pulled back his arm, glaring at the display. Breathing heavily, he collapsed into a chair beside the desk.

"Damn you for a fool, Randall!"

When the marbles rolled to a halt against the baseboards, Randall stepped over clear glass shards and began picking them up, his back to his father.

Disgusted, Fletcher Tyree watched him retrieve his treasures. Kicking aside slivers of glass, Randall walked the room's perimeter, dropping handfuls of marbles into other jars. He settled into a chair across from his father and studied the damage that littered the floor.

"I assume you'll send one of your niggers to clean up your fit of temper," he said.

His father lighted a cheroot and yanked an ashtray closer, his movements panicked.

"Disaster." Fletcher's voice broke as he looked around the room in disgust. "You've seen Caine's posting?"

To Randall's eyes the once vibrant figure wore his age like a dispirited prisoner of war, older and beaten with no hope of repatriation. "The entire city's most likely seen it," he said. "We couldn't ask for a more propitious occurrence."

"You're a fool," his father repeated. "People have brains, despite your assertions." Lost for words, his head collapsed against the high-backed chair.

"You see ghosts where none exist," Randall said. "Caine's given us the perfect opportunity. After tomorrow there'll be no one to oppose us."

Fletcher considered the display of swords behind his son's handsome head. No doubt he already counted Jesse Caine as a dead man, but the assurance did nothing to salvage their family name. He saw himself again rushing from the City Exchange steps, waving off inquiries. Ashes flaked down his vest and he frantically brushed them away, his voice grating.

"Nailed to the damn front door."

"I'm sure Sanderson was most unhappy."

Fletcher crushed the cheroot in the ashtray, looked at the smoldering stub and flung it at the window. "'Murderer, thief, and coward.' That's what Caine's labeled you. And *me* by association. He sullied our name within the confines of a single sheet of paper."

Randall waited until his father's rage quieted. "The entire city knows we've been at each other's throat for weeks," he said. "There'll be no surprise when we meet. No suspicion will attach to us."

"It's not just Caine, dammit. Our family name's involved, publically assailed."

"Family name." Randall made an amused sound and scooped a handful of marbles from the urn beside his chair, a gesture calculated to infuriate his father. A sliver of broken glass nicked his thumb and he sucked away the blood before allowing the orbs to tumble noisily into the jar, suddenly sad that anger and distrust were the only emotion in the room. He imagined the older man grateful for the distance between their chairs, torn between protecting their name and regretting having brought him into the world. Randall pretended to study a marble in his palm, a yellow cat eye. He held the orb toward the ebbing sun and squinted into its golden depths, a smear of blood turning its depths muddy orange.

"Where our family's concerned," he said, "we've merely joined a long line of dubious ancestors that grabbed whatever came to hand."

He rolled the bloodied marble between his thumb and forefinger, seeking to placate his father. "But you were most helpful, dear father. I could not have undertaken this venture without your thoughtful advice."

"I never anticipated killing anyone," Fletcher snapped, "Ambrose Caine's health aside. But I certainly never wanted the parade of funerals you instigated." He ran a hand through his white mane of hair as though wiping away the past weeks.

"Did you have anything to do with the attack on the Pendleton woman?"

"No," Randall lied. The dark street had rendered him invisible. "A failed robbery, nothing more."

"And Victoria Danford? You were more than close to her."

Randall shook his head. "It appears someone is preying on our city's women." Surprised his father knew about the affair, he congratulated himself for never revealing her role to his father.

"Such a lovely creature," Fletcher mused. He kicked an overlooked marble and sent it rolling toward the hallway. "A damned waste of feminine beauty."

"She was that," Randall agreed, recalling her perfume and sweat-stained sheets. He dismissed the regret, his next trip to New Orleans planned, an attractive and available female companion selected earlier in the day. He dropped the marble into the urn and weighed his father's misgivings. He watched the nervous movements, concerns mounting as his father retreated into a closed universe of his own making. Like Victoria, he seemed on the verge of disassociating himself from reality. Not lost to Victoria Danford's depths, Randall thought, but barricaded behind his possessions with little thought other than acquiring the next bauble. In the beginning, Randall had seen himself as the dutiful son, ensuring the old man's final years were pleasurable, allowing him to acquire whatever satisfied him. The charade satisfied what little remained of his conscience, but also assured their lifestyles, disparate as they might be. Neither, however, would enjoy the bounty if his father lost his will to win the race in the last furlong.

Unaware of his son's scrutiny, Fletcher tapped the edge of the ashtray with nervous intensity, hunched as though expecting a blow. Randall wondered if he imagined the existence of a vengeful God rampaging through time, seeking him out, a sword of retribution clutched in His hand? Did he see hordes of cheated friends marching on his home, howling for vengeance? Randall thrust away a stab of apprehension; they'd both be fortunate to escape with their lives if it fell apart now. Kill Caine now, he thought, and be done with it.

Randall rose and lit lamps around the room, partially to keep his father's growing uneasiness at bay. He settled back into his chair, annoyed by the crunch of unseen broken glass under his boots. The lamps reflected off the rows of gleaming blades behind his chair. His father glanced at them and looked at the front door.

"Stop imagining ghosts," Randall snapped. "I'll end Caine's interference and your fears in the same moment."

"What if the woman from Boston survives?" his father persisted. "Even with Caine dead, Cohen will employ her to disprove our documents. We're then left to the whims of a jury."

"The documents are flawless. Her claims will contradict what jurors see."

"I assume our forger's well hidden?"

Randall smiled. "Completely."

He opened his humidor in a conciliatory offering. His father's mottled hands steadied as they clipped the proffered cigar and allowed his son to apply a match without meeting his eyes.

"The Pendleton woman's an outsider," Randall continued. "If she lives, she'll be dismissed as a crank, a desperate subterfuge by Cohen. A judge and jury will see her bias in favor of those who hired her. She'll return to Boston, and we'll never hear of her again."

Fletcher squinted at him through the smoke "Conjecture. Cohen's a damned bulldog."

"He has no case once Caine's dead and his father's found guilty."

Candles wavered in their battle to brighten the morose room. Light reflected off broken glass on the floor and created the illusion of fireflies at rest. Randall studied the tip of his cigar. A hollowed husk sat cross from him, so different from the force he once feared and admired. He waited for the older man to resume the quarrel.

"A damned dangerous thing, Randall. Don't underestimate young Caine. Remember, he bested Belden and your man on the ship."

Weary of the sparring, Randall sat back. "Instead of your fat friend Belden," he said, "the half-breed will meet me."

Chapter Forty-Nine

April 16
Daybreak
Old Jewish Burial Ground

The hem of the elderly Jew's long black woolen coat hung heavy with dew as dawn's first glow touched the cemetery walls encased in morning fog. Stooped with age and burdened by his thoughts, the caretaker settled his tattered hat firmly on his head as he studied the expanse of weeds bordering four brick walls. He leaned on the scythe's two wooden handles and allowed a small measure of pride to ease his coming labor. The sacred burial ground contained so many revered names. He experienced a rush of pride in his menial labor before he dismissed the sensation. What kind of work was this for an old man, he thought?

I should be wearing soft slippers, my children and grandchildren bringing me hot tea, not standing knee-high in cold wet weeds.

He dismissed the daydream, sorrowful no children or grandchildren waited at home for him. Worse, the necessity of money cared nothing for age, but at least the cemetery trustees did not care how much time his task consumed. So, he sighed, I'll take my time. Finish two walls before noon. Then, brew a cup of tea and eat my lunch.

He spat on his ragged gloves and swung the scythe's curved blade at his weedy foe. As he worked the morning heat found the cemetery and he removed his coat. The few dollars seemed small recompense for such labor, but few others appeared interested in keeping the grounds presentable, and he needed to live. Had he not required the money, or lacked pride in the holy place, he would have gladly relinquished the burden to a younger zealot.

Footsteps crunched along the path behind him, and he turned to see finely-dressed men emerge from the fog. Several stared at him as they walked past and opened the double doors in the cemetery wall, disappearing inside. He stared after them and spat on the ground, knowing what they represented. As a younger *mensch*, he might have put an end to it, but no longer. Sighing again, he aimed the scythe at an offending cluster of rebellious dandelions and cut them down.

Eight blocks east of the caretaker, the first light etched patterns on Jesse's bedroom ceiling. Fog smothered the streets below as he lay in bed and listened to the morning sounds beyond the window. He longed to turn over and touch Lizzie. Instead of her murmurs and warm nakedness, there were only the murmurs of doves and a horse's whinny as a sutler's wagon lumbered past the house. If she lay beside him now, he might find words to defend his decision. He tried to splice together a rational defense, but the effort collapsed. If he survived, he hoped Lizzie understood no alternatives had been left to him. If Tyree killed him, she'd be alone again, his father ashamed that his son died in the desolate graveyard. Given time, his father might come to see Jesse's blood tipped him beyond civilization.

Harper Jerrard, Tyree's perpetual second, had appeared the previous night to deliver terms of the duel. His long face had twitched nervously as Jesse opened the door, remembering their previous meeting. He began to stammer out the arcane rules when the door slammed in mid-sentence.

Jesse struck a match to the lamp and laid out his clothes. A white shirt and black trousers. Low-cut patent shoes. He looked down at his hands as he buttoned his shirt, content they evidenced no tremors. He picked up a black ribbon to tie back his hair, then stared at his image in the mirror. He tossed the ribbon on the bed before turning back to his reflection. His straight black hair reached his shoulders, and he saw his mother's son disguised in gentleman's clothing.

If they consider me a savage, I may as well look the part.

Mesmerized, he stared at the transformation. The long black hair framed his face his neck and framed his face, and he nourished a fleeting thought his appearance might cause Tyree to hesitate.

With Lobeau's bare epée tucked beneath his arm, he found Cohen waiting outside on the top porch step. He turned when Jesse opened the door, pointing at the loose hair.

"A statement?" he asked.

"Of sorts." Jesse said. "It seems appropriate, given the circumstances."

"Will you tell Lizzie where you're going?"

"No. If I'm left standing, it won't matter. If not, I expect you'll explain my reasons."

Cohen frowned. "And what do I say to your father?"

"Tell him I inherited my mother's blood."

He locked the front door and handed the key to Cohen with a grim smile. "In case my lessons were insufficient."

Kerrigan waited at the front gate with the horses. He nodded at Jesse without speaking.

"I asked him to accompany us," Cohen said.

Jesse secured Lobeau's epée across the pommel and recalled Charles Rushton had born his sword in the same manner to the deserted plantation. He stroked the horse's neck and mounted, as gray mist swallowed the three riders.

Sister Mary Katherine materialized from the fog in front of the hospital, her white habit an offering emerging from the fog. Hands locked in front of her, she watched their approach, her form half-hidden by two men, one a giant with a red bandanna around a bulging neck, the other a smaller man with a flattened nose. Jesse heard metallic clicks of two pistols being cocked, and Cohen waved to them.

"Friends," he said quietly to Jesse. "I provided Lizzie with more tangible guardian angels."

The nun eased between the two sentinels. "Mr. Caine. Mr. Cohen." She nodded to Kerrigan and indicated the two men flanking her with a shy smile. "I didn't know what to think when Jacob and Mickey arrived, but I understand your concern, given the circumstances." She smiled benevolently. "They appear to like our coffee."

Jesse peered through the doorway. "How is she?"

"Improved. She slept the night, and the bleeding's subsided. The doctor stayed most of the night and left an hour ago."

"Can I see her?"

"For a minute."

Kerrigan eyed the two men. "I'll wait here."

The nun led Jesse and Cohen to Lizzie's room. The larger guard stationed himself beside her door, and the second man remained at the head of the corridor. Jesse stepped inside.

Alcohol and fresh linen suffused the cramped space; a single lamp added a thin vapor of oily smoke. The faintest trace of color suffused Lizzie's face, and Jesse saw no signs of pain. The laudanum held her in its grasp, but she looked up at the sound of his footsteps and smiled weakly. Jesse bent over the bed.

She touched his hair. "You forgot to tie your hair," she said dreamily, stroking the black tresses with her fingertips.

"I need you to remind me to be a gentleman," Jesse replied softly. He lightly caressed her bare arm as though the limb might break under the slightest pressure. The ache in his chest mounted. She'd danced with death and barely escaped its clutches. He lightly squeezed her arm. "You're better now." He inclined his head toward the door. "Samuel's assigned two friends to watch over you. They'd frighten the devil himself."

"I don't imagine the sister will allow me one small cigar," Lizzie murmured.

The nun appeared at the bedside and smiled down at her. "If you're a good girl, I might allow you a single indulgence. According to the Dr. Barrow, tobacco has a positive medicinal effect."

Lizzie closed her eyes, and Sister Mary Katherine pulled the sheet to her chin. She glanced at Jesse and tilted her head toward the doorway. Jesse leaned down and kissed Lizzie's cheek.

"I'll see you this afternoon," he whispered, but she had drifted away.

He followed the nun outside and glanced back at the pallid figure. A second sister appeared and sat in the chair beside the bed as Sister Mary Katherine partially closed the door. Jesse inclined his head at Cohen's man propped against the wall. The guard returned his nod, a long-barreled pistol tucked into his wide belt, a mug of steaming coffee in one hand. Doors to most rooms stood open where their occupants slept or awaited another painful or uncertain day.

In the vestibule, Sister Mary Katherine returned to her desk. Jesse studied the contained figure, so serene in her religion. He remembered wondering what he'd become if he attended Charlie's funeral, but events had moved far beyond the dinner table admission to his father. Now he would attempt to destroy a man, drawn by the siren's call of his ancestors, a rite of purification, gripped in its power.

A cold cast iron stove stood in one corner. The impulse overtook him and he unbuttoned his waistcoat and stripped off the neck stock. He loosened the top buttons of his shirt and bared his upper torso. Reaching inside the stove's door he pressed his index finger against the charred interior and withdrew his hand. He looked down at the blackened finger and closed his eyes in silent prayer to whomever cared to listen. He drew a breath and pressed the fingertip against his hairline. Slowly, he drew a black stripe down the center of his forehead onto the bridge of his nose, then over his chin. Placing his hand back into the stove he gathered more soot and drew two horizontal lines across his cheeks and chest, imagining the stains bore a weight against his skin. He pictured the conversations in candle-lit dining rooms; shocked faces beneath glowing chandeliers, outrage reflected in silver and crystal settings. If he accomplished little else this morning, he'd leave the pretenders with reminders of their fabricated piety, a fish bone in their throats.

Cohen stood, unable to conceal his surprise. "What are you doing?"

Jesse walked around him to the desk. He reached for Sister Mary Katherine's hand before remembering his stained hand. She gaped at the drawn markings, the face unconnected to the gentle figure at Lizzie's bedside. He thanked her, and she managed a nod, transfixed by the heathen she'd seen only in books.

Outside, sunlight had chased fog from the street. Jesse patted Aristotle's neck with a calming gesture. Neither man spoke until Jesse heard a tinny chime and removed the chained hunter from his coat pocket.

"Our appearance is expected at the cemetery." His eyes lingered on the watch. He clicked the case shut, rubbed his thumb over the gold cover, and held the piece toward Cohen. "A gift from my father on my twenty-first birthday. Will you see it's returned?"

"Come back inside with me and there's no need."

"I can't do that."

Cohen stared at the painted face, and Jesse returned his friend's inspection.

"The city sees me as a savage," he said. "I wouldn't want to disappoint its citizens."

Chapter Fifty

Mid-Morning
Old Jewish Burial Ground

The three men rode past the abandoned trenches where men had fought and died fifty years earlier. A few hundred yards below the redoubt's remains a picket line of horses that stood along West Broad Street tended by young Negro boys. Wide-eyed, they stared at Jesse's face as he dismounted and handed a coin to a startled youngster. He untied the epée's retaining straps and lifted the naked blade from the saddle.

Eager for the bloodletting, men milled around the gate as Jesse walked past them trailed by Cohen and Kerrigan. Fog persisted in the swamp, thinning at the edge of the western wall. An ancient man in an ankle-length black coat leaned on a scythe and distanced himself from the proceedings. Jesse stepped inside the walls with a surge of exhilaration. He looked at the north wall where Elias had fallen with surprising calm, the narrow corridor trodden flat, all reasoning washed away when Lizzie fell in the muddy street. Stone vestiges of forgotten men and women dotted the earth around him, submerging him in reality. In all likelihood he would die today, but Lizzie would be safe. Cohen's law books would see to that. Vaguely aware of faces turned his way, he managed a smile as a sudden stillness settled over him. He would never step back.

A tiny brown bird swooped down and perched atop the open gate door, its head cocked at the gathered men. Distracted, Jesse watched it flutter to the nearest wall, its song innocent of what was about to transpire below. Kerrigan, dressed in a long overcoat, walked away to lean against the far wall, hands jammed in his coat pockets.

Cohen glowered at the fashionably dressed crowd that was unaware or uncaring they stood on holy ground. He scanned the crowd, memorizing faces for legal retribution if the opportunity presented itself. "I asked these gates be bolted," he said, "but our city fathers seem intent on desecrating hallowed ground."

"A cemetery seems appropriate."

"Don't do this."

Jesse recalled his own warning to Charlie Rushton minutes before he died, a lifetime ago now.

Cohen lowered his voice. "Tyree will stand trial for attempted murder. You'll live to see it if you walk away with me. Kerrigan will make certain nothing happens to you."

Walk away, Jesse thought.

He wondered if his face mirrored Charlie's belated recognition of what awaited him. Tyree had tried to murder Lizzie, and Jesse could not risk a capricious courtroom. Only a blood reckoning would atone for her suffering. He pushed aside the vision of Lizzie's bloody bandages and calmed his mind, remembering Lobeau's warning. Charles Rushton and Elias Pendleton had died like lambs led to slaughter, and only Lobeau's training stood between him and the same fate. He needed an opening, a single mistake he could exploit. More than that, the small chance he'd survive the morning depended on his willingness to kill Tyree.

His painted face drew whispers from the crowd. A group was gathered around Randall and his father, and John Sanderson and Jacob Belden nodded at whatever was being said until they saw Jesse. He started toward him when Jerrard blocked his way. Taken aback by Jesse's painted face, he hesitated before speaking in a broken voice. "Only seconds may communicate now. The principals may not speak directly to—"

Jesse shoved him aside and continued walking. Randall Tyree stepped away as the crowd of admirers met him. Eyes alight with a hunter's anticipation, Tyree cocked his head and studied the markings.

"A tribal ritual? Something passed down by your mother who found herself on the fortunate side of a trade blanket?"

"You read the posting?"

"I trust it provided satisfaction," Tyree said. "It will be your last pleasure on earth."

"Murderer, cheat, and coward," Jesse said loudly for the onlookers' benefit. He found Fletcher Tyree in the throng and turned toward him. "Did I miss any family attributes, Colonel?"

Fletcher's face darkened. "You'll be brought to account today."

Cohen stepped in front of Jesse and faced Randall. "Miss Pendleton identified you as her attacker. I plan to lodge an attempted murder charge against you."

Randall fixed his eyes on Jesse and ignored Cohen. "Look around you. This will be a beautiful day, but these old walls will be your last memory." He leaned closer, his lips almost touching Jesse's cheek. "One last thought to take to hell," he whispered. "Your lady friend will never see the inside of a courtroom."

Jesse reached for Randall's lapel when the iron doors slammed shut. A uniformed figure stood just inside the gate, epée case tucked beneath a gilded braided sleeve. Dressed in scarlet trousers and green hussar's dolman, the outlandish figure wove his way past rows of gravestones. Casting a quick glance at Kerrigan, Lobeau stopped in front of Randall, then took a half-step back as if reprimanding a wayward child. He pursed his lips with an indifferent grunt that carried to the onlookers.

"I understand you possess sufficient skills to attack mere boys."

Randall, aware every ear heard the slur, inspected the eccentric attire with a sardonic smile.

"This is a private matter, little man."

Lobeau raised his eyebrows and stroked his groomed moustache with a long-practiced gesture. "*Mais non*, it is no longer a private affair."

Tyree glanced at the circle of faces, the smile strained. "And you are?"

Lobeau lifted his chin and silently brought his heels together. "Etienne Lobeau."

Randall studied the epée case. "If you insist, I'll accommodate you in a few moments." He turned back to Jesse, but Lobeau shook his head and stepped closer.

"*Non, non.* You will accommodate me now."

He slapped Randall's face. The open-handed blow resounded off the brick walls and gravestones like a musket shot, and before he could recover, Lobeau slapped him again, the second blow more forceful. Speechless, Randall took a half step back and tasted blood.

A pitiless smile crossed Lobeau's face. "Ah, then, *Monsieur* Caine only told the truth. You are indeed nothing more than a puppy and coward."

Face burning, Randall stripped off his coat. He tossed it to a startled Jerrard and motioned for his sword. His father pushed Jerrard aside and grabbed Randall's arm. Randall ignored him and pointed at Lobeau.

"You have your wish, little man," he fumed. "Your friend can wait a minute longer."

Lobeau bowed and opened the lavishly decorated case. He removed a slender blade elaborately scrolled with eagles. Frowning at Jesse's blackened face he handed him the case.

"If you will be so kind."

Jesse recovered his voice. "I can't allow this."

Lobeau shrugged and removed the embroidered jacket to reveal a pristine cream-colored shirt. "I am left with no choice," he said, handing the jacket to Jesse. "You heard him insult my height."

"This isn't your fight, Etienne."

The barest of smiles touched Lobeau's lips. "Many times you do not select your fights. They select you."

Jesse took a step toward Randall but Cohen grabbed his arm, a light in his eyes. "No. He's made his choice."

Before Jesse could reply Lobeau faced Randall again, the epée loosely gripped in one hand. "We have no need of seconds, you and I, *n'est pas?*"

"No seconds are needed, since you lack a gentleman's credentials."

Lobeau bowed. "*Précisément.* I have never debased myself with such labels."

Fletcher Tyree pulled his son aside and glanced at Kerrigan who had not moved. "Randall, you don't know this man."

Randall, breathing heavily, glared at Lobeau. "Look at him," he snapped. "A gnome gotten up like one of my toy soldiers."

His father led him away and looked back at Lobeau. "Think for once in your life," he grated. "He means nothing to us. Caine first, then do what you will with this fool."

His face ablaze, Randall ignored him and walked back to Lobeau, the scar on his cheek glacial white. He waved his hand toward Jerrard, who handed him the epée.

Kerrigan pushed from the wall and started toward them.

"Etienne?"

Lobeau turned his back as though he'd not spoken.

"Etienne, what in hell are you doing?" Kerrigan called.

"I came to find you, Patrick, but other matters now demand my attention," Lobeau said.

He followed Randall to the opening beside the wall. He rolled up his right sleeve, without taking his eyes from Tyree's face, the elegant sword at his side.

Randall lunged without warning, surprised when Lobeau snapped aside the thrust. Circling, Lobeau pointed the sword tip at the ground as though inviting another attack. Randall with his usual opening gambit feigned two thrusts, assessing his smaller opponent. Lobeau inclined his head and parried the feints, his teeth brilliant beneath the luxurious moustache.

"Is this all they teach at your school?" he goaded.

Randall stepped away and unconsciously bit his lower lip, experiencing a rare moment of uncertainty. Lobeau turned aside the next thrusts without ripostes and disengaged, content to measure the rushes. Encouraged by the lack of response, Randall unleashed a flurry of attacks. The clash of steel chimed off the old walls, eliciting murmurs from the crowd who waited for the inevitable. Again, Lobeau turned aside the attacks.

An odd sensation gripped Randall's bowels. Aware the crowd watched with renewed interest, he cast aside the alien feeling, fleetingly wondering if his face mirrored the alarm he'd seen in his victims' eyes.

No, he chided himself. The little bastard hasn't touched him. Hadn't come close.

As always, there'll be an opening and I'll end it.

Randall increased the fury of his attacks, each onslaught more complicated than the last. He used his height advantage and pursued the will-o-wisp along the wall. Lobeau's tiny feet danced past the grave markers without looking down, and Jesse marveled at the Frenchman's skill. Shod in supple boots, he skated effortlessly over the grass, a dance master who occasionally nodded approval at his partner.

"*C'est mieux comme ça!*" Lobeau laughed. "That's better!"

Moving out of reach, he allowed Randall to catch his breath. Lobeau's smile faded.

"Today is different, *n'est pas?*"

Randall stepped back. He lowered his guard to study the smaller man. When Lobeau made no effort to attack, Randall suddenly understood. He faced an imposter! Whoever this interloper is, he thought, he hasn't attempted a single thrust. He turns aside attacks with no riposte, content to show off his cleverness, lacking the grit to kill. He straightened and sidestepped a gravestone, circling to his right, seeking a single opening to end it. He risked a glance at his father. The old man had never bothered to attend one of his duels, never appreciated his talent. Randall would gain his esteem after all the years. He'd end the charade and—

Lobeau's thrust pierced Randall's chest, passed upward through his heart, and exited his back. He deftly withdrew the blade and stepped back.

Randall gasped in astonishment as a crimson flower spread over his shirt.

"You..."

The epée slipped from his fingers and he sank to the ground. Jerrard and a physician rushed forward. With a strangled howl, Fletcher Tyree shoved them aside and knelt by the still figure. Randall's butter-colored hair obscured sightless eyes that looked past him at the morning sky.

"No," Fletcher moaned. After a moment his trembling hand gently closed the unresisting eyelids, unaware of the shocked crowd that looked on in disbelief.

Lobeau removed a handkerchief from his waistcoat and strode past the kneeling figure without a glance. He wiped the epée blade and took the case from Jesse who gaped at him. Lobeau returned the weapon to its home and shrugged into the dolman, oblivious to the bewildered faces around him. He cocked his head at Jesse as he buttoned the ornate jacket. "Your face is dirty," he said.

He strode to Kerrigan and withdrew the note, holding it in front of him. "You dropped this at the cabin."

Kerrigan reached for the paper but Lobeau dropped it, regret softening his voice as the note fluttered to earth.

"Such a small piece of paper, *mon ami*," he said sadly.

Lobeau handed the IOU to Jesse without taking his eyes from his former comrade. "They say the Sanhedrin paid Judas 30 pieces of silver. It appears you made a better bargain."

Jesse opened the note, saw Kerrigan's name, and felt the last pieces fall into place.

"Patrick?"

Kerrigan backed away until his shoulders touched the wall. He drew a pistol from beneath his coat and thumbed back the hammer, pointing the muzzle at the lifeless body.

"I tried to help you," he said to Jesse. "I didn't care if you killed the bastard. I got paid either way."

Still on his knees, Fletcher Tyree's head snapped up. "Shut up, damn you!"

Kerrigan leveled the pistol at the distraught figure kneeling on the ground. "To hell with you."

Lobeau faced him without emotion. "Filling your pockets in war is good fortune, but you became a common thief, *mon ami*, a traitor to your friend."

Kerrigan shifted the pistol to Lobeau, the crowd frozen in astonishment. "You and your island, Etienne," he sneered. "You and your fancy furniture and fine wine, but you never shared a dollar with me."

He looked back to Jesse, a touch of regret in his expression. "They told me it would be easy. Greedy fools investing their money. No risk. Let your father take the blame." He wiped his mouth with the back of his hand, alert to any shift in the crowd. "They said he was sick and wouldn't live long, so it wouldn't matter in the end." He grinned crookedly at Cohen. "The fire at your office should have destroyed the woman's work, but you're blessed with Irish luck."

Jesse stared at the flushed face. "You'd have seen me killed and my father dead in jail."

Kerrigan shrugged. "I survive, that's what my kind does." He backed away and swung the pistol at the crowd that kept its distance. "Money's the great leveler." He gestured at Lobeau. "Hell, even an old soldier knows that. Fine clothes and principles come easy when you've gold in your pockets."

He looked at Lobeau and back to Jesse. "I hoped for a better outcome if Etienne taught you well. You disposed of one Mincey on the ship, and I took care of his brother." He looked at Randall's body and gestured around the walled enclosure. "It would have worked except for the woman."

"Lizzie?"

Kerrigan made a disparaging sound. "The actress. The lovely bitch put me and the Tyrees in harm's way."

"Shut up, damn you, Kerrigan, " Fletcher rasped.

"*You* killed her?" Jesse asked in disbelief.

Kerrigan swung back to him. "Too late in the game for her loose mouth. The Tyrees couldn't dirty their fine hands." He edged toward the gate as onlookers backed away. "I've money enough to disappear back to the old sod now where no one remembers me." He glanced at Fletcher Tyree, who got to his feet. "You can do what you will with this old rogue."

Fletcher swayed to his feet. "You'll hang, damn you black soul."

"Then you'll hang with me," Kerrigan yelled at him.

Kerrigan turned back to Jesse as though contemplating a final explanation when Fletcher pulled a pocket pistol from his waistcoat and cocked it. Kerrigan recognized the sound a second too late to save his life. Fletcher shot him in the temple and the sparrow darted from the wall. Kerrigan staggered and toppled to the ground amidst the veil of smoke. Cohen ripped the pistol from the old man who collapsed with a sob beside his dead son.

The sparrow, frightened, swirled upward, then fluttered back to its perch as small groups silently slipped through the gates. A few men nodded at Jesse without speaking. Jesse looked at Fletcher and pity welled up until he remembered the dead: Charlie, Victoria, Elias. After a moment Cohen led him toward the gate. He looked back at Kerrigan's body. "I never believed Pat would—"

"Money," Cohen said. "A sickness for his kind."

"The Colonel..."

"The Colonel will stand trial, his former friends will see to that."

Jesse looked at Randall's ruined body. "I promised my father..."

"Tell him you kept your promise."

Jesse scanned the cemetery for Lobeau but he was gone. Whatever his flaws, the Frenchman's code had saved Jesse's life. Remembering the drunken night on the island, Lobeau's rules for friendship left no room for Kerrigan's treachery. With a price still on his head, Jesse guessed he'd never see him again. The former hussar would collect his dogs and vanish from the island to seek peace elsewhere. He only hoped Prussian gold bought escape from his memories.

Fletcher Tyree remained on his knees beside the body, the graveyard empty. Cohen looked at him, then placed his hand on Jesse's back and guided him through the gates. "We'll go to the hospital, then wake Judge Fraley to have the charges dismissed."

Jesse looked back he saw the old Jew swing the scythe as though nothing had happened inside the graveyard. "My father won't understand."

"He'll understand."

Cohen was right. He'd kept his word. One son's life had ended, but another had been reborn. Jesse's spirits lifted until he suddenly remembered his face and stopped.

"Lizzie can't see me like this."

"You can wash up at the hospital," Cohen said. "I'm more concerned that Sister Mary Katherine's coffee has converted my two associates."

The solitary sparrow fluttered to the top of the wall and watched the two men tread up the footpath. A burst of sunlight outlined the way ahead of them and Jesse fell in step with his friend.

About the Author

Will Ottinger's first novel, *A Season for Ravens,* was selected by Reader Views as a top three historical novel for 2014-2015. An earlier non-fiction work was published in Great Britain on the art of painting military miniatures, an endeavor in which he earned the title of Grand Master painter. He also wrote a magazine column for seven years and has published numerous articles.

A graduate of Emory University and Northwestern Graduate School, he spent most of his early life in Savannah and coastal Georgia. He and his wife owned an art gallery in Chicago, and he founded a wealth management consulting firm where he was an acknowledged trainer, speaker, and writer. He's an inveterate fly fisherman, moving from Chicago to Houston ten years ago.

He has just completed his third novel, *The Last Van Gogh.*

www.ingramcontent.com/pod-product-compliance
Lightning Source LLC
Chambersburg PA
CBHW071815020726
47502CB00004B/1116